THE TRICKSTER FIGURE IN AMERICAN LITERATURE

THE TRICKSTER FIGURE IN AMERICAN LITERATURE

Winifred Morgan

THE TRICKSTER FIGURE IN AMERICAN LITERATURE
Copyright © Winifred Morgan, 2013.

Yusef Komunyakaa, "Touch-up Man," and "False Leads" from *Pleasure Dome: New and Collected Poems* © 2001 by Yusef Komunyakaa. Reprinted by permission of Wesleyan University Press.

Barbara Babcock-Abrahams, "'A Tolerated Margin of Mess': The Trickster and His Tales Reconsidered," *Journal of the Folklore Institute* 11 (1974): 159–160. Reprinted by permission of Indiana University Press.

First published in 2013 by
PALGRAVE MACMILLAN®
in the United States—a division of St. Martin's Press LLC,
175 Fifth Avenue, New York, NY 10010.

Where this book is distributed in the UK, Europe and the rest of the world, this is by Palgrave Macmillan, a division of Macmillan Publishers Limited, registered in England, company number 785998, of Houndmills, Basingstoke, Hampshire RG21 6XS.

Palgrave Macmillan is the global academic imprint of the above companies and has companies and representatives throughout the world.

Palgrave® and Macmillan® are registered trademarks in the United States, the United Kingdom, Europe and other countries.

ISBN: 978–1–137–34471–7

Library of Congress Cataloging-in-Publication Data

Morgan, Winifred, 1938–
    The trickster figure in American literature / by Winifred Morgan.
        pages cm
    Includes bibliographical references.
    ISBN 978–1–137–34471–7 (alk. paper)
        1. American literature—History and literature.
    2. National characteristics, American, in literature.
    3. Tricksters in literature. 4. Self-knowledge in literature. I. Title.

PS169.N35M67 2013
810.9'355—dc23   2013018071

A catalogue record of the book is available from the British Library.

Design by Newgen Knowledge Works (P) Ltd., Chennai, India.

First edition: October 2013

10 9 8 7 6 5 4 3 2 1

CONTENTS

Acknowledgments   vii

1   Introduction   1
2   African Americans and an Enduring Tradition   15
3   Coyotes and Others Striving for Balance   47
4   Trickster Seeking His Fortune   73
5   Heirs of the Monkey King   103
6   Rough Mischief, Irreverence, and the Fantastic   131
Conclusion   167

Appendix I: The Monkey King   171
Notes   175
Bibliography   229
Index   249

ACKNOWLEDGMENTS

I thank the gracious library staff at Edgewood College who tracked down everything I asked of them. I also am indebted to many friends and colleagues, who have read, commented on, and criticized parts or all of this text. I want to especially thank Andrea Byrum, Ashley Byock, Binbin Fu, Lisa King, Jill Kirby, Lauren Lacey, Mary Paynter and Larry Shanahan. The flaws are still mine, but due to my perceptive readers, they are fewer. I also thank Lisa Rivero for compiling the index when I was too sick for the task.

CHAPTER 1

INTRODUCTION

America is woven of many strands.
I would recognize and let them so remain.
Our fate is to become one and yet many.
This is not prophecy but description.

—*Ralph Ellison*[1]

THE CHALLENGE

In 1952, before the civil rights legislation of the 1960s, even before Brown versus the Board of Education in 1954, a far-seeing Ralph Ellison envisioned a United States of America where despite its flaws and limitations, its all-too-different citizens worked to understand and work with one another for the common good. His great novel, *The Invisible Man*, moved the nation closer to the future he predicted.[2] Today, for all the dissonance surrounding the fact, the United States of America *is* a multicultural, multiethnic nation.[3] Groups that were once hidden or ignored minorities populate swathes of mid-American small towns as well as large coastal cities, the traditional entry immigrant points into the country. Latinos live in Iowa and Georgia; second-generation Vietnamese have settled into large areas of the Gulf Coast; and Hmong and Somali immigrants have found a home in Minneapolis. Most American Indians have at least some European-American or African-American ancestors. A biracial man has been elected president. Yet, since the United States is a nation made up of many nations, the heterogeneous composition of its population as well as its contradictory values inevitably still produce conflicts among its citizens. Americans belong to the United States by right of citizenship, yet that is only the legal tie. At a deeper, more emotional level, they belong by virtue of subscribing to a common set of principles. In the United States, the citizenry is bound to the nation primarily by its promise of an equal chance to succeed and equality before the law—the Declaration of Independence's "life, liberty, and the pursuit of happiness" and the Preamble to the Constitution's promise of "justice,...domestic tranquility,...common defense,...general welfare, and...blessings of liberty." The United States is unique among modern nations in that it has chosen both to define itself in terms of its ideals and to become a country of dissimilar peoples bound primarily by those ideals. If a case can be made for American exceptionalism, this is it.[4] From time to time—after an election where the other side has won, when someone from an untraditional background or ethnicity takes over leadership in business or public life, being part of a neighborhood or crowd where no one seems familiar—this situation leads to every American feeling like an outsider, a member of the minority.

Furthermore, the United States of America is a nation of individualists professing egalitarian ideals. Even those who vehemently espouse the concept of equality tend to think they want to be equal with those who are "ahead" or "above" them in society, rather than those whose status is "beneath" or "behind" them. Reality is far messier than the intellectual principles. Most Americans are more enamored with the idea than the reality of equity. As the speaker in Langston Hughes's "Theme for English B" says, "Sometimes perhaps you don't want to be a part of me. / Nor do I often want to be a part of you, / But we are" and a few lines earlier, "That's American."[5] Every day, Americans deal with the contradiction between the idea that everyone is equal and a common yen to get ahead regardless of the means. So what or who gives hope to disparate groups faced with this impasse?

In 2011, William T. May, a leading ethicist, weighed in on the tug-of-war between the desire for personal gain in American life and the ideals offered in the Declaration of Independence and the Preamble to the Constitution. *Testing the National Covenant* calls readers to consider the covenantal biblical origins of both documents as well as their Lockean origins and that the country thus has an ongoing covenantal responsibility to complete what has been "projected" by the two documents. May closes by saying that

> Of the voiceless there are always plenty—the repressed in hierarchical societies, the excluded in communitarian societies, and those hobbled at the gate in competitive, egalitarian societies. In its imperfection a

nation that boldly declared at its outset, "We the People," recognizes some mix of all these faults in its own life, as it keeps covenant with the unfinished political agenda ahead.[6]

Angela Glover Blackwell and her colleagues, Stewart Kwoh and Manuel Pastor, are more pragmatic than May, but they too believe that the United States needs to recognize that, regardless of individual preferences, the future of the country will be multicultural. That fact, Blackwell argues, demands that only by working toward not just legal equality but also providing significant equity and inclusion among all of its people can the nation flourish. Without access to educational, health, and transportation systems, access to adequate grocery stores and protection from displacement as their neighborhoods "improve," for example, citizens are offered an empty promise. Even worse from a political point of view, the country impoverishes itself by not investing in the people whom it needs to prosper in the future. The future of everyone, after all, depends on the existence of a healthy and educationally prepared young population capable of paying taxes to support health care and social security.

Beyond May's legalistic and altruistic approach and the more pragmatic approach of Blackwell and her colleagues, I suggest an examination of trickster stories produced by American men and women who belong to five different ethnic/racial groups in response to their experiences of inequity and exclusion. In addition to May's and to Blackwell and her colleagues' rational expositions of the problem, I believe Americans can learn from tricksters who encode a collective emotional response on the part of groups that feel they have not been treated right. Niigonwedom James Sinclair speaks of stories being the vessel that carries the cores of Anishinaabeg life.[7] Stories, and particularly trickster stories, encapsulate the self-awareness of both oral and literate cultures. As "outsiders," people call on the trickster's contrariness in dealing with what they perceive as injustices. Trickster stories thus allow the rest of us to experience vicariously another culture's deepest discontents. In addition, tricksters often suggest routes around the impasse between the promise of but lack of equity that any group is experiencing. Their neighbors, of course, may not appreciate the trickster's alternative solutions; so perhaps they might want to revisit those proposed by May, Blackwell, and others.

Just as educators increasingly use the "salad bowl" rather than the "melting pot" metaphor to help students understand American society, Americans of every background are coming to recognize that they need to develop greater understanding of one another since differences such as historical backgrounds, current needs, and aspirations remain significant to how individuals and groups approach common social concerns. The "we" and "ourselves" in American culture is far broader than the particular parochial background each citizen comes from; the simple nineteenth-century understanding of American culture, repeating the notion that everyone else will "melt" into ways established by upper-class Anglo-American males, does not match twenty-first-century reality. The American "we" encompasses all its citizens, and the country works best when it recognizes the fact. Fortunately, American literary tricksters offer readers insights about people who might otherwise always remain "other." Especially when Americans read the imaginative literature of other Americans with whom they do not automatically identify, they have the opportunity, as Toni Morrison says, "to examine centers of the self and to have the opportunity to compare these centers with the 'raceless' one with which [they] are, all of [them] most familiar."[8] Race and ethnicity offer one area where American citizens rub against one another; differences in class and gender lead to further touchiness and sometimes major conflicts, and contemporary trickster literature explores all of these dissonances.

WHAT IS A TRICKSTER?

The short answer is to think of the story about Br'er Rabbit and the Tar Baby. Br'er Rabbit and every trickster is transgressive in the cause of creativity. In the best-known American versions, the core of the Tar Baby story finds the undeserving but guileful Br'er Rabbit escaping his just punishment. In most versions of the tale, he is lazy; usually, he is a thief as well. In the Tar Baby tale and others, Br'er Rabbit encapsulates many trickster qualities. But the trickster is more than just a lazy thief with a talent for evading even cunning traps. Every culture's tricksters have a lot in common with what a *Smithsonian* article refers to as the "puny pip-squeaks" in the animal world who often, research is discovering, "get the girl" despite all expectations.[9] They are the "little guys" who overcome overwhelming odds to triumph despite their apparent lack of stature, heft, or promise.

The long answer is complicated. Tricksters represent freedom from all restraint. They frequently astonish with their ability to achieve creative breakthroughs. But they also embody what Carl Jung would call the shadow side in human nature and frequently engage in what most humans consider unacceptable, even taboo, behavior. Tricksters fascinate Jung and others because—like the male birds in Richard Conniff's *Smithsonian* article who manage to impregnate the prize females despite their inability to win the female's favor in a fair fight—tricksters reverse expectations. They are apparent weaklings who theoretically should not, but do, beat the competition. They are the losers who win: Among oral trickster traditions, Pedro Urdemales not only steals his boss's herd of pigs, he leaves the man thinking that the pigs are salvageable, only caught in a bog. The Monkey King—only a monkey after all—connives so successfully that he almost oversets heaven. Jack bumbles along and sells his mother's cow for beans. Yet he manages to kill the giant and end up with a fortune. Although his foolishness wipes out his achievement, Coyote *almost* eliminates death. And Br'er Rabbit, of course, regularly outwits the much stronger Br'er Fox and Br'er Bear. These and other tricksters from oral culture overset expectations and thus have long appealed to people who yearn for something other than the usual outcome.

Tricksters cannot be pinned down. They are "both/and" creatures—both villains, for example, and culture heroes; likely to do good or evil to humankind; usually highly sexed males whose closest connections are nonsexual attachments to older women. Nonetheless, all tricksters share many of the characteristics that folklorist Barbara Babcock-Abrahams explains in "A Tolerated Margin of Mess."[10] Pulling together much of the earlier critical anthropological literature about tricksters, Babcock-Abrahams elaborates a series of central points about tricksters. They are, first of all, marginal—not in a pejorative sense but as a reflection of all the in-between and "anti-structural" states Babcock-Abrahams is discussing. Next, tricksters are not put upon. The Spanish Pedro Urdemales of oral literature, for example, may be stuck at the bottom of the country's socioeconomic scale but successfully spends every waking moment throwing disquiet into the hearts of his oppressors. Rather than worrying about banishment or fitting in, tricksters invite chaos; in their hands it becomes a farce,[11] and hence a source of relief from otherwise absolutist norms. Thus, in modern literature, but picturing a postmodern landscape, Gerald Vizenor's Fourth Proude Cedarfair and his family navigate a violent land almost devoid of fossil fuels where only the clowns make sense. Tricksters are both "central to the action" and capable of "dissolv[ing] events" and "throw[ing] doubt on the finality of fact."[12] Tricksters explode preconceptions, so Nina Marie Martínez' s *¡Caramba!* makes a joke of male pretensions to superiority. Barbara Babcock-Abrahams lists 16 interrelated forms of "anomalousness"[13] that characterize tricksters. Whatever category a trickster encounters, he[14] blurs and confuses the distinctions that make it a category. Yet Babcock-Abrahams argues that even the apparent "antistructure [in trickster tales] implies structure and order"[15] because the trickster *consistently* disrupts order.

WHERE ARE TRICKSTERS FOUND TODAY?

These days, tricksters—and trickster tales—proliferate in those social spaces where people from different backgrounds rub against one another; and that includes most parts of the United States. When the promises in the Declaration of Independence and the Preamble to the Constitution are not realized, contemporary trickster literature takes realistic details from the lives of people intimately acquainted with the flaws of the world they live in and suggests where and how Americans might bring reality into closer alignment with the nation's ideals. While trickster discourse[16] certainly outlines major sources of social discontent in the United States, it also proposes ways in which Americans might overcome that discontent and come closer to the ideals encompassed in their official rhetoric.

Tricksters are aptly fashioned to spot the contradictions between American rhetoric and practice, deflate its self-satisfaction with humor, and suggest alternative approaches. In *Trickster Makes This World: Mischief, Myth, and Art*, Lewis Hyde asks readers to notice that tricksters proliferate wherever a society has "dirt" (Hyde's word) to hide, whenever it clings to something it would prefer remained unexamined. In response to that implicit challenge, tricksters invariably rise up and challenge any attempt to gloss over what those in power prefer to ignore. Americans value freedom, and tricksters embody ultimate, even anarchic freedom. In fact, to quote Mark Twain's response after Matthew Arnold complained that Americans lacked awe and reverence, "A discriminating irreverence is the creator and protector of human liberty."[17] Twain might also have mentioned the way American irreverence is often wrapped up in humor. Some of America's most memorable public tricksters, from Mark Twain himself to Will Rogers and more recently from Red Foxx to Steven Colbert, have always been best known as humorists. Tricksters excel at irreverence, and American literature continues to call upon a world of trickster traditions to preserve the liberty of its peoples.[18]

PARTICULAR TRICKSTERS REFLECT PARTICULAR OUTLOOKS

Because the trickster traditions of each ethnic group encode each group's hopes and its communal interpretation of life in the United States, contemporary trickster literature is especially helpful in understanding the aspirations and frustrations of people from different backgrounds. Although American tricksters' ancestors come from earlier cultures, they have become American and reflect ingrained attitudes of groups now living in the United States. No one traditional culture's trickster, however, can speak for all Americans; and each group's tricksters view American culture from their own perspective. Br'er Rabbit, for instance, takes a different approach than the Monkey King in dealing with American multiculturalism while Coyote understands getting along and getting ahead quite differently than Jack.

When they are aware of their folk roots, in order to express their strongest feelings about what is occurring in their country, writers often resort to trickster discourse they have heard from their friends and family. Thus it is helpful to lay out, as this text does, the lineaments of five prominent trickster traditions and trace them into their contemporary avatars. In doing so, this text also explores significant discontents among American racial and ethnic groups. Sometimes, the stories also reflect economic and gender discontents. Given the nation's core challenge to meld divergent peoples together as they strive to come closer to the ideals laid out in the Declaration of Independence, the United States is fortunate to have access to multiple trickster traditions. Contemporary American literature shows tricksters—to use the American Indian phrase associated with the trickster—still "going along" and urging all Americans to examine more closely their common culture and ways in which their society has yet to make its reality match the rhetoric of its ideals. Trickster tales offer a fresh look at what American culture deems "settled," "true," or "factual." Instead, tricksters offer alternatives, creative insights into how things could change for the betterment of a particular group and perhaps everyone.

Despite some commonalities among all trickster traditions, the historical experience of African Americans, American Indians, Euro-Americans, Asian Americans, and Latino groups has differed in what is now the United States; thus, their trickster tales take on different colorations. African American trickster tales, for example, carry the DNA of African tales forged in a culture that honored both its religious sanction for social hierarchy and the individual's traditional right to challenge arbitrary use of authority. Transported to America and forced to endure chattel slavery that reduced them to the status of domestic animals, African Americans adapted ancestral trickster tales from Africa and reworked them so that the tales reflected the "no-win" circumstances in which they found themselves in America. The slave's favorite trickster, Br'er Rabbit, his later human slave avatar John, and contemporary literary tricksters, including those in the mystery novels of Walter Mosley as well as the fiction of Alice Walker and Toni Morrison, know that they exist in an innately unfair and dangerous universe; they assume that the only way to survive, much less thrive, is to make use of every devious trick they can think of.[19]

Before contact with Europeans, American Indians too had well-developed trickster traditions. Traditional American Indian tricksters were tied to the land; this was true whether they were given animal forms such as coyote, rabbit, or raven or human figures such as the Black Foot Old Man. In many ways traditional Indian tricksters reflect the unforgiving nature of primitive existence. Making foolish choices, for example, can lead to famine; trusting the wrong individual can lead to one's children being devoured; choosing the self over the community can lead to death. On the other hand, American Indian tricksters are also full of earthy humor. Sometimes, the humor involves penis and farting jokes; sometimes, it involves laughing at the trickster's foolish choices. In addition, American Indians have often used trickster tales to explain natural phenomena such as why there is both a sun and moon or why all living beings experience death. Contemporary American Indian literature including, for example, that written by Sherman Alexie, Louise Erdrich, and Gerald Vizenor is often haunted by an aching sense of separation from the land and the degradation of the land.

Euro-Americans also have access to multiple well-articulated trickster traditions from many European nations. The Greek Hermes, for instance, and Scandinavian Loki offered immigrants from Europe entire trickster cycles. In America, however, the Euro-American tradition that took hold most strongly as oral literature in the broader culture was a series of tales from the British Isles about the youthful Jack who, among other marvel-filled adventures, slew a man-eating giant. A common theme in the "Jack" cycle, as in the stories of the Old Southwest that continued the tradition, is an individualistic pursuit of personal gain, the need to "get ahead." Jack's pursuit of his fortune continues to be evident in Mark Childress's female tricksters and Clyde Edgerton's scruffy malcontents as well as in John Kennedy Toole's even scruffier Ignatius Reilly. Just as the oral Jack tales carry a whiff of the marvelous, modern Euro-American trickster stories tend to relate the larger-than-life adventures of off-beat, nonconforming malcontents such as Elmore Leonard or Ken Kesey's characters.

While immigrants from other parts of Asia brought other trickster traditions, Chinese immigrants brought with them the mischievous, powerful, ever-changing Monkey King; the sheer number of Chinese immigrants to America has led to the Monkey King becoming the best-known Asian trickster. Found in both a literary colossus, *The Journey to the West*, as well as in the oral culture of the poorest peasants who immigrated to America, stories about the Monkey King who could transform himself at will pervade Chinese thinking. The Monkey King is both a mischievous trouble maker and champion of right order. Having to deal with both racism and culture shock, Chinese immigrants to the United States and their descendants continue to call on the Monkey King's resilience. His spirit informs the thinking of characters in both Maxine Hong Kingston's fairly traditional novel *Tripmaster Monkey* and Gene Luan Yang's graphic novel *America Born Chinese* as in some ways the books' young heroes are forced to and in some ways choose to change. Ironic transformations, for good and ill, occur in much of Chinese American literature, including, for example, in David Henry Hwang's *M. Butterfly*.

More than other ethnic groups, North American Latinos have melded multiple traditions. Quite often, they build on tales that originally feature Spain's peasant folk hero, Pedro Urdemales, who usually cuts the rich or powerful down to size; more often than not, however, Pedro Urdemales is mischievously irreverent rather than vicious. He is funny. Contemporary Latinos/as broaden their trickster focus, and the objects of trickster humor frequently include gender and racial as well as class inequities. Thus, while Rudolfo Anaya's fiction deals with class inequities, Latina writers such as Nina Marie Martínez or Denise Chávez go after gender bias. In the short fiction of Dagoberto Gilb and Junot Díaz, race and class often entwine. Furthermore, the fantastic forms a particularly strong trope in Latino fiction. Ron Aria's *The Road to Tamazunchale* is uniquely representative of this tendency, but other writers commonly employ touches of what some might call magical realism.

WRITTEN VERSUS ORAL TRICKSTERS

Since all contemporary literature—including American literature—lacks the "sacred context,"[20] the ritual setting of traditional trickster tales, it cannot duplicate the mythic power of tales in oral literature. Instead, contemporary stories are—to use Ralph Ellison's phrase—"time haunted"[21] rather than timeless; even the best literary tricksters are often epigones of the mythic trickster. Nonetheless, the use of trickster motifs allows writers to access at least some of the figure's power in modern settings.[22] Thus even writers who have little or no conscious intention of telling modern trickster tales still do so because tricksters reflect something very human. In the process of moving from oral culture, the literary trickster loses some qualities found in his uncontrolled and uncontrollable ancestor because—in

contrast with their traditional ancestors who *cannot* be constrained—
tricksters in modern literary culture are *allowed* latitude. Yet while
they lack the unbridled power of their predecessor, in the best literary
tricksters, readers still encounter the verve, the humor, and the wild
card unpredictability inherent in the original.

In popular culture, the Blue Man Group might be a good illustration of modern audiences authorizing tricksters to be transgressive:
The group may embarrass late arrivals by following them to their
seats with a spotlight, but no one is hurt. They may splash the first
few rows of the audience with colored liquid; however, the audience
has already been provided with plastic rain hoods. The production
may flash on their screens more words and phrases for derrieres than
most of the audience even knew existed; still in this communal space,
both the polite and rude words are all "acceptable."

SINCE 1960

The upsurge of trickster literature since 1960 reflects insistence, particularly on the part of groups affected by inequality, that the country live up to its ideals. Members of disparate groups probably felt
dissatisfied before the 1960s, but the increase in their numbers and
concomitant encouragement to speak out has been more evident since
then. Trickster discourse provides one means of tracing and analyzing
some of these developments in the stream of time. Thus, the literature
examined in this text goes back only to 1960. That date sets a limit,
but also, and more importantly, takes into account significant changes
during and since the 1960s. Social, political, and cultural upheavals
experienced by the United States during and since the 1960s have
brought into prominence the contradictions between American ideals and practice. The decade of the 1960s itself was pivotal in United
States history: Not only did the war in Vietnam shake the country's
confidence in its ability to impose its will anywhere in the world, the
United States' internal discord over civil rights culminated in the Civil
Rights legislation of 1964 and 1968, forcing Americans to reexam-
ine and reaffirm the country's commitment to its official rhetoric
trumpeting equality among races and between the sexes. Following
the same impetus, reform of immigration law, particularly the 1965
Immigration and Naturalization Law, altered centuries of bias in favor
of Western Europeans. Title IX, the upsurge of women entering into
full-time employment outside their homes, and easy access to oral con-
traceptives, all contributed to an unanticipated alteration in gender

relations. The Vietnam War, those laws, and cultural shifts continue to affect the attitudes and composition of American society.

In response to cataclysmic changes in American culture, recent generations of American writers have dug deep into different traditions of trickster lore to draw attention to inequities that America's egalitarian ideals and laws have failed to address. Each of this book's following five chapters explores a racial/ethnic trickster tradition and how the group has updated the tradition as it holds up a mirror to contemporary American society. Paralleling literary culture, oral traditions perdure and sometimes merge with pop culture as tricksters discombobulate established power relations among races, classes, and genders.

Lewis Hyde's insight—that the presence of a trickster indicates that a society is trying to ignore something important—and Mark Twain's insight—that irreverence, the trickster's forte, bolsters freedom—have particular relevance for American literature because over more than 200 years, the United States has led the world in proclaiming the rhetoric of equality and individual worth while practicing racist slavery, fostering policies that diminish nonwhite peoples, and oppressing its weakest populations. Readymade for this situation, tricksters undercut self-satisfaction even as most Americans prefer focusing on the country's ideals rather than its inadequacies—a very human failing. In addition, while black slavery, wars against American Indians, Asian exclusion laws, legally enforced sexism, blatant land grabs of Hispanic-owned lands, and crushing economic inequities even among Euro-Americans no longer characterize American culture as blatantly as they once did, basic inequalities persist. Furthermore, since the rich and powerful have always been a minority, the overwhelming majority of Americans sometimes feel the pinch of being treated differently. So not surprisingly, every major and a number of smaller groups of Americans have resorted to trickster discourse from time to time in order to "speak back" to their perceived oppressors. Much of the most memorable, most trenchant trickster discourse emerges from the most oppressed peoples.

HUMOR'S ROLE

Toying as they do with each society's most sensitive discontents, trickster tales embody bedrock truths so paradoxical and unsettling that they need to be treated warily and wrapped in humor. The fact that tricksters are always treated with some kind of humor—whether

giggles, guffaws, high comic art, or irony—registers someone's dis-
gruntlement beneath a seemingly placid social surface; the trickster's
comic role complements his role as a naysayer, providing a release for
socially unacceptable instincts. Cloaked in humor, tricksters also offer
a kind of palliative to the pain and discomfort inherent in difficult
social interactions. Through the ages, humor has often marked, as well
as shaped, shifts in political, social, and religious power. Particularly
through their humor, tricksters can offer a distraction or a release
because humor at once reveals tension between groups and holds up
to scorn one side or another. Humor often makes it possible for its per-
petrators and audiences to literally laugh, letting off emotional steam
and getting a new perspective; and people with a new perspective have
a better chance of being able to alter an untenable external situation.
The audience of a trickster tale moves beyond victimhood; trickster
humor makes them members of a community with a strategic edge.

Earlier Critical Attention to Tricksters

Although a number of fine books and articles have been published
about literary tricksters, no one text has placed the major traditions found in the United States side by side and compared how the
work of contemporary writers updates those traditions. No text has
examined these five trickster traditions for what they tell Americans
about America. That, however, is the focus of this text, *The Trickster
Figure in American Literature*. As a rule, book-length treatments
have focused on tricksters in one or more cultures, on tricksters in
the work of a limited number of writers, or in the work of writers
before the 1960s. In addition, given that thinkers from various backgrounds continue to be fascinated by tricksters, many of the best
texts are collections of essays by experts from multiple disciplines.
The essays edited by William J. Hynes and William G. Doty, *Mythical
Trickster Figures: Contours, Contexts, and Criticisms*, for example, is
less interested in literary tricksters than those from oral literature.
At least a couple of books, Elizabeth Ammons and Annette White-
Parks's *Tricksterism in Turn-of-the-Century American Literature:
A Multicultural Perspective* and Ruthann Knechel Johansen's *The
Narrative Secret of Flannery O'Connor*, use trickster discourse to
examine American writers working before 1960. The introduction to
Jeanne Campbell Reesman's edited volume, *Trickster Lives: Culture
and Myth in American Fiction*, parses different theoretical approaches
to and understandings of tricksters as emanations of human understanding and as cultural constructs. In Reesman's collection, the

essays by major critics utilize multiple theoretical approaches to explore trickster discourse in the work of various writers from multiple ethnic backgrounds through the years. Jeanne Rosier Smith's *Writing Tricksters: Mythic Gambols in American Ethnic Literature*, taking a feminist look at the trickster discourse in the works of Maxine Hong Kingston, Toni Morrison, and Louise Erdrich, reflects on the ties between these writers' contemporary tricksters and their roots in ethnic culture. Lewis Hyde's *Trickster Makes This World: Mischief, Myth, and Art* weaves the origins of tricksters in psychology and myth with their continuing roles in visual as well as literary culture. More recently, the essays in Deanna Reder and Linda M. Morra's *Troubling Tricksters: Revisioning Critical Conversations* take issue, on the one hand, with overgeneralizations they have encountered about pantribal tricksters while, on the other hand, they follow current creative and critical ruminations about tricksters particularly in indigenous Canadian literature.

Instead of these approaches, *The Trickster Figure in American Literature* attempts in successive chapters first to briefly review some significant oral tales demonstrating the uniqueness of different tricksters from large segments of the Unites States' population: tricksters from African American, American Indian, Euro-American, Asian American, and Latino/a backgrounds, and then to demonstrate the persistence of that trickster energy in recent American literature written by men and women from these same backgrounds. The persistence of these traditions offers insight into how large blocks of the United States' population view themselves and their fellow citizens.

The number of books about tricksters or featuring literary tricksters should be no surprise. Literary tricksters intrigue readers, provide lively action, and almost always supply a laugh. They continue to flourish in recent American literature because they are lively and interesting; their stories reflect real emotion and engage readers who recognize the contemporary dilemmas being played out in fiction. In addition, tricksters are good for taking the pulse, so to speak, of a society. In a country such as the United States of America, tricksters remind listeners and readers that the ideals espoused by the law and traditions have not been achieved. Nor will they or can they be finally achieved; they are ideals. As Robert D. Pelton tells readers, the trickster serves as "hermeneutics in action."[23] But the fact that the actuality does not jibe with reality is an uncomfortable truth, so many readers and especially consumers of popular culture prefer to avoid that bit of unpleasantness. Nonetheless, as American literature has grown beyond a canon of works by dead white men, it has also come to encompass the work of men and women from disparate backgrounds and to value the trickster's creativity and humor; knowing that these are just a stage, American readers have come to value even the destruction and chaos tricksters create. Tricksters from many cultural backgrounds combine in American literature to provide the richness that is American culture. The trickster's creativity and humor engage readers and make the stories popular while the trickster keeps stirring things up in contemporary American culture but moving everyone closer to what the country professes.

CHAPTER 2

AFRICAN AMERICANS AND AN
ENDURING TRADITION

In the crucible of American racial slavery, the trickster traditions of Africa became African American; these traditions have persisted throughout African American culture to contemporary times.[1] The spider Ananse morphed into the Caribbean Nance and Aunt Nancy. The West African Esu-Elegbara changed into the signifying monkey, while the African rabbit or hare turned into Br'er Rabbit. Characteristics of African American tricksters were intensified in the dire circumstances of chattel slavery. Thus, for example, given the minimal food allotments slaves received, the trickster's theft of food pointed the way for starving people to survive.[2] Slaves always lacked power beyond the power of their wits; they knew that like the trickster Br'er Rabbit, in this milieu, they constituted prey. They knew that their circumstance behooved them to be wary of becoming dupes themselves or underestimating their masters.[3] They needed to use all their skills at manipulation and chicanery while they appeared to act with decorum and apparent politeness toward those who might devour them.[4] In John W. Roberts's words, "Slavery itself was a trick—a trick with words that turned a human being into a piece of property. In the world of enslaved blacks, the ways of the treacherous had to be learned, mastered, and dealt with on a daily basis."[5] In America, from slavery through contemporary times, African Americans have revised and updated their African trickster traditions to address lingering power imbalances.

Differentiating them from most other trickster traditions, African and African American trickster tales are characterized primarily by the trickster's sheer pleasure in the use of cunning to overcome a more powerful foe. In contrast with the tricksters from Euro-American and from American Indian trickster traditions, for example, African and African American tricksters seldom take on the fool's role. When the trickster does act foolishly, the results are apt to be fatal. Thus in an African Bakongo tale resembling the African American "Br'er Rabbit and the Tar Baby," after Rabbit gets caught in birdlime following his theft of water from Antelope's well, he does not get away to a briar patch refuge. Instead, Antelope laughs at Rabbit and kills him.[6] In addition, unlike most American Indian tricksters, for the most part, African and African American tricksters are more intent on eating rather than sexual gratification. Unlike Euro-American tricksters, they seldom resort to magic. The African trickster slaves brought to America functioned in a world where access to outside help including magic was unavailable; that reflected life in America as well.[7] Finally, far more than Asian American tricksters, for example, African American tricksters delight in verbal tricks.[8]

So much has been written about the horrors of slavery in North America, it is difficult to decide where to begin. The facts of chattel slavery are enough. To illustrate, while Annette Gordon-Reed's objective tone reflects her background in law, her saga about *The Hemingses of Monticello* lays out in chilling detail the combination of de jure and de facto powerlessness suffered by African and African American slaves in even the most "benign" of circumstances where some slaves were "favored."[9] Despite their close physical proximity and ties of sanguinity to the people who held them in bondage, from about 1735 when Elizabeth Hemings was "born a slave" to a full-blooded African slave woman, she and most of her progeny— including Sally, the concubine of a United States President—were defined primarily by their status as slaves until after the American Civil War; and as Gordon-Reed says, none of today's worst conditions "approach the systematic degradation and violence of American slavery sanctioned by state and church."[10]

A combination of greed, brutality, hardness of heart, and codified racism ensured that African American slaves were denied motivation to contribute to the good of the plantation society. Long-term cooperative efforts with either their masters or fellow slaves offered slaves little benefit.[11] Trickster tales, however—both those tales slaves brought with them from Africa and those they encountered in other traditions[12]—suggested duplicitous strategies for maximizing short-term goals. On the one hand, slaves were cut off from achieving long-term goals and becoming acknowledged members of a "commonwealth"; on the other hand, they did gain some short-term advantage by means of of trickster behavior.[13] Thus, since working for the slave system served no advantage, slave tricksters worked against it.

AFRICAN TRICKSTERS

The traditional African cultures in which African trickster tales developed were socially cohesive with strict roles for each member of the community and strict sanctions for violators; rigid customs repressed the lowest and most vulnerable members.[14] The trickster role, however, gave those who had no other recourse a means to challenge "irrational authority."[15] Robert D. Pelton thinks that the West African tricksters he studied "symboliz[e] the transforming power of the imagination as it pokes at, plays with, delights in, and shatters what seems to be until it becomes what is"[16]; in fact, he finds tricksters "the living core of [traditional] West African societies."[17] Pelton repeats an Ashanti tale, one that he considers quintessential because it includes characteristic touches from many trickster tales: the trickster's tendency to fall prey to contradictoriness, his arbitrary manipulation of what is physically possible and socially acceptable, and finally his power and his rootedness in the present human world.

In the Ashanti tale Pelton relates, the spider Ananse defeats Hate-to-be-contradicted whose contrariness has led to the death of "all the animals."[18] In this tale, Ananse visits Hate-to-be-contradicted but manages to avoid contradicting his host—and thus being beaten to death. Ananse then invites Hate-to-be-contradicted to visit him. On the way home, having chewed and spit out the palm nuts he has pilfered from Hate-to-be-contradicted, Ananse leaves a trail of red juice. The next day when Hate-to-be-contradicted arrives to return Ananse's visit, Ananse's children inform the guest that their father has had to take his extraordinarily long penis to the blacksmith for repairs while their mother is engaged in catching the water pot she almost dropped and broke the day before. Hate-to-be-contradicted may wonder about what he has been told but accepts that what he has seen on the path to Ananse's home is blood from Ananse's broken penis.

When Ananse returns and orders the children to cook food for Hate-to-be-contradicted, they cook a stew with one small fish and a great many peppers. Since the stew burns the mouth of Hate-to-be-contradicted, Ananse sends his son for water. However, presumably prompted by his father, the son explains to Hate-to-be-contradicted that "Our water is of three different kinds. That belonging to my father is on top, that of my mother's cowife is in the middle, and that belonging to my own mother is at the bottom. I want to draw for you only the water belonging to my mother, and if I do not take great care, it will cause a dispute."[19] At the boy's explanation, Hate-to-be-contradicted bursts out, "You little brat, you lie!" contradicting the boy and calling down on himself the fatal punishment he has dealt out to others.

Noting Ananse's contrariness, Pelton calls him "both fooler and fool, maker and unmade, wily and stupid, subtle and gross, the High God's accomplice and his rival."[20] In another context, Pelton refers to the "doubleness of life" that the West African trickster symbolizes, being at once "holy and ordinary, rooted yet open to transformation, mortal and enduring."[21] In Africa and elsewhere, traditional tricksters demonstrate preternatural qualities; nonetheless, Pelton believes that tricksters are symbolic of all people trying to work out how to live human lives in social groupings, how to develop a community despite daunting challenges. Along the way, like the trickster, humans make an abundance of bad and some good choices. Ananse and other West African tricksters[22] were a vital part of the cultural baggage that slaves managed to bring to America.

In North America, slaves adapted the trickster's limited protective mantel to their lives in chattel bondage. The slave tricksters' comic masks sometimes allowed them to avoid retaliation for occasional transgressions against the system while scoring points in a contest they could not win. Providing a core story for African American literature, slave narratives graphically detail the lives of slaves who were in no way "favored" despite the theoretical "care" provided by the system's paternalism. These narratives, as well as the trickster tales embedded in them, perdure in contemporary literature written by African Americans where the trickster humor of black slaves survives as a bitter commentary on contemporary race relations.

SLAVE TRICKSTERS

For most African Americans, the antebellum South meant a slave culture with dehumanizing taboos that hemmed them in at every turn. What better ally could they find than what Laura Makarius calls "the necessary Breaker of Taboos."[23] After all, the trickster rule breaker ignores all discipline and defies the laws of both mortals and immortals—often with impunity.[24] While slaves themselves could act out such behavior only at peril of their lives, in their tales, they could and did identify with heroes who knew the "trick" that could alter the way things are.[25]

ANIMAL TRICKSTERS

The precarious conditions of subsistence in Sub-Saharan Africa had worked against the ideals of "harmony, friendship, and trust…while deception, greed, and cleverness emerge[ed] as valuable behavioral traits."[26] In the slave culture of the antebellum South, conditions had not improved. In fact, surviving necessitated that slaves become tricksters. From the slaves' standpoint, they were still struggling to endure intolerable conditions; furthermore, their masters' mistreatment of slaves justified any stratagem; "cleverness, guile, [or] wit [were] the most advantageous behavioral options for dealing with the slave masters in certain generic situations."[27] In addition, animal trickster tales reminded slaves how important it was to deal inventively and creatively with any situation arising from the slave–master relationship.[28]

Even the doubleness of the trickster could be made to work for slaves. Masters recognized the trickster acting the fool while slaves knew the trickster was also a conniver. The trickster's double-sidedness was part of the protective "secrecy and subterfuge"[29] that characterized all public slave humor. Some animal trickster tales, those that elicited laughter without too clearly identifying slave owners with the oppressor's role, were shared with masters. Since the time when some tales first circulated beyond oral culture, these have continued to be the best-known African American trickster tales. However, in addition to the almost universally familiar "Brer Rabbit and the Briar Patch," African Americans told a wealth of animal trickster tales,[30] the point of which was that being a dupe could be fatal but wile could prove as valuable as natural strength. In any case, as a whole, the oral tales of African Americans were not intended for consumption beyond the slave community. An indulgent Euro-American *might* find Brer Rabbit or another trickster amusing; but ultimately—since almost any Euro-American would disapprove of the trickster's amoral treachery in dealing with the ultimate treachery inherent in slavery[31]—sharing the tales could prove dangerous.

John and the Massa

Riskier than animal tales were the "John" tales because these clearly involved a slave and a master; the slave character went by a number of names, mostly commonly John, but also Jack or Nememiah or Pompey, sometimes Golias. The two central characters in these tales, "John" and the master, are locked in an ongoing conflict; they engage in a series of skirmishes in which each wins occasional victories, but neither triumphs all the time or forever.[32] In addition to being a human trickster, John is set apart from the animal tricksters by his ability to talk his way out of trouble.[33] More often than not, his tongue saves his hide. Besides language, humor plays a central role in these tales. Euro-Americans as well as African Americans could and did laugh at the tales; however, Euro-Americans laughed at what they saw as the puffed-up absurdity of John, someone who always needed to resort to tricks in order to substitute for his lack of substance.

John W. Roberts believes that many of the John and the Massa tales use the complex relationship of African American drivers and their masters as a paradigm. Drivers had a modicum of power and responsibility; to a certain extent, they had the master's ear. Although legally chattel with no more rights than the furniture their masters sat on, they also had a human relationship with those who held them in bondage. Yet, even black slave drivers knew that whatever they did, whatever their status within the slave culture, their masters nonetheless regarded them as "little more than trained animals."[34] The system of black chattel slavery relied on this assumption. Thus, using *human* wit and wile was paramount. Many of the tales depend on the very human knack of using language to assert superiority. Just as one of objectives of the slave narrative was to affirm the humanity of the slave despite an inhuman system, one objective of the John and the Massa tales was to insist that slaves had both human intelligence and feelings. John is boxed in by slavery; however, as "The Coon in the Box" illustrates, he uses every bit of his small area of maneuverability to gain whatever limited advantage he can garner. John cannot "win" but he can and does score some points. John is not an animal of prey; if he is to survive, he must make use of his *human* gifts.

The tale most commonly found in collections, often labeled "The Coon in the Box,"[35] relates the story of a slave who has convinced his master that he is preternaturally knowledgeable. The master is so convinced of the slave's ability to predict outcomes that he bets his neighbor an outrageous sum, sometimes his entire estate, that his slave cannot be tricked. The neighbor hides a raccoon in a box or under a pot; then he and the master call John to guess what is hidden there. Naturally, John does not have a clue. So he finally gives up and tells them, "Well, you got de ole coon at last."[36] Sometimes, the trickster is smart; sometimes he is just lucky—or unlucky although in this case both white men are overwhelmed by John's prescience. In

Zora Neale Hurston's retelling, John quits fortune telling after this experience; in some versions, John is well rewarded; in others, he just escapes with his hide intact.

The root tale is ancient and not necessarily tied to Southern slave culture; yet it would appeal to Euro-American Southerners because even though John effects an escape from punishment, that escape is only temporary. Reflecting a worldview, John even refers to himself with the deprecating "Coon." John is still a slave, and his "escape" has resulted from dumb luck rather than any innate intelligence. Hearing the tale, white racists could still feel free to despise John and other wily slaves. Not having lost anything of value, former slave owners could enjoy the joke as a reassertion of their legal position and innate superiority over the poor slave who has escaped only because of a fluke. In this, as in other John and the Massa tales, to Euro-American ears, humor probably softened the social criticism. Perhaps, only alert listeners even heard the critique of the cultural situation, yet the African American community that lived the reality of it would absorb every nuance. The tales are both humorous and critical. What the audience heard, however, may have been a matter of readiness and perception.

The tale's play on a double meaning reflects a familiar pleasure in words. This one and later stories share in savoring what crafted language can do. Sometimes, John's nimble tongue saves him—as when the colonel, the man for whom he works shares, accuses him of stealing watermelons out of the colonel's field. First, John tells the colonel, "Things ain't always what dey seems, Boss." Then when the colonel notes that John and his sons are coming from the direction of the colonel's watermelon patch, John responds, "What direction got to do wid a hones' [honest] man?" The colonel is "outdone by John's reply."[37]

In another frequently reprinted tale (and presumably frequently told before that), a trickster slave finesses his competition after he has convinced his master that he is a prodigious swimmer. In one version, "John" hides aboard a ship and then, after jumping overboard, swims toward it for a short while and gets the master and his wife to believe he has swum the Atlantic Ocean.[38] In another version of the same tale, "Tom" just brags that no one can outswim him.[39] In still other versions, the slave cannot swim but will not admit it. In all the variants, he brings so many heavy "provisions"—food, for example, maybe a cook stove, a bed, a dresser, and a gun—that his competitor decides that anyone who can swim with all of this extra weight is too strong to defeat. In all of these tales, Euro-American audiences could view John as paltry and dishonest if humorous.

As important as speaking out and using language to out-fox the master is, the John and the Massa tales also emphasize the paramount importance of knowing when to be quiet. That is certainly the point of the tale in which John finds a talking turtle in the bayou. The turtle responds to John's complaints about his hard life with the unsympathetic comment, "Black man, you talk too much."[40] Later, when John shows off the turtle to a white man, it refuses to speak and John gets a beating for his pains. The next time John is drawing water, the turtle tells him, "Black man, didn't I tell you you talked too much?"[41] The point, of course, is that in a situation where the "other" has irrational but overwhelming power, the prudent choice is to remain silent. This point is similarly reinforced in Frederick Douglass's *Narrative* where he recounts the tale of one of his master's numerous slaves, who—not realizing to whom he was talking—admits to a kind and friendly "stranger," actually his owner, that he has not always been well treated. For that offense, he is "sold South."

Although some "John" tales end with his achieving a short-term success, others exhibit a particularly bitter humor, illustrating all too well that the slaves recognize how inequitable their situation is—as well as their present inability to alter it. In Hurston's *Mules and Men*, one of the last two tales in the chapters devoted primarily to John stories tells about

> a nigger dat useter do a lot of prayin' up under 'simmon tree, during slavery time. He'd go up dere and pray to God and beg Him to kill all de white folks. Ole Massa heard about it and so de next day he got hisself a armload of sizeable rocks and went up de 'simmon tree, before de nigger got dere, and when he begin to pray and beg de Lawd to kill all de white folks, Ole Massa let one of dese rocks fall on Ole Nigger's head. It was a heavy rock and knocked de nigger over. So when he got up he looked up and said: "Lawd, I ast you to kill all de white folks, can't you tell a white man from a nigger?"[42]

The last John and the Massa story in *Mules and Men* has Ole John saving Ole Massa's beloved children from drowning, then producing an extraordinary crop, and being rewarded with the master's cast-off clothing. Finally, John is freed; however, the tale continues with the master's refrains that "de children love yuh...I love yuh...And Missy *like* yuh" as well as the iterated reminder, "But 'member youse a nigger.' John wisely keeps right on steppin' to Canada."[43] Both John and those who heard about his experience recognized that not even astounding service and preternatural loyalty would alter the basic situation: He was chattel. The best he could hope for would be to be treated as a favored animal; even that would be contingent on continued perfection. Getting as far away as possible was the only reasonable course.

AN UNBROKEN TRADITION

Concurrent with the oral John tales, other tricksters appearing in print during the latter part of the nineteenth century emphasize many of the same points. For example, Jake Mitchell and Robert Wilton Burton's series of newspaper tales published in Alabama during the late 1880s and early 1990s bridge oral into written culture. In Marengo Jake's tall tales told to and written up by Burton, trickster Jake continues the balancing act between the races as Burton and other white "massas" condescend to "uncle" Jake and other black men. In the meantime, Jake vies for whatever advantage he can from the relationship: In one sly tale, supposedly about the extraordinary mud in Marengo County, a Mr Jinks changes from a white to a black man when he slips into a "bottomless" slough whose mud works into his hide and kinks his hair.[44] The tales furthermore illustrate abundant crossovers and connections between African American and Euro-American oral and literary humor with touches of Baron Munchausen and the American tall tale tradition from the Old Southwest frontier familiar to most readers at least from Mark Twain's *Adventures of Huckleberry Finn*. In addition, Jake's stories recall both Twain's "Celebrated Jumping Frog of Calaveras County" and his "How to Tell a Story." Insisting on his own veracity, for example, Jake promises, "Hit's de truth, an' I ain' gwine to tell you a lie"[45]; yet he also reminds auditors that they must be dubious about some of anything they hear "becc'se, folks tells sich big lies dez days you never knows what to 'pen' on."[46]

From slave tales to contemporary writers, a line of tricksters in African American tricksters runs through Charles Chesnutt's Julius McAdoo in *The Conjure Woman* and Paul Lawrence Dunbar's short fiction through Countee Cullen's trickster-convert Sam to Ralph Ellison's *Invisible Man*.[47] Among these, Charles Chesnutt's late-nineteenth-century Uncle Julius takes prominence. While the white Robert Wilton Burton retells the oral tales of black Jake Mitchell, the African American Charles Chesnutt takes on the persona of an apparently indulgent Northerner telling about his encounters with a former slave, his coachman Julius McAdoo. One of the most chilling stories, "Po' Sandy," encapsulates the humor, extravagant imagination, and tragedy the narrator believes characterizes Negro stories from slavery times.

The central figure in "Po' Sandy" has the misfortune to be too cooperative: He resembles a dependable plow horse who is handed around
the family and accepting even when his master sells off Sandy's first
wife to a passing speculator willing to pay cash. Worn down from
being passed around and having no place of his own, Sandy complains
to his new wife, Tenie, a conjure woman. She turns him into a tree
near the swamp but turns him back in the dead of night so that they
can get together to talk. Abruptly one day, just before they plan to flee
as foxes, the master insists that Tenie go 20 miles away to nurse one of
his daughters-in-law; and while she is away, the tree is cut down and
sawed into lumber so that the master can have a new kitchen built. The
story does have elements of humor such as the bloodhounds returning again and again to the tree when set upon "run-away" Sandy's
trail. The imaginative details are also extravagant, especially the lurid
details of what happens to the deaf and dumb but presumably still
sensate Sandy as he is hacked down and finally cut into pieces of lumber. But the tale cleverly makes Sandy and Tenie's fates stand for that
of all slaves whom not even conjuring could help. The only one who
succeeds is the trickster Julius; having convinced Annie, the narrator's
wife, that the lumber of the old shack her husband was going to use
for their new kitchen has haunted associations with slavery's cruelty, he
gets her to give it to him and his friends for use as a church.

Traditional African American tricksters also turn up in the works
of Langston Hughes and Zora Neale Hurston. Tricksters are not confined to consciously literary works. Two recent biographies of Lincoln
Perry, the Stepin Fetchit of early talkies, celebrate his work playing
the fool during the early years of film talkies.[48] During the 1930s and
1940s, a contemporary and close friend of Richard Wright, Oliver
Harrington, regularly published popular cartoons featuring a trickster character called "Bootsie" in the Chicago *Defender*; and during
the 1960s, the "bad nigger," already a staple of African American culture, broke into the stand-up comedy of Red Foxx and later Richard
Pryor.[49] Tricksters remain just below the surface of a great deal of
contemporary literature with mystery writer Barbara Hambly comparing the interactions between Lapin the rabbit and his adversary,
the ugly and stupid Beuki the Hyena, to the action of her novel set
in pre–Civil War New Orleans.[50] Whatever form it takes—from the
routines of stand-up comedians to the consciously literary fiction of
accomplished writers—the African American trickster, having evolved
beyond his West African trickster forebears, has become a staple of
African American culture. In addition, like the oppression of slavery and racism that formed it, African American trickster humor is

frequently bitter; but in contrast to much of African American history, much of African American trickster humor remains flat-out funny.

Survivors of centuries of chattel slavery based primarily on skin color, African Americans have needed humor. Their tricksters encapsulate an attitude toward life's inequities: bear what you must, strike back when you can. The recognition that the wheel of fortune will turn, implicit in all trickster lore, surfaces in modern African American as well as in traditional tales. The trickster always bounces back. His roots identify him as a demigod and indestructible. Not surprisingly, human tricksters in literature are also irrepressible.

The African American trickster tradition has proven remarkably strong and resilient. It is not, however, an undiluted stream. On American soil, traditional African tricksters did develop into Br'er Rabbit and the slave John. However, the humor of the Old Southwest found in the work of Mark Twain and others also influenced African Americans. In fact, Gillian Johns not only argues for the centrality of humor in twentieth-century "African-American literary sensibility,"[51] she contends that the humor of the Old Southwest has a primary role in that sensibility. Johns believes that several representative works by George A. Schuyler, Zora Neale Hurston, and Ralph Ellison use elements from Southwestern humor to critique "racial tenets or assumptions in American literary culture."[52] In addition, as William Bernard McCarthy demonstrates in *Cinderella in America*, African slaves also absorbed a great many European cultural influences; they also adopted and adapted American Indian elements into what became apparently quintessential African American tales.[53] So modern African American tricksters may appear to derive only from African sources; but as one should expect from a people intent on signifying, they are influenced by multiple other sources as well. Yet what else could one expect from a living tradition? As Toni Morrison says in an interview with Nellie McKay, "The stories are constantly being retold, constantly being imagined within a framework."[54]

TWENTIETH AND TWENTY-FIRST-CENTURY TRICKSTERS

On Stage: "Contribution" (1969)— Killing with Kindness

The humor and engrained bitterness of slave tales remain in contemporary black literary tricksters.[55] The African American trickster's skill at manipulation and chicanery are equally apparent. Presented

Off-Broadway in 1969 by the Negro Ensemble Company, copyrighted in 1970, and anthologized several times since then, Ted Shine's "Contribution" brings the trickster tradition to the 1960s Civil Rights Era; the one-act play encapsulates and reflects many of the same elements of trickster humor familiar from antebellum tales embedded in slave narratives and traditional African American oral culture. A hard-working, hymn-singing woman just short of 80, the central character is ironically named Grace Love. On her wages as an underpaid servant, she has long since put her son through college but refuses to join him up North. Instead, she bakes corn bread for the racist sheriff; and she demands that her grandson, Eugene, visiting from the North to join a lunch-counter sit-in, present a good appearance. She scolds him for wearing a bathrobe around the house and insists he wear freshly pressed slacks, a white shirt, and a tie to the sit-in. She also wants his hair combed and parted.

In reality, she is someone who might be labeled a psychopath;[56] she is certainly a mass murderer. She insists, of course, that she does not hate anyone. Gracie Love's doubleness as a sweet old lady and vengeful angel of death marks her as a trickster.

Gracie Love has used her "Auntie" status as cook and caregiver, her apparent acceptance of the town's racist assumptions, to poison the men who have harmed her family; for good measure, she has also killed off some of their families, and no one in town has an inkling of how she has paid back and continues to pay back the town's racists. She counts on the Euro-American townspeople's expectations: They think she grieves for the people she has "nursed" and "cared for." The townspeople assume she, like other "nigras [,] is scared of death."[57] She has duped the doctors who refused to care for her sick husband into thinking of her as a kindly nurse. She tells her grandson that she has tried to get along with the town's rabid sheriff. She explains that she knows Sheriff Morrison "means well."[58] That does not stop her, however, from poisoning his corn bread rather than allow him to harm Eugene and the other sit-in participants.

The play is full of verbal and dramatic ironies. As the play opens, Mrs Love is singing a hymn and sipping a beer. She demands that her grandson maintain appearances by dressing appropriately even as she prepares to kill the sheriff. After the successful sit-in, Eugene tells her what has happened on Main Street: that the sheriff "said he'd die before a nigger sat where a white woman's ass had been. 'God is my witness!' He shouted. 'May I die before I see this place integrated!'"[59] And, of course, as Mrs Love has planned, Sheriff Morrison gets his wish. In true trickster fashion, at the end of "Contribution," Mrs

Love is moving on, thinking about getting a job as cook for the family of the racist governor of Mississippi. Implicit in the use of the African American trickster tradition is the assumption that an unfair imbalance continues, particularly in relations between blacks and whites. The underdog has no choice but to use the oppressor's blindness against him.

LITERARY FICTION

Flight to Canada (1976)—Revising the Record

Ted Shine's 1969 "Contribution" seems to look toward progress in relationships between African and Euro-Americans in the United States. The sit-in has been successful. Mrs Love has defeated a number of unregenerate racists; both she and her grandson are committed to working toward a more equitable society. The play ends with the sense that a more equitable society can be achieved. In contrast, the tone of Ishmael Reed's *Flight to Canada* is less hopeful. Reed seems to imply that "progress"—both after escape from slavery and during the late twentieth century—is illusory. Although Reed has a great deal of fun with several slave and fugitive tricksters' outmaneuvering of Swille, their grotesquely villainous master, the novel implies that fleeing a site of oppression—even moving to Canada—does not alter the basic imbalance of power between blacks and whites. The novel's arch villain, the slave owner Arthur Swille, tells Abraham Lincoln that he controls the world through "gold, energy, and power."[60] Even after the Emancipation Proclamation, even after the American Civil War, even after Swille's death, Euro-Americans still maintain control over those three commodities.

Just as the title of Claude Brown's fictionalized 1965 memoir, *Manchild in the Promised Land*, throws ironic light on the contrast between the hopes and expectations his parents had in moving to the North and Brown's upbringing amid a culture of violence in Harlem, Reed's novel argues that intractable structures of racism are at least as difficult to elude as slavery; and they remain obstinate because many people think the struggle is over. According to Reed, much of the problem lies with people of theoretical goodwill and in others who do not care what happens as long as their own economic interests are served. The Nebraska Tracers, for example, who track down fugitive slaves for Swille, defend their work as just a way to pay for their graduate school tuition. The pirate Yankee Jack defends his smash and grab approach to acquisition by explaining that he is just a middleman.

Despite some qualms, even Abraham Lincoln accepts the individual's right to private property—and slaves as private property. The slaves and former slaves in the novel are hardly better: like Stray Leechfield, they are intent on acquiring money no matter how tainted—accepting roles in pornography and in paid groveling as viable options—like 40's, holing up in some sort of survivalist mode; or like the free tradesman Carpenter, fleeing to Canada only to discover that that country is no better than the United States.

In his constant references to other literary and historical events as well as the off-the-wall quality of his narrative style, Reed resembles a trickster aficionado from the American Indian tradition, Gerald Vizeneor.[61] Unlike Vizenor, Reed may not consciously employ trickster tradition[62]; however, the effect is the same.[63]

Using an African American rather than an American Indian trickster, Ishmael Reed's *Flight to Canada* is also exploring the margins. An imaginative tour de force, *Flight to Canada* demands an active reader as it breaks down focus on dominant Euro-American history, culture, and aesthetics. Quickskill the character and Reed the author are both tricksters,[64] and what Patrick McGee says of Quickskill, "his words are his weapons,"[65] is equally true of Reed. Updating the paradigmatic eighteenth- and nineteenth-century slave narrative form, in *Flight to Canada*, Reed combines a stunning imaginative whirlwind with delight in the sound and meaning of the novel's words. In this novel, Reed plays with the taboos and bugbears, the unspoken fears and unease that permeate American race relations.

Following an enigmatic line, "Evil dogs us" by the poet James Bertolino, a line that actually sets the tone of the novel, Part I of *Flight to Canada* begins with a poem in which the fugitive slave, Quickskill, taunts his Virginian "master" with a projection of Swille's worst fears. The poem lays out the novel's themes and sets its anarchic tone—as well as beginning the novel's merry reliance on anachronism. Raven Quickskill, the poet and the novel's central character, pretends to have flown to Canada in a jumbo jet, slept in the master's bedroom with his concubine, tricked Swille's wife into giving him money from his safe, and left rat poison in his master's favorite whiskey. As the narrative's first page wonders, "Who is to say what is fact and what is fiction?"[66] In the imaginative world of the trickster, anything is possible. And the past continues into the present as race relations continue to be poisoned by black slavery's legacy. In this poisoned atmosphere, recognizing the situation's lack of viability and as a necessary "precondition for laughter and communitas," in a kind of "institutionalized clowning,"[67] Reed's trickster violates not just irrational social and legal norms but even those of time. In the trickster's world, even time and space lose their unyielding solidity.

Reed's novel plays with history and myths, with stereotypes and language. Arthur Swille, Raven's "owner" is a multinational capitalist, intent on his own aggrandizement and only tangentially interested in who wins the Civil War. He can work with either Lincoln or Jefferson Davis; in fact, he rather prefers Lincoln. Unfortunately, "Abe" allows moral scruples to get in the way of business; so he has to be assassinated. Harriet Beecher Stowe and Edgar Allan Poe, Queen Victoria and Prince Albert, Prime Minister Gladstone and the Marquis de Sade wander in and out of the narrative. The literary references are as varied as *The Idylls of the King, Our American Cousin*—the comedy playing at the time when Lincoln was shot—and *Hello, Dolly!* The novel's form itself parodies the narratives of fugitive slaves intent on establishing their humanity, intelligence, and intense desire for freedom. Reed's twentieth-century text recalls the earlier form but speaks to a new century and new challenges. Unlike earlier slave narratives, *Flight to Canada* is funny, but also harsh and angry, where the original slave narratives tended to understate commentary on even the cruelest events they spoke of. All of this is, of course, the sort of "double-voiced" literary signification—what in another place Henry Louis Gates calls, "voices in texts…that somehow talk to other texts"[68]— that he finds characteristically African American.[69] In this novel, the quadroon overseer, the Uncle Tom, and the black mammy, the Southern belle—stereotypes from other fictions—frequently work against type. Uncle Robin, the novel's apparently classic Uncle Tom, for example, turns out to be two-faced and devious. At his own peril does any white man trust Uncle Robin's ostensible servility.

Reed also plays with the meaning of names. Names, of course, often suggest character; and they do in *Flight to Canada*. Thus, one fugitive is named Stray. The master's piggish family name is Swille. His land is known as Swine'rd, Virginia. In a nod to the romantic illusions of antebellum Southern plantation, culture Reed portrays Arthur Swille as thinking of himself as the king of Camelot; his "kingdom" is equally ephemeral and fantasy-ridden as the original. Raven Quickskill's first name recalls a trickster animal atavar, the raven; the first name also suggests both the raven's innate need to fly and his glossy black color while his last name suggests his ability to maneuver through any situation. Reinforcing the notion that the African American's only safety lies in deception, the black character who defeats Swille is the Uncle Robin. What could be more innocent that a robin?

Ultimately, however—despite its comic tone and incidents—the novel is quite serious and makes abundantly clear just how thoroughly the odds are stacked against Quickskill and his compatriots. The sources of economic power are controlled by men like Swille and Yankee Jack; the people and places that promise surcease from slavery prove unreliable. Robin muses that "Canada, like freedom, is a state of mind."[70] Still, physical freedom matters. Until Swille dies, his slave Robin is tied to a role of shuffling pretense. Until Robin—the man to whom Arthur Swille inadvertently leaves his property—employs Quickskill, he is always on the run. It turns out that Quickskill's compatriots, both those who flee Swille's plantation when he does and his sometime lover Quaw Quaw have been often willing to settle for less than freedom. As Robert Elliot Fox notes, for the characters in *Flight to Canada*, the "promised land of freedom…proves to be an ever-receding horizon."[71]

In *Flight to Canada*, the tricksters actually have the largest vision: Raven offers hope and insight with his poetry; and after conning Swille for years with fulsome crass lies such as, "It's such a honor to serve such a mellifluous, stunning and elegant man as yourself, Massa Swille,"[72] Uncle Robin takes advantage of Swille's dyslexia to alter Swille's will and make himself the major beneficiary. In oral tales, the trickster's successes are short-lived and limited; even Raven Quickskill's and Uncle Robin's may be as well. The people of color in *Flight to Canada* move through mazes of obstacles, navigating one only to be confronted by another. In 1976, two centuries after the Declaration of Independence and despite the 1954 Supreme Court's decision in Brown versus the Board of Education, despite legal emancipation from slavery, despite the Civil Rights legislation passed by the United States Congress during the mid-1960s, the novel proclaims that as long as a blatant racial power imbalance exists, African Americans need to employ their trickster skills to even approach justice The trickster mode of Reed's narrative suits its message since, as Henry Louis Gates comments on one of the African trickster tales, "The folly…is to insist…on one determinate meaning, itself determined by vantage point and the mode one employs to see."[73]

Engaging emerging issues during the early 1980s, two women, Toni Morrison and Alice Walker, also invoked the African American trickster tradition in *Tar Baby* and *The Color Purple*. Racism is paramount among those issues; however, in their different ways, both women additionally recognize the workings of sexism in African American culture.

Tar Baby (1981)—An Old Tale Illustrating New Tensions

Tar Baby is about power imbalances between blacks and whites, of course, but also about inequities between the sexes, those who have money and those who do not, those who have youth and strength and those who do not. The novel's title would make almost anyone who grew up in the United States recall the folk tale about Br'er Rabbit and the Briar Patch;[74] furthermore, during a heated argument between the central characters Son and Jadine, he retells her an abbreviated version of the tale with the clear implication that all the gifts that her patrons, the Streets, have given her are so many sticky toys that have immobilized her and made her their dupe.[75] All the gifts the Streets have given her—clothes, education, a relatively easy job as social secretary and a luxurious place to stay while she considers her career options—actually bind her to them and their culture instead of leaving her free to find her own. Another character later warns Son that Jadine has "forgotten her ancient properties";[76] the implication is that she has become an admired copper goddess for magazine covers—a beautiful surface—but has lost track of who she is and where she came from, her connection to her family and people.

However, the parable of the Br'er Rabbit and the tar baby could apply equally to others, particularly Son, who becomes so bewitched by Jadine that he loses his way and turns away from the ideal of community and fraternity that has been his guiding star. Or perhaps, Son himself might be enticing Jadine from her goal of self-determination. Son recalls watching Jadine sleeping and breathing into her his "smell of tar,"[77] so his macho ethic might be the tar baby who captures her for a while. The Sweets have married for illusory gains; Jadine's Uncle Sydney and Aunt Ondine Childs serve the Sweets for illusory security. So while critics often write in terms of Jadine being enamored of false values, the novel's title and the tale it refers to resonate with multiple possibilities. It would be simplistic to think of *Tar Baby* in terms of villains and the virtuous or even in terms of tragedy. A realistic novel, *Tar Baby* disallows either frame of reference. Most of the novel's characters, including Jadine and Valerian Sweet—the retired candy manufacturer who employs Jadine's uncle and aunt and becomes Jadine's patron—are flawed human beings rather than villains. So too are William Green—so identified with his place in his family and community that he thinks of himself as "Son"; Valerian's wife Margaret; and Jadine's aunt and uncle, the Childs. (In a patriarchy, the Childs remain children.)

Although other characters also act as tar babies, ensnaring others and keeping them from their true paths, Jade certainly tempts Son away from his beliefs. Yet Jadine is not a villain. Orphaned early in life and presumably cut adrift from her culture, Jadine has been emotionally scarred by a prepubescent experience of seeing a street pack of male dogs impregnate a powerless bitch. Even then, only half-understanding the experience, Jadine determines "Never, Never, Never" to accept a quiescent female role. When Jadine first encounters Son in her bedroom, she is put off by his sexuality and her own sexual desire because his smile brings into view "small dark dogs."[78] Even after Jadine falls in love with Son, dominant Western culture values have become so engrained in her psyche that Jadine rejects Son's backwater but beloved hometown and all it stands for. It is incompatible with who she is. By the time Jadine meets Son, she is hardly capable of basic change. She has come to prefer high art and high fashion, wealth and luxury over ties to community and family culture; she prefers dressing well, presenting a glittering—although hard—appearance, and being in control of her personal choices to submerging herself into another person's will, even that of someone she loves, or to losing herself among what she perceives as the inferior and despised masses.

The image of Jadine flying first class to Paris and away from Son is overlaid with images that reinforce her lack of volition. In the airport washroom and before boarding, Jadine muses in terms of the lack of safety from stray dogs even in New York. Later, when she is onboard the airplane, the novel's imagery associates Jadine with "shamelessly single-minded" soldier ants, almost all of them female, who "have no time for dreaming."[79] Even the colony's queen has just a short "marriage" flight, but most of her life is given to "Bearing, hunting, eating, fighting, burying"[80]—although toward the end of a long life, she might experience a moment of regret. Jadine chooses; but rather than a tragic choice, hers is a predetermined one. Jadine thinks in terms of a forced choice: either submersion in Son's patriarchal world or single-minded focus on her own objectives. Framed in these terms, she makes the choice that apparently preserves her self-hood. She turns away from Son and her sense that she would be erased if she stayed with him. Paris offers at least the illusion of volition—choosing a career, a lover, a life. So Jadine is neither a villainous temptress nor entirely free. Despite her seeming freedom, she is someone formed—like the tar baby from oral literature—by forces outside of herself.

Like the white farmer who fashioned the tar baby in Son's retelling of the tale, Valerian Street seems at first to be guilty of forging the lures that have tempted others away from their own best interests. His wealth and power support the comfortable lifestyles of his wife Margaret, Jadine, as well as Jadines's aunt and uncle, and for a while, even Son. Street presents a lot for readers to scorn. But on closer examination, he too turns out to be someone molded by his background of wealth and privilege. Street, whose last name rimes with *sweet*, is aptly named after a Roman emperor who ruled during a part of the empire's long decline. Presumably, he means well, but he does not pay attention. He pays his loyal servants well and helps their niece as well, but he treats them all as conveniences rather than people. He marries the beautiful Margaret Lenore but rather than providing her with the emotional "safety" she craves, he does not consider her insecurity. Twenty-two years younger than Valerian, Margaret comes from a significantly lower socioeconomic class; and rather than helping her find her way in his world, he belittles her inadequacies when he disparages her for not recognizing a line from Edwin Arlington Robinson's "Richard Cory" and, worst still, not recognizing the poem's limitations. During their small son's defenseless childhood, Valerian Street had not been sufficiently engaged to realize that Margaret abused the child. Valerian allows a starving and filthy black man, Son, to live in a guest room in his home on Isle de Chevaliers; he even has his butler find one of his old suits and shoes for Son, and further Valerian has the Yardman help Son get a haircut, shoes that fit, and underclothes; still, Valerian—as are most of the characters—is intractably racist. Ironically, by the end of *Tar Baby*, the aging and physically dependent Valerian has lost his will to dominate and relies almost entirely on the decisions of his wife and butler, people he once took for granted.

For the characters in the novel, racism itself is a tar baby, immobilizing them as they get further entangled. Although the ways in which most dominant characters have been shaped by racism become clearer as the novel progresses, from the early pages of *Tar Baby*, the characters' language and unconsidered actions make racism one of the novel's preoccupations. Valerian has accepted a lifetime of impeccable service from his African American servants, Sydney and Ondine; and while he has intimated that they will be taken care of well in his will, when they displease him, they fear—presumably with good reason— that they will be let go in their old age. Valerian and Margaret Street have never learned the real names of the occasional help, Yardman and the two "Marys," Yardman's relatives. Of course, some of the black characters, Sydney, Ondine, and Jadine, also never learn to call Yardman and the Marys by name. When Eugene (Yardman) and one of the Marys, his aunt Thérèse, filch some apples, they are summarily dismissed. Before flying to Paris, when Jadine meets Alma Esmèe, Eugene and Thèrése's relative, in the airport washroom, she still calls her "Mary." Racism entangles the actions and thought processes of all the characters in *Tar Baby*.

Perhaps, because she cannot take her place for granted as the imperial Valerian does, throughout the novel, the emotionally vulnerable Margaret's language and attitudes are more overtly racist than those of Valerian. Margaret refers to Sydney and Ondine as "Kingfish and Beulah" and implies that they are Valerian's slaves, "for life."[81] Valerian, after all, always "gets his way"[82] and expects others to serve his needs. Although the candy named after him has never sold well, it has after all only been made from scraps, "syrup sludge," but is good enough as a steady seller to poor African Americans. When Son hears his name, he assumes that Valerian has been named for the candy and not the other way around. Although a young Margaret, arguing in favor of her incipient friendship with Ondine, once said that Ondine "(if not all colored people) was just as good as"[83] she and Valerian, neither Margaret nor Valerian believe or accept the argument. Angrily recalling finding Son curled up in the back of her walk-in closet, Margaret's language repeats both the worst stereotypes about African American men ("this nigger [who Valerian] lets in[,] this real life dope addict ape"[84]) and the assumption that the black man must have designs on her. Subtler in the rest of the novel, the language of racism remains pervasive.

The tar baby of racism especially affects the relationship between Jadine and Son and their inability to view one another untouched by their separate experiences. Throughout the novel, Morrison uses contrasting imagery to show that what comforts Son oppresses Jadine, and what comforts Jadine oppresses Son. Thus, Son hears the sound of women crying and envisions blank-faced men in New York, while Jadine finds affirmation in the city that has treated her as a celebrity. On the other hand, Jadine is affronted by the patriarchy and lack of amenities in Son's beloved hometown, Eloe, which he associates with warm welcoming women's voices and community. Son's dreams of being coddled and welcoming women's voices calling, " 'Come on in here, you honey you,' their laughter sprawling like a quilt over the command."[85] Jadine, on the other hand, is oppressed by dreams of heavily matriarchal black women whose full breasts and the role they represent suffocate her. Despite her loyalty to Euro-American values, Jadine does have moments of doubt such as after her encounter in a Parisian market with a heavy, tar-colored woman in a long canary dress. The woman's authenticity unnerves Jadine and makes her question the value of her success in a European world. Nonetheless, that is the world she ultimately chooses because she does not see a place for herself in the world that has nurtured Son. In contrast to Jadine's worldly sophistication, Son is associated with the warm Caribbean waters of Dominique that welcome him at the start of the novel and the "Lickety split, lickety split, lickety lickety split" of his movement on the last page of *Tar Baby*. Son finds his comfort in the briar patch of Isle de Chevaliers's undergrowth. This is the same frightening swamp that almost engulfed Jadine when she stepped off the road. Jadine prefers Parisian salons.

Racism is a tar baby, but so is easeful acceptance of privilege whether that privilege is bestowed by wealth or patriarchy or insularity. Images reinforce the contrasting pull of the conflicting values embodied by Jadine's patrons, the Streets—and by extension—by Jadine and her uncle and aunt and those of Jadine's lover, Son. The color black, for instance, is associated with tar as are the 90 baby seals sacrificed for Jadine's Christmas gift from her Parisian suitor. So is the peat swamp that captures Jadine when she steps off the road on Isle de Chevaliers. Both are traps. On Isle de Chevaliers, the poor eat fresh avocados off the trees while the white inhabitants of mansions eat slightly wilted produce shipped in from the States. Valerian goes to great expense and trouble to raise rather common temperate-climate flowers but ignores that lush beauty of the island on which he lives. The natives are attuned to the local myths, including the tar women in the swamp and the blind horsemen on the beach, while Valerian and Margaret live in a house with lovely carvings but awkward plumbing built by poor workers with a greater sense of beauty than craft.

Beyond the racial imbalances that the novel emphasizes, the age and class differences between Valerian and Margaret, the age differences between Sydney and Ondine, and the differences in wealth between the Sweets and all of the black characters constantly remind readers of other imbalances. All of these underscore the object lesson implied in the title: many things in life can tempt one to destruction. Although Americans think in terms of Br'er Rabbit escaping to his briar patch, some African versions of the tale end with his death because he cannot return to his roots. While the demigod Trickster is indestructible, the trickster in any given story may allow him or herself to be duped and destroyed. In her gendered reading of *Tar Baby*, Jeanne Rosier Smith emphasizes the trickster roles that Jadine, Son, and Thérèse take—according to the trap each needs to avoid. Many things can be traps although no one can be caught without choosing to grab them; swatting a tar baby involves a cost.[86] The novel suggests that avoiding the trap involves other costs.[87] None of the characters in *Tar Baby* escapes unscathed. In an essay first published in the *Michigan Quarterly Review*, Morrison herself talks about how the novel's beginning and ending bookend the characters' search for "safety"[88]—an illusive goal in the real world. Perhaps not as despairing in tone as Reed's *Flight to Canada*, Morrison's *Tar Baby* still has her characters grappling with slavery's legacy of racism. Unlike Reed's Uncle Robin, none of her characters ultimately manages the necessary combination of apparent acquiescence and trickster chicanery required to redress innate power imbalances. They use the stories, however, in attempting to find a way to deal with those imbalances.

The Color Purple (1982)—Remaking Ugliness into a Fairy Tale

In contrast to *Tar Baby*, *The Color Purple* is grittier—with incest and violence playing a major part in the action—and something of a fairy tale[89]—complete with an ending that includes a community of equals organized for the healing of the characters who have suffered. In a series of letters that at first she dares to write only to God, Celie, the central character, tells of her rape by the man she thinks is her father, his stealing her two babies, his selling her in a marriage to Mr ___, then Mr ___'s chasing away Celie's beloved sister Nettie so that Celie is entirely isolated in his violent household. Once Celie moves to his house, her story becomes bound up with those of her husband's family, especially Mr ___'s son Harpo and Harpo's wife Sophia. The violence of racism and sexism affects all of their lives as well as those of the novel's minor characters. When healing does come about, it is in large part through the efforts of a series of female tricksters.

Although the most apparent of Walker's female tricksters is Lillie "Shug" Avery, most of the women characters in *The Color Purple* are tricksters. With this authorial choice, Alice Walker challenges a long African American folk tradition. The tricksters in almost all African American oral tales are male—although Louis Henry Gates, Jr., mentions that the West African trickster Esu is female as well as male, or perhaps more properly both.[90] Shug reflects Esu's sexual ambivalence. She is bisexual, having born three of Mr ___'s children, but she also becomes his second wife's long-term lover. Although his wife Celie quickly tells him she finds Shug's admirable qualities womanly, Mr ___ asserts that Shug acts "more manly than most men."[91] In true trickster fashion, Shug leaves her children for her mother to raise. Emotionally, tricksters are children rather than paternal or maternal. Their role is not to build the community through nurturing children.

Shug is the most individualistic character in *The Color Purple* and the least willing to accept her culture's mores. Instead, she works to balance power inequities. As is common among heroic characters, her antecedents are unclear. For all that she disrupts, she heals; for all that she betrays, she demonstrates intense loyalty. Her musical talent and personality draw others as surely as the sugar her nickname recalls; regardless of what the preacher and church ladies call her, Shug is "Queen Honeybee." Shug dominates through her personality rather than personal beauty. Her black skin, pointed nose, and fleshy mouth may not fit the usual norm of beauty; but even sick and worn out, she has a commanding presence and refuses to allow Mr ___ to smoke in her sick room. She has a prodigious talent as a singer. She is prodigal with both her personal gifts and her money. Shug displays the engaging—and sometimes off-putting—mix of opposites one expects in tricksters. Unfettered by boundaries, Shug does not care what anybody else thinks; and she says whatever comes to mind regardless of the company. In a casual show of power, she single-handedly makes a success of Harpo's juke joint by starting her comeback there. In no time, Shug is singing all over the country and again earning ample salaries. Shug starts Squeak—the woman Sophia's husband, Harpo, takes up with after Sophia leaves him—on her path to a singing career; Shug filches Nettie's letter from Mr ___'s pocket and gives Celie hope for the first time in her adult life; Shug frees Celie from Mr ___'s dominance and takes her away to Memphis; Shug starts Celie on her path to a job and then a business making distinctive, comfortable pants for both men and women. Shug makes things happen.

Celie, the downtrodden central character in *The Color Purple* at first may seem an unlikely trickster. In fact, in multiple ways, Celie too is a trickster. While she can indeed be "tricky," she is first a trickster in that her letters to God and then to her sister Nettie allow her to write herself into understanding herself and her world. She creates a new world. Having come from a fractured world, Celie—the most vulnerable and least likely of heroines—also takes on the powerful role of the African trickster Esu, a "classic figure of mediation and of the unity of opposed forces."[92]

In the last chapter of *The Signifying Monkey*, Henry Louis Gates, Jr. lays out in detail how Walker—through Celie's writing herself into being—has "Signified"[93] upon Zora Neale Hurston's Janie in *Their Eyes Were Watching God*. Janie too found her dialect voice and also spoke herself into being. Gates believes that both Walker and Hurston belong to an African American literary tradition, Signifying in order to speak to and reflect upon the words and ideas of earlier

African American and Euro-American writers. According to Gates, this process of Signifying connects Walker's Celie back through time and folk culture to the monkeys of African myth who instructed the African trickster in the divination of human fate. This is noteworthy since through the dispersion and mixing of Africans in the Americas, the signifying monkey came to take on a central place in the trickster's role of interpreting the meaning of events.[94] As narrator, Celie translates all the characters' words and actions in addition to mediating between them and the reader. Both of these roles according to Gates are traditional trickster roles since tricksters are fundamentally mediators between gods and humans.[95]

On a more obvious level, as her writing helps her to gain a sense of self and with a lot of help from Shug, Celie also takes on the trickster roles of initiating jokes that contend with those in power and eventually manipulating major events. Her first small evidence of rebellion comes when Celie puts a bit of her own spit into her vicious father-in-law's drinking water and then on his next visit decides to put Shug Avery's urine in his drinking water. In time, Celie is able to curse her abusive husband, declare independence, and start her pants-making business. Perhaps even more impressive, she even gets her husband to listen to her.

Actually, in this fairy tale–like story, not only Celie but also most of the female characters demonstrate some trickster behavior.[96] This is true of even Squeak and Eleanor Jane—the white woman whom Sophia raises when forced to work for a white family. Squeak tells her uncle-violater a Br'er Rabbit and the Tar Baby lie in order to get Sophia out of prison. In the course of the novel, she also literally finds her voice and demands to be called by her real name, Mary Agnes. Even Eleanor Jane manages, better than anyone else, to disguise yams in appetizing dishes that Susie Q—Squeak's daughter—will eat even though Susie Q hates the tubers as much as she needs them to combat her sickle-cell anemia.

Capturing and expressing as they do, "the social and moral dilemmas of people living under conditions of enforced political and economic marginality,"[97] tricksters and their antics appeal to women as well as men. In *The Color Purple*, an overtly "womanish" novel, Alice Walker focuses on female tricksters working to subvert the engrained patriarchy of traditional African American culture as well as the engrained racism of mainstream American culture. Given the centrality of Walker's message, the firestorm of criticism against *The Color Purple* by black male reviewers is hardly surprising.[98]

Yusef Komunyakaa's Poetry (1980s and 1990s)—Lethal Subservience

Commonly encountered in the fabric of literary novels and plays, the trickster motif of apparently accepting unfair social structures in order to mask rebellion also surfaces in poetry and popular culture. For instance, though probably best known for his often reprinted poem "Facing It,"[99] Pulitzer Prize winner Yusef Komunyakaa occasionally makes use of tricksters as social commentary.[100] Thus, the speaker in "Touch-up Man," first published in *I Apologize for the Eyes in My Head* (1986), seems to obliterate the horrors he lives with; but he does so as a trickster—hiding his real thoughts, altering the evidence.

1 I playact the three monkeys
2 carved over the lintel of a Japanese shrine,
3 mouthing my mantra: *I do*
4 *what I'm told.* I work
5 from Mr. Pain's notecards;
6 he plants the germ of each idea.
7 And I'm careful not to look
8 at his private secretary's legs,
9 as I turn the harvest through the dumb-mill
10 of my hands. Half-drunk
11 with my tray of bright tools,
12 I lean over the enlarger,
13 in the light table's chromatic glare
14 where I'm king, doctoring photographs,
15 airbrushing away the corpses.[101]

The speaker playacts "the three monkeys / carved over the lintel of a Japanese shrine," reminding readers of the oft-repeated "see no evil, hear no evil, speak no evil" monkey icons. In addition, the icons recall at once the trickster monkeys of Chinese mythology and those associated with African trickster figures. Furthermore, in line 5, the speaker signifies on *The Invisible Man*, echoing the invisible man's grandfather as he works from Mr Pain's (rather than Tom Paine's) notecards. In fact, the theme of deception and hiding anything that might lead to punishment figures throughout the poem. In line 8, the speaker refers to that bugbear of race relations, the mere idea of recklessly eyeballing "his private secretary's leg." Presumably, the woman is private in more than one sense. Instead, the speaker concentrates on the images that his hands and mind are also supposed to ignore—the corpses in the photographs of memory. Yet the speaker is also "king" (line 14), "half-drunk with [his] tray of bright tools" including an "enlarger" (lines 10–12). Even as he speaks of "doctoring photographs, airbrushing away the corpses" (lines 14–15), he is committing them to his memory and those of his readers. A trickster, the speaker breaks down time periods, merging the echo-in-the-blood of slave–master relations with the details of twentieth-century photographic technology.

Another trickster, Br'er Rabbit morphed into the Bad Nigger, surfaces in "False Leads"—originally published in Komunyakaa's *Copacetic* (1984).

1 Hey! Mister Bloodhound Boss,
2 I hear you're looking for Slick Sam
3 the Freight Train Hopper.
4 They tell me he's a crack shot.
5 He can shoot a cigarette out of a man's mouth
6 thirty paces of an owl's call.
7 This morning I glimpsed red
8 against that treeline.
9 Aïe, aïe, mo gagnin toi.
10 Wise not to let night catch you out there.
11 You can get so close to a man
12 you can taste his breath.
13 They say Slick Sam's a mind reader:
14 he knows what you gonna do
15 before you think it.
16 He can lead you into quicksand
17 under a veil of swamp gas.
18 Now you know me, Uncle T,
19 I wouldn't tell you no lie.
20 Slick Sam knows these piney woods
21 & he is at home here in cottonmouth country.
22 Mister, your life could be worth
23 less than a hole in a plug nickel.
24 I bet old Slick Sam knows
24 about bloodhounds & black pepper—
26 how to put a bobcat into a crocus sack.[102]

The speaker in "False Leads" warns his listener, "Mister Bloodhound Boss" (line 1), that the man he intends to hunt, "Slick Sam / the Freight Train Hopper" (lines 2–3) is a dangerous trickster. The speaker himself has also trickster power. Self-named "Uncle T" (line 18), the speaker says he "wouldn't tell you no lie" (line 19); however, this Uncle

Tom may prove just as chameleon-like as Ismael Reed's Uncle Robin. Although he couches it with a relatively safe "could," the speaker warns Sam Slick's would-be stalker, "Mister, your life could be worth / less than a hole in a plug nickel" (lines 22–23). The speaker's threats are crouched in images—fitting usage for a poet who says of himself that he "think[s] in images,"[103] and the unsettling images in the poem (shooting, a trace of red, quicksand, swamp gas, cottonmouth country) are disturbing. The poem's speaker takes the role of the traditional Br'er Rabbit to Slick Sam's Bad Nigger. Trying to stay safe, the speaker still revels in Slick's deeds.

The Slick Sam the speaker reports on is a "crack shot" who can "shoot a cigarette out of a man's mouth / thirty paces of an owl's call" (lines 5–6). The red against the tree line the speaker saw earlier in the day was only a glimpse (lines 7–8) and all the more worrisome for not being more explicit. One does not have to speak Creole to feel the threat of "Aïe, aïe, mo gagnin toi" (line 9) (translated more or less—"Oy, Oy, gotcha"). The images suggest preternatural stealth: the predator and prey close enough to not just smell but even "taste" the other's breath in the dark without being seen (lines 11–12); Sam Slick is a mind reader (line 13), someone who leads his prey to "quicksand / under a veil of swamp gas" (lines 16–17) someone "at home here in cottonmouth country" (line 21), a hunter who can "put a bobcat into a crocus sack" (line 26)—such "prey" might just turn the tables on and "bag" the putative hunter. Befitting the badman tradition, the poem even evidences the rhythm of the dozens.[104]

POPULAR FICTION—THE TRICKSTER MORPHING INTO THE BADMAN FOLK HERO

Popular writers continue to make frequent use of the trickster, particularly the badman tradition, in popular mystery tales. Walter Mosley has developed more than one mystery series that employs tricksters; in his Easy Rawlins's series, Easy's childhood friend Mouse is a trickster;[105] in his Fearless Jones series, the narrator, Paris Minton, and his friend Fearless share the role. Pearl Cleage's character Blue also skirts conventional morality in the badman tradition.[106]

John W. Roberts devotes the fifth chapter of *From Trickster to Badman* to showing how, stressed by the legal, political, and social exigencies of the South during the late nineteenth-century, the African American antebellum trickster merged with the traditional conjure man to evolve into a badman folk hero. The conjurer adds a preternatural strength and sometimes almost magical powers to the traditional trickster. This new folk hero's characteristic actions, according to Roberts, offered late-nineteenth-century African Americans living in the rural South a "model of behavior" for dealing with Euro-American power that threatened the community from without through a rigged legal system organized to leave blacks powerless and from within through the destructive actions of the "bad nigger" who threatened the community.[107] Both the legal system organized to circumscribe and keep African Americans in check[108] and the bad nigger whose violent behavior brought down the wrath of the law on the community threatened the entire African American community. Jerry H. Bryant offers a further distinction between the "bad nigger" and the badman when he notes an anonymous source who thought that, like a trickster, a badman fights with his brain as well as his emotions.[109]

Walter Mosley

Starting with *Devil in a Blue Dress* in 1990, by 2007, Mosley had published ten novels featuring Ezekiel "Easy" Rawlins and his friend Raymond Alexander, called Mouse. Although Easy narrates these novels and is the central character, Mouse—the trickster—consistently saves Easy and their community. Even in the 2002 *Bad Boy Brawly Brown* when Easy fears his friend is dead, Mouse remains a force. Easy hears Mouse's voice advising him, for example, to kill the policeman who wants to coerce him into informing on some local black organizers. Throughout the novel, Easy thinks about Mouse, their friendship, and what Mouse would do even though Mouse is supposedly dead. Riding along with another friend and aware of his friend Sam's envy of Easy's friendship with Mouse, Easy thinks,

> Raymond Alexander was the most perfect human being a black man could imagine. He was a lover and a killer and one of the best story-tellers you ever heard. He wasn't afraid of white people in general or the police in particular. Women who went to church every week would skip out on Sunday school to take off their clean white panties for him.[110]

The popularity of Mosley's Easy Rawlins's novels was helped along by several factors: great one-liners,[111] his evocation of African American reality before and during the Civil Rights Era,[112] and finally by Denzel Washington's starring role in a 1994 film adaption of *Devil in a Blue Dress* with Don Cheadle playing Mouse. It also probably did not hurt to have Bill Clinton mention that Mosley was one of his favorite writers. With 18 adult mystery novels and 16 other books in print by 2009, Mosley has indeed been a popular writer. As one would expect from such a prolific writer of popular fiction, his novels are formulaic. To say that his fiction is "formulaic" is not necessarily pejorative. As John G. Cawelti explains, popular fiction is of its nature formulaic.[113] Part of the reader's pleasure derives from the way a particular writer works with the formula. Groundbreakers alter the popular formulas. Walter Mosley has been a groundbreaker, embedding African American trickster badmen in popular noir fiction set in a post–World War II California African American working-class culture relatively unknown to the larger reading public.[114]

While Easy sometimes skirts the law because he recognizes that the world he lives in is unfair, he is an essentially fair-minded and honest man.[115] A World War II veteran, he is a workingman who holds down a job when he can. He also has an inner voice that speaks about functioning in his treacherous racist milieu: "Bide yo' time, Easy. Don't do nuthin' that you don't have to do. Just bide yo' time an' take advantage whenever you can."[116] While he is physically large, Easy is not a powerful man; in a 1996 National Public Radio (NPR) interview, Mosley calls Easy a "normal everyday person" whom the interviewer notes has "to live in an imperfect world."[117] When Easy dies in a traffic accident at the end of *Blonde Faith*, readers do not expect Mama Jo—a healer and perhaps a witch—to be able to revive him as she did for the supposedly fatally shot Mouse. Mouse is a trickster and almost indestructible; Easy is not. Although small in stature, Easy's friend Mouse is powerful; in fact, Mosley calls him a hero because he is fearless.[118] Even the most dangerous men respect Mouse. He is totally amoral: quite willing to kill Easy's enemies, willing to kill even Easy should Easy come between him and what Mouse sees as his money; Mouse is always looking for monetary gain and uninterested in how he accumulates wealth. Self-serving as all tricksters are, Mouse nonetheless protects his friend and does not foolishly cause the police to make life any harder for Easy and his other friends than they already do. For all of his seeming uncontrolled violence, he is, in fact, a calculating planner. He is definitely, in Roberts's parlance, a badman.[119]

Mosley's novels satisfy readers at many levels. First of all, he successfully melds African American trickster with fictional American noir and hard-boiled traditions. George Tuttle uses phrases such as concision and "fast pace," a "feeling of despair and cynicism" with an "emphasis on sexual relationships and the use of sex to advance the plot" to describe the fictional genre.[120] Many critics have noticed how well Easy fits Raymond Chandler's formula for the literary private investigator.[121] All of these characteristics are readily evident in Mosley's fiction. Mosley's characters differ from those in earlier Euro-American noir fiction in that Mosley's characters are intent on survival rather than self-destruction, but their milieu makes that goal challenging. In addition, Easy is always reflecting on the action. As Jerry H. Bryant says, "Amidst the moral detritus of the streets, idealism and cynicism are in a constant interplay in Easy's mind, touching on race and ethics, history and philosophy."[122] The trickster-badman helps to equalize the power disparities that threaten to overwhelm members of the African American community.

One of the ways that Mosley the writer plays the trickster is by signifying on the work of others, including African Americans.[123] One of the most evident of these events appears in the dedication at the beginning of *Blonde Faith*, "In Memory of August Wilson." Much of Easy Rawlins's commentary has the flavor of Langston Hughes's Jesse B. Semple. The series itself, with its homage to African American trickster badmen and noir fiction, signifies on the writing Mosley expects his audience to be familiar with. The conjure woman, Mama Jo, makes readers recall Charles Chesnutt's conjure woman and perhaps other nineteenth-century men and women from oral culture. In *Bad Boy Brawly Brown*, Easy works at Sojourner Truth Junior High. Mosley's Paris Minton might almost be Ralph Ellison's invisible man as he explains,

> I was wily but numb. That was my defense against the law. I didn't have the slightest antagonism toward those peace officers. That might come as a surprise to anyone who hasn't had the experience of being a black man in America. I wasn't angry, because we were just actors playing parts written down before any one of us was born.[124]

In a further exchange, bookseller Minton trades questions and answers with the police officers who are amazed that he really does know who wrote *Madame Bovary* and *The Mysterious Stranger*.

Mosley's Watts settings are also appealing for their sense of place. Just as readers enjoy Sara Paretsky's and Donna Leon's crime novels for their evocation of Chicago and Venice, Anne Perry's evocation of Victorian England or the World War I front, and Boris Akunin's evocation of Czarist Russia, in Walter Mosley's fiction, readers get to explore a fictional Los Angeles and Watts of generations ago. If anything, Mosley crushes his readers with a plethora of action and characters; but over the course of his 18 mysteries, Mosley has managed to paint a broader and broader picture of community. While the novelistic world of *Devil in a Blue Dress* feels satisfying and complete, it is still very much a black world with white edges. As the Easy Rawlins's novels progress, they are increasingly populated by a multiracial, multicultural cast of African Americans, of course, but also Africans, Caribbean blacks, Mexican Americans, Vietnamese Americans, Chinese Americans, and Euro-Americans. These characters demonstrate a variety of ethnic backgrounds within their racial heritage, as well as differing levels of morality and understanding. A number of families are interracial through blood or adoption. The groupings held up for admiration are the people such as the Mexican American Primo and his black wife Flower who nurture generations of children and Easy's adopted son Jesus, or Juice, who is always looking out for someone vulnerable.

With their trickster discourse, writers comment on and interpret interactions in their culture. Walter Mosley belongs to a long line of African American writers focused on this task. African Americans continue to "Signify" on Euro-American as well as their own folk sources. One has only to read one of Yusef Komunyakaa's many interviews, for instance, to be aware of the multiple poetic sources and influences he credits.[125] Nonetheless, the deepest, most lasting influences continue to be those forged in years of indispensable concealment and subversive resistance. Many African Americans still see themselves in Br'er Rabbit, outnumbered and besieged by a dominant culture whose oppression is all the more painful for lack of acknowledgment. In dealing with this environment, nothing has proven more effective than the trickster discourse inherited through several hundred years of slave experience from their African ancestors and then nurtured by generations of oral discourse and literary signifying. In the hands of generations of speakers and writers, African American trickster humor has served as beacon of hope, insisting that neither slavery nor racism and neither gender nor racial oppression have to triumph.

CHAPTER 3

COYOTES AND OTHERS STRIVING
FOR BALANCE

American Indian tricksters present a contrast with African and African American tricksters who above all exult in outwitting a stronger, more powerful opponent; African American oral tales and later written tales are about power imbalances and gaining an advantage even when the advantage proves ephemeral. Br'er Rabbit will always lose in a physical confrontation with Br'er Fox or Br'er Bear; John cannot overcome the Massa's entrenched power. Racism and sexism set up equally impossible odds in contemporary stories such as *The Color Purple*. So, rather than attempting a suicidal frontal attack, African American tricksters concentrate on whittling down the odds in their favor by using their wits and employing guile.

American Indian tricksters also enjoy winning against more powerful opponents. However, American Indian trickster tales from traditional oral cultures tend to emphasize jockeying for sex and food; for all the romanticizing about them in popular culture today, pre-European-contact American Indians often lived precarious lives characterized by cycles of abundance and starvation. The environment itself was often the most dangerous opponent. Theirs was not a world that encouraged lone wolves. Everyone needed the group; so more often than not, oral tales from the period before anyone was writing them down featured self-focused tricksters as object lessons demonstrating foolish or dangerously antisocial behavior. American Indian tricksters are particularly complex.[1] After contact with Europeans and more particularly in contemporary times, written tales continue to reflect the oral tradition. Since contact, however, besides having to contend with the environment, American Indians have had to cope with encroaching Euro-Americans. Modern written stories focus especially on all the losses that American Indians have endured as individualistic Euro-Americans altered just about everything: relationships with the land and the environment, the ways an individual succeeds. Contemporary trickster stories are about attempts to compensate for losses. They explore the borderlands between what was and what is, between the imposed white world of individualism and the traditional American Indian world that values the communal.

Thus, like the coyotes, ravens, and spiders that adapt to urban areas as well as the wild, animals that American Indians have chosen as avatars of the trickster, American Indian tricksters that once thrived in oral literature continue to flourish in written literature though they also cross cultural boundaries and mix traditional culture with modern experiences. The elemental challenges of American Indians' traditional past—staving off the elements, getting enough to eat, dealing with enemy forays into their territories—have given way over the years to other, less obvious, but no less life-threatening challenges: the loss, for example, during the eighteenth and nineteenth centuries of most of their land; the diminishment and sometimes loss in recent years of their languages and traditional ways—all the cultural trappings that allow people to self-identify. Cultural ravages have been made worse by further harm caused by racism, family disruptions, violence, and alcoholism. In Sherman Alexie's *The Absolutely True Diary of a Part-Time Indian*, the adolescent narrator laments, "We Indians have LOST EVERYTHING. We lost our native land, we lost our languages, we lost our songs and dances. We lost each other. We only know how to lose and be lost."[2] Nonetheless, although central to American Indian lives, the story of their losses does not represent the entire story; and the fact that tricksters and trickster stories remain a major part of American Indian culture indicates that, like their tricksters, American Indians are still "going along."

In traditional oral literature, what are sometimes called folk tales, Indian tricksters generally appear as animals with human traits. In contemporary written literature, they usually take on human form. Even in oral literature, animal tricksters act in such a human fashion that one forgets they are animals. Given the large geographic area of the North American continent, it is hardly surprising that American Indian tricksters from all over the continent take on a multitude of animal forms and names. Traditional Indian tricksters from oral literature include Coyote, Raven, Blue Jay, Raccoon, Dragonfly, South Wind, Kamukamts, Iktomi—a spider; and Old Man or Old Man Napi but also Veeho, Nixant, Sitconski, Masau'u or Skelton Man, Gloosap, Nanabozho, and still others. Of course, these tricksters from all over the continental United States are not identical. As Franchot Ballinger reminds readers, even the same tale told by story tellers from different tribes may have different meanings according to each tribe's cultural values.[3] Since the original tales were oral, their meaning might also alter over time. At least superficially, the tricksters found in the work of the writers featured in this chapter suggest diverse approaches to understanding the trickster's role in contemporary culture. Writers feature particular tricksters from their own tribal and personal backgrounds. Yet, even though James Welch's Old Man Napi, Raven, and Wolverine share some trickster characteristics with Robert J. Conley's Rabbit, and just as Leslie Marmon Silko's Coyote, Sherman Alexie's Coyote, Louise Erdrich's skunk, and Gerald Vizenor's bears teach trickster wisdom to fictional characters and to readers, they are not all the same trickster. They are affected by the different areas where the oral culture originally flourished and by the contemporary authors' closeness or lack of closeness to their tradition's oral cultures and by their individual approaches to their work.

The trickster's animal forms—everything from mink and turtle, to the wolverine and the blue jay, and maybe the skunk Lipsha Morrissey encounters in Louise Erdrich's *The Bingo Palace*—always belong to relatively weak but adaptable creatures. Among animal tricksters, coyote is preeminent, but a common characteristic among all animal trickster avatars is their ability to explore new territories and to fit in wherever they find themselves. On the extensive reach of Coyote in popular culture, Gerald Vizenor comments sarcastically that "it's become a kind of American 'kitsch,' the trickster . . . and it's spreading rapidly, like killer bees."[4]

Although the facile way Coyote has become synonymous with Trickster in popular culture annoys Vizenor, the rapidity with which this has happened reflects the physical animal's invasion of new terrain. The coyote's adaptability is legendary. Metropolitan newspapers and magazines regularly carry stories about the ways coyotes have made themselves at home in seemingly unlikely places. Often the stories feature conflicts between urban dwellers who cherish the *idea* of having wildlife in the city and the tendency of actual coyotes to make meals of small, untended pets. In any case, coyotes are ubiquitous: Their current range covers most of the North American continent. They are fairly prolific, with females sometimes bearing up to 19—though usually between 3 and 6—pups a year. Although coyotes are carnivorous and prefer fresh kill, they will also eat carrion or fruits, vegetables, and berries if that is all that is available. Coyotes will hunt by themselves, with another coyote, or in packs. To suit altered circumstances, coyotes change their breeding habits, diet, and social dynamics. Considering how pervasive they are in North America, visual sightings of coyotes are amazingly infrequent. Taking a moonlight walk in the country, however, often leads to hearing their vocalizations. Well before the advent of Europeans to North America, American Indians had noticed the coyote's adaptability; since coyotes persist like cockroaches, the grudging admiration accorded to them by contemporary popular culture has been well earned.

Although far from being the only animal trickster avatar among American Indians, coyotes are one of the most common. Wherever they live, real coyotes remain wild animals; Indians whose ancestors lived in close contact with coyotes for millennia are unlikely to confuse them with either domestic animals or the Wile E. Coyote of Saturday morning cartoons. Real coyotes have earned respect as survivors. They do not challenge large predators, including adult humans, in either the wild or in urban areas. Instead, they forage for whatever food is available; they explore and adapt to new environments. Furthermore, in common with the trickster of oral literature, coyotes are not cute. Nor are the tricksters in contemporary literature written by American Indians.

RESTORING BALANCE

Finding one's place in a group and the environment plays an important role among animals like the coyote. Fitting in, finding a balance, is also important to American Indians. As Paula Gunn Allen notes in her introduction to the stories in *Spider Woman's Granddaughters*, balance, or as Allen says, "right relationship...right kinship" is the bedrock of American Indian aesthetics.[5] Consonant with this value, Trickster serves to first upset the balance, to introduce a disharmony, and then to rebuild the relationship in a new fashion. Members of any culture are periodically impelled to upset something that is deeply imbedded in their culture. Thus, after examining Coyote tales from the Oregon country, Jarold Ramsey posits that among the Indians of the area, trickster tales provided emotional release for people oppressed by a shame society[6] where a perceived loss of honor inexorably leads to a crushing sense of unworthiness causing individuals to feel they lack personal value.

As a rule, American Indian communities value balance but do not perceive any particular moment as a final balance. Trickster-generated chaos never achieves a stasis because the trickster is always "going along." A moment is just one moment. In addition, neither innately good or bad, beneficent nor evil, American Indian tricksters mirror the animals that are part of the physical world. Animals present humankind with gifts but remain inherently unpredictable and potentially dangerous. American Indian oral literature conveys the sense that tricksters, including those who appear in human form, should be treated as cautiously as one would deal with a wild animal. Tricksters are more than animals, however; they demonstrate animal, human, and god-like qualities.[7] Tricksters from traditional oral literature belong to mythic time. Although narrators and listeners feel a close bond to the tricksters whose exploits are being related, the tricksters still harbor a wild animal's threat; so everyone needs to be wary around them.[8] Just as the tricksters of traditional oral culture generally offered their listeners risible object lessons about destructive paths, the tricksters in modern written tales are generally surrounded by humor; but their choices are equally questionable. Almost invariably funny, American Indian tricksters from both oral and written literature offer dubious models for emulation. Nonetheless, they do suggest ways others might negotiate borders between individual desires and communal needs.

ORAL LITERATURE

Traditional

Although traditional American Indian tricksters found in oral culture, products of the imagination, sometimes function as culture heroes and explore the borders for flesh-and-blood men and women, they can also cause considerable harm. Sometimes, they both benefit and harm others. In one Okanogan tale from the far Northwest, "Coyote Kills Owl-Woman," Coyote saves the children who have been stolen by the evil Owl-Woman;[9] but in another tale, "Coyote Cooks His Daughter," Trickster kills and eats his own daughter.[10] In still another tale, he sleeps with his daughter.[11] As Rabbit in Omaha lore, Trickster serves the people with a good turn when he kills a monster in "How Rabbit Killed Hill-That-Swallows";[12] but as Ictinike in "Ictinike and the Woman and Child," he also kills and eats a child with whose care he has been entrusted.[13] The mix of good and bad in trickster tales reflects the especially American Indian recognition that life is also mix; after all, according to many interpretations—the trickster "is in charge of the world in which we live"[14]—a real rather than ideal world.

Even though people have to be wary of tricksters, American Indian tales also tell of ways in which tricksters have benefited the community. They are culture heroes. For example, in a typical tale that also appears in other Indian traditions, an Inuit story tells how Raven steals back the light from a shaman who has taken it away and hidden it in a couple of bladders. Through a trick of course, Raven impregnates the shaman's wife with a child (Raven himself) who, after he has been born, appears fascinated by the bladders. Naturally, no one—not even the thief of light—can refuse a child, so the baby is allowed to play with the smaller bladder. Once the bladder rolls down the passageway to the outdoors, Raven takes back his own shape; and in their own shapes, he and his friend Fox take turns, passing the bladder back and forth between them as they flee. When it appears that the evil shaman may catch them, they peck and tear at the bladder, releasing the light. They have stolen only the smaller bladder, however; so daylight now alternates between different parts of the earth. Had they gotten the larger bladder from the shaman, the world would know light all of the time.[15]

American Indian tales commonly paint the trickster as someone whose thoughtless lack of foresight has caused the world to be the way it is. Thus in a Nez Perce tale that parallels the story of Orpheus and Eurydice, Coyote does not "guard against [his] inclination to do foolish things"[16] and ignores the death spirit's warning against touching his dead wife's spirit until five days have passed. She vanishes, and Coyote has "established for [humans] death as it is." He tries to retrace his steps and repeat the ceremonies that almost brought her back to life, but he cannot undo what he has done.

Probably most common are those American Indian tales in which the trickster is *both* wily and foolish. Thus, in a Salish-Kootni/Flathead tale from the Northwest, through trickery, Blue Jay builds up the appearance of his legs so that they look "larger and stronger than anyone's"[17] and so wins a chief's daughter. In usual trickster fashion, however, he forgets that the clay and moss with which he has created his illusion will rinse away in water. So when he attempts to carry his new wife across a stream, of course, everyone recognizes him for himself and he loses his prize.

In still another tale, this one from California, Spider is spinning a thread to let Coyote down from the sky where he has been marooned after hunting the sun; Coyote has been warned that under no circumstances should he look up and certainly not laugh. But Coyote *cannot* resist looking up at the Spider's behind and laughing.[18] The editor of this text situates this and other trickster tales in the dark of winter where the tension of months of close quarters is chafing every-one.[19] For the entire community, therefore, the stories served many purposes; but "the dominant experience of listening to Coyote stories was the longed-for feeling of being united with others in laughter, everyone liberated and joyful."[20] Malcolm Margolin's interpretation thus conjoins the emphasis of Babcock and others on Trickster as lib-erator with the emphasis of Ballinger and others on Trickster as object lesson.[21] The Coyote knows better but cannot resist what will surely defeat his purpose; on the other hand, everyone knows that while his choices would destroy anyone else, Coyote is a trickster; so he will bounce back to repeat his disruptive behavior.

Perhaps most characteristic of the American Indian trickster is his unpredictability; this characteristic might be allied to the Indians' expe-riences of having to navigate one unpredictable milieu after another. Accordingly, a Creek tale portrays a trickster Rabbit who is weak and cowardly yet willing to take on and best a lion (Big Man-eater). Nonetheless, because Rabbit's creativity is at best "haphazard,"[22] he may steal fire for humans or protect them from dangerous forest ani-mals or he may kill an orphan and offer the child to the lion to win the carnivore's confidence.[23] In this Creek tale, Rabbit is the weakling who needs to resort to trickery to survive, but he is also a sorcerer capable of altering the width of a creek.[24] About all the listeners can be sure of is that at some point, a trickster will overreach himself and lose his temporary advantage.

In the Tradition of Oral Literature

As do others,[25] American Indians continue to delight in making up and elaborating trickster tales.[26] A book popular during the 1990s, Clarissa Pinkola Estés's *Women Who Run with the Wolves*, retells a tale, "Coyote Dick," that her informant had heard " 'from a Navajo who heard it from a Mexican who heard it from a Hopi.' "[27] Peter Blue Cloud also makes up new coyote tales with the feel of traditional oral tales. For instance, capturing the trickster's self-absorption and vanity, "When the Sun Was Very Young" explains the appearance of sunshine by having Coyote urinate into what he thinks is a rabbit hole and inadvertently flushing out the sun who has been living inside a mountain. Instead of being fearful or astounded, Coyote congratu-lates himself and his "powerful" penis.[28] In another tale set in con-temporary Berkeley, "Street Scene," Blue Cloud has Coyote selling supposedly wax candle penises at a sidewalk table. Coyote sticks his own penis up through the tabletop so that women customers can caress it in order to feel the authenticity of his products.[29] Blue Cloud's tale captures the exuberant lasciviousness found in many traditional oral trickster tales.

Another foray into making up new oral tales, David Smith's collection of Winnebago tales includes a tale, "Wak'djunk'aga and the Car,"[30] in which Trickster cracks his head open on a telephone pole because he has not bothered to wear a seatbelt. In one of my classes, students who had read Richard Erdoes and Alfonzo Ortiz's *American Indian Trickster Tales* also delighted in writing original trickster tales; the students set many of their tales in contemporary times and places.[31] At least as much as Blue Cloud, the undergraduates reveled in tricksters' toilet humor and sexual grossness in addition to their power and flair for the unexpected. They understood as well as tellers of traditional tales that the trickster offers an alternative to any society's strictures, an opportunity to explore the edges of what is deemed acceptable and venture over into the socially unacceptable. In the classroom's communal space, they enjoyed listening to one another's tales of the trickster's excesses. The students' tales showed that they understood Roger Welsch's encapsulation that the American Indian trickster's "logic is not an extension or denial of our own but actually an alternative, neither better nor worse, simply equivalent... his madness, contradiction, cruelty, kindness, random behavior, his uncertain nature, and erratic identity... reflect the nature of god or of divine intent."[32]

For American Indian tricksters, "the world as it is" is not always necessary or fixed; they are intent on suggesting alternatives. With some frequency, this acceptance of change is reflected in their association with gambling. Both early and recent oral tales reflect what popular medieval and ancient European tales called the wheel of fortune: Neither good times nor bad times last indefinitely. Someone is always winning; others lose. The wheel is always spinning, however; so what everyone is currently experiencing not only can, but probably will, change.

WRITTEN LITERATURE

Tricksters as Background Fabric: *Fools Crow* (1986), *Reservation Blues* (1996), and *The Dark Way* (2000)

The trickster naturally appeals to peoples whose lives have been characterized by loss. Almost incidentally, late-twentieth-century American Indian writers have commonly woven tricksters or traditional trickster tales into the background fabric of their stories. This tendency is

apparent, for example, in James Welch's *Fools Crow*, an elegiac historical novel set during the decade after the Civil War, when the Blackfoot
Indians were decimated by Euro-American encroachments accompanied by smallpox, diminishing buffalo herds, and diminished cultural
identity. In a similar fashion, Robert J. Conley weaves traditional
trickster thinking into one of his historical novels drawn from oral
sources, *The Dark Way*. In Conley's novel, a young Cherokee priest,
Like-a-Pumpkin, sent on a mission to the west of the Mississippi to
bring Thunder to the Real People (the Cherokee) and thus to break
a drought, is captured and enslaved though he finally escapes.[33]
Conley's novel features Jisdu, the trickster rabbit, as an adventurer-
guide. Setting his fiction much later—in the late twentieth and early
twenty-first centuries—Sherman Alexie picks up the theme of dealing
with losses and weaves trickster imagery and themes throughout his
work, but especially in the character of Thomas Builds the Fire, the
central character in *Reservation Blues*, in the earlier linked short stories
found in *The Lone Ranger and Tonto Fist Fight in Heaven*, and the
1998 movie *Smoke Signals*, for which Alexie wrote the script based on
characters from the short stories.

In *Reservation Blues*, set ten years after *The Lone Ranger and Tonto
Fist Fight in Heaven*, Thomas is alone—lacking even the solace of
his loving grandmother's companionship.[34] Nonetheless, even alone,
Thomas—like Coyote and Raven—is almost indestructible. He lacks
the physical strength of other characters; but he has survived the fire
that has killed his parents, the regular beatings and taunts he takes
from his peers, the breakup of his Indian band, and the slights he
suffers for just being an Indian whenever he leaves the reservation.
Trickster inhabits stories; in Alexie's tales, Thomas Builds the Fire
constructs stories that revise and contend with Euro-American versions of both the past and the present.[35] Through his stories, Thomas
Builds the Fire reworks the historical past in which American Indians
lost their land and had their culture relegated to secondary status, part
of the background in currently dominant Euro-American culture.[36]

In Conley, Welch, and Alexie's fiction, the trickster recedes into the
background, but that actually reinforces the pervasiveness of tricksters
and their promise of change in addition to their value in negotiating
change—in Conley's novel from a priestly to a more secular society, in
Welch's novel from a traditional hunting culture to one that will have
to accommodate itself to the intrusions of Euro-American people and
culture into Indian territories, in Alexie's fiction from a despairing
minority to a people cobbling together a new story.[37]

EMBODYING TRICKSTER IN MODERN TIMES

Although they are not alone in making trickster sensibility central in their work, in recent times, the fiction of three American Indian writers in particular—Leslie Marmon Silko, Louise Erdrich, and Gerald Vizenor—showcases different trickster approaches and tribal traditions.[38] Each writer makes extensive use of trickster motifs, but the characters in their work also embody the trickster in modern garb proposing alternative means of dealing with monumental changes in the American Indian's physical world and zeitgeist. Silko's Tayo, for example, has to deal with disruptions brought about by war, guilt, alcoholism, and loss of cultural integrity. Erdrich's characters are trying to find their footing in the shifting sands of multiple cultures. Many of Vizenor's characters are awash in a postapocalyptic world brought on by greed and a refusal to care for the common good. All deal with racism. All of the characters find balance in their traditions, particularly in the trickster's ability to explore the margins, to alter what is, to negotiate, and to adapt.

Silko's major novel *Ceremony* was written before the other authors' work and—though responding to political and social tensions of her own time—deals with events of an earlier generation. All of Erdrich's novels feature tricksters using wile to overcome crushing circumstances; Vizenor—born earlier than the others,[39] publishing prolifically during the 1970s through 1990s, but no longer as active as the younger Erdrich, for example—makes tricksters central to both his fiction and his academic prose.

Leslie Marmon Silko and the Wicked
Trickster: *Ceremony* (1977)

As Americans reacted with repulsion to ways in which the Vietnam War had and continued to tear apart their nation during the 1970s, Leslie Marmon Silko published *Ceremony*, a novel that explores the necessity of balance and right relations for the sake of a healthy world and the need to pass through the borderlands, taking what is useful from the outside without giving up the essence of one's heritage. Silko's central character is a World War II veteran named Tayo. In the course of the novel, Tayo comes to understand that since both his balance and that of his community have been ripped apart through violence, hatred, and war, they both need ceremonies to restore what has been lost; but ceremonies by themselves are not enough. Part of what the community needs is the disruptive trickster, someone who can literally and figuratively cross borders and trick the witches, evil tricksters. A Laguna Pueblo Indian, Silko, portrays a trickster different from those from other parts of the United States. Tayo needs to become a trickster in order to defeat a series of evil tricksters. Southwestern tricksters associated with witchery are not playful and usually more overtly malicious than those from other Indian cultures. The evil tricksters in *Ceremony* are closely associated with the death-dealing events that bedevil Tayo. The horrors of World War II jungle warfare, his guilty feelings about his uncle's and cousin's deaths, the army hospital's lack of understanding and attempts to deal with his post-traumatic stress disorder (PTSD) primarily with drugs, his own and his friends' internalized racism, their shared alcoholism, and the land's environmental degradation reflected in the extended drought are all "tricks" that he needs to overcome. Old Betonie's ceremonies help, but Tayo himself needs to grow beyond simplistic reliance on either old Pueblo traditions or Euro-American medicine. Over time, Tayo comes to realize that hanging out and drinking with his fellow Indian veterans is destroying him. Equally destructive is the violence with which Tayo is tempted to meet his friends' violence.[40]

Tayo finally moves in a new direction when he recaptures and starts to make his uncle's spotted cattle his own. By reappropriating the cattle stolen from his uncle, he is dealing with the drought, getting beyond his guilty feelings, sloughing off the false principles taught by his Euro-American teachers, reconnecting with the uncle who raised him, plus working with and for his community. The cattle are an old breed, adapted to the arid land; but they also represent the future because Tayo—following the example of his uncle—plans to breed them into a new herd that can withstand the rigors of the arid Southwest and support his family. Tayo takes what is health-giving from his past and his people's past, but he adapts it to a new future. Having repudiated the violence and self-destructive lifestyles of his drinking companions, Tayo is actually going "home"[41] and in the process casts off the "dead skin Coyote threw on him."[42] In order to defeat the witchery[43] in his life, Tayo learns from his enemies and outwits them with his unanticipated adaptation. Ever the trickster-transformer, Tayo keeps developing—as Gretchen Ronnow notes—new selves.[44] Unlike his calcified opponents, Tayo is able to move beyond his insecurities. His losses—the deaths of his loved ones and his diminishment through participating in combat—are real; yet Tayo grows into understanding his failings and limitations. The witchery of the degraded land, racism, war, and self-hatred is real; but the trickster in Tayo is able to change himself and thus deal with them.

The youth who had once been influenced too easily by his cousin, by Euro-American racism, by crushing remorse over his own weak choices, and by his self-destructive friends grows up, and as a strong member of his community resists the forces that, in destroying him, would further diminish his people. His adult ability to accept what he has learned from outsiders as well as his culture's wisdom figures mark him as an integrated man whose life is in balance.

VIZENOR'S DANGEROUS MERRY PRANKSTERS

Writing both academic prose about and fiction featuring trickster discourse, as he would say, a "mixed blood" Ojibwe from the upper Midwest, Gerald Vizenor, has written extensively about American Indian tricksters. For Vizenor, trickster discourse involves warping what readers expect in traditional novels written in English. He delights in the disjunctions that a postmodern approach produces and often overlays that postmodern mindset on his trickster narratives. Thus in Vizenor's fiction, the usual directional signals such as character motivation as well as time, gender, spatial, and historical limitations often blur rather than clarify relationships. The very structure of Vizenor's fiction can be as slippery as tricksters themselves. Anthropologists have written more extensively about American Indian tricksters than Vizenor; however, he despises anthropologists whom he believes waste too much time on analysis and miss the elusive spirit of trickster tales. In fact, Vizenor objects that social scientists generally miss the core of tribal peoples as a whole.[45] Specifically, according to Vizenor, the "methodology [of anthropologists] is narrow, bigoted, and colonial...most of what they say...about colonial people is...at very best, bullshit."[46] Vizenor goes on to say that anthropologists have "never been right once"[47] because "[t]he methodologies of the social sciences separate people from the human spirit."[48] Since he believes that trickster stories in particular inherently resist dissection, Vizenor balks at social science approaches that dissect and isolate one or another part of tribal life. Instead, for Vizenor "[t]he trickster is a comic liberator in a narrative and the sign with the most resistance to social science monologues."[49] Instead of an anthropological approach, Vizenor proposes tricksterism as a strategy for bridging the growing gap between contemporary and traditional American Indian worlds, between contemporary and traditional American Indian worlds, and between internal psychological divisions among peoples such as the Chinese and Americans who think they are entirely different.

In writing and speaking about tricksters, Vizenor iterates phrases and ideas that have special significance to him. He says, for example, "the trickster is comic nature in a language game" and that "tricksters are embodied in imagination and liberate the mind,"[50] and "the trickster is a communal sign in a comic narrative."[51] He sees tricksters offering the possibility of something new happening—and thus reifying an alternative, an imaginative "comic liberation"[52]; hence, Vizenor believes that trickster stories are a healthy response on the part of American Indians to the disruptions and dislocations, the losses, visited upon them in their encounters with Euro-Americans. Vizenor notes that no one narrator or tribal entity owns the trickster, but together "listeners, readers and four points of view in third person narratives" share the trickster as a communal sign.[53] Even more explicitly, Vizenor says, "In trickster narratives the listeners and readers imagine their liberation; the trickster is a sign and the world is 'deconstructed' in a discourse."[54] He is making the point that people who can imagine something different have a chance to achieve an alternative to things as they are. Yet angry as individual American Indian narrators may be, the trickster himself remains a comic figure. In fact, Vizenor himself repeatedly refers to the trickster as "compassionate."

With particularly imaginative flair, Vizenor fleshes out this world of comic liberation in his novels: *Griever: An American Monkey King in China* (1987), *The Trickster of Liberty: Tribal Heirs to a Wild Baronage* (1988), *The Heirs of Columbus* (1991), and especially, *Bearheart: The Heirship Chronicles* (1990).[55] Vizenor uses fiction to illustrate and argue in favor of his ideas. Thus, his notion of "mixed blood" is important because he resists the idea of purity belonging to individual people or things. Vizenor's vision is international though it is a comic mix of internationalism that entwines the fates of humans and the natural world. Those of his characters dealt a bad hand by fate use luck and wile to achieve success. In Vizenor's fiction, inventiveness and creativity trump mere intelligence and education. His stories mock history as it is taught in schools, substituting his own version for the ones commonly found in textbooks. Characters and ideas weave in and out from one of Vizenor's fictions to another. His novels are often graphically violent. In his fictional work, Vizenor replaces the sad tale of the symbolic dying Indian with trickster humor, inherently communal, always open to possibility.

In an interview given to Laura Coltelli, Vizenor says that when he left to teach in China at Tianjin University in the fall of 1983, he had no intention of writing a novel or anything else.[56] Nonetheless, he was intrigued by the Chinese Monkey King, whom he recognized as a first cousin to the American Indian trickster. Vizenor's dedication of *Griever: An American Monkey King in China* to "Mixed Bloods and Compassionate Tricksters"[57] thus refers to both the American Indian and Chinese tricksters. *Griever* is an episodic story following the surreal adventures of Griever de Tianjin, originally Griever de Hocus, a mixed blood from the White Earth Reservation who becomes one with the Monkey King. An exuberant wanderer, Griever moves about upsetting the authorities and freeing the oppressed. The novel is full of ironies but a major irony is that the story shows "socialist" China absorbing the worst aspects of capitalism while the "liberal" West does its best to kowtow to China. The novel's comment on the détente between the Reagan administration and the Communist leaders is that "[t]he trickster...was severed from his shadow in a culture that pretended to understand the monkey king and trickiness."[58] In fact, according to Vizenor, only the downtrodden and outcasts within the Chinese culture, certainly not the repressive Communist leaders, understand the monkey king's liberation of spirit. Vizenor says that the ordinary Chinese people he met in Tianjan first found his woodland trickster embarrassing; but "[o]nce they recognized him in the category of the Monkey King, they loved him. He could do anything and he was compassionate about it...they knew he wasn't going to destroy anything—he was just going to screw up and they just loved it."[59]

In *The Trickster of Liberty*, something of a prequel to *Griever* and *Bearheart*, Vizenor continues in a similar vein; but as he warns readers in his Prologue, the trickster in this novel—and in much of his thinking—is a communal language game, a "comic *holotrope*,"[60] no more something that can be pinned down than a figure of speech written in light. The stories in this book also abound with characters, mostly the descendants of Luster Browne who, having been handed the worst allotment in Minnesota, turn it into a "barony." The novel follows the adventures of various descendants, including those who visit China, and pokes considerable fun at all things connected with social science. The characters are wildly successful with inventive ways of creating new money-making ventures—selling ginseng, for example, to the Chinese and developing an ultralight industry on the baronage; in addition, Browne's descendants are consistently in conflict with the US government but somehow manage to arrive at a settlement both sides can accept. Unlike Ishi, the last of the Yahi Indians, who was housed and studied at the University of California, Berkeley, during the early part of the twentieth century and who appears in one of the stories, Browne's descendants are constantly growing, changing, adapting, and surmounting challenges from a dominant culture that would try to study and define them to death. Luster Browne's descendants are *not* the last of their kind. Instead, they have figured out how to meld their heritage and traditions with those of the dominant culture so that they, rather than their oppressors, control the outcome of their encounters.

In *The Heirs of Columbus*, another stew of tricksters—many of them surnamed either Browne or Columbus—continues to contend with the forces of modern culture and defeat them, of course. If there is a central character in *Heirs*, he is Stone Columbus who runs a late-night radio talk show and a floating (thus offshore and beyond government control) tribal casino named the *Santa María Casino*. In another inventive combination of comic characters and action, everyone is crossing human, animal, and logical boundaries as they go about stealing back Indian inheritances. The book itself steals back Columbus. As much as anything, the theme may lie in the line that "humor rules and tricksters heal"[61] since the central conceit in this text published several years before the United States' sesquicentennial is that Christopher Columbus was actually a descendant of the Mayans, who took civilization to the Greeks. The story thus redraws cultural boundaries as it redraws the history of Columbus and European encounters with the American Indians. In *The Heirs of Columbus*, Columbus was coming home to America in 1492. When he lost the support of the Spanish crown as the value of his "discoveries" came into doubt, according to *Heirs*, Columbus's spirit moved to the headwaters of the Mississippi. The men and women of this tale are his spiritual descendants.

BEARHEART: THE HEIRSHIP CHRONICLES

Probably his strongest attack on "terminal creeds," Vizenor's *Bearheart* recapitulates themes from other texts but also packages them in his most explicitly trickster novel. While everything Vizenor writes deals with tricksters, *Bearheart* is structured—if that word is not too contradictory—to show off trickster tale contrariness.[62]

The story is also, as Vizenor himself admits, "the darkest" of his visions.[63] In *Bearheart*, the "buffer zone of organized society" has already been destroyed.[64] The novel opens in an apocalyptic, post-petroleum future; and the "sovereign cedar nation"[65] that the Fourth Proude Cedarfair's family has defended for generations is again under siege by a federal government that covets the family's cedars for fuel. This time, despite some successful holding actions, Fourth Proude

decides to leave rather than fight further. His choice is appropriate for
a trickster who is always "going along." Fourth Proude certainly recalls
his father's conviction that "beliefs and traditions are not greater than
the love of living."[66] As important as the land is, the story implies that
the cultural essence of the people and the stories that embody them
are more important. His daughters have already abandoned the Cedar
nation and presumably their heritage. Rather than be obliterated, forever losing the stories, Proude and his wife, Rosina Parent, leave. On
the road, they are joined by other travelers—a pilgrim circus of mixed
bloods and some Euro-Americans in what Vizenor calls "a mythical
and a historical thematic reversal" of the popular myth of "a Western
expansion [of whites] encountering the savage" Indians.[67] Toward the
end of their journey, after Proude trades a powerless medicine bundle
for his group's train passage to Santa Fe, Proude explains to Rosina,
"the power of the human spirit is carried in the heart not in histories
and materials. The living hold the foolishness of the past."[68]

Only apparently foolish, Proude toys with his opponents; and the
anger in *Bearheart* repeats the anger in *Darkness* written years earlier
following the fuel crisis of the early 1970s. The putative narrator,
Saint Louis Bearheart, as well as the novel's author, Gerald Vizenor,
are angry about human—though particularly at Euro-American—
arrogance that has led to the degradation of the land as well as people
and animals. The novel links all of these: Humans are a link in a chain
of being that includes animals and the land. The human greed that
has led to a vicious and dangerous world without fossil fuel in the
novel also reflects a refusal to recognize human, animal, and cosmic
interdependence. Brutality against women and native peoples reflects
individualism gone wild. The violence visited on both women and
men in the novel is graphic and cruel. Vizenor chooses this, and he
defends the novel's violence noting that it differs from the violence
people encounter in popular media where "We are denied the tragic
wisdom of the violence we must endure. Our violence becomes entertainment, but not tragic wisdom."[69]

Rather than making human greed alone the central villain, however, Vizenor rails against "terminal creeds" that he believes lead to
inhumanity in the mad world of this novel.[70] Woven through the
novel are parodies of Christian, particularly Roman Catholic, prayers,
rituals, and beliefs. Vizenor replaces Christian religion with belief in
oneness of being: Proude Cedarfair with his male ancestors, humans
with animals, humans and animals with the earth. American Indian
as well as Euro-American characters in the novel succumb to terminal creeds; in one way or another, the members of Proude's pilgrim

circus who die or leave his group have ignored their relationship with all that exists beyond them in the natural world. Their embrace of terminal creeds makes them vulnerable.

Louis Owens points out that *Bearheart* parodies the *Canterbury Tales'* pilgrimage but additionally reverses the triumphalism of the "westering pattern of American 'discovery' and settlement."[71] Vizenor's novel gathers as motley a group of travelers as found in the *Canterbury Tales*, and the name of at least one character, Justice Pardone Cozener, even echoes the cozening pardoner.[72] Except for a few, however, most of Vizenor's pilgrims are physically and emotionally twisted. No worthy knight nor salt-of-the-earth plowman joins Proude's band. Their progress to the American Southwest is anything but triumphal, and the novel ends ambiguously.

Instead of recognizing a unity at the heart of creation, each of the failed pilgrims substitutes another terminal creed. From whatever tradition or authority it arises, a terminal creed limits human possibilities and interactions. The mostly gory demises of the pilgrims who succumb to terminal creeds reflect the inadequacy of terminal creeds, even those that seem to honor American "Indianness." For instance, Lilith Mae immolates herself after losing to the evil gambler, Sir Cecil Staples. According to the evil gambler, she has been a gambler but also a "fool[ ] who believe[d] in luck."[73] Lilith lacks the balance and innate trickiness of Proude who does defeat Staples.[74] In the person of the sociopathic Sir Cecil Staples, Proude contends with an unequivocally evil opponent who embodies the sickness of the society Proude has to defeat. He gambles, and like Erdrich's Nanapush and unlike Lilith Mae, Proude combines quick wit with his willingness to take chances and the knowledge that he cannot control chance.

Only a few of Proude's pilgrims survive to the end of the novel. In response to a vision bear's instruction, Proude and the orphan Inawa Biwalde (who has joined the circus pilgrims in St. Paul and become Proude's disciple) turn into bears and during the winter solstice, enter the fourth world through a spirit window at New Mexico's Pueblo Bonito. Rosina and the parawoman arrive too late to join them. Rosina finds the bear tracks but nothing else. She is left behind while the old medicine men laugh and tell stories about Changing Woman and vision bears. Given the association of the Navajo Changing Woman with recurrent new life, a possibility exists that even the dead world of this novel might revive. Proude, however, the novel's most consistent trickster, has moved on. As part of the novel's fictional frame, the putative author, an old shaman functionary about to retire from the Bureau of Indian Affairs, has warned his female American

Indian Movement interrogator that the book is "about" "sex and violence"[75]—but also, more explicitly in *Darkness,* the novel is about "Spiritual and material travels without oil through sex and violence, time and evil . . . Travels through terminal creeds and social deeds escaping from evil into the fourth world where bears speak the secret languages of saints."[76] In revising *Darkness in Saint Louis Bearheart* to *Bearheart: The Heirship Chronicles,* Vizenor may not have wanted to be quite as explicit as this line from the previous novel. The intention, however, remains. The end of the novel remains not just another, a "fourth world,"[77] but an imaginative disentanglement via trickster discourse from preconceived mental straight jackets. Since no one—except the fictional shaman, Fourth Proude, and his apprentice Inawa Biwald—ever entirely "arrives," the journey is crucial because survival demands constant adaptation in order to arrive at a balance.

Playing with Chance—Louise Erdrich's Larger-than-Life Comic Tricksters

The central Ojibwe characters in Louise Erdrich's fiction are full of life; they are often funny. However, in a cycle of seven roughly connected novels—*Love Medicine* (1984; rev. 1993), *The Beet Queen* (1986), *Tracks* (1988), *The Bingo Palace* (1994), *Tales of Burning Love* (1996), *The Last Report on the Miracles at Little No Horse* (2001), and *Four Souls* (2004)[78]—Erdrich concentrates on how these Ojibwe tricksters respond to the vicissitudes and losses visited upon the Ojibwe by Euro-Americans during the twentieth century. Many of her characters are mixed bloods, working the margins of their truncated physical reservations[79] and finding ways to use their mixed heritage to their own and their people's advantage. Traditionally, the Ojibwe have accepted that listeners can learn from hearing stories of tricksters' adventures, their failures and their triumphs. They also believe that the stories have the power to transform listeners. Since the tricksters in this series of novels make plenty of mistakes, their misadventures lead to instructive comic tales.

A key lesson is that nothing is certain. Accepting with Nanapush, Erdrich's paramount trickster, that "Time is a fish and all of us are living on the rib on its fin"[80]—and thus apt to be brushed off at any moment—the Indian characters in Erdrich's novels are especially aware of the tenuousness of their existence. Accordingly, gambling has a particularly important role for the novels' tricksters; all of Erdrich's Indian tricksters are accomplished gamblers. Gambling is innate for tricksters because as a wisdom figure, an Arapahoe elder, tells the priest-sleuth in Margaret Coel's popular mystery novel *Killling Raven*, "life's a chance...Nothing's for certain. Can't take nothing for certain."[81] The only way to deal with so much uncertainty is to gamble.

Toward the end of *The Last Report*, the musings of the fading Agnes/Damien reinforce with a series of "if onlys" the uncertainty of the Ojibwe world—and hers since she has chosen to make the Ojibwe world her own. The tipsy Agnes/Damien thinks back to her youth and wonders,

> "If only she'd banked an hour earlier or later. If only she'd managed to fall off the moving car. If only Bernt hadn't been going to Upsala to fix the harrow...If only the priest, the first Damien, hadn't visited me with his doubts and stories. If only, if only. If only I'd thought to get out of the way when the river came for me."[82]

But, of course, since the world is a world of chance, change, and uncertainty, things did not happen that way. So as tricksters, the very embodiment of chance, Erdrich's central characters adapt to their shifting worlds. In contrast to the malevolent Coyote Silko's Tayo has to deal with or even Alexie's put-upon Thomas Builds the Fire, Erdrich characters are generally playful tricksters; and they endure and even triumph as comic characters playing with chance.

Displacement touched almost everyone living during the twentieth century. But this is particularly true for a handful of Native American families in Erdrich's novels—the Pillagers, Kashpaws, Nanapushes, Morrisseys, Lazarres, Lamartines, Adares, and Mausers[83]—who intermarry in and around the fictional town of Argus, North Dakota. For the most part, Erdrich's characters lack a sense of cultural common ground: Neither their partially assimilated Roman Catholicism nor the traditional forms and relationships that once gave meaning to their lives satisfy their present needs. Instead, Erdrich's characters depend on decreasing circles of support: since they cannot be sure of how much support to expect from even their cousins, much less the larger community, they trust only their immediate families and sometimes only their own innate ability to navigate the shoals of chance and change. In addition, since their world is already irrational and unpredictable, a core of characters call upon the trickster's comic preference for upsetting order—whatever the cost. These characters need "humor in a desperate situation,"[84] and trickster humor proves essential to their survival. While some cultures split the trickster into opposite but complementary figures such as Prometheus, who considers beforehand, and his brother Epimetheus, who reflects only after the fact, in her Argus Indian novels, Erdrich spreads out the trickster's qualities among an interrelated family of characters.

Nanapush

Even many of Erdrich's minor characters in this series of novels are tricksters; some major characters, however, stand out in part because of their skill at gambling. All are liminal characters dealing with substantial changes in their worlds. This is especially evident in the first of Erdrich's human tricksters according to chronological time, Nanapush—the old Indian who saves and informally adopts the teen-aged Fleur Pillager in *Tracks*. He is not only named for the Ojibwe trickster,[85] his actions embody his name. In *Tracks*, Nanapush is the last to live the old life of hunting and gathering; but later, in order to overcome his tribal and bureaucratic federal government foes, he uses not only his native trickster skills but also the skills he has been forced to learn at a Jesuit boarding school. An obviously liminal figure, he has witnessed the "last" of many things, and he nurtures the future in the form of Fleur's daughter, Lulu. Nanapush's house overlooks the crossroads: He likes to know what is going on. He is a storyteller, a talker. Although he lies "when it suits,"[86] he prefers to talk his way out of difficulty. He uses his skill at bluffing to wear down the local Catholic priest, Father Damien; to outfox his enemies, even to cheat Death as everyone around him dies. He is a healer, saving Lulu's frost-bitten feet, a "clever gambler,"[87] "curious,"[88] a thief who steals food from Margaret Kashpaw's house and communion wine stored in the Sisters' cellar.[89] Nanapush would be a trickster in earlier times as well; however, in the transitional period following the Dawes Act,[90] his trickster skills save an enduring remnant of his people.

Typical for an Ojibwe trickster, Nanapush demonstrates legendary sexual appetite. Having buried three wives and all of his children, as an old man, Nanapush takes up with Margaret Kashpaw and despite their monumental fights, wins her over.[91] Above all, Nanapush is tricky—aiding Fleur's suitor in winning her affections, claiming Lulu as his legal child and winning her back from the government, liter-ally ensnaring his enemy Clarence Lazarre. In revenge for an insult to Margaret Kashpaw, Nanapush uses a piano-wire snare over a shal-low pit to trap Clarence and then abandons the choking man who will remain alive only as long as he can straddle the pit. With an eye to Euro-American culture's reverence for written forms and records, Nanapush gets Father Damien to list Fleur's child—no blood relation to Nanapush—as Lulu Nanapush so that he becomes her legal father.

Nanapush is a force of nature, and his "secret jokes"[92] have an earthy, sometimes cruel flavor. For example, he mesmerizes Pauline Puyat with storytelling and an excess of tea in order to mock her foolish attempt at a silly penance (allowing herself to urinate only once a day) and to lay her open to public ridicule.

Nonetheless, for all of his mythic stature and unlike the Nanabozho for whom he is named, the human Nanapush exhibits an appealing humility and knows his limitations. When he is being smart, the trickster takes chances, plays with chance, but does not pretend to control it. Even the trickster of oral literature is at most a demigod. Like the coyote and other animal tricksters, Nanapush is successful only when he recognizes his limitations. As Nanapush explains to Fleur,

> Power dies, power goes under and gutters out, ungraspable. It is momentary, quick of flight and liable to deceive. As soon as you rely on the possession it is gone. Forget that it ever existed, and it returns. I never made the mistake of thinking that I owned my own strength, that was my secret. And so I never was alone in my failures. I was never to blame entirely when all was lost, when my desperate cures had no effect on the suffering of those I loved. For who can blame a man waiting, the doors open, the windows open, food offered, arms stretched wide? Who can blame him if the visitor does not arrive?[93]

Nanapush's ultimate secret is that he laughs "at everything."[94] Chance, after all, can go either way. Nanapush's secret is a communal one: His adopted daughter Fleur and her descendants share his wisdom although all of them—including Nanapush—fail from time to time when they give in to the temptation to try to control chance.[95]

In *The Last Report*, readers learn from Agnes/Damien of Nanapush's last days. He is still trying to find the easiest way to kill a moose and having his efforts turn out disastrously. He apparently dies but comes back to life, fights and engages in energetic sex with Margaret, and indeed finally dies.[96] Nanapush dies as he has lived: a magnificent comic hero. His flawed but larger-than-life spirit lives on to inspire the Ojibwe.

Fleur

Although female tricksters are uncommon among American Indians, Fleur Pillager, Nanapush's adopted daughter, and her daughter Lulu are, in fact, powerful tricksters. Both women are phenomenally adaptable and use whatever comes to hand. Women who might be considered inconsequential because of their gender in male-dominated societies, they use their gender to bring men into line; and they enjoy sex. More than any of Erdrich's other tricksters, however, Fleur tries to control chance and for all of her success comes close to being a tragic figure. Moreover, she is a vindictive trickster. Thus night after night in *Tracks*, the adolescent Fleur flaunts her almost preternatural skill as a card player, consistently winning a single dollar after a whole night's gambling. Frustrated and angry, the male butchers she has been gambling with rape her. But Fleur wrecks creatively cruel vengeance on them. While the narrator never makes absolutely clear if, instead of Fleur, perhaps 9-year-old Russell Kashpaw (the stepson of one of Fleur's tormentors) or 15-year-old Pauline (a tormented orphan who eventually turns into an adult tormenter) is guilty, during a tornado, *someone* locks Fleur's rapists in a meat locker where they are sheltering from the storm and leaves the men to freeze to death. The tornado is a natural occurrence, but the trickster uses whatever presents itself.

Fleur also has revenge on the men who cheat her out of her ancestors' land.[97] First, in *Tracks*, Fleur destroys the trees her oppressors covet; then she goes after the men who took advantage of her. When the Turcott Lumber Company buys the land on which she has not been able to pay taxes, Fleur seems to cause the surveyors a plague of inexplicable accidents. Finally, she notches the trees so that, ruined, they all crash down during a storm. *The Bingo Palace* narrates how—in the late 1930s—she returns to the reservation, dressed to kill, her hair in warrior's braids,[98] and wins back the Pillager land from the former Indian agent, Jewell Parker Tatro, who has bought the land from the lumber company. She entices him into playing cards with her and wins everything he owns. He thinks he can weasel her car away from her "just like he had acquired her land."[99] Instead, she defeats him.[100]

Fleur preserves her grudges and does her best to destroy her enemies. In *Four Souls*, readers learn that while she was away from the reservation, she ensnared the lumber baron who had profited from the original sale of her land. Instead of literally eviscerating John James Mauser, she marries him. He tells her, "My spirit is meant to be the slave of your spirit. I will make you my wife and give you everything I own. And more than that, I will love you no matter what you do to me, as a dog does. My spirit is meant to be g'dai, your animal, to do with as you wish, let live or kill."[101] What he predicts happens. A character in *Four Souls* comments, "He hadn't a notion in the world that it would have been easier for him if she'd used her knife."[102] As the narrator in *The Bingo Palace* comments, "Fleur was never one to take an uncalculated piece of revenge. She gave back twofold."[103] She uses what chance has given her. In later life, she also supports adaptation to the late twentieth century when she tacitly agrees to the gaming hall built on her ancestral land. Fleur realizes that the unappealing Lyman is the "fish that knows how to steal the bait, a clever operator who can use the luck that temporary loopholes in the law bring to Indians for higher causes, steady advances."[104] Although "[a]nnoyed,"[105] she chooses to trade her death for the life of her great-grandson. Much more calculating than Nanapush, Fleur considers her own actions and the world around her and only then gambles on her best chance, but from time to time, she too fails.

Lulu

Although far more humorous in her approach, Fleur's daughter Lulu proves at least as adaptable as her mother. She is also a card player and teaches her grandson Lipsha how to mark a deck. Even as an old woman in *The Bingo Palace*, she connives to give her son Gerry a chance to escape yet another jail and then makes fools of Federal Bureau of Investigation (FBI) agents searching for him. A "powerfully mindless female,"[106] in *Love Medicine*, *The Bingo Palace*, and *The Last Report*, Lulu effortlessly and endlessly seduces all sorts of men. In *The Last Report*, Agnes/Damien recognizes how even in the 1990s, the elderly Lulu thoughtlessly bewitches the middle-aged Father Jude Miller.[107] In common with her mother and her legal father, Nanapush, Lulu cannot control all that happens to her and her loved ones. Too much of life involves chance. Nonetheless, Lulu uses and even adjusts chance just as she adjusts the odds in card games. She never entirely recovers from her mother's abandonment and seems emotionally cut off from pain; but like the quintessential animal trickster, Coyote, Lulu keeps "going along." In common with her "father" Nanapush,[108] Lulu knows that "the grand scheme of the world is beyond our brains to fathom, so" the best one can do is not "try, just let it in."[109]

As much as any of her family, Lulu embodies Kimberly Blaeser's description of the trickster who "plots...gambles...sings, talks, and brags his [in this case, her] way along; [s]he breaks the rules just because they are there; [s]he repeatedly indulges h[er] gluttonous appetite for food and sex; and [s]he laughs as heartily as [s]he lives."[110] In addition, Lulu shares Nanapush's ability to navigate between apparent opposites. She is adjustable. On the one hand, she gets buffalo back grazing on the reservation; on the other, she drives the latest model Chevrolet. As do Nanapush and Fleur, Lulu adapts. Thinking back on how she ensnared (and was ensnared by) Moses

Pillager, her son Gerry's father, Lulu comments, "*The greatest wisdom doesn't know itself. The greatest plan is not to have one.*"[111] Instead, Lulu follows her trickster instincts.

Gerry

Suggesting that both chance and change in the lives of Nanapush's descendants and their adaptation will continue into the twenty-first century, Lulu's sons, Gerry Nanapush and Lyman Lamartine, as well as Gerry's children, Lipsha Morrissey and Shawn Nanapush, continue to demonstrate trickster skills. Chance lands Gerry in prison after a bar fight. Gerry's conviction for his "crime, which was done in a drunken heat and to settle the question with a cowboy of whether a Chippewa was also a nigger"[112] leads to a life sentence because Gerry is "so good at getting out of the joint and so terrible at getting caught."[113] Although his cousin Albertine thinks, "It hadn't been much of a fight" after Gerry kicked the cowboy in the scrotum, in court, the cowboy's Euro-American witnesses prove effective against Gerry—"because they have names, addresses, social security numbers, and work phones,"[114] while Gerry's Indian witnesses lack such middle-class credentials. Gerry does not help his defense by explaining that he cannot possibly have caused "that much damage since the cowboy's balls were very small targets, it had been dark, and his aim was off anyway because of two, or maybe it was three, beers."[115] Tricksters have no sense of when not to joke.

Gerry spends his adult life escaping, getting caught, being sent back to increasingly secure prisons, and then escaping again. When still another prison transfer finds him flying to a new maximum-security prison in Minnesota, he reflects that

> sitting in the still eye of chance fate [is] not random. Chance [is] full of runs and soft noise, pardons and betrayals and double-backs. Chance [is] patterns of a stranger complexity than we [can] name, but predictable. There [is] no such thing as a complete lack of order, only a design so vast it [seems] unrepetitive up close, that is, until you [sit] doing nothing for so long that your brain [aches] and, one day, just maybe, you [catch] a wider glimpse.[116]

Chance allows Gerry to escape after the plane crashes and later, aided by his son Lipsha[117] in *The Bingo Palace* and later still by his daughter Shawn and by one of his former wives, Dot, in *Tales of Burning Love*. The novel leaves Gerry presumably still running; but particularly for tricksters, nothing ever stays the same. Gerry has told Lipsha, "I

won't ever really have what you'd call a home"[118]; the last that readers hear of him in *Tales of Burning Love* is that Gerry is still running.
Gerry, all of Erdrich's male tricksters in fact, are traditional Ojibwe
tricksters, each of whom "upturns the world and runs off until it falls
again to rights and he can return. Or who, by virtue of bad choices, is
himself up-ended or killed until the world sets him to rights."[119]

While for the most part, the novels focus on these and other Indian
tricksters, Euro-American tricksters such as Wallace Pfef in *The Beet
Queen* and Agnes/Father Damien are also adept at gambling, catching
at chance and adapting to change. Over the years, Agnes/Damien, in
particular, so identifies with the Ojibwe, with whom she has worked,
and becomes such a close associate of Nanapush as to have become
by Alan Dundes's definition, a part of the folk group.[120] Her trickster
spirit is apparent when she tells Father Jude, "I have never seen the
truth without crossing my eyes. Life is crazy."[121]

Reflecting American Indian vicissitudes during the twentieth century, the world of Erdrich's Argus novels teems with trials and Indian
responses to the alterations, losses, and occasional gains in their
lives—the breakup of tribal lands, poverty, disrupted families, racism,
alcoholism, and Indian gaming. Erdrich's novels are not, however,
drear reports of Indian losses but accounts of larger-than-life trickster
responses to those woes.[122] The tricksters in Erdrich's novels do not
entirely defeat their enemies nor do they halt the changes in their
world. Yet, they live full lives, and they give their people heart. They
adapt and thrive. They thrive because they make Nanapush's wisdom
their own. "Even our bones nourish change, and even a people who
lived so close the bone and were saved for thousands of generations
by a practical philosophy, even such people as we, the Anishinaabeg,
can sometimes die, or change, or change and become."[123]

Part of the complexity of modern American Indian tricksters
derives from their having to deal with the less obvious challenges they
encounter in modern times. During precontact times, their opponents
were clear—the elements and opposing tribes. Following contact, the
nemeses causing the most damage often proved to be Euro-Americans
who thought of themselves as well-meaning friends. Thus, for example, Henry Rowe Schoolcraft and the early anthropologists who followed him thought of American Indians as a dying race but hoped
to preserve some of their interesting lore. These Euro-Americans had
little sense of how Indian stories inhered in American Indian culture
and how divorcing one from the other distorted both. In a similar
way, Senator Henry L. Dawes recognized that Euro-Americans were
usurping Indian lands. He hoped that his plan—what was eventually

enacted into law as the 1887 Dawes Severalty Act—would save Indians from Euro-American encroachments. He lacked understanding, however, of the deeply communal nature of American Indian society. His Severalty Act further fractured Indian reservations and exasperated the tensions in Indian communities. The fruits of such well-meaning efforts are apparent in modern American Indian literature as tricksters reconnoiter the new territory of dominantly Euro-American culture to reassert what they find useful for their own traditional culture.

Yet, despite the dire circumstances they navigate, American Indian tricksters often seem to be playing, even having fun. Whether working in oral or written tradition, American Indians often use the trickster as Shakespeare uses comic touches in his great tragedies—as a means of relieving the terrible tension of living through numbing destruction. On the other hand, narrators sometimes create trickster tales like Shakespeare's comedies—for the fun of it in a world that takes itself too seriously. American Indian tricksters tend to be at once transformers and comic characters. In either case, since they are not powerful as, for example, the Chinese Monkey King, they use their humor to deal with what they cannot control.

From different parts of the continent and different tribal backgrounds, American Indians continue to draw upon trickster traditions. In so doing, however, they emphasize the need to adapt as well as the coyote and raven do to suburban, urban, and rural areas. The world has changed radically since Indians wandered over the unfenced American continent; no one is more aware of the fact than American Indians. Yet contemporary American Indian writers remind everyone that as the traditional and recent oral tales show, a trickster keeps going along. Rejecting the poison of self-hatred and guilt, Leslie Marmon Silko's major trickster, Tayo, calls on the wisdom of the past but also takes what is good and useful from the contemporary world. Relentlessly creative, Gerald Vizenor's tricksters laugh at the world even as they connive to defeat their enemies. Shortening the odds in their favor when they can, Louise Erdrich's tricksters play with chance. Studying their tricksters' maneuvers, sometimes learning from the tricksters' weakness and foolish mistakes, American Indians strive for balance.

CHAPTER 4

TRICKSTER SEEKING HIS FORTUNE

More often than not, Euro-American literary tricksters are hustlers with a sense of entitlement; they are hardwired to believe in their own superiority. Yet, even though they see themselves as the center of the universe, the arrogance of Euro-American tricksters is often matched with an appealing innocence or maybe naivete. Mark Twain's Huckleberry Finn, for instance, repeatedly fools Jim and others he meets on the Mississippi; yet Huck also sympathizes with victims of greed and violence. Fewer Euro-Americans suffer under the oppressive inequities that have caused African American and American Indians to turn to trickster discourse; plenty of them, however, are dissatisfied with their lot. Actually, writers as disparate as Charles Murray and Peter Adelman argue that Euro-Americans who find themselves in the lower economic half of American population have good reason to be dissatisfied as, particularly since the 1970s, what had been a good life and a chance for "the American Dream" has been rapidly eroding.[1] But Euro-Americans and the tricksters they tell about believe they can change their circumstances, and they do. Furthermore, Euro-American trickster tales frequently retain a whiff of wonderment even though modern realistic fiction, including Euro-American trickster stories, has lost the literal wonderment found in early oral tales as well as their oriental predecessors. Euro-American trickster tales and the European tales they derive from quite often appear fantastic, magical, with an element of a child's wish fulfillment to them.[2]

As a group, Euro-Americans tend to have an ambiguous attitude toward authority. On the one hand, to outsiders they can seem ludicrously law-abiding: The overwhelming majority actually stop at stop signs in the middle of the night when no one else is in sight. But they are also individualists, as Alexis de Tocqueville noted, constantly juggling—with uneven success—the demands of self and common interest. Their tricksters reflect a Euro-American obsession with personal freedom and liberty. From time to time, their popular culture even associates outlawry with freedom. Whatever the social or economic system in place, Euro-American tricksters will attempt to meddle with it. As Charles Murray reminds readers in the "Prologue" to *Coming Apart*, what he calls the American project "consists of the continuing effort, begun with the founding, to demonstrate that human beings can be left free as individuals and families to live their lives as they see fit, coming together voluntarily to solve their joint problems."[3] Any class, gender, or social stricture that impinges on what Euro-Americans see as a literally God-given right to personal freedom will be opposed by Euro-American tricksters.

Unlike men and women raised in African American or American Indian cultures who are aware of their own trickster traditions, many Euro-Americans retain only a superficial awareness of their ancestral traditions. Thus, instead of drawing on their European ancestors' tales, some Euro-American writers freely filch tricksters from multiple other trickster traditions. Yet, pockets of contemporary Euro-Americans are quite familiar with the European trickster traditions that migrated to America with early settlers to the Eastern seaboard and Appalachian Mountains. In addition, some Jewish Americans with strong ethnic roots retain a feeling for traditional Jewish tricksters.

The more prominent place of ancestral tricksters in African American and American Indian literature makes sense since as transformers and culture heroes, but particularly as liminal figures, tricksters appeal to groups who feel marginalized. For those who feel excluded, tricksters restore proportion in a world of imbalance; in US history, more often than anyone else, peoples with the darkest skin have been those excluded from a society dominated by the fair skinned. While ancient peoples designated those who were "others" by class, custom, or religion, in the United States, skin color or "race" has been the primary means by which outsiders have been stigmatized: they are *not* Euro-Americans.[4] As Bessie Delany forthrightly comments in a best-selling memoir told by her and her sister, another East Coast African American centenarian, "The darker you are, honey, the harder it is."[5] Compared to the world at large, most Euro-Americans live enviably comfortable lives. For the most part, Euro-Americans are "entitled." Most Third-World inhabitants would consider Ken Kesey's Merry Pranksters, for example, spoiled children.

Euro-Americans have been so dominant in the United States that even their humor has often been characterized as "American" humor as if it were normative for the entire populace. The African American Ralph Ellison, for example, characterizes the traditionally Yankee trickster pose of the "smart man playing dumb"—a ploy frequently and particularly employed by Euro-Americans—as American[6] and America itself as "a land of masking jokers."[7] Abundant historical evidence supports Ellison's contention that others too recognize a cloak of slow-wittedness thrown over sly humor as American; pretending to slow-wittedness was first recognized as "American" in the white-skinned hayseed Yankee, Jonathan, about the time the American colonies rebelled against English political control. Before the American Civil War, the figure of Brother Jonathan appealed to readers of the popular press and to stage audiences because he reminded them of flesh-and-blood Euro-American connivers they had already met. In a 1854 newspaper cartoon, for instance, an English traveler asks whether he is on the right road to Hartford and finding that he is, asks how far he has to go to get there. Jonathan replies, "Well, if you turn reound and go 'tother way may be you have to travel abeout ten mile. But if you keep on the way you are going, you'l have to go abeout eight thousand, I reckon."[8] Mark Twain's humor too was built on the same straight-faced pretense of innocence or ignorance. Twain maintains, in fact, that this is *the* American way to tell a joke.[9] Thus, what many writers label "the" American trickster is often a Euro-American trickster.

Euro-Americans continue to dominate American culture, and the United States still dominates the world. Although Euro-Americans are hardly unique in their ethnocentrism, during much of American history since the earliest European-Native encounters, most Euro-Americans have demonstrated their belief that, of course, they belonged to *the* superior race and that the social and economic inequities that favored them were part of the natural order.[10] Since they feel "entitled" and the culture as a whole advantages them, many Euro-Americans do not feel the need to join Trickster in slipping, as Lewis Hyde would call it, culture's "trap."[11] So the notion that with the privileged status granted by their lighter skins, some Euro-Americans still feel downtrodden may sound counterintuitive. More often than not, those Euro-Americans who do feel slighted appear as apart from the mainstream of Euro-Americans; they are con men (flimflam men, scalawags), rebels, or outsiders (outlaws, malcontents, the socially or economically disadvantaged). Yet, although their skin color keeps them advantaged in some ways by their culture, and they seem like cousins rather than siblings to tricksters from other traditions, these characters are still tricksters. They recognize their oppression, especially by economic or social systems structured in terms of winners and losers that leave them more or less permanently in the latter category.

While tricksters offer minority populations "a different plot,"[12] another way of reading any situation,[13] trickster discourse also appeals to discontented members of dominant groups. At times, everyone rebels against life's strictures. Invariably, therefore, some individual Euro-Americans are excluded from something they want. They find themselves religious or regional outsiders, or they are limited by their economic, educational, or social status. After all, in any group, even among those who belong, even among families, even among those with the status automatically granted to the dominant group, someone feels slighted. Appealing to every malcontent, the trickster, Louis Hyde's "creative idiot,"[14] then breaks the impasse between his society's, or sometimes life's, rules and his heart's desire. The texts discussed in this chapter show that some Euro-Americans rebel against religious hypocrisy, male inability to recognize female frustration, intellectual smugness, a sense of displacement, and self-complacency. In addition, Euro-American tricksters do not suffer their dissatisfactions with patience; they can be as dangerous as any other tradition's tricksters.

Although they present a threat, Euro-American tricksters are also cultural heroes, admired as well as feared; so they have spread as widely in Euro-American literature as those from other cultural groups. They transform their worlds whether those around them want them to or not. Noting the ongoing popularity and widespread currency of trickster tales in America's popular culture dominated by Euro-American producers, Richard M. Dorson mentions tales in which Davy Crockett takes on a trickster role,[15] but probably more telling is a recurring anecdote about the soldier released from service during the Civil War. Because he keeps using a gun to fish, his superiors decide he is mentally incompetent. His reaction: "That's what I was fishing for."[16] Such tales and anecdotes recycle through *MASH*'s Corporal Max Klinger and beyond as they present the concerns of common men and women rather than those of "those in charge."

SOURCES IN ORAL, LITERARY, AND POPULAR TRADITION

Hermes, Loki Et Al.

Although they are influenced both by American settings and popular culture, especially the American fascination with con men,[17] contemporary Euro-American trickster renditions are also heirs to multiple oral and literary European tales. By high school, most American students have learned about the Greek and Roman Olympians and have heard about Hermes, the shrewd and cunning Olympian master thief. Secondary school students may also read about Loki whose trickery leads to the death of Balder, the most beloved of the Norse gods. Students may even encounter Til Eugenspielgel, the incredibly brave, clever, stupid, cruel, and obscene German trickster; or they may have heard of Baron Münchausen, the German malingerer of a more recent fable. Students might have encountered Renard the Fox or more likely the less villainous Puss-in-Boots in children's tales. As Paul Williams's *The Fool and the Trickster* illustrates, European literature has several long and well-developed trickster traditions that intertwine with stories about the fools they often resemble.[18] Nonetheless, the details of these tricksters evidence little direct influence in American literature. Instead, for the most part, Euro-American tricksters are con artists with roots in Anglo-American folklore.

Jack Tales

Although related to still earlier con men, the con artist or flim-flam man of American popular and literary culture can be traced back to oral traditions about Yankee peddlers[19] and the backwoods schemers found in the humor of the Old Southwest. These traditions themselves have ties to Appalachian Jack Tales[20]—best known in the relatively "safe for children" story of "Jack and the Beanstalk" that continues to flourish, especially in American popular culture. An August 2003 *Bizzaro* cartoon, for instance, depends on the audience's recollection of the oral tale.[21] So does a *Non Sequitur* cartoon appearing in March of 2004.[22] Since children have been the primary contemporary audience of most Jack Tales and since these trickster tales have been best preserved among people with close ties to their small Primitive Baptist mountain churches, most of the tales lack the salacious content of other trickster traditions. Nonetheless, according to Carl Lindahl, Joseph Daniel Sobol, and Cheryl Oxford—contributors to William McCarthy's collection—as one would expect of trickster tales, Jack Tales have been and sometimes remain ribald except for audiences containing women and especially children.[23] The core of some of the more suggestive Jack Tales can be traced back to stories that also appear in Chaucer's *Canterbury Tales*. Thus, "How Jack Solved the Hardest Riddle" told by Donald Davis is traceable to "The Wife of Bath's Tale."[24] In addition, Davis's "The Time Jack Fooled the

Miller"[25] relies on the same trick as Chaucer's "The Reeve's Tale." Apparently, outside the hearing of women and children, Jack Tales can take on racy overtones.

"Jack and the Beanstalk" and other Jack Tales belong to a cycle in English and Irish oral literature that migrated to North America during the seventeenth and eighteenth centuries. The tales have parallels in much of European oral literature.[26] Quite often, Jack is a blatant trickster[27] who pretends to be foolish, while sometimes he is indeed foolish. In America, particularly among the Appalachian hills and hollows where they developed most prominently and where they were influenced by other traditions, the setting of the Jack Tales became Americanized; as one would expect of a culture hero, Jack himself became a local boy with qualities the community valued. He is in transition between youth and adulthood. Although often devious, he is usually a hard worker, generous, and imaginative. Since Jack is always on the lookout for ways to get ahead, he has to leave home and go on the road. And, despite the occasional giant or magical object he encounters, the road he travels is an Appalachian trail rather than an English lane.

In Jack Tales, the line between Jack's feigned and real foolishness blurs because sometimes, as one writer says, his "foolishness borders on stupidity."[28] But one can never know for sure: Often his "foolishness" is a form of wisdom. One tale has Jack trading down a sizable inheritance for objects of decreasing material value until he has gotten rid of all of these encumbrances and is "happy."[29] Whether Jack is a wise fool or just stupid is left to the listener/reader to decide. He is the one who never got as much as others. Sometimes, the youngest of several sons, Jack often has to fend for himself because his older brothers have already received all of their father's bequests. In some stories, the family doubts his ability and worries that Jack is "a little foolish and uncertain...and quare."[30]

More than that in the African American or American Indian trickster traditions, Euro-American Jack Tales call upon magical objects to help the hero. Hence, the tales highlight the storyteller's rather than the trickster hero's ability to imagine "something else." At least one commentator makes much of the Jack Tales' *märchen* spirit.[31] Many of the Jack Tales bring the reader back to childhood and listening to fairy tales such as "East of the Sun and West of the Moon," which is echoed in Donald Davis's "The Time Jack Helped the King Catch His Girls."[32] Nonetheless, although the Jack Tales are full of marvels, the tricksters of oral folk literature are not gods, just fortunate in both their wit and, upon occasion, their fortuitous access to magical artifacts.

While Euro-American tricksters and particularly Jack have to depend on one sort of chance or another, Jack's chance belongs to a particular type. Jack has personal qualities that prepare for good luck: Either he performs good deeds for others and they reciprocate with magical gifts or he uses his native wit to outmaneuver opponents and achieve his good fortune. The American Jack differs from his European predecessors in that his success depends less on using magic than his own "mental resources" and perhaps encouragement from other mortals when he confronts a magical creature.[33] Regardless of how they succeed, Jack and latter-day Euro-American tricksters are unstoppable. Like their counterparts in other traditions, they just keep going along. They are, as a former American Folklore president says of Jack, "unafraid, iconoclastic, and inventive."[34]

Not always, but often, Jack uses his innate wit to right a wrong; he balances justice's scales, as in "Big Jack and Little Jack,"[35] when Little Jack turns the tables on a cruel "king" who hires workers but does not feed them and then uses his whip to cut "strops"[36] out of their backs if they complain. Perhaps more typically, Jack balances the social and economic scales by improving his own lot. In one Jack Tale, "The Time Jack Stole the Cows,"[37] Jack is caught in the woods at night after he has been hunting. He finds a house with no one home; so he has something to eat and falls asleep. Unfortunately, this is the home of 14-foot giants who have not "brushed their teeth in 27 years" or bathed in 31 or 42 years. The giants are robbers and do not believe Jack when he pretends he is too. However, they let him try to back up his lie; and on three successive days, he manages to trick a local farmer out of a cow. The giants like eating the cows Jack brings them, so they let him live a while longer. Then Jack brags that he can steal as much in an hour as they have in a year. Of course, they do not believe him. So he goes to the sheriff, turns in the giants, and earns a half of their ill-gotten gains as his reward. Being a good son, he brings his mother to live in the giants' now-empty house.[38] Obviously, Jack differs from African American and American Indian traditions in that the people who tell his tales are dissatisfied with their lot rather than oppressed. Jack does not start in a state of utter deprivation; and while he may be temporarily low on the economic or social totem pole, he has the very expectation of bettering his condition. His "pursuit of happiness" is usually centered on seeking his fortune.[39]

YANKEE PEDDLERS AND SOUTHERN FLIM-FLAM MEN

Even with their close ties to Europe, the Jack Tales accommodated themselves to North America as their characters took on American attitudes; and although traces of their *märchen* origins persist, their settings became localized. Jack's descendants, Yankee peddlers and Southern flim-flam men, are clearly related to Old World rogues; yet, in their speech and attitudes, they are even more American than Jack.

Brother Jonathan

The Yankee trader and the Southern scalawag from the humor of the Old Southwest form two major links between the Jack Tales and contemporary trickster tales. For much of the period between the American Revolution and the Civil War, the preeminent Yankee trader—often personified in a rube named Brother Jonathan—became the popular culture embodiment of the American. Jonathan, indeed most of the Yankee Peddlers encountered in popular stage comedies, broadside cartoons, newspaper verse, and almanac anecdotes of the early nineteenth-century as well as others related to him, reflect the insecurities of America's "new men" during the first half-century of the new nation's existence, insisting on their rights and superiority but falling back on tricks and sly humor to stay ahead of competitors.[40] Jonathan was the bumpkin-trickster whom both British and American popular culture portrayed as a reflection of the ordinary American. He appears as the comic servant in Royall Tyler's *The Contrast*, where he apparently mistakes the "fourth wall" of a proscenium stage as reality rather than illusion and reflects on the "little cherubim consequences" a young woman carries about nine months after dallying with a villain.[41] His humor almost invariably carried a sly sting. In 1846, an almanac anecdote describes trial of speed between American and English schooners. After the American ship wins, the English captain gallantly swears that his ship "had never been outsailed before. 'Just like me,' said Jonathan, 'my Jemina never beat nothing before.' "[42]

Con Men from the Old Southwest

The struggles of New England's Jonathan and early nineteenth-century Southern frontiersmen as they elbowed their way ahead, insisting on their place in the sun, continue to find an echo in fiction about late-twentieth and twenty-first-century tricksters. Before the Civil War, the Old Southwest—the territory south of the Ohio River and west of the Appalachian Mountains—was frontier territory. The area that became Tennessee and Kentucky, western Georgia and the Carolinas was a raucous territory; then as the frontier moved west and south, what are now the states of Alabama, Mississippi, Louisiana, and Arkansas became the frontier. In Old Southwest literature, most of the central characters are confidence men; and many of them are the particular band of confidence men recognizable as "a distinctly American version of the archetypal trickster."[43] During the antebellum period, sketches about wily backwoods con men memorialized the humor of the Old Southwest.[44] William E. Lenz finds the roots of American confidence men in the "ambiguities" inherent in the "new country" of the frontier [45] from the 1820s through the 1840s and up to the Civil War.[46] Lacking traditional social supports on the frontier in a land that was neither "traditional nor nice,"[47] the old verities, social structures, and even moral absolutes blurred. In tales about the Old Southwest, brutality is a commonplace means of survival; and much of the humor derives from laughing at the physical discomfort others suffer. In these tales, laughing becomes a sort of "desperate triumph in the face of awfulness."[48] Readers need to remember, however, that the men who published tales of the Old Southwest in New York's *The Spirit of the Times*, the St. Louis *Reveille*, and the New Orleans *Picayune* as well as other local newspapers were almost all Whigs, suspicious of both encroaching national power and "populist agitation."[49] So they reported on what they encountered but also despised many aspects of frontier society, and the attitudes of those writers permeate the tales.

The frontier world depicted in Southwestern tales is both violent and full of energy. The tall talk and humor with which the men who populate this violent world respond make for vivid language. In addition, there is something so ingenuously bold-faced about the confidence games rapscallions from Old Southwest sketches play that readers laugh both at and with them—as in a favorite anecdote that relates how Johnson Jones Hooper's Simon Suggs escapes from jail dressed in his "widow's" clothes while she takes his place in his coffin. He gets safely away too even though she "obstinately refuse[s] to be buried in [his] place when she [gets] to the grave."[50] Hooper built upon earlier as well as contemporary tales of frontier pranksters and sharpers to establish in Captain Suggs a pattern for the frontier and the American trickster.[51] Details of that pattern—such as Suggs's defeat of equally or even more dishonest opponents, his status as an individualistic outsider, his penchant for ingenious escapes, his focus on personal gain, his consistent manipulation of those who think they are using him, the way readers want to laugh at his shameless shenanigans—reappear repeatedly even today in American literature, especially in Southern literature.

By comparison with some other tricksters from the Old Southwest, notably George Washington Harris's Sut Lovingood, Suggs is an almost endearing prankster. Despite the irony of his last name, Sut is a cruel conniver: coarse and brutish, at war with a world he believes has failed him, and lacking in empathy for others who live on the harsh Tennessee frontier. Total lack of thought as to how his actions might affect anyone else certainly characterizes the tales about Lovingood. By dint of narrative disengagement, however, Harris encourages readers to laugh at the earthy mishaps visited upon both Sut and his antagonists. Both the narrator and readers, after all, are safely uninvolved in the mayhem. A misogynist, Sut values only the kisses and whiskey he expects to get out of "Mrs. Yardley's Quilting"; and, rather than Mrs Yardley's death, he recalls the event primarily because of the mayhem he enjoyed causing and the prodigious kick in the pants he received from Mr Yardley. Despite the anecdote's dark undertones, the humor lies in the language as, for example, Sut revels in the thought that "quiltins, managed in a morril an' sensibil way, truly am good things-good fur free drinkin, good fur free eatin, good fur free huggin, good fur free dancing, good fur free fitin, and goodest ove all fur poperlatin a country fas'."[52] In another tale, as he explains why his "white lightning" is preferable to ole Bullen's, Sut notes that Bullen "puts in tan ooze, in what he sells, an' when that haint handy, he uses the red warter outen a pon' jis below his barn; makes a pow'ful natural color, but don't help the taste much."[53] A useful commentary on appearances.

In addition to its brutality and coarse jokes, the humor of the Old Southwest contains a significant amount of satire. In fact, Harris intended many of his tales as political satires.[54] The tales do not so much comment on as they describe characters and situations that encourage readers to come to their own conclusions about, for example, the trustworthiness of preachers and politicians. Although the male authors did pen a limited number of tales containing female tricksters,[55] for the most part in this male-dominated literary form, women are consistently marginalized when they are not disparaged. Yet, amid all this, the Old Southwestern tricksters are helping to shape the values of their time; many of the attitudes from their time persist into contemporary times. Extreme distaste for hypocrisy, admiration for individualism—even extreme individualism—a willingness to settle conflict through force, the sense that dupes often deserve their fates, grudging admiration for the scruffy underdog, earthy jokes that imply rather than state what has occurred, pleasure in colorful language, subtle jests as well as outlandish ones: All of these Euro-American values pre-dated the humor of the Old Soutwest. Euro-American culture was already characterized by distaste for hypocrisy, admiration for even excessive individualism, willingness to settle conflict through force, the sense that dupes often deserved their fates, grudging admiration fo the scruffy underdog, earthy jokes that implied rather than stated what had occurred, pleasure in colorful language, and subtle jests as well as outlandish ones. The sketches of the period, however, reinforced and handed on these values.

The protagonists of Old Southwest tales assume that dupes deserve their ignominious fates and generally glory in language that rubs in their opponents' defeat and their own triumph. The contemporary notion that "No one can cheat an honest man" has close ties to the contention that the society as well as the person confiding in con men often reveals an inherent moral flaw in itself. To the trickster, such a confiding personality reveals at least naiveté, an invitation to manipulation. This is apparent in Augustus Baldwin Longstreet's "The Horse Swap" when the man who is "a *little* the best man at a horse-swap that ever [anyone] got hold of" gets a bit "snappish" on realizing he has traded a pathetic-looking little horse with an open sore on its back for one that looks fine but is deaf and blind.[56] The citizens of Mark Twain's Hadleyville demonstrate the same mistaken assumption of their superiority to flawed humanity.

Contemporary Americans are most often familiar with the tricksters of the Old Southwest from encounters with the work of Mark Twain, probably its greatest practitioner. Twain was quite familiar with the conventions of the form and even his earliest successful story, "The Celebrated Jumping Frog of Calaverous County," revolves around a sharper winning a bet from Jim Smiley who has trained a frog to jump better than others. (While Jim is distracted, the stranger fills Jim's frog with buckshot.) In addition, the story's frames themselves are something of a trick: The narrator finally realizes that he has been sent to listen to a garrulous storyteller incapable of answering the question asked even if he did know the answer; the stories themselves are bound to be more fabulous than factual; and Twain himself is tricking his readers with a further bit of indirection. Twain also moves the form forward in combining the detached narrator with the butt of the joke.[57]

Twain's other well-known tricksters from *The Adventures of Huckleberry Finn*, the Duke and the Dauphin, might have come directly from one of Harris's tales. Reminiscent of Harris's "Parson John Bullen's Lizards,"[58] Twain's self-proclaimed king excels at collecting money at a camp meeting and kissing the pretty girls. The primary joy of the swindling Duke and the Dauphin comes from scamming their marks, and they are conscienceless. All of Twain's tricksters are decidedly American in language and attitude. The Duke and Dauphin, for example, are just as cruel and soulless as Lazarillo de Tormes's tormenters; on the other hand, their exaggerations are more comical. Huck himself is far more innocent than Lazarillo. There is something timeless about rogues such as Huck's Duke and Dauphin: The assumption is that every society grows its own malefactors; yet in the American heartland, the good-hearted Huck manages to sidestep their machinations and finally wiggle out of the traps they set for him. The same cannot be said of Lazarillo de Tormes.

In contrast to the good-heartedness and youthful mischievousness of Huckleberry Finn, humor about con men in the Old Southwest often feels vindictive and assumes the worst of human behavior. The tricksters of Old Southwest humor demonstrate the worst aspects of individualism while Huck demonstrates the best. Readers or listeners to the tales of Harris and others have to achieve a level of intellectual detachment to find the humor in what are often cruel jokes. Old Southwest tricksters are opportunists, adapting to circumstances. Although the phrase "confidence man" came in to currency in the United States only during the 1840s, tricksters from many eras would agree with Simon Suggs's aphoristic encapsulation of his "ethical system": "IT IS GOOD TO BE SHIFTY IN A NEW COUNTRY."[59] Huck is also something of a trickster and he may shave a few ethical corners; however, he does not purposely set out to cheat good people. In fact, he is even capable of pitying the fates of the tarred and feathered Duke and Dauphin.

Southern Literary Tricksters

Lucille Vinson in Mark Childress's *Crazy in Alabama* (1993)

Both Jack Tales and the humor of the Old Southwest are rooted in the American South East. Not surprisingly then, over-the-top avatars related to earlier tricksters continue to thrive especially in recent Southern fiction. Part of what characterizes Euro-American—particularly Southern—tricksters is the sense that no matter what they do, no matter how unlikely the outcome, they will somehow not only survive but even triumph. Certainly, Lucille Vinson, the narrator's aunt in Mark Childress's *Crazy in Alabama* demonstrates this quality. Early reviews of the novel use phrases such as "craziness rules"[60] and "gruesomely entertaining."[61] At first glance, Lucille Vinson does not seem particularly put upon; but a husband who is inattentive to her needs, six children in a presumably short span of time, plus frustrated ambition finally get to her. So she alters her situation. The narrator's Aunt Lucille hacks off her husband's head, leaves her children with their long-suffering grandmother, flees across the country, gets her chance to make a splash as a new country-femme fatale on *The Beverly Hills Hillbillies*, and is finally caught and convicted of murder, but still gets off with a suspended sentence and then lives happily afterward with a smitten beau. While she is "going along," Lucille manages to escape one trap after another, win a small fortune at roulette, and thoroughly enjoy a series of sexual encounters. At the novel's end, she is almost 30 years older but still intent on inveigling her nephew into getting her a part in a new movie.[62] Except for her gender, Aunt Lucille is a typical Euro-American trickster. Her original circumstances have not been cruel; but once she decides they warrant extreme action, she quickly deals with her husband's petty tyranny and her demanding children before doing the twentieth-century version of Huck's "lighting out for the territory."

Wesley Benfield in Clyde Edgerton's *Walking across Egypt* (1987) and *Killer Diller* (1992)

Another Southerner, Wesley Benfield in Clyde Edgerton's *Walking across Egypt*, is something of a trickster wannabe. A 16-year-old thief and braggart with murky antecedents, he seldom considers anything beyond how to satisfy his appetites for food and sex. His driftless existence reminds readers of the minor stories they encounter in the daily paper. He escapes from a youth correctional center; but having borrowed first a choir robe to blend in at church and later a car from one of the churchgoers, he is still cornered by the sheriff and his deputies at the home of Mattie Rigsbee, the woman Wesley rather wishes were his grandmother. (In common with traditional tricksters from oral literature, Wesley's most significant feminine relationship is with an old woman.) Mattie is his protector while Wesley resembles the feisty stray Mattie feeds against her better judgment. Wesley is an unprepossessing hero, young, awkward, a relatively ineffective schemer. Yet, he is also a transformer, and as he says—though with considerable exaggeration—to the deputy who has missed capturing him in a church choir loft, "I can just about be anywhere I want to at anytime I want to."[63] In any case, wherever Wesley lands, somehow, he never settles down.

In *Walking across Egypt* as well as the next Edgerton novel featuring Wesley Benfield, *Killer Diller*, Wesley demonstrates traits commonly encountered in Euro-American tricksters: He is individualistic and wants to focus entirely on his own needs and desires; he has an outsider's penchant for spotting the failings of those around him. Yet, he is also drawn to Mattie Rigsbee, someone fostering the communal good in his society. This tension between self-serving individualism and communal needs lies at the core of Edgerton's two novels. American individualism has always strained against the pull of the common good. While in their extreme forms these values are always at odds, the United States glorifies both the lone individual and collective effort. That tension is expressly reflected in Euro-American tricksters. In Wesley's case, although he can be a hustler, he is more mischievous than acquisitive. Like Huck, he is a young innocent looking askance at a world of hypocrisy.

In *Killer Diller*, Wesley is older—24—and if not exactly mature, somewhat toned down due to Mattie Rigsbee's authentically Christian influence. He is still a trickster—switching a donor's name plate from a classroom to a broom closet just for the fun of it, still lying without compunction, still fixated on sex; yet he also ponders moral questions in a fashion that would never occur to a full-blown traditional trickster. Innocent, rather than the totally amoral character a traditional trickster is, Wesley turns his intelligence and honesty on the pseudo-Christianity that surrounds him in his cleaning job at a fundamentalist Christian university. In spite of Wesley's trickster instincts, influenced by Mattie, and in contrast to that of his bosses, Wesley's Christianity is sincere.[64] More than mere agitators, characters who take seriously Christianity—or any ethical system—generally prove challenging for authorities to deal with. Honest and open, Wesley keeps grappling with the literalist interpretation of the Bible taught by the school's faculty and administration; in the process, readers come to recognize both the absurdity of his bosses' theology and ways in which they fail to live up to the gospel they purport to teach.

Whether a trickster, most protean of characters, represents a savior or destructive force is a matter of perspective. Folk sayings have always emphasized this point: "It's all in where you sit, how far the man in the balcony can spit" and less crassly, "It depends on whose ox is gored." A reader who despises religious hypocrisy or unreasonable authoritarianism will, of course, root for a Wesley Benfield, who is as charming and devious as George C. Scott's character was in the 1967 movie *The Flim Flam Man*. But powerful men and women instinctively recognize that tricksters can upset their carefully constructed plans. It is in the genes of tricksters to be transgressive for the sake of change. Not wanting to lose their control, powerful people especially try to marginalize the tricksters.

In *Killer Diller*, the ensconced leaders who administer a small Baptist university more focused on fundraising and encouraging small, careful virtues than on either education or the gospel know that tricksters are bound to stir up trouble. Oblivious to the absurdity in his language as well as its flat-out inaccuracy, in *Killer Diller*, a new dean explains to Wesley's band of musicians the university administration's belief that, "Hierarchy is...the cornerstone of American democracy."[65] Almost all of Ballard University's administrators come from a military background and prefer compulsion to debate; they confuse coercing with convincing others. At the pinnacle of the school's hierarchy, Ballard's all-male administrators believe that their role is to limit the damage nonconformists might inflict on their closed system. They become the dupes, however, when they decide Wesley is someone they can brag about as one of their success stories; so they invite local radio, television, and newspapers to cover his Christian "testimony." The problem is that Wesley has been reading the Bible and thinking about it. With the same combination of naive honesty and courage one would expect of Huckleberry Finn, Wesley gets all the coverage the leaders of Ballard were hoping for. However, he tells his audience,

> *If you believe every word in the Bible is absolutely true like some kind of steel trap then you believe both of these versions* [of the creation story in Genesis] *are absolutely true and if you believe that then you ain't using the brain God gave you.*[66] [Emphasis in original.]

Having thrown a fright into Ballard's leaders, at the end of the novel, Wesley and his band, the Wandering Stars (an exemplary trickster name), are headed out on Interstate 95. Edgerton paints Wesley's opponents as totally unsympathetic, even larcenous; but in any case, they and the milieu they foster seem deadly because they lack intellectual and moral substance though they pretend to have both. The limited virtues and simplistic "correctness" of Ballard's administrators beg for a trickster's flare at trouble making. So Wesley stirs up trouble, makes fools of the men who would use him, and then takes off down the interstate with his Wandering Stars.

Ignatius Reilly in John Kennedy Toole's *A Confederacy of Dunces* (1980)

Even funny tricksters are destructive; at the center of John Kennedy Toole's *A Confederacy of Dunces*, waddles a trickster happy to contribute his bit of chaos to a universe he despises. Ignatius Reilly is totally anarchic, certainly hard to pigeonhole. One writer settles for calling the novel itself an example of "comic grotesque" fiction.[67] Toole's central character is so self-absorbed and so delusional that his tricks flow from only a few motives: ensuring his physical comfort, his self-glorification, and his self-protection. Yet, regardless of his motives, Reilly effectively changes everyone he encounters.

Although many readers have found the mix of characters in Toole's *A Confederacy of Dunces* satisfying in themselves, Random House editor Robert Gottlieb finally passed on the novel because he could not find any "reason" for its anarchy. Rather than a plot, the novel offers readers a concoction of characters and contrivances. Lucinda MacKethan characterizes the novel as representing a comic "immersion in a city representing the perverse heart of modernity";[68] however, she also points to Toole's trickster opposing not injustice but modern attempts to quell creativity and imagination. No trickster will stand for that. Toole's Ignatius Reilly does not. As a Euro-American trickster, he does not need oppression to rebel against. He just needs to feel put upon.

Years after Toole's suicide, his determined mother finally badgered Walker Percy into reading the manuscript, and Percy in turn persuaded Louisiana State University Press to venture a limited press run of 2,500 copies.[69] Despite the novel's farce and over-the-top satire, another difficulty Toole and then his mother encountered in getting the book published may lie in the central character: Reilly is physically disgusting and morally limited—a trickster. Walker Percy's foreword referring to Reilly as a "slob extraordinary"[70] is probably too gentle a description. Reilly is unwashed and grossly overweight; he belches and masturbates into his already filthy sheets while he pencils half-baked but overwritten ideas in Big Chief tablets. When he does leave his mother's house, he is comically attired and socially inept. He spouts spurious academic jargon,[71] is quick to demand his own prerogatives, but loves to point out the quirks and limitations of other characters; his misguided self-importance parallels that of Flannery O'Connor's overeducated and unfeeling characters. Presumably applying for a job, he berates would-be employers. Particularly as the novel opens, readers find little to like or admire in Reilly; yet his trickster spirit holds the novel together, and the other characters' relative success is directly related to his whims.

In the course of the event and character-stuffed novel, Reilly encounters a swirl of lively characters from a chosen few New Orleans settings: outside a department store, in a dreary bar that is at once sleazy and pathetic, and at Reilly's two work places.

Reilly precipitates anarchy and chaos. For no better reason than he feels like it, he composes an insulting letter to a customer, forges his boss Gus Levy's signature, and mails the letter. The recipient's reaction threatens to bankrupt Levy. Later on, realizing that his actions might have some unwanted consequences for himself as well as Levy, Reilly rather ineffectively lies to protect himself. For the most part, however, his lies have little purpose other than annoying his listeners. He believes in his own innate intellectual superiority though his language—a mix of cliché and bombast—gives little support to his conviction.

However, despite his apparent ineptitude and without actually intending it, Ignatius Reilly creates a new world. By the novel's end, his actions have caused his mother to realize she can find a new mate. Gus Levy realizes that he can revive his company and control his termagant wife. A bungling policeman is credited with breaking up pornography sales to children. Even the incompetent bargirl is offered her dream job as an exotic dancer, and a malingering janitor is slated to receive an award while the pornographer and her minion are arrested by the police. Reilly has changed the world he inhabits. In a fictional world where tricksters function, anything can happen— though perhaps not what or in the way the tricksters intended. In their single-minded focus on what they want, both Wesley Benfield and Ignatius Reilly are seeking their fortune. Their success may spell success for others as well; yet for these tricksters, those effects are peripheral. Both Edgerton's Benfield and Toole's Reilly have a little Jack in them, even more of the con man. Although they are not as competent or as in charge as other major European tricksters, they even have a bit of Hermes and Loki in them. For the most part, however, the mischievous focus of these characters on their own purposes overshadows any inherent malice. Ignatius Reilly might remind readers of Sut Lovingood, Wesley Benfield might remind them of Huck, while Lucille comes closer to Captain Suggs; but they all belong to the same con-man tradition.

RULE BREAKERS TAKING ISSUE WITH SOCIAL CONTROL

While the American South has contributed a wealth of Euro-American tricksters to literature, the rest of the country has also contributed its full share. Harking back to their ancestors, Jack and the bumpkins and frontier tricksters who followed his lead, Euro-American tricksters throughout the United States are particularly uncomfortable with any type of social or economic hierarchy. Like their Southern cousins, they cannot abide conformity or excess order. This propensity toward disruption flourishes in all of Ken Kesey's work, but especially in *One Flew over the Cuckoo's Nest*.

Ken Kesey's *One Flew over the Cuckoo's Nest* (1962)

The central character of *One Flew over the Cuckoo's Nest*, Randle Patrick McMurphy, embodies the trickster's elemental force, intent on breaking down strictures against natural behavior. McMurphy is larger than life: physically large, earthy, a braggart, a gambler, a con artist proud of his reputation for "fight[ing] too much and fuck[ing] too much."[72] To accept him as a heroic figure, the reader must accept the proposition that much of the society McMurphy rebels against, certainly the mental health system and perhaps much of American culture during the 1950s and early 1960s, is repressive and unhealthy. Kesey does.

As much as any trickster can be tragic, Kesey makes McMurphy into a tragic figure. Given the trickster's close affinity with comedy, this is an extraordinary feat. The character of McMurphy starts out relatively simple: as Nurse Ratched recognizes, he aims to disrupt the ward just for the fun of it. He has only gotten himself locked up in a mental ward because he has mistakenly believed that life there will be warm and lazy. Any trickster would do that. By the end of the novel, however, McMurphy has grown beyond such an uncomplicated purpose. He has controlled his anger and frustration in the face of repeated assaults and taught the rest of the men how to do the same so that when the sadistic aides make them go through some sort of demeaning proctologic scrub, the men can actually laugh at the aides' attempt to make the patients react—and merit punishment. As the novel progresses, McMurphy becomes more than a totally mindless trickster.[73]

From his first days on the ward, McMurphy is appalled by the treatment the patients receive and quickly recognizes that it is vicious rather than therapeutic, designed to humiliate and control rather than return healthy patients to society. In most untrickster-like fashion, McMurphy comes to empathize with the other men in lockup. Over time, McMurphy's brand of therapy—primarily laughter and spunk, just living regardless of the challenges—provides the therapy the men need. They learn to emulate him, to live with themselves; and one by one, they sign themselves out of the ward, away from the ward's pathological treatment. McMurphy has changed the dynamics of the ward. Each of the "Acutes"—men whom the narrator calls "sick enough to be fixed"[74]—has caught the infection of tricksterism from McMurphy.[75]

The process, however, involves the hero's physical destruction; in this case, Nurse Ratched manages to have McMurphy undergo a lobotomy. Even so, the rest of the inmates recognize that his essence no longer inhabits the inert figure lying on McMurphy's bed; yet, rather than allow the apparent proof of Nurse Ratched's success to throw doubt on McMurphy's power, Chief Bromden, the novel's narrator, smothers the almost mindless wreck that McMurphy has become and crashes out of the asylum, leaving another of the inmates to insist that McMurphy had been "up and moving around"[76] after Bromden left. The novel implies that that trickster spirit, not just being "cagey"—a frequently repeated word used to connote playing it safe—will also allow the damaged, but at least functioning, inmates to defend themselves against unreasonable and pointless coercion.

Kesey's *Cuckoo's Nest* demonstrates the trickster's serious function, the way that nay-saying need not be as humorless as Henry David Thoreau's grain of sand.[77] McMurphy's bawdy clowning can be just as effective in destroying a rigid structure—whether that is a sick mental health ward or a whole culture of conformity. McMurphy—and, influenced by him, the rest of the men in the *Cuckoo's Nest*'s microcosmic psych ward resemble the trickster Jack whose family thought was "quare" because he traded away his inheritance. Jack and McMurphy both recognize more than one way to seek one's good fortune in order to be happy. Demonstrating the social complexity of attempting to act out Jack's and McMurphy's philosophies becomes apparent in Tom Wolfe's work of New Journalism,[78] *The Electric Kool-Aid Acid Test*.

In-the-Flesh Tricksters—Ken Kesey's Merry Pranksters in Tom Wolfe's *The Electric Kool-Aid Acid Test* (1968)

In-the-flesh tricksters—men and women who are not fictional but people encountered in corporeal bodies just like those people who are reading about them—can also alter the worlds in which they live; but depending on one's perspective, they may prove more unnerving than humorous. Caught up in the charm of most literary tricksters, readers can lose sight of the trickster's power and potential for destruction. Readers who see tricksters in a positive light have to see their antagonists as villains—or, at the very least, as in the case of Kesey's Merry Pranksters, "dear-but-square ones."[79] In-the-flesh tricksters are difficult to pigeonhole: they can be dangerous, and any authority who attempts to control a trickster subtly or even through force quickly encounters their ability to inflict damage. Nonetheless, tricksters often function as culture heroes and exert major influence on their society.

The success of Ken Kesey's *One Flew over the Cuckoo's Nest* and his next work, *Sometimes a Great Notion*, published in 1964, eventually funded Kesey and his Pranksters. *The Electric Kool-Aid Acid Test* follows their trips and immerses readers in the mindset of a group of real-life tricksters who, more or less guided by Ken Kesey and influenced by lysergic acid diethylamide (LSD) and marijuana, led a life-without-social-limits existence from about 1963 through 1967. During most of this time, they functioned with a group mind and will that they characterized as being "on the bus," recalling the multicolored and decorated bus on which they traveled through the United States and Mexico. Wolfe's detailed description makes the last year sound ever more chaotic and physically repellent. (The warehouse where they are living in San Francisco, for example, lacks plumbing, and even the Pranksters inured to the need for social niceties cannot bear the open-sewer smell of places others have already used as urinals or worse and thus traipse over to a local Shell station to use its toilet.)

On the other hand, along the way, the Pranksters are also exuberant. Together, they embody the trickster's verve. During the 1960s, Kesey and the Pranksters played a central role in changing American culture.[80] They become culture heroes, influencing language (e.g., as they "go with the flow"),[81] mores, and American youth culture. The Pranksters affect Day-Glo colors and outrageous costumes; they connect with and gain respect from both earlier generation radicals such as the Beatniks and contemporary outlaws such as Hell's Angels. During this period, they become lightning rods galvanizing college students and disaffected youths as well as the young lawyers who ably defend Kesey in court. They begin, anticipate, or encourage the psychedelic scenes at the Avalon and Fillmore West and the music of Jerry Garcia's Grateful Dead. They play with drugs but they also play with the police and the public; and in response to the high seriousness of world events, they make their lives a "game."

Wolfe portrays the Pranksters as shape-shifters, changing their clothes and physical environments as well as rewiring their brains and perceptions through LSD. In true trickster fashion, they were always moving on to another "current fantasy." Even if their aims and achievements seemed to fizzle after 1967, in true trickster fashion, the Pranksters had already fostered chaos and changed—to play on the title of Lewis Hyde's book on tricksters—*this* world. Since they did not care about acquiring what later generations often refer to as "toys" such as cars, boats, motorcycles, electronic equipment, and such, they considered themselves admirable free spirits. The Pranksters' admirers would argue that the Pranksters performed an essential social function in turning many Americans away from the 1950s' penchant for acquisition and the high seriousness that had led the United States into a Cold War with the USSR and a hot war in Vietnam. The Pranksters' critics, on the other hand, would point to their mindless destruction and their antisocial ego-centricism. The Pranksters, in common with many fictional Euro-American tricksters, were innocent hustlers. Individual Pranksters, caught up in a sort of groupthink, apparently rejected guilt or social censure for anything they did; but they were hustlers, intent on their own self-aggrandizement, although in their cases, this involved gathering limitless sensual experience with no thought to how their actions might affect others such as a vulnerable naked woman who becomes psychotic and has to be removed from their bus.[82]

NOT JUST CENTRAL TRICKSTERS FOSTER CHANGE

Because novels are character driven and tricksters make wonderfully quirky characters, tricksters often fuel plot turns in Euro-American novels even when the whole novel does not revolve around a central trickster figure. Such characters especially appeal to authors known for off-beat, outsider characters. Minor trickster characters in the novels of Anne Tyler and John Irving, for example, often provide an impetus, moving the situation and other characters to change. The tricksters in secondary roles in the novels of Anne Tyler and John Irving reconnoiter discords in the lives of the main characters.

Anne Tyler's *The Accidental Tourist* (1985)

In Anne Tyler's *The Accidental Tourist*, for example, the choices made by Muriel, Macon's eccentric and self-involved siblings, even the choices of Macon's still more idiosyncratic corgi Edward, offer Tyler the opportunity to explore the themes of needing to get involved with life by being involved with other people and thus leaving oneself less self-protected.

Ralph Ellison warns readers against too close an identification of modern fictional characters with the trickster archetype since by definition modern novels are almost at least "implicitly realistic."[83] And, in fact, because *The Accidental Tourist* is a novel about characters that readers need to accept as real, for all of Muriel's trickster qualities, she lacks either the marvelous *märchen* tools Jack acquires in some of the Jack Tales or the relentless cunning con men from the tales in humor from the Old South West. In Tyler's novel, Muriel cannot make Macon return to her. Given his inert character, however, that he does return to her is humanly marvelous. In fact, in this—as in many of Tyler's novels—the central character chooses to associate with idiosyncratic and odd people because despite their flaws they are appealingly human. Muriel is so appealing that she makes Macon want to change.

John Irving's *A Son of the Circus* (1994)

In *A Son of the Circus*, the cloud of characters populating Irving's crowded comic novel[84] but especially his central character, allow John Irving to probe what it means to not belong but also the need to avoid becoming too comfortable. Set mostly in India with a cast of for the most part Indian characters, Irving's novel still deals with modern Euro-American themes. The behavior of the novel's crowd of characters provides the impetus for the novel's action. The tricks, ploys, and hangups of supposedly minor characters, rather than the altruism of the central character, drive the plot.

The most prominent trickster is a serial killer called Rahul who, over time, transforms himself into the second Mrs Dogar. His or her sexual ambiguity, as well as his or her refusal to accept limits imposed by gender, age, or morals supply a major plot engine. Psychotic though he is, Rahul is the engine whose unexamined needs and anger drive the plot and cause many of the difficulties that Dr Farrockh Daruwalla, the central character, and other characters get into. Rahul, rather than Dr Daruwalla ultimately pushes Dr Daruwalla to participate in a real murder investigation, to confront the real lives of the people he has built into fantasies, and finally to put aside his successful but totally false screenwriting. *A Son of the Circus* does indeed offer, as one reviewer called it, a "rich, contradictory" stew of a setting.[85] The trick-ster behavior of Irving's characters is an important part of that stew. By upsetting the balance, the trickster/murderer allows Dr Daruwalla and other characters to reorder their lives.

Tricksters, including tricksters devised by Euro-American writers,[86] can function as positive or negative forces. Both Rahul/Mrs Dogar and Muriel are tricksters and alter the world around them. Rahul/ Mrs Dogar is a psychotic killer. Muriel Pritchard is a more obviously benign Euro-American trickster. She lacks malice; she bustles ahead but ultimately works to forward the good of her small enclave. But both characters change their worlds by getting others to change their lives. Neither has to deal with the racial/ethnic oppression that African American and American Indians confront; nonetheless, Muriel's hard-scrabble existence at the edge of economic and social subsistence and Rahul's lifelong maneuvering on the edge of his psychological obses-sion with gender identity give them serious reasons for discontent.

UNLIKELY BEDFELLOWS

More fully developed tricksters and trickster tales appear in the fic-tion of an unlikely pairing, Saul Bellow and Elmore Leonard. The writers generally appeal to different readerships, yet the tricksters of both men are distinctly Euro-American, reflecting Euro-American ambitions and discontents that among other places, find echoes in thirty-second political ads on television. Euro-American tricksters reflect a common refrain, "I deserve more; and if you're not going to give it to me, I'll find another way of wrangling it."

A Jewish Trickster in Saul Bellow's "A Silver Dish" (1984)

The father in Saul Bellow's short story "A Silver Dish," a Jewish trickster,[87] has relatively little in common with the Appalachian Jack and his literary descendants but a close connection with tricksters from the shtetls of Eastern Europe. Thus, Saul Bellow's short story "A Silver Dish" published in1984 still resonates with the con-man tradition that best characterizes Euro-American trickster tales. In "A Silver Dish," Bellow accesses a powerful European Jewish trickster tradition that remains alive in the United States. In this story, Bellow enriches a trickster con-man character with Jewish humor and, fur-thermore, turns the story into a reflection on what it means to be an

American. In his introduction to *A Treasury of Jewish Humor*, Nathan Ausubel characterizes Jews as "jesting philosophers,"[88] managing to take the stings out of life's cruel absurdities by laughing at them. Ausubel thinks that Jews assume that life is full of inevitable disaster; yet in common with tricksters everywhere, the world "invariably starts all over again."[89] The folk tradition of Jewish laughter is ironic and even bitter but, according to Ausubel, never cruel or harsh. As with many trickster tales, the purpose of laughter in Jewish tales is to criticize or correct. "Jewish tradition encourages all wise men to be fools sometimes as a moral corrective because if a man is wise all the time, he's just one big *schmiggege!*"[90]

To illustrate this point, Ausubel repeats a tale about a minor dealer in wheat who goes to Minsk to sell his grain but promises his wife to send her a telegram telling her the results. Having successfully sold his wheat, he writes out a telegram that says: "*Sold wheat profitably return tomorrow embrace lovingly Itzik.*" But then he realizes he does not absolutely need the word *profitably*. Next he decides *sold wheat* is redundant. And then he decides that, of course, she knows he will *return tomorrow* and that phrase *embrace lovingly* is what she would expect under any circumstances. Finally, "*[l]ooking down at the telegram, he notice[s] that there was only one word left now—Itzik.*" He does not want to waste 50 kopecks on a single word; so he decides against sending the telegram.[91] The point this and other tales make is that while one should be on guard against making a fool of oneself or of being taken advantage of, the most vigilant person of all is especially prone to fooling himself, and the foolish pursuit of trying to avoid *all* human error is just that, foolish. The wise man accepts that.

In "A Silver Dish," the trickster father, Morris, tries to impart to his son, Woody, the secret of "what life is" because he wants his son to be like him, "an American."[92] By implication, an American is a trickster—always on the make, needing to take chances, and prone to cutting ethical corners. The pensive third-person narrator, reflecting Woody's grieving recollection after his father's death, says, "You could never pin down that self-willed man. When he was ready to make his move, he made it—always on his own terms. And always, always, something up his sleeve. That was how he was."[93] In the course of the story, Morris has plenty of things up his sleeve—and in the case of the silver dish he steals from Woody's benefactor Mrs Skoglund—down the front of his pants.

Although Morris's son, Woody Selbst, professes to be unsure of what life is all about, the narrative reflecting Woody's musings and recollections show how well Morris has passed his trickster sensibility on to his son. Although the son does a better job of disguising his trickster streak, both Morris and Woody are tricksters. Woody continues to puzzle over life and death, but—like his father—"he like[s] taking chances" and revels in the "wonderful stimulus"[94] inherent in risk taking. On the one hand, Woody wears a staid and responsible mantle of respectability: He is the owner of Selbst Tile Company, drives a Lincoln Continental, and supports not only his aging parents and middle-aged sisters but also his father's aging mistress. On the other hand, he grows marijuana in a patch behind the company warehouse next to where he parks his car. Once, at the end of one of his yearly vacations, he even smuggles hashish into the United States from Africa. (He then laces the hashish into the stuffing of the family's Thanksgiving turkey.) As the narrator tells readers, "There [is] no harm at all in Woody, but he d[oes]n't like being entirely within the law. It [i]s simply a question of self-respect."[95]

In addition, Woody supports his own mistress as well as his estranged wife. He differs from Morris in that Woody actually does support these households. Woody has a passion for "honesty" and realism, which generally translate into physically sensible artifacts. Another American innocent, he has developed an ethical system that combines his father's refusal to follow his society's mores and a personal code that finds comfort in appearing to be a responsible businessman, family man, and citizen—an admirable American—while also thumbing his nose at the codes that regulate each role.

After Morris steals Mrs Skoglund's silver dish, Woody realizes that Morris "simply *had* to live, his free life...in the billiard parlor, under the El tracks in a crap game, or playing poker at Brown and Koppel's upstairs."[96] When Woody confronts Morris about the stolen dish, Morris admits that "maybe [I] tried a few more horses."[97] In retrospect, Woody comes to realize, Pop "was always pointing [him] toward a position—a jolly, hearty, natural, likable, unprincipled position. According to his father, if Woody[98] has a weakness, it is his unselfishness. This works to Pop's advantage, but he criticizes Woody for it, nevertheless."[99] Morris, Woody's "Pop," is a consistent trickster few would want to live too close to, but he is earthy and full of life. He lives free. Something of Morris's tricksterism, Woody comes to realize, is part of him as well. And Woody is grateful for that legacy. In the course of his grieving musings, Woody comes to realize that his trickster father with his not-entirely-neat edges has helped him become who he is and that has also made Woody's life fuller and more enjoyable. Because of his father, Woody is no longer constrained by the rigid Puritanical code of his one-time patron. Morris's Jewish trickster tradition has taught him that he cannot—and should not—always follow the wise or socially sanctioned course lest he become a big *schmiggege*. With his father, Woody has come to be what Morris considers uniquely American—a trickster who is always willing to cut corners for the sake of freedom to make his own choices.

City Toughs in Elmore Leonard's Fiction

In contrast to Saul Bellow's work, Elmore Leonard's work, though prolific, is less known to most Americans in hard- or soft-cover fiction than as the source of a number of movies. The list of men who have starred in movies made from Leonard's fiction reads like a Who's Who of leading Hollywood actors and includes among others Robert Mitchum and Paul Newman and also Russell Crowe, John Travolta, and George Clooney. On the other hand, Leonard's novels and short stories are also extremely popular and regularly top sales charts. American tricksters appear in just about every one of his books though the stories usually contain trickster traces rather than well-developed ones.

In *When the Women Come out to Dance*, Elmore Leonard's 2002 short-story collection, for example, about people skirting the edge of morality and social acceptability, life itself seems to be a trickster, an existential coin toss. Yet, even in Leonard's tales, readers hear an echo of Jack. To use the final story in the collection as an illustration, perhaps in a nod toward one of the Jack Tales about Jack killing "many" at once,[100] Leonard's Ben Webster, the Caucasian central character, adopts the Indian surname "Tenkiller" as a screen name. Not all of Leonard's characters are traditional tricksters although they are often con men or women; just about all of them are liminal characters, operating in a moral landscape somewhere between the socially sanctioned and totally outlawed. Thus, one of Leonard's novels, *Pagan Babies*, published in 2000, revolves around a con man/"priest" called Terry Dunn, a quintessential Euro-American trickster, more intent on seeking his own fortune than righting any imbalance; he is typically amoral, yet somehow creates a somewhat better world. At the close of the novel, when someone asks him what he will do when his money runs out, he replies, "I can always get more,"[101] and, knowing that Dunn is unrestrained by ethics, the reader believes his boast. Leonard's heroes belong to the Euro-American con-man tradition of tricksters. The con men and women in Leonard's stories do not necessarily intend anything beyond improving their own lot; however, for the most part, their hearts are in the right place; so along the way, they also improve the lot of those whom they favor while puncturing the self-satisfaction of those who think of themselves as morally superior. Euro-American tricksters refuse to accept the presumed moral superiority of any master. They confront power in whatever form they encounter it.

Paring down Inequity—But Only within Limits

Euro-American tricksters share the general outlines of all tricksters and serve the same purposes: to shake up the status quo, to equalize imbalance, to offer alternate ways in which things could be different; nonetheless, the ways Euro-American fiction writers make use of trickster discourse differ from other American traditions. They are less focused on racial inequities and more apt to pay attention to disparities in economic, social, and gender advantages. Thus, Morris Selbst and Ignatius Reilly are intent on slimming down the economic advantages enjoyed by Mrs Skoglund and Gus Levy; Wesley Benfield finds absurd the supposed superiority of his administrative bosses; and Lucille Vinson sees no reason why men should control her world. To some degree, all modern work tones down the trickster; but this is particularly true of Euro-American fiction, demonstrating that mainstream consumer culture is able or willing to accept only relatively limited trickster discourse. In *A Son of the Circus*, for example, lesser tricksters flourish, but the transgendered murderer proves unacceptably beyond human social norms.

In the original Jack Tales as well as contemporary stories, the community seems to reflect a core belief that all Euro-Americans have a right to succeed. Even so, luck plays a role; luck, in turn, definitely favors ambition, native wit, and willingness to work with—rather than disregard—others. Unlike some American Indian trickster stories that explain how death came about or why the sun shines during the day and the moon at night, Euro-American stories tell about their tricksters transforming some part of the social order. While lacking the high seriousness and purpose of Henry David Thoreau's "Resistance to Civil Government," Euro-American tricksters are also intent on casting a "grain of sand" into the machinery of the established structures of social and economic tradition. In contrast to the Jack Tales of oral literature that are full of wonders, the con men of contemporary American trickster literature are rooted in human nature: They make

their own breaks. Nonetheless, their successes appear equally fantastic. As part of their culture, of their nature, Euro-American tricksters
are always challenging its social and economic sureties. If tricksters
are more evident in Euro-American popular literature and culture
that appeals to the hoi polloi than the literati, this might reflect more
dissatisfaction on the part of consumers of popular than literary culture. Frequently, Euro-American tricksters evince a puzzled sense
that things just are not the way they are supposed to be.

All tricksters promise the chance that, regardless of how well
planned or seemingly settled or secure a situation is, something could
change. While the sources of dissatisfaction among Euro-Americans
may seem relatively insignificant to outsiders, any personal discomfort
is significant to the person who suffers it. The dissatisfactions of the
characters in these stories are not insignificant; however, they illustrate that people do not need to suffer rampant racism or appalling
social or economic inequities to need the services of a trickster. A society that trumpets the value of egalitarianism is bound to note every
inequity. Euro-American idealism gives rise to an innocent assumption that the system can work; and in the meantime, Euro-American
tricksters hustle to achieve their own notion of what is due to them.
Perhaps, Euro-American tricksters reflect among Euro-Americans a
belief that they *should* be privileged and puzzlement at gender or economic oppression that frustrates their sense of entitlement. One has
to wonder how much of the Euro-American trickster's optimism and
innocence is the result of privilege: Huck is a poor *white* boy in a slave
society.

Although no Euro-American literary trickster tales of the last
50 years can match Saul Bellow's 1953 novel *The Adventures of Augie
March*, some Euro-American writers continue to build their fiction
around memorable tricksters. What sets a Euro-American trickster
apart? As Bellow's Morris Selbst realizes, he is always on the make.
He usually alters the world around him, sometimes improving the lot
of others, though not necessarily on purpose, as does Toole's Ignatius
Reilly. Yet, in common with Leonard's Terry Dunn, he is amoral and
totally confident of his success and generally with good reason. Euro-
American tricksters are often compelled to kick others into action as
Tyler's Muriel Pritchard and Irving's Rahul/Mrs Dogar do. Secure in
their sense of entitlement, Euro-American tricksters like Edgerton's
Wesley Benfield and Childress's Lucille Vinson, demand their share
of sex, wealth, or the right to ignore other people's rules. To one
degree or another, that same sense of entitlement produces an aura of

innocence and also characterizes Kesey's Randle Patrick McMurphy as well as the Merry Pranksters who accompanied Kesey across the country. Even when they feel they have been short-changed, these men and women are neither politicians nor social activists taking on society's major problems. Instead, they are individualists focused on their own betterment; and sometimes, in achieving their own ends, they often improve the worlds they live in.

CHAPTER 5

HEIRS OF THE MONKEY KING

A common trope among immigrant literatures, transformation is especially prominent in Pacific Islander and Asian American, particularly Chinese American, fiction. In typical fashion, Asian American stories, particularly those that deal with the liminal space people negotiating major changes in their lives need to navigate, often feature tricksters or at least trickster discourse. The trickster is comfortable in his skin and uses his ability to work the margins of different milieus to his advantage and often that of his community. With his unique talent for altering himself, he presents an invaluable ally to people who need to either successfully navigate the shoals of transformation or be destroyed by it. Immigration to the United States with its significantly different culture, language, and racial prejudices demanded major transformations of first-generation Asian Americans; even later generations have been marked by those challenges. The trickster, however, and trickster discourse have allowed both immigrants and their children some control over those changes. A great deal of Asian American literature since the 1960s are tales of immigrant transformation,[1] but the characters in these stories, even trickster stories, cannot help considering the price they have paid to achieve those transformations.

While contemporary Asian American writers could draw on other well-developed trickster traditions as well, just as the sheer geographic and demographic bulk of China dominates Asia, the Chinese Monkey King figures most prominently among Asian trickster traditions.[2] Of course, others, including India's baby Krishna and the Polynesian Maui, are also major tricksters. In a similar fashion, while *The Adventures of Amir Hamza* grew out of Arab culture, the tales about Amir Hamza's close friend and follower, the trickster Amar Ayyar, have enjoyed wide appreciation in the South of Asia, especially in India and Pakistan. Asia has many trickster traditions; and though many twenty-first-century Euro-Americans retain only vague notions about and tenuous ties to the specific countries from which their ancestors emigrated, Asian Americans generally identify themselves as, for example, Japanese American. They have a better sense of their ancestral cultural heritage than most Euro-Americans, who have so many national heritages that they do not know much about any one of them. In fact, as one writer stresses, at root, all that Asian Americans as a group actually have in common is that at one time or another, all have been excluded from US citizenship.[3]

All Asian trickster traditions are no more identical than all Chinese, Indians, Filipinos, Japanese, Indonesians, Thais, and Polynesians are; but attempting to address each Asian American trickster tradition individually would hopelessly bloat this chapter. Nonetheless, although this chapter deals exclusively with Chinese American texts, these texts cannot be assumed to reflect *all* Asian American traditions. Being aware that each national group of Asian Americans arrived in the United States with its own trickster tradition is important. The term *Asian American* is, as Sau-ling Cynthia Wong notes, used by many groups but in pursuit of separate goals.[4] The Chinese Monkey King that this chapter concentrates on does, nonetheless, have more in common with other Asian and Pacific Island tricksters than those from other areas of the globe. Assuming a literary panethnicity (i.e., what can be said of one can be said of all) of Asian American writers in the United States can lead to what Stephen Sumida and Sau-ling Wong call "an uneasy conglomeration of texts."[5] Yet Asian American tricksters share some commonalities. Asian tricksters and particularly the Monkey King often deal in the marvelous and battle monsters; unlike other traditions, the tricksters almost never make foolish choices. Instead, they have good reason to be proud, even arrogant. They are often outsiders who need to be integrated with the community. As culture heroes, transformers, and demigods, Asian tricksters obviously belong to the genus "trickster," yet they are not underdogs like Br'er Rabbit, given to clownish foolishness like Coyote, or apt to slip on the community's "good old boy" cloak as Jack and his descendants sometimes do. They are so powerful that they seldom need to be sly as the tricksters from other traditions often are.

THE MAKING OF A MODEL MINORITY

As African Americans still deal with the legacy of slavery and American Indians are haunted by the loss of their land and traditional cultures, as a group, Asian Americans confront a different but still perverse challenge. After a century of legal exclusion, in recent decades, Asian Americans have been saddled with the "nonchoice" of either accepting exclusion or taking on the mantle of being a model minority.[6] Rather than being known for political agitation or riots, Asian Americans have developed a reputation for hard work, for banding together and building small businesses, and for demanding that their children excel in school. The Japanese proverb about the nail that sticks out getting hammered down has crossed the Pacific to America. Few Asian Americans want to be known for their inability or refusal to fit in. Americans may chuckle about Garrison Keillor's Lake Woebegon where all the children are above average, but demanding above-average success and almost preternatural self-discipline of oneself and one's confreres comes at a high personal cost. The model minority stereotype becomes even more pernicious because it suggests that most, if not all, Asian Americans and Pacific Islanders have done well in the United States. That is not so.[7]

Historically, along with other minority groups, Asian Americans have dealt with racism during long years of physical exploitation and legal exclusion from American citizenship. When large numbers of Chinese immigrants began to appear in the American West during the gold rush of the 1840s and then as Chinese workers took part in building the intercontinental railroad after the Civil War, the dominant Euro-American society assumed that Chinese immigrants were incapable of being assimilated into American society. In common with African Americans and American Indians, Chinese immigrants encountered racist stereotypes that portrayed them as totally "other." While not technically slaves, nineteenth-century Chinese laborers were treated barely better than slaves and sometimes, since they were considered expendable, they were treated worse.[8]

A Message Massaged by Popular Media and Powerful Elites

During the century that saw the transformation of Asian Americans from a group of foreigners who could not possibly be absorbed into American culture to an admired group of model Americans, popular culture helped to mold popular perceptions. During the first part of that century, the late nineteenth century, and into the early twentieth century, much of American popular culture perceived little threat in Asian American men.[9] When Japan came to be recognized as a competing colonial power, however, that perception changed. During the early twentieth-century, Hollywood films reflected worries about the rise of Japanese prominence with Japanese males portrayed as villain-ously sly—wily and underhanded. The Hearst newspaper chain also prepared American readers for the Yellow Peril scare whipped up dur-ing the 1920s and even the internment of Japanese American citizens during World War II. Nonetheless, until World War II, popular cul-ture tended to lump Asian men and women into faceless masses.[10]

During this swath of time, significant social and economic forces also contributed to the manipulation of mainstream Euro-American per-ceptions of Asian Americans. Company owners frequently hired Asian Americans as strikebreakers when either Euro-American or African American workers proved recalcitrant. In addition, government policy makers were prone to setting up one Asian American group as supe-rior to another. Thus during World War II, popular media encouraged the rest of America to view Chinese Americans as good citizens while Japanese Americans were demonized. One has only to catch a few war movies from the 1940s on late-night television to be on familiar terms with the stereotypes. This led to a situation after World War II where no one group of Asian Americans had the political influence of, for example, African Americans. All of these experiences in the United States taught Asian Americans to lie low, avoid the limelight, and con-centrate on demonstrating their patriotism and good citizenship. In contrast to African Americans, American Indians, and Latinos, Asian Americans appeared to embrace the same work ethic and belief in edu-cation that the dominant culture espoused. So by 1966, *U.S. News & World Report* was touting Asian Americans as a model minority.[11] Of course, this stereotype carried its own self-destructive seeds, setting up what Zeng Li calls an "ethnic dilemma."[12] The external and inter-nal repression involved begs for a trickster response.

CHINA'S MONKEY KING

Caught in this bind and forced to accept the limitations of their lives in America along with its promise, since the 1960s, Chinese American writers have embraced the Monkey King. While at first, the mythical Monkey King put his ability to transform himself into the service of anyone else only under duress, over time, he does come to serve the common good in the guise of the T'ang monk. For indi-viduals weighted under discrimination and misunderstanding, want-ing to personally succeed but steeped in a tradition of cooperation, the Monkey King offers a positive transformative path to follow. Still vibrant in both Chinese and Chinese American culture, the trickster

Monkey King is a prince of transformation on his own terms, changing himself and his circumstances at will. Embedded in both oral and literary culture, the Monkey King is most fully delineated in Wu Ch'êng-ên's *The Journey to the West*,[13] one of China's four great classical novels. In the course of 100 chapters that relate fantastic adventures eclipsing even the most imaginative twenty-first-century fantasy tales, at its core, *The Journey to the West* remains a reflection of late-sixteenth-century Chinese social and religious thinking. The central narrative follows the Buddhist monk, Hsuän-tsang, as he travels west to India in order "to seek scriptures from Buddha in the Western Heaven"[14] and bring these scriptures back to his T'ang master, the emperor. Hsuän-tsang's is a perilous religious pilgrimage.[15]

The text has many levels of meaning. It is a polemic religious text: The fiends and monsters that manage to escape death for opposing the T'ang monk—so called because he has been commissioned by the T'ang emperor—and his disciples convert to Buddhism. The villains are often Taoists. In addition, the story is a symbolic journey to Buddhism's highest levels. The story reinforces Buddhist beliefs in reincarnation, the prohibition against taking human life, the importance of vegetarianism, of celibacy, and the monks' mental as well as physical detachment. Yet, despite the preference for Buddhism, woven through the books runs the theme that China's three traditional religions, Confucianism, Taoism, and Buddhism, are all "honorable";[16] the T'ang monk's disciples all need to learn to see themselves as part of society rather than as individuals. Throughout the tale, the characters argue their philosophical, religious, and personal positions using folk and Confucian proverbs.

As well as a reflection of traditional Chinese culture and society, the narrative is also an exciting adventure tale, a story of personal growth, a story of intriguing interaction among the core cast of strong personalities, and a wildly imaginative series of fantastic encounters with marvelous creatures. Along with a host of more insulting names, the central, most memorable character in *The Journey to the West*, the Monkey King—who eventually becomes the T'ang monk's most trustworthy defender—is variously called Stone Monkey, Handsome Monkey King, Sun Wu-K'ung, Pi-ma-wên, Great Sage Equal to Heaven, Fiery Eyes and Diamond Pupils, and Sun Pilgrim—or just Pilgrim. A quintessential trickster, the Monkey King can transform into 72 different forms. Early on, his actions are completely self-serving; in time, however, under the influence of the T'ang monk, he puts his ability to transform himself at the service of his mission and moves beyond self-aggrandizement, finally achieving Buddha status.

An established part of traditional Chinese culture, the Monkey King and his gross alter ego, Pa-chieh, another of the T'ang monk's followers, transitioned quite effectively to the Gold Mountain in America. Even today, every Chinese school child is thoroughly familiar with stories from *The Journey to the West*. (The stories are not equally familiar to most Americans, so for more on *The Journey to the West*, readers should refer to appendix I.) Not surprisingly, the Chinese Monkey King is a central element of both the oral and literary culture Chinese immigrants brought to the United States, and the Monkey King plays a major role in Chinese American literature.

A TRANSITIONAL GENERATION OF IMMIGRANTS AND THE TRICKSTERS IN THEIR FICTION

Eat a Bowl of Tea (1961)

A trickster with elements of both the Monkey King—the trickster leader—and Pa-chieh—the trickster as totally self-absorbed sensualist, capable of limited growth—appears in what Jeffrey Chan calls Chinese America's first[17,18] novel, Louis Chu's *Eat a Bowl of Tea*. Ah Song[19] invades the nest of the young bridegroom Ben Loy and leaves his cuckoo chick for Ben Loy to raise. Ah Song is an inveterate gambler, a hanger-on at the mah-jong club owned by Ben Loy's father, Wah Gay. Ah Song is also a flashy dresser though he never seems to have held down a job. Additionally, he is wildly imaginative and "fabricate[s] a fantastic family background"[20] as part of his plan to seduce Ben Loy's young wife. What is more, Ah Song has a way with women; Mei Oi is not the first wife he has seduced. As happens with tricksters, however, he does not escape unscathed: Wah Gay slices off his ear and the local tong exiles him from New York for five years. Furthermore, Ah Song has also been forced to pay a 1,000-dollar indemnity for his earlier association with another wife. Ah Song's trickster character is summed up in Chu's description of him as Ah Song "straighten[s] his tie and peer[s] at himself in the full-length mirror in the living room. It reflect[s] a nonchalant, cold, and calculating individual. He [can] get what he want[s], he t[ells] himself."[21] A "lone wolf"[22] and a "rascal,"[23] Ah Song is predatory and dangerous but eventually brought down by his isolation in a milieu that values connection—bonds of family and friendship, of reciprocal gift and favor giving, the Wang Association, the Ping on Tong. In *Eat a Bowl of Tea*, the trickster Ah Song functions as an object lesson, illustrating how no member of society should act.

Ah Song recognizes Mei Oi's youth, naivety, and vulnerability. Yet, while she is still a teenager and new to the community, and he is middle-aged, a participant of long standing, she belongs in a way he will never belong. Eventually, she accepts that she has offended her husband and damaged the community. By the end of the novel, she feels "a desire and a responsibility of sharing her husband's problems."[24] From the standpoint of the community, Mei Oi is far more mature than Ah Song since he remains emotionally a preadolescent, unable to get beyond his own desires.[25] From the analytical perspective of Paul Radin and Franchot Ballinger, Ah Song illustrates the unsocialized trickster's usual behavior. Ah Song alters the community but unlike the Monkey King never changes himself.

In typical trickster fashion, Ah Song incites action: He gives the young couple—as well as the Wang family and the Chinese community—a child and thus the promise of a future for the otherwise barren bachelor society of exiles. In a perverse sort of way, he is responsible for helping to heal the rift between the impotent and shamed young man and his insecure young wife. While as one writer notes, all the major characters are pursuing the American dream of happiness,[26] only Ah Song's devious ways can move them beyond the oppression implicit in their society's rigidly traditional familial attitudes.[27] Nonetheless, Ah Song remains a foolish villain. He does not fit in. In contrast, Ben Loy and Mei Oi reconcile and come to love her child and one another. Ben Loy accepts some guilt for Mei Oi's seduction by Ah Song since Ben Loy recognizes that "I have ruined my health"[28] by consorting with prostitutes before his marriage.

The novel ends with a promise of further reconciliation—the young couple's agreement that when (not if) they have a second child, they will invite their fathers, who have lost face because of the son's cuckolding and the daughter's infidelity, to that child's haircutting ceremony. The young couple, therefore, as well as their fathers—all of whom who have fled New York in shame—will reconfigure a new community. Unlike African Americans, Euro-American, or American Indians, this Chinese community does not admire the trickster who does not change—as the Monkey King does—to serve the larger group. This Chinatown community is a world of *relationships* complicated by tong politics and the necessity of saving face. In this unexpected way, the world of *Eat a Bowl of Tea* parallels the complicated—but heroically predictable world of monsters and adversaries in *Journey to the West*.

Ah Song has typical trickster's powers: luck and power to seduce; with these powers, he alters the moribund bachelor society of Chinatown in a way that neither Ben Loy nor Mei Oi, much less their fathers, Wah Gay or Lee Gong, could. As Jinqi Ling notes, what has really changed by the end of the novel is that the young couple have transformed their marriage and now negotiate gender relations.[29] They need to change. That would be impossible in the bachelor society where they first live; Ben Loy and Mei Oi need to move on to negotiation, and that would not have occurred without Ah Song's disrupting their settled though unhappy lives. Far more than any other character, the outsider Ah Song acts independently of Chinatown's self-reflexive male society where—until the late 1940s when legal Chinese women immigrants were allowed into the United States—racial segregation and socioeconomic barriers kept the community moribund. Even though he pays the high personal cost of five years' exile, ironically, the outsider Ah Song alters the world for all of the characters as he transforms the lives of Ben Loy and Mei as well as the New York Chinese Americans. His antisocial actions thrust them across an adaptive bridge between the traditional cultures they have come from and the American culture they now need to navigate. In common with Pa-chieh from the *Journey to the West*, Ah Song is capable of transformation although his powers and his utility to the community are limited. Nonetheless, Pa-chieh achieved Buddha status; and Ah Song, regardless of his selfish motivation, has altered the community for good. He remains a member and presumably will return to join the community after his exile.

Crossings (1968)

While Ah Song is an outsider impelling the other characters to change, in the next two works, tricksterism is at the core as the central characters' attempt to reconcile traditional worldviews and realities that conflict with them. Perhaps all immigrant literature must, of its nature, reflect the immigrant's sense of dislocation and longing for home—whether "home" denotes a place or a people. Chinese American immigrant literature of the 1960s and 70s reflects the transformations inherent in the painful transplanting from one culture to another. All too painfully accurate, Francis L. K. Hsu opens the preface to *American and Chinese* with the statement that "I am a marginal man."[30] In much the same fashion, Tsai Chin says of herself, "Bi-cultural, accepted in both the East and the West, I am never a stranger, but always an outsider."[31] Immigrants are natural tricksters, liminal creatures functioning between separate entities.

Chuang Hua's narrative *Crossings* shares the liminal quality found in many trickster stories but emphasizes the aching discontent of the uprooted. Even Chuang Hua's name situates her between her older and younger siblings, her American and Chinese cultures, her family's expectations and her separate inclinations. Narrator Chuang Hua (Fourth Jane) has two names, one Chinese and one English. Her Chinese name gives off ambivalent signals: "Chuang" associates her with the sons born after her. She is the fourth child in her Chinese American family and the four situates her among her parents' children. Fourth Jane's lack of place combined with the family's assumption that her place is immutable lead to her contradictory combination of compliance and rebelliousness. In common with other tricksters, she is always "between."

In a multitude of large and small ways, she strives to please her parents and to satisfy their expectations, but she also rebels. She conforms to their notions of acceptable etiquette and chooses to work with her father in the investment market. On the other hand, she also refuses to marry any of the men her father suggests for her. In time, she separates herself from her family, living in Paris and taking a French journalist for a lover. Perhaps most painfully, she accentuates a familial rift when she refuses to acknowledge her brother's "barbarian," that is, Euro-American, wife even though Fourth Jane's father accepts his daughter-in-law once she has given the family a child. Were Fourth Jane a thorough-going trickster, she would find a way to negotiate the seeming impasse between the rigid rules of her upbringing and the change implicit in accepting her brother's wife into the family. By the end of the novel, Fourth Jane is returning and presumably reconciling with her family. But this reconciliation seems primarily a submission to her dead father's wishes. Rather than Fourth Jane, her unnamed sister-in-law has played the trickster's role—altering the known world and herself by marrying into a Chinese American family. In contrast, at the close of *Crossings*, instead of causing change, Fourth Jane adjusts to it, thus relinquishing some of her power as the rebellious trickster. In the milieu of her family that demands unanimity, however, that makes her admirable.

The family Fourth Jane has grown up in is a totality; that totality belongs to, is loved by, and reflects her father, Dyadya. His life and that of his family are ruled by everything being "very well done," being "proper."[32] Fourth Jane's mother, Ngmah, too needs "order" in her house and in her family. For example, Ngmah cannot sleep until she has thoroughly cleaned her bedroom. The assumption by First Michael's wife that she will share her husband with his family instead of his belonging first and foremost to his father elicits an outburst of Dyadya's anger. Nonetheless, because of his grandson, Dyadya eventually accepts his son's wife. Fourth Jane, however, cannot accept such an ultimate "other." Fourth Jane has come to see the family's unity as its "first principle."[33] She has invested so much of herself in that unity and destroyed so much of herself in the process that she cannot "stand around waiting to see the old destroyed...[while she remains] unconvinced about the new."[34] So for most of the book, she is in exile, "becalmed"; she takes up with a married Frenchman; neither commits to the other.

At the end of the book, despite her lover's current pleas to marry him, Fourth Jane is packing to go home for her father's funeral. Even though she is bringing her trees back to the garden her father carefully tended, the unity that once sustained the family no longer exists. A false note exists in this trickster's somber acceptance.[35] The humor, if only irony, that readers come to expect in trickster tales is absent in *Crossings*. In contrast, Fourth Jane approaches everything seriously. The novel leaves Fourth Jane lost in a painful void between what was and what will be. Tricksters generally inhabit an area between polarities, but for the most part, they do so with verve rather than acceptance.

Fourth Jane reverses the order of the Monkey King's journey. He moves from total independence to integration into the society of immortals. She moves from total integration as a member of her family to rebellious disruption. The novel's ending suggests a possible reintegration but to a new reality. Since she is a human being, the process is as painful and perhaps as potentially fatal as the uprooting of one of her father's beloved trees. Shu-yan Li believes that the story describes Fourth Jane growing into an "Asian American." Thus, no longer blindly submissive to her father's words, her thoughts and actions are still influenced by her father's ideas; and yet she also recognizes that many members of the dominant American culture view all Asian Americans as "other."[36]

Fourth Jane evinces many of the trickster's qualities. Although inhibited by gender and her assigned role in her family's traditional Chinese American culture and while her "subversion" remains circumscribed, she does attempt to bring down the dominant patriarchy that characterized her upbringing.[37] In common with other tricksters, Fourth Jane is a clearly liminal character. Even her transformation, however, is limited. Despite her determination, she never quite breaks from her early cultural moorings. To do so would be just too self-destructive. Her inability to change herself or her family's assumptions about her attests to the strength of the roles her cultural background ascribes to individual members. Finally, Fourth Jane exemplifies the tricksterism defined by Huining Ouyang as: "Typically characterized by disguise, ambiguity, disruption, and adaptation, tricksterism refers to the rhetorical and cultural strategies practiced by the powerless to achieve some vindication, validity, or balance of the scales."[38] In Fourth Jane's case, the emphasis has to be on "some." Fourth Jane garbs herself in roles that hurt herself and her family. Her relationships with her family and her lover remain ambiguous right to the narrative's end. For all of her adaptation—to her family, to American, Chinese, and French cultures—her life is constantly disrupted by her father's demands, her brother's choices, and her lover's inconstancy. As do Ah Song and other tricksters, Fourth Jane pays a steep price for her limited trickster role in a severely defined culture.

Neither Louis Chu nor Chuang Hua explicitly references the Chinese Monkey King trickster. They do illustrate, however, that among this early wave of Chinese American writers, some have been particularly adept at appropriating and reworking the myth of the Monkey King so that while it remains a potent archetype, it has also become private and mythopoetical—to use Joan Chang's term[39]—speaking to an Asian American present as well as to a ancient Chinese past.

M. Butterfly's (1989) Sophisticated Reversals

Neither the supremely competent Monkey King nor the gross Pa-chieh appears in David Henry Hwang's *M. Butterfly*. Instead, the self-deluded Pa-chieh again predominates in the role of Gallimard. Hwang uses Gallimard as the focal point in a story about illusion and self-delusion. Galliard as well as Hwang's other Westerners in *M. Butterfly* are caught up in the orientalism that Edward Said warns ignores "brute reality"[40] and says more to and about the West than the East. Hwang rejects orientalism as he would reject any self-reflexive "grand narrative" more intent on itself than the rest of the world. Hwang's personal history has prepared him to doubt any all-encompassing system of thought including the Christian fundamentalism he encountered during his childhood and youth.

His rejection of his family's Christian fundamentalism has been a key event in Hwang's personal history. Talking about religious beliefs, Hwang explains that any "belief becomes fundamentalist when those who question it become the enemy, the heretic."[41] Hwang seems to extend his definition of religious fundamentalism to political and social arenas. Thus his satire of communism in the drama may also derive from his rejection of grand narratives. Choosing to question his family's beliefs when he was in college obviously cost Hwang the comfort of tribal identity. At the same time, that habit of questioning has helped him to utilize the trickster's fluidity.

Hwang's significant youthful rejection has given him insight into the fact that other seeming immutables—for example, cultural assumptions about gender and race—are also constructs. Constructs carry inherent dangers. Defining one's self in terms of what one is not—not Asian or not female, for example—is particularly risky. It demands that the "other" stay other; once one starts to recognize similarities, one can lose one's own identity. Constructs also tend to project one's psychological shadow onto the "other."[42] Starting with its title, *M. Butterfly* places considerable emphasis on "seeming" and lazy inattention. The play also warns against the danger of constructing "the other" according to one's own notions rather than recognizing what is there.

The success of Hwang's play[43] and its subsequent reformulation as a film relies in part on its modernity and in part on its tapping into mythic trickster roots. *M. Butterfly* is eminently modern, even postmodern[44] in its insistence on the untrustworthiness of what its characters—and presumably its audience—believe and act upon. From the start, nothing is quite what it seems: Many of the cast play multiple roles; time and place are collapsed and confabulated; the language itself is full of double entendre and dramatic irony; and as Gallimard tells the audience, "In life...our [his friend Marc's—apparently the 'sensitive soul of reason'—and his] positions were...always reversed."[45] Thus, even as the play opens, the action itself proves untrustworthy. As Hwang's "Playwright's Notes" reprinted right after the cast of characters in the Plume paperback edition of the play explains, the play is based on an incident reported in a 1986 *New York Times* news story. For years, a French diplomat had passed on information to China for the sake of his Chinese lover whom, the diplomat insisted, he never realized was a man masquerading as a woman.

For the most part, Gallimard, the central character in *M. Butterfly*, and the play itself, skirt the issue of homosexuality; Gallimard refuses to entertain the possibility that he knew and accepted Song Liling as a homosexual lover. Instead, Gallimard insists that he accepted Song Liling's "modesty."[46] Gallimard is willfully ignorant of Chinese customs[47] including sexual practices. Even so, his assumption that the sexual dysfunction in his relationship with Song Liling derives from his acceptance of the Song's Chinese reticence rings false since the play demonstrates Gallimard's inability to sustain either a marital relationship with his wife or an extramarital affair with another woman.

Gallimard's affair with Song Liling involves a fantasy about all Asian women, as if they were all clones of Giacomo Puccini's Butterfly; however, the play also literally substitutes a homosexual relationship for a heterosexual one. Once Gallimard has to accept at the end of the play that his "other" has changed, so does he. If Song Liling will not play Butterfly, he will.[48] One of the men in the relationship has ceased to play the submissive woman's role, so the other takes on the role. The ending of *M. Butterfly* leaves audiences with more questions than answers leading David Eng to conclude his essay on Gallimard's closeted existence with a paragraph of questions:

> In the final analysis, who in *M. Butterfly* is afforded the last laugh? Who is the ultimate artist and trickster figure, the queen in control? Is it the caustic Song whose provisional foray out of the paternal order is quickly suppressed by Gallimard's heterosexual conversion and homo-sexual abjection? Or is it Gallimard, the white Frenchman diplomat, whose flawless performance as the awkward straight lover subdues the oriental diva and assures us that all will be well in status quo sexual and racial politics?[49]

Eng belongs to a company of critics who complain about the manner in which the play raises but does not resolve questions about gender roles and their metaphorical association with political relations.[50]

Hwang himself believes "our capacity for self-delusion [is] fairly boundless. Yet it is also part of the human dilemma to try and under-stand ourselves."[51] In *M. Butterfly*, Hwang all but exhausts the idea that illusions are dangerous, and perhaps most destructive are those with which people fool themselves. Galliard is so ignorant of China, the country to which he has been posted, that he does not realize that although by the 1920s some theater managers had begun to cast women in female roles, in traditional Chinese opera, the female roles had all been taken by men. Thus, a man might well play a female opera role. Galliard is enamored by the Mme. Butterfly trope of sub-missive women and submissive Eastern countries. Yet, human beings thirst to be known as who they really are. Hwang himself explains that "in act 3, scene 2 of *M. Butterfly* when Song disrobes, Song is really trying to say, 'Look at me, get past the make-up, get past the archetype. You were in love with me.'"[52]

As in the 1986 news report upon which the play is based, power relations between the sexes and between the East and West are central to *M. Butterfly*. Gallimard's false sense of virility and cultural superior-ity, of the prerogatives granted by his masculine authority and Western birthright, initially furthers his career. Ultimately, of course, both his delusion and that of the West contribute to their defeats: his conviction for spying; the French and American defeats in Vietnam. The play is also about the power of mindless belief and of lies. At the end of *M. Butterfly*, Gallimard takes on the role of Puccini's Butterfly and commits seppuku rather than accept (Hwang's phrase) "the devastating knowledge"[53] of the truth. In the last scene, Gallimard chooses to be the discarded archetype. He cannot "get past" it. Such convoluted themes and characters are appropriate to the trickster tradition. In *M. Butterfly*, as is common in trickster tales and especially in the Monkey King tales, transformation and fluidity of identity are central. Actually, Hwang admits "all my work in some sense confronts the issue of fluidity of identity and explores the idea that who we are is the result of circumstance, the result of things that are not necessarily inherent but instead come out of our interaction with our contacts."[54] Used as a name and an image a century ago by Puccini and more recently by Hwang, the butterfly embodies change in its life cycle. In Hwang's play, Song Liling's costume changes are apparent changes, but Gallimard's psychological changes go deeper. The play recapitulates his insecure youth, cold marriage, passionately involved love affair with Song, and his final choice of a romantic death over acceptance of pedestrian reality. The power of *M. Butterfly* arises from modern myths of gender and racial superiority and the more ancient trickster archetype. But Hwang's play reminds viewers and readers of how the popular myth best known from Puccini's opera can blind its adherents.[55]

The Monkey King likes to brag about his power to achieve 72 transformations; even Pa-chieh has access to 36. While Pa-chieh's impetuosity is more evident, both tricksters are most vulnerable, most susceptible to hubris, when they depend solely on their own strength and wits. The same proves true of Gallimard and Song Liling. The Monkey King-Pilgrim is known for his diamond-eyed vision and power; nonetheless, on a regular basis, he has to appeal to his heavenly patrons for special knowledge and sometimes for physical help. Otherwise, he could not defeat the fiends and monsters he encounters on the pilgrims' journey to the West. In Hwang's play depending only on himself, Gallimard condemns himself to Pa-chieh's buffoonish role. Like Pa-chieh, Gallimard focuses on himself, his own needs; he lacks truthful relationships with his wife, friend, and lovers. If he had a mutual relationship with any of them, he would not be so alone. If like the Monkey King, he finally converted to some belief or cause beyond himself, he would not be so pathetic. Gallimard considers himself the center of the action when, in fact, Song—himself and as the surrogate of other people and ideas—has manipulated Gallimard and continues to manipulate him. Gallimard's only defense is further self-deception.

Both Gallimard and Chang Hua are trapped between cultural truths they have accepted—even when they kicked against them—as certainties and different worlds that contradict those certainties. For all that Chuang Hua has resisted her father's and her culture's paternalistic dominance, it is, nonetheless, the bedrock of her worldview. Her rebellions—refusing the men her parents suggest as husbands, moving to France, taking a French lover—represent negotiations rather than true separations from what she believes are her father's immutable interpretation of his life and by extension that of his family. By accepting his daughter-in-law, however, he demonstrates that he can change. His trees flourish; the trees that Chang Hua brings to his garden seem to be in more peril. Gallimard too is caught up in the dynamics of incomplete tricksterism. His certainties have been illusionary notions of national and male superiority. Both have blinded him to hard reality. Neither Gallimard nor Chang Hua has been able to learn from the Monkey King's ability to transform when necessary but to stay in control of his transformations both for his own sake and for the sake of his community. Rather than calling upon their trickster cores, Gallimard and Chang Hua fail to transform and, caught between worlds, remain fatally vulnerable to the dangers in both.

Tripmaster Monkey (1989)

A character that far more successfully inhabits his inner trickster appears in Maxine Hong Kingston's *Tripmaster Monkey*. Jeanne Rosier Smith considers all of Kingston's three best-known books, *The Woman Warrior* (1976), *China Men* (1980), and *Tripmaster Monkey*, "transformational trickster texts."[56] However, Kingston's fourth book and first novel, *Tripmaster Monkey*, makes the Monkey King central to the novels. Kingston's central character, Wittman Ah Sing, takes on the role of the trickster Monkey King; and, as Kingston herself says, "The monkey's task was to bring chaos to established order. So Wittman has that also."[57] Reflecting the Monkey King's energy, the novel is crowded with allusion, incident, and almost more word play than a reader can keep track of.

Wittman Ah Sing's both/and qualities quickly mark him as a trickster. This lack of clear definition to his character frustrates some critics such as Amy Ling who complains that Wittman is "simultaneously heroic and inane, daring and ridiculous, vulnerable and ego-centric, sensitive and insensitive"; he is at once "heroic and ridiculous, admirable and pitiable."[58] All true, all typically trickster-like. Yet, in his Monkey King persona, Wittman jousts with [white Americans'] "dreams about us [Chinese Americans]"[59]; and with Wittman, Kingston insists that instead of Euro-American orientalist projections, "I am a human being, standing right here on land which I belong to and which belongs to me"[60]; *mine* [emphasis added] "is an American face."[61] Wittman stresses that while he is Chinese American, he is certainly no less American than, for instance, any Italian American or German American. All are capable of asserting an American identity and still valuing their own rich ethnic heritages.

Kingston feels strongly that as post–Cultural Revolution Chinese artists have discovered, without cultural roots, artists are left with nothing; rather, all artists need the many cultural layers that enrich a work.[62] Thus both her characters Wittman and Kingston herself insist on all of the elements in their rich, multilayered heritages. Although five generations away from China, Wittman claims the literary heritage of China he learned through oral culture and his own study; he also claims the literary heritage of Europe and the United States that he learned in American schools. Additionally, he is heir to the popular culture of twentieth-century America. They all belong to him.

Set primarily in a 1960s San Francisco preoccupied with race and antiwar ferment, the novel also echoes and sometimes criticizes Beat attitudes. The witty Wit Man (as his mother calls him) of the early novel is as consciously American as Walt Whitman,[63] as much a literary name-dropper[64] as a newly minted English PhD. Aware of his Chinese heritage and his American roots, Wittman is irritated, on the one hand, with FOB (fresh off the boat) Chinese Americans who cling to third-rate elements of both Chinese and American culture; but on the other hand, he is also annoyed with other Americans (including his fifth-generation American self) who mimic immigrant accents. But also, like his predecessor the Monkey King, Wittman grows and changes, transforming himself as well as his world. Early in the novel, he recalls the costumes he wore as a child for his parents' stage shows. The child Wittman performed in a monkey suit, collecting money for a huckster and for his father's performances; he also dressed as a miniature Uncle Sam for his mother's patriotic World War II performances. Like his name, his costumes reflect his consciously non-hyphenated Chinese American self. He is an American with an ancestral Chinese heritage and an American heritage; he refuses to give up either; he refuses to mush them together.

To pursue his own journey, already *in* the American West, Wittman
has to keep going along. The novel's chapters take him through the
physical and metaphorical fog of the Golden Gate Park; through the
commercial world of his mind-fogging job selling toys in a department
store; through his friend/antagonist Lance's riotous party and its after-
math including Wittman's "marriage" to the blonde Taña; through
visits to the abodes of his mother, Ruby Long Legs, and her gambling
friends and of his father, Zeppelin Ah Sing; and to the surreal world of
the unemployment office. The novel crescendos in the last several chapters setting up several days of theatrical performance reinvolving most
of the characters introduced earlier; the show itself features a series of
vignettes exhibiting Chinese and American myth as history.

Finally, as a standup comedian, Wittman confronts Euro-American
clichés and stereotypes about Asian Americans in his sarcastic in-your-
face one-man show. Along the way, Wittman also progresses from
someone who "has lessons coming to him"[65] in how to deal with
women and who complains that Taña "hasn't cleaned the apartment"[66]
to someone who can publicly declare to her, "You don't have to be the
housewife. I'll do one-half of the house-wife stuff. But you can't call
me your wife. You don't have to be the wife either. See how much I love
you? Unromantically but."[67] Wittman's altered relationship with Taña
reflects his hope for the larger society's change from roles of dominance and subservience even though his "ideal resolution," as Zeng Li
notes, is likely to be "an unsettled and ongoing one."[68]

Wittman moves physically from one place to another in the San
Francisco area, briefly to Las Vegas and Sacramento; but more significantly Wittman moves psychologically beyond the depressed loner, a
loser who—as the novel opens—daily considers suicide. By the end
of the novel, Wittman has married, reconnected with his family, and
developed notable ties with the community. He also has a way to go.
Wittman has set out to transform the Chinese American community
and all of American society so that everyone recognizes the multicultural nature of the United States. His grandiose production more
than tolerates minority groups: It embraces multiplicity and insists
that diversity has always been a source of America's strength.

In an interview with Marilyn Chin, Kingston identifies with her
omniscient Kuan Yin narrator and says,

> She is actually pushing Wittman Ah Sing around, telling him to shut
> up...she has a memory that goes back to China. She has a memory
> that sees a little bit into the future, toward the end of the Vietnam

war...And she is also sometimes very tough on Wittman, and she captures him...[Yet] Kuan Yin...is very merciful. I mean, nobody is going to get killed or hurt. She keeps giving people wonderful opportunities.[69]

The omniscient narrator promises still more change as she addresses Wittman: "Dear American monkey, don't be afraid. Here, let us tweak your ear, and kiss your other ear."[70] Mischievous as he is, even the Chinese Monkey King is expected to change on a more profound, more personal, level than his flashy, superficial transformations into mere fleas or multiple monkeys. In her interview with Marilyn Chin, Kingston envisions a future for her 23-year-old Wittman, one in which he has grown up to be "a socially responsible and effective, good man—forming a community around him."[71]

By the novel's last page, Wittman has recognized that "[s]tudying the mightiest war epic of all time," has changed him "into a pacifist."[72] Thus as an American trickster, he refuses to be fooled by the "clanging and banging"[73] of either the Chinese *War of the Three Kingdoms* that he has just staged or by the contemporary war drums being beaten for the conflict in Vietnam. In *The Journey to the West*, the Monkey King arrives at wisdom and becomes a Buddha. In *Tripmaster Monkey*, Wittman arrives at a bit of 1960s' wisdom: Even the most brilliant military stratagems and justifications lead to loss. He will have no part of any war. Instead, he will flee to Canada.[74]

Kingston's novel involves so much fancy dancing, so much humor, so many traditional and contemporary events and literary allusions that a reader might be distracted from its powerful intent. Blending Chinese and American tradition and myth, literary and popular culture, the novel focuses the Monkey King's laughing diamond eyes to argue the futility of both racism and war. Initially, the novel earned mixed reviews.[75] Reading Kingston's novel can be as challenging as keeping track of all the details from a psychedelic dream. Nonetheless, the novel reflects an American Monkey King's trip to enlightenment. He is no longer solely Chinese; yet he retains important elements of his Chinese ancestry and cultural memories. At the novel's start, he demonstrates the Monkey King's self-absorption. Only as the novel progresses does Wittman, the American monkey, integrate his Chinese and American backgrounds and become someone capable of sharing his enlightenment with his community.

Kingston's novel does not follow the novel's expected narrative arc; instead, it rejects the neatness of the well-made novel and substitutes a transforming and transformative anti-structure. At least one critic finds the text's non-structure functioning as a trickster.[76] Commentators note that in common with Wittman, Kingston functions as a trickster.[77] A trickster herself, Kingston refuses to be limited by the confines of any of these conceptual boxes. Kingston uses intertextuality as a tactic, making one part of her text speak to another. The fact that most readers will not recognize some allusions mirrors the breadth and complexity of America's multicultural reality.

A good deal also has been written[78] about Kingston using *Tripmaster Monkey* as a trickster response to the objections a number of male Chinese American critics leveled at *Woman Warrior* and *China Men*. The subtitle of *Tripmaster Monkey*, "his fake book," subtly jabs at Frank Chin's 1988 parody of her earlier works.[79] In addition, the female narrator, allied to the powerful but compassionate Kuan Yin of *The Journey to the West*, allows Kingston to indirectly undercut the deep-seated sexism and arrogance of her male protagonist.[80] Kingston herself has taken a trickster position, writing with confidence in the power of her pen rather than a penis—her own magical "Compliant Golden-Hooped Rod"—and asserting that a new world of diversity and equality is emerging in America and that this is its future.

The Middle Heart (1996): Survival Only in Transformation

Seven years after Alfred A. Knopf published Kingston's *Tripmaster Monkey*, the same publisher brought out Bette Bao Lord's *The Middle Heart*, a historical novel again utilizing the Chinese trickster trope of transformation. The novel reverses the order of this chapter's other works, however. Lord immigrated to the United States as a child with most of her family, but in this novel, she looks back to the country of her birth and where she lived as an adult when her husband served as the ambassador to China. This novel tells about men and women forced to change during the mid- and late twentieth century in China rather than America. In common with Chinese immigrants to the United States, the novels' characters change to survive; and in common with those immigrants, they have only limited control over their circumstances: foreign invasion, civil war, and cataclysmic social disruptions. In *The Middle Heart*, the lives of Lord's three central characters reflect the experiences of large portions of the Chinese population intent on surviving first the upheavals of Japanese occupation, then civil war, and finally the turmoil instituted by alterations in communist policy during the Mao Zedong years.

While they all lack his power, the characters that prove most successful are the most like the Monkey King.

Before writing *The Middle Heart*, Lord had written a number of other books, blending fact and fiction in a sprawling earlier historical novel dealing with the first part of the twentieth century and in a fictionalized retelling of her own childhood experience of learning to blend her new American culture with her ancestral Chinese traditions yet retaining both cultures. In addition, she had written about her younger sister's experience of growing up in communist China and a series of tales describing experiences of individual Chinese under communist rule during the latter half of the twentieth century. *The Middle Heart* combines Lord's interest in the sweep of historical events, their effects on ordinary people, and her choice to use fiction in making sense of them. Despite the dire times the novel chronicles, *The Middle Heart* can seem at times predictable or romanticized. The sections about Cinders, her guardians, and her encounters with Loyalty, for example, take on a fairy-tale aura during a grim historical period. What is striking, however, is the way the main characters and most of the minor characters are forced to change in order to survive a series of historic upheavals. Dramatic as events may seem in fiction, readers recognize actual horrors behind the characters' fictional transformations.

The central characters' reinventions of themselves are the most evident transformations though many of the novel's characters alter something in their lives: In order to survive through threatening times, they alter their names, their occupations, and their residences. An unlikely trio of three central characters become friends as prepubescent youths. Steel Hope, an heir of the once illustrious House of Li; Mountain Pine, his book mate–tutor/study companion/confidant/moral compass; and Firecrackers, the grave keeper's daughter masquerading as a boy, become boon companions, pledging opposition to the oppressive Japanese invader and loyalty to one another during the Japanese occupation. Although they share youthful patriotic fervor, they come from distinctly different social and economic backgrounds. While his family has lost much of its past wealth and glory, Steel Hope comes from a privileged background. The crippled Mountain Pine receives an education with Steel Hope only because he is Steel Hope's book mate. Firecrackers's position is even more precarious: Her father, devastated by grief, has lost his living as a boatman and been forced to take the position of a grave tender for the Li family. When he cannot deal with even that work, Firecrackers pretends to be a boy in order to sweep the graves in his stead. As a girl, she would never be allowed to do such work.

Their relationships change Steel Hope, Pine Mountain, and Fire-crackers; but so do events. In response to history and circumstances, they change their occupations and names. But that sounds too bland to describe the profound alterations in their lives. Firecrackers changes her name to Summer Wishes in the course of becoming a successful Chinese opera star during the war with Japan and still later during the Communist Era. She also marries Mountain Pine but then, in order to protect their son from the ignominy of his father's taint as an intellectual Rightist, divorces him; later, she marries Stone Hope but has to publicly revile and beat him, an accused Revisionist, to save both of them from worse harm. At her death, she plaintively tells her grand-daughter, "I wanted to be a human being."[81] To achieve that end, she has attempted multiple transformations; they have almost destroyed her. For all her resilience, she is not a natural trickster. Her transformations have been superficial; she has reacted to circumstances rather than channeling the Monkey King's changes.

Steel Hope too has to change from a "young master" to an engineering student carting books on his back to the war-time nationalist capital of Chonqing, to an aspiring bureaucrat, to a youthful lover, to a marked man faking his death in order to save his life, to a communist follower, to a dedicated revolutionary cadre fighting side-by-side with the peasants, to the feared Party Secretary of Wen Shiu, to a Revisionist condemned to ten years in solitary, to the powerful Vice-Minister of Administration, to a loving grandfather willing to risk everything he has achieved for Firecracker/Summer Wishes's grand-daughter, North Star.

Of the three central characters, the most successful at transformation is apparently the weakest, the lame Mountain Pine. Although he also goes through multiple transformations from book mate to writing hack to tubercular lamplighter,[82] he eventually becomes a husband and father. In fact, he takes on these roles twice. He goes from being a copier of manuscripts to a writer whose own manuscript is presumably going to be published in the United States. Although he is shipped to a forced labor camp, he not only survives 15 years as part of a work gang, as prisoner 5799, Mountain Pine becomes subtly powerful. Mountain Pine recognizes that his life has been a series of successful escapes and reversals:

> "When the flood came, I could have died, but I lived. When my leg wouldn't grow, I could have become a beggar, but my sister found us a home where we were clothed and fed, where the master's son treated me like a brother. Even so, I could have grown up ignorant.

Instead, the mistress sent me to school. When the House of Li no longer needed me, I found a Christian mission where I was needed. When the war came, I escaped harm. When my health failed, I could have wasted away, but you [Firecrackers/Summer Wishes] and the monks made me whole. When love was only a word, you taught me how to feel every nuance of its meaning. When we thought our oldest friend was dead, he came back to us."[83]

In the work prison camp, Mountain Pine develops his subtle "mischief"[84] and gallows humor to the point where he becomes a hero to his fellow sufferers and someone to be reckoned with by the authorities. The warden values him as the prisoners' only source of medical help. In his ability to accept what cannot be avoided regardless of the most stringent of circumstances—as when he and his 19 kang-mates, forced to sleep so closely head to foot lest they freeze in the night that they need to heel-tap one another on the nose in order to shift as group—Mountain Pine becomes not the powerful Monkey King but a trickster nonetheless who not only survives but survives with a smile.[85]

Suggesting that change is the only route to survival, numbers of minor characters go through similar transformations. Little Panda, the loving son of Summer Wishes and Mountain Pine, takes on the role of Loyalty, the leader of a group of Red Guards until he is denounced and excluded from their ranks; he then moves off with 17 million other junior and high school students who volunteer to go "Up to the Mountain, Down to the Village" to be "educated by the peasants." Padlock, a poor child, morphs into CC, a tycoon; and presumably, with the triumph of the communists, he will change again into a refugee. Physical locales also change with the backdoor to the House of Li becoming first the school where Mountain Pine teaches and then School #3 and then May Seventh School. Not everyone does survive, of course: Jade, the powerful wife of Steel Hope's father diminishes throughout the novel, losing almost everything she values. Hua, the petty tyrant of School #3, is overset by Red Guards. Loyalty commits suicide as does Lincoln Chen, Steel Hope's mentor; only by dint of abasement and scouring off their most precious relationships and mementoes do most of the characters manage to continue.[86]

For all the changes and transformations in the novel, the characters seem to be caught up in a maelstrom over which they have no control. In *The Middle Heart*, Lord uses the form of a "revolutionary epic"[87] to reflect on the disruptions to Chinese society over most of the last century. She personalizes the sweep of history, humanizing it through the stories of her central characters and a large supporting cast. In the course of her novel, she depicts extraordinary heroism and perfidy as the country transforms itself. She also allows the characters' experiences comment on the human cost of the country's and personal transformations to achieve "the world as it is." Although the weak and submissive Mountain Pine comes closest to altering his fate, even he seems wafted by the winds of change rather than consciously choosing to transform himself for the sake of himself and his community. His former book mate, Steel Hope, attempts to control the transformations in his life; but he too is swept along by forces he can barely influence much less control. Most of the novel's characters are destroyed by the perfidy of communist political whims; and that may be Lord's major point. Unlike most trickster tales, in *The Middle Heart*, the characters—partial tricksters—have little control over their transformation and they are thus caught on the border between what was and what will be.

American Born Chinese (2006): The Monkey King Speaks to Adolescent Angst in a Graphic Novel

Befitting his youth relative to the other writers discussed in this chapter, Gene Luen Yang utilizes the consciously up-to-date form of the graphic novel in updating the Monkey King's wisdom for contemporary young people.[88] Juxtaposing Jin/Danny's story with excerpts from the Monkey King's adventures, Yang's text forefronts the transformation motif at the heart of the Monkey King story and draws new insights from the original tale. As a youngster, Yang's central character and narrator listens to his mother's tales about the powerful Monkey King who defeats almost everyone with the nerve to attempt limiting him. The Monkey King is appealing to the child Jin because unlike Jin, he is powerful, a deity who brooks no disrespect. As a child, Jin Wang identifies with him and plays with plastic transformer toys while he aspires to abilities and power similar to the Monkey King's. The wife of the herbalist his mother is visiting warns that his ambition of becoming a transformer is fine—as long as Jin Wang does not forfeit his soul; but lost in imagination, pretending that he too controls the Monkey King's transformations, the child barely adverts to the warning.

The narrator transforms his name from Jin Wang to Danny and imagines himself with curly blond hair, someone who flawlessly fits in among his Euro-American classmates. He drools over the blond Euro-American girls with whom he attends grade and high school.

In time, Danny does seem to blend in with his Euro-American high school classmates. But along the way, the narrator is tripped up by Wei-Chen Sun, a new transfer to his school from Taiwan, and later by a "cousin," Chin-Kee. For the most part, the boys' classmates and teachers do not understand any of the three boys. While Wei-Chen Sun is a recognizable little boy, Chin-Kee is a composite Chinese American drawn from current and historical pop culture stereotypes. Invariably, Chin-Kee embarrasses Danny. Only in the last section does Jin come to realize that it is not the Monkey King's ability to smash his opponents that is admirable; instead, his acceptance of himself has made his power worthwhile.

Although fashioned for a youthful audience, the craft of *American Born Chinese* reaches beyond its relatively simple theme. Visually depicted by the bifurcated graphic on the novel's dust jacket, for example, the message of needing to fit in with his peers accentuates the American-born Jin's discomfort with his visually apparent Chinese heritage. The child and his transformer toy are cut in half by the book's spine; and in the background, crushed but unrepentant under his punishment mountain, lies the furious Monkey King. The text itself literally draws the child and youth Jin's subtle but nonetheless real oppression by his "friends" and teachers in his American schools: His teacher in the first predominantly Euro-American school he attends seems oblivious that he has come from San Francisco rather than China and even her suppression of a bully's insult contains a further insult. His new teacher "defends" him by telling the class, "Jin's family probably stopped that sort of thing [eating dogs] as soon as they came to the United States."[89] Schoolyard bullies call Jin "bucktooth," and his seemingly sympathetic curly haired blond classmate at best makes only gentle nudges toward quieting the bullies. Later on, he implicitly suggests Jin's unacceptability when he discourages Jin from dating his crush, Amelia, because since she is almost in high school, "she has to start paying attention to who she's hanging out with."[90] After a polite brush-off, another girl in high school insults him further by giving him the card of her uncle, an orthodontist, so that Jin can have his buckteeth taken care of. The message is clear: Jin is never quite acceptable. By high school, visits from Chin-Kee (an obvious play on the derogatory Chinky) just makes things worse because Chin-Kee, the embodiment of every negative Asian American stereotype, is *his* cousin. In the last section, Jin and the readers find out that Chin-Kee is actually an avatar of the Monkey King.

As usual for trickster tales, the message—in this case, that "to find your true identity . . . within the will of Tze-Yo-Tzuh [He Who

Is]...that is the highest of all freedoms,"[91] releasing the Monkey King from his mountain and Jin from his self-loathing—comes wrapped in humor. Much of that humor carries a whiff of the trickster's earthiness with references to farting and penises; some of it is subtler and more bitter. The biology class's donated animals, for instance, appear to be rejects from failed cosmetic experiments, and the teacher names the coldest animal after his ex-wife. Some of the humor, such as the teenaged boy's misadventures as he tries to suppress underarm odor while he is on a date, is universally recognizable.

Part of what makes the graphic novel intriguing is the use of Chinese characters for "lightning," "thunder," "cloud," "fire," the imperative for "close up," "transform," and "get bigger," much as readers expect to see the English words "Boom" and "Crack" as visual comments.[92] More intriguing is the way Yang tweaks *The Journey to the West* and his suggestion that some part of Western wisdom originated in the East. Lan Dong rightly refers to Yang "rewriting" the story of the Monkey King.[93] The Monkey King does not achieve an epiphany that he needs to accept himself at the start of *The Journey to the West*; in fact, at first he serves the monk only under duress. In Yang's graphic novel, when the deities battered by the Monkey King beg Tze-Yo-Tzuh's emissaries to have Tze-Yo-Tzuh "do something" about the Monkey King, the text identifies Tze-Yo-Tzuh as "He Who Is," a Hebrew rather than Buddhist concept. At the same time, Tze-Yo-Tzuh is called the "creator" of all things including the Monkey King. Such a concept is foreign to Buddhism.[94] Buddhists would not confuse Buddha with the Y*HW*H of Exodus. In Yang's graphic novel, the monk Wong Lai Tsao travels 40 days and nights, a familiar number for readers of both the Hebrew and Christian Bibles, to find his first disciple, the Monkey King. The notion too that the Monkey King has sent his son to help Jin through life is more Christian than Buddhist. When asked who he is, the Monkey King tells Jin, "I am the Monkey King, Emissary of Tze-Yo-Tzuh." "I have stood in his holy presence—since the completion of my test of virtue, my journey to the West."[95] The graphics depict first a "heavenly" scene with, their hands folded, the monk Wong Lai Tsao and the Monkey King along with other prominent emissaries standing in the presence of Tze-Yo-Tzuh. Another panel depicts the Monkey King and Wong Lai Tsao's two other disciples, as wise men from the East, offering gifts to the Christ child in his mother's arms with Joseph looking on. The novel thus not only delivers its central message about "True Identity" but also blends Eastern with Western culture as American-born Chinese need to do, accepting all of who they are but also making connections instead to antipathies out of the differences they encounter. In that, Yang's work makes use of the trickster's liminality.

FROM LEGAL TO CULTURAL CHANGES

The texts discussed in this chapter show Chinese Americans making significant use of the trickster, especially the traditional Monkey King and picking out characteristics of the Monkey King that allow them to address their particular concerns. Just as the Monkey King has always been characterized by his transformations, Chinese American literature often follows the role of transformation in the lives of its characters. The writers' concerns can be as dissimilar as Louis Chu's and Chuang Hua's puzzling out the ways in which Chinese immigrants to the United States need to change and to adjust to a new culture. This early wave of identifiably Chinese American literature concentrates on the pain entailed in the transformation and certainly lacks the triumphalism of the Monkey King's successful change. Nonetheless, the writers are working out what that change means to individuals and to the community.

Part of the major civil rights legislation of the mid-1960s, the Immigration and Nationality Act signed by President Lyndon B. Johnson in 1965, finally knocked into oblivion more than 100 years of exclusionary legislation designed to limit the number of Asians in America. Yet, that legislation is culturally far in the distance for the immigrants whose stories Louis Chu and Chuang Hua tell. Reflecting a new era later in the twentieth century, works such as David Hwang's *M. Butterfly* and Maxine Hong Kingston's *Tripmaster Monkey* provide more sophisticated explorations of transformation. Hwang and Kingston have moved beyond mere adjustment to a new culture. Nonetheless, with other children of immigrants who share only their common language, English, and a disquieting sense of "feeling like the hyphen" between Asian and American,[96] Hwang and Kingston still utilize the powerfully subversive Chinese trickster, the Monkey King, to make complex comments on orientalism, gender roles, power relations between countries and genders, and on the difficulty of getting beyond gender politics, blending cultures without "melting" them down, and finally on the futility of war and racism in the human community.

Bette Bao Lord's *Middle Heart* and Gene Luen Yang's *American Born Chinese* attest to the pervasiveness of the transformation trope and the persistence of the Monkey King's ability to inspire Chinese Americans with new ways of understanding the past and moving into the future while dealing with the present. Along the way, these and the other writers in this chapter have proven adept at using Monkey King to question deep-rooted, mainstream, Eastern and Western pathologies. Hwang and Kingston's stories aim to transform not just the characters but also the cultures of which they are an integral part. Chinese American tricksters point to transformations that could forge a new American identity valuing the past but also looking forward to a better future.

Immigrating to America, all Asian immigrants, including the Chinese, have had to take on minority status and transform themselves into Asian Americans. The cost of that transformation into a model minority has become a recurring refrain in literature as writers return again and again to the danger of the liminal space between cultures and the importance of being true to oneself and to one's heritage even as "Asians" become "American."

CHAPTER 6

ROUGH MISCHIEF, IRREVERENCE, AND THE FANTASTIC

WHERE TRICKSTERS DWELL—THE BORDERS

All tricksters inhabit the space "between" entities: This is especially true, however, of Latinos[1] and their tricksters. Whatever their ancestors' countries of origin, the Latinos encountered in contemporary American fiction use their identity as border dwellers to somehow balance national, racial/ethnic, linguistic, cultural, and sometimes economic and political divides and to shed light on both sides of these divides. Latinos are well suited to this function since every day they rub up against and negotiate one or another of these borders. Richard M. Dorson adverts to a profound reality in Latino lives when he mentions the border between "alien cultures" connecting as well as separating Latinos of the American Southwest to those around them.[2] Latinos who live far from physical borders with Mexico or from other Latin American countries as well as those whose families have lived in the Southwest of the United States for hundreds of years often still have close familial and cultural ties on both sides of the international borders. The border is deeply woven into their being.

Many Latino writers then appropriately resort to border writing, which forces readers to loosen their holds on the necessity of a linear narrative, on images with simple referents, on traditional roles of dominance, and on assumptions of superiority. Rolando J. Romero believes that creative artists and academics alike tend to "project their own assumptions and Utopias,"[3] particularly on the United States–Mexican border; so border writing of either the theoretical or artistic

stripe contributes new perspectives on perceived political "certainties." In response to their own cultural fantasies, people on either side
can come to think of the border as the division between civilization
and barbarism, as a site of military conflict, or as a line between a pol-
luted landscape and a healthy one. They can think of "the other side"
as full of unhappy families while their side has "right" relationships
or that "the other side" has a corrupt approach to civil organization.
Perhaps they think of the border as a site of incursion by aggressive invaders or dangerous ideologies, perhaps as a division between a
"pure" race and a bastardized one; yet for the most part, these remain
projections rather than realities. In response to this challenge, border
writing discombobulates those projections and attempts to portray
clearer realities.

Among theoretical literary approaches, border writing stands out
for its endeavor to lead comfortable onlookers to empathize with
marginalized people by imaginatively experiencing some of the disruption that people pushed to the edges deal with. Rather than teaching or intellectualizing about what a border theoretician would call
"the cultural, social, and political boundaries that demarcate vary-
ing spaces of comfort, suffering, abuse, and security that define an
individual's or group's location and positionality,"[4] creative writers
engaged in border writing take readers imaginatively across dominant "cultural spaces and social formations" and those that resist that
dominance.[5] Thus, engrossed in imaginative border literature, readers stretch beyond their comfort limits and gladly explore what might
otherwise be literally unthinkable. Literary critics frequently analyze
Latino writing through the prism of border theory because much of
Latino literature deals with marginalization of one sort or another,
especially *mestizaje*—the racial and ethnic mixing of Latinos in the
Americas. As Henry A. Giroux reminds his readers, while schools
engage in teaching, so do many other "cultural workers,"[6] including
writers. Those cultural workers include visual and folk artists as well
as writers spreading trickster discourse.

In all border writing and especially in trickster writing, readers
encounter fragmented experiences and reassemble them into a holographic representation of existence:[7] what they come to understand is
no longer the simplistic ordering of their preconceptions but something new. In the introduction to their collection of essays on border
theory, Scott Michaelsen and David E. Johnson suggest the appeal of
borderlands: While often places of violence and controversy, borderlands also offer those who inhabit them "politically exciting hybridity,

intellectual creativity, and moral possibility."[8] Hardly "complete," that understanding nonetheless includes increased multidimensional historical and political realities. Paying attention to the fragments and reordering them allows readers to build a more complete understanding of the larger world they too inhabit. Benjamin Alire Sáenz tries to convey the complexity of this both/and situation in his description of dealing with his reaction and that of his graduate students to being labeled Chicano since they are heirs to both elite North American higher education and the lived experience of their *familias*.[9] The label oversimplifies the reality.

In addition, one critic of border theory's intellectualizing, Eduardo Barrera Herrera, points out that border theoreticians can confuse the image as a metaphor with physical entities and lose sight of the migrants, real human beings, whose lives are affected by "discusión teórica."[10] While border theory posits useful changes derived from the disruption inherent in being "caught between," Barrera Herrera objects that these "teóricos privilegían lo simbólico"[11] and pay little attention to the human suffering undergone by, for example, the workers in the "Zona de Libre Comercio" in northern Mexico. Concentrating on the situation in northern Mexico, Barrera Herrara correctly reminds theoreticians that in real time, real people bear the consequences of being caught between entities. Particularly those first to dwell on the border find the position more painful than merely uncomfortable and less exciting than overwhelming.

Those who tell and listen to trickster tales know full well that real people suffer when they are caught "between"; and trickster discourse does not confuse labels with reality. Yet, one of the strengths as well as limitations of trickster discourse is its *lack* of the high seriousness found in border theory and in most forms of literary criticism. For the most part, contemporary Latino trickster tales involve more satire and irony than ludicrous moments. But whether or not contemporary Latino trickster stories are hilarious or not, they verge on the comic rather than the tragic. More than theoretical, trickster writing is about how people can imaginatively escape or even overturn unhealthy situations. Since tricksters live on borders, many of the insights of border theory apply to trickster tales. Mixing, transgression, crossing borders, living on the edges: All belong to the nature of the trickster. Just as borders are a place of possibilities, tricksters—and particularly Latino tricksters—inhabit borders and constantly test the limits of the possible. As does border writing, trickster stories "dislocate" readers and encourage them to pay closer attention to economic, political, linguistic, and sometimes gender realities to which the readers' worldviews might otherwise blind them. These stories so successfully dislocate readers that, conjoined with the massive influx of legal and illegal immigrants from Mexico[12] and Central America during last 25 years, some writers and politicians have referred to what has occurred as a "reconquest."[13]

What then distinguishes trickster discourse from border writing as a whole? Although many are, not all border denizens are tricksters; still, tricksters thrive in the borderlands, places that are the opposite of the settled and staid, the intellectually ossified. Writers of trickster discourse stand out from other border writers chiefly because they treat dichotomies with irony and satire, or sometimes even with whimsical mirth. They are willing to joke about the most serious realities; most border writing tends to treat serious matters with a serious tone. The writers of trickster discourse may be angry; in fact, more often than not, they probably are; yet their writing is so overlaid with and disguised by humor that readers swallow the hook of the writers' ideas before recognizing what has happened. Yet, Latino–trickster discourse is almost always also border writing though it often moves beyond realistic modes. In fact, in trickster discourse, exaggeration is the norm rather than the exception. Realism would undercut the trickster's almost preternatural ability that imagination grants to "slip the noose" of constraint. So humor and the fantastic characterize Latino trickster stories. Neither is requisite to border writing.

LATINO TRICKSTERS AND "EL DISIMULO"

Members of all ethnic groups have their reasons for discontent and thus resort to trickster discourse. People of Latino descent have the tradition of what Octavio Paz refers to as "*el disimulo* or 'the process of concealment.'"[14] Forced to accept a great deal of Spanish culture and religion, indigenous Indians and later African slaves sequestered some parts of their cultures from their masters. They did this so successfully that even 500 years later, in Mexico alone, 52 indigenous languages still survive, and on many levels in all Latin American countries, cultural syncretism is the norm. As the writers whose work is discussed in this chapter illustrate, the trickster's particular brand of *disimulo* continues to have a hand in this process of concealment and suppressed rebellion whether the master is a Spanish conquistador or an Anglo government, power-hungry boss or an entitled male. Trickster discourse takes many forms in the United States, sometimes as machismo morphs into a form of cultural resistance or as Latino tricksters learn to take on the coloration of the city or resist the macho norm.

"HISPANIC": MORE MÉLANGE THAN AMALGAM

Suddenly aware of the flood of usually brown faces they are encountering in new areas of the country, media and governmental groups as well as ordinary citizens are talking about the new immigrants they are frequently bumping into in workplaces, marketplaces, and neighborhoods. They may feel that the border itself has shifted. In fact, the language used to denote Latinos is shifting. While media outlets and governmental agencies refer to people with Spanish-speaking ancestry as "Hispanics," the people themselves are more apt to refer to themselves as Latinos or Latinas, the terms used in this chapter.

The political jockeying over competing 2006 immigration demonstrations, more recent law enforcement sweeps to pick up illegal residents, as well as legislative bills and presidential action to regularize the status of undocumented immigrants have presented only one, though a very public, face of Latino presence in the United States. The political maneuvering responds to late-twentieth and early-twenty-first-century demographic realities: Men and women whose grandparents and great grandparents spoke Spanish as a first language form an increasingly visible part of the contemporary United States.[15] One 2003 estimate put the number of undocumented immigrants in the United States at 8 million, the vast majority from Mexico and Central America.[16]

Contemporary Latinos and their children, many born in the United States and thus by law US citizens, are only the most recent group of primarily Spanish-speaking people living within the borders of what is now the United States. Before other Europeans, Africans, and Asians came to America, Spanish-speaking men and their descendants had settled large stretches of Florida, what are now the Southwestern states, and California. Nonetheless, various conflicts and treaties, probably most notoriously the 1848 Treaty of Guadalupe Hidalgo, altered the borders and the balance of power, effectively making the Spanish-speaking population a subjugated people on land where they had lived for centuries. The tidal wave of immigrants from south of the border during the last 25 years represents a return of Latinos rather than a new ethnic/racial group coming into US territory. But those facts are political; the place of Latinos in the United States is far larger and more complex than the political brouhaha over legal and illegal immigration.

Undocumented immigrants actually supply a small proportion of the 50 million Latinos and the over 300 million people that the 2010 United States Census Bureau estimated resided in the country. In addition, despite their large numbers relative to other Latinos, Mexican Americans—that is, Chicanos, men and women of Mexican ancestry who self-identify as Americans—represent only part (less than 60%) of the Latino population in the United States.[17] Not only that, Latinos in the United States are impacted by a mix of cultural influences including multiple linguistic backgrounds. Thus, for example, in discussing experimentation in early Chicano poetry, Rudolfo Anaya mentions anywhere from two to five linguistic influences, "English, Spanish, Black rhythm, Mexican Nahuatl, Indian, and our street Pachuco talk,"[18] impacting the sound of the poets' work.

Given the diversity among Latinos and thus among Latino writers, the diversity of trickster traditions among the group should be expected. While most Latino tricksters draw from American Indian and Spanish cultural roots, some Latino writers make use of other trickster traditions as well. Cristina García, for example, suffuses her novel *Monkey Hunting* with trickster images from Asia and Africa as well as *criollo* Cuba. Although the monkey of the novel's title proves elusive, García's character Chen Pan and his descendants hunt for it all their lives. The novel suggests that, like Chen Pan, his descendants need to learn to listen to the Old Monkey quoted in the inscription to the novel's first chapter and "discern good and evil." In old age, Chen Pan tells his youngest grandson about "the incorrigible Monkey King, who'd stolen peaches from the immortals' sacred grove and eaten his fill." Then Chen Pan tells the child, "The most important thing about life is to live each day well."[19] The novel is not, of course, a trickster tale; nonetheless, the blending of cultural heritages—Cuban rhythms, Asian poetry, African wisdom, and especially a modicum of Chinese trickster thought reflects a not uncommon blending especially in Caribbean cultures.

Even when they are not necessarily inscribing a trickster tale, Latino writers are apt to incorporate characters with trickster attitudes. Readers of Latino literature rather typically encounter characters like the narrator's Aunt Piña in Denise Chávez's first novel, *Face of an Angel*, who, readers are told, always irritated the narrator's grandmother. In her "go-get-'em-I-deserve-it attitude, her silly, superstitious, blind, childlike faith in herself and the powers of her mind,"[20] Piña flaunts a typically trickster attitude toward the world she inhabits.

A "Double Weave" and More

Although they arrive at the response through a multitude of trickster traditions, most literary Latino tricksters subscribe to Pina's attitude. Many Latinos view themselves as almost inherently both/and: They grow up with what has been called a "double," actually much more complex, weave of the facts of history, language, religion, individual and cultural experience and expectations, plus ties to rural and urban settings. In his own self-aware way, Junot Díaz reflects this when he tells an interviewer:

> I have multiple traditions...I'm part of the mainstream "American" literary tradition. I'm a part of the Latino literary tradition. I'm a part of the African Diaspora literary tradition as well as the Dominican literary tradition. But there's also the oral tradition and the rhythmic tradition of the music I grew up with which deeply influence how I write a sentence and how my work sounds.[21]

Latinos belong unequivocally to mainstream American culture; but as border dwellers, they remain mindful of and sensitive to more than one linguistic, racial, and social heritage.[22] For the most part, Latinos in the United States can boast of a minimum of two racial and cultural heritages, Euro-American Spanish and American Indian; and their tricksters reflect that crossing of racial and linguistic borders. Thus at times, Latino tricksters are clearly descendants of the Spanish peasant Pedro Urdemales, but sometimes they remind readers of the foolish Coyote of American Indian tales. Sometimes they resemble the equally foolish, though usually more fortunate, "bobo" inherited from Spanish Jewry.

A Major Source for Latino Tricksters: Pedro Urdemales

While Spain has contributed La Celestina and Lazarillo de Tormes, two of its wiliest tricksters, to world literature, trickster discourse in Spanish-speaking America is more often closely related to oral tales about Pedro Urdemales ("plotter of evil").[23] In these tales, Pedro Urdemales functions as an out-and-out rogue. The Euro-American trickster heritage from Latin America aligns most closely with the Spanish trickster Pedro Urdemales. In Spain, the name is a shorthand reference standing for amoral skullduggery. Ironically, no tales of his exploits can be found in Spain anymore. In the New World, however, tales about Pedro Urdemales are widespread. The Spanish Pedro Urdemales comes from a settled society with clear economic and social classes; he belongs to the lowest class. Like his Anglo-European cousin Jack, Pedro Urdemales is always scrambling to rise though he lacks Jack's humor or innocence. Unlike Huck Finn, Jack's descendent, Pedro Urdemales feels no sympathy for any underdog but himself. Always discontented, Pedro wants "more" of any asset. While oral American Indian trickster tales reflect a primordial land and are apt to include talking animals, if an animal speaks in a story about Pedro Urdemales, Pedro is probably acting as a ventriloquist.

Although his origins appear to belong in late medieval Spanish tales, Pedro Urdemales has totally acculturated to the Americas. In fact, although the name is synonymous with knavery in Spain, by the early part of the twentieth-century, Ramon A. Laval could not find any actual current tales about Pedro Urdemales still told in Spain.[24] In America, however, Chileans, Argentineans, Columbians, Central Americans, Puerto Ricans, and New Mexicans have made him their own. American Indians including the Aymara in Bolivia and Peru, the Maya in Guatemala and Mexico, as well as some Indians in the Southwestern United States tell Pedro Urdemales tales. Just as Euro-American Jack has an admixture of multiple traditions, in the Latino world of America, Pedro Urdemales sometimes shows a tinge of indigenous tricksters. The original Pedro Urdemales has pícaro roots and while retaining his essentially trickster character,[25] Urdemales has taken on the role of a modern folk hero in the Americas and is often associated with men who have striven to repair injustices perpetrated by the dominant social order.

Like Coyote and Br'er Rabbit, Pedro Urdemales is a survivor and an underdog, so the butts of his tricks tend to be the powerful or well-to-do or self-satisfied, the smug—anyone who pretends to superiority: Churchmen, the wealthy, gringos, everyone who makes the lives of ordinary people more difficult. The mischievous irreverence that often characterizes just about all Latino trickster tales seems to derive from Pedro Urdemales. More than being just mischievous, however, the original Pedro Urdemales seems primarily intent on transferring the wealth of others to himself. Thus, for example, he convinces a traveler coming along on a horse (and therefore obviously someone of wealth) to take over holding up a heavy stone lest the world come to an end. Pedro Urdemales then absconds with the horse in order, he tells the traveller, to find others who will relieve him. The traveler, of course, is still waiting.[26]

Pedro Urdemales can also be flat-out vindictive; but his tricks depend on the moral weakness, especially cupidity, vanity, and pride, of his victims. In one tale,[27] Pedro Urdemales sets up an avaricious old man whom he has gulled earlier and whom he knows wants revenge. This time, Pedro works with a confederate whose tattered and torn clothes he splashes with lamb's blood, and then the confederate plays dead. In the presence of his dupe, Urdemales appears to revive his "dead" companion by playing his flute. The old man negotiates to buy the flute from Urdemales for "only" 3,000 pesos. Elated and eager to brag about his success at getting such a bargain, when the man returns home, he gathers his staff and—positive that he can revive her—knifes his wife in the chest. Naturally, he is arrested and condemned to death. In tales about Pedro Urdemales, his prey often contribute to their own downfall; they are so focused on their own goals, they ignore good sense.

Spanish stories about Pedro and their translations into English retold as children's tales avoid references to Pedro's potential for gross sexuality or frightening mayhem. Instead, Pedro engages in mischief, invariably upsetting one sort of order or another. One frequently retold tale, for example, has Pedro Urdemales cutting off the tails of the pigs he is supposed to have watered and sold, planting their tails in a marsh, selling the pigs—and then telling his master that the pigs have all have been swallowed by the swamp.[28] Attempting to extricate the pig's tails, Pedro's boss gets dragged deeper and deeper into the swamp while Pedro takes off with his boss's horse and the money from selling the pigs. In another tale, this one with the magical elements common to many Euro-American tales, Pedro Urdemales tricks Jesus and St. Peter into letting him get into and then stay in heaven.[29]

Of course, a Latino trickster from oral culture does not have to be called Pedro. Among the *leyendas* reprinted for beginning readers of Spanish in Genevieve Barlow's *Leyendas Latinoamericans*, for example, is a trickster tale from Mexico whose central character goes by the name of Juan Bobo.[30] Another tale, this one from Columbia, features a humorless and proud Spaniard repeatedly tricked by anonymous pranksters on the Feast of the Holy Innocents, December 28, a date on which many countries and cultures have celebrated the temporary overturn of hierarchy.[31] Another group of trickster tales from New Mexico feature Don Peanut, theoretically a numbskull, whose talent in bluffing his opponents resembles those of his cousin, the African American "John."[32]

A rather typical trickster tale from Peru features an incorrigible corporal named Montañez who is addicted to gambling and, since he is a trickster, to winning. In this anecdote, he outwits the officers, both his captain and his general. First, he bets his captain 20 gold coins that he can get their general to take off his wig and uncover his bald head; Montañez then wins that bet by betting the general ten gold coins that the general's head is covered by large, ugly warts. The general wins because he takes his wig off to show that he does not have any warts on his pate, but the captain loses his 20 gold coins; and the corporal is 10 gold coins ahead.[33] The corporal is the usual "little guy" who works the system in his favor. In the real word, the officers would not let him win, but the story is a nice little fantasy. The corporal's name is irrelevant; he stands for all the "little guys" who are scrambling to get ahead in a world that grants them little leeway.

A "Bobo" Tradition

In addition to generic trickster tales including those featuring Pedro Urdemales, Latino trickster tradition has inherited, perhaps from Spanish Jewry,[34] a corpus of tales about foolish tricksters, "bobos," who make absurd choices yet somehow always fall on their feet. A bobo does not learn from experience[35] or perhaps learns the wrong lesson. While American Indians also have a parallel tradition of tales about foolish Coyote, for example, not only are these tales object lessons showing what not to do, the presumption is also that the Indian trickster is not considering his choice and deserves whatever ill befalls him. So in American Indian tales, the foolish trickster usually comes to a bad end. In contrast, the Latino[36] bobo survives his stupidity.

In addition to the character explicitly called Juan Bobo, the Don Peanut tales belong to this group. One fool tale, this one from Mexico, relates how a good-hearted but all too literal bobo inadvertently irritates and offends the well connected and wealthy of his town. Although he uses the directions he has garnered from each previous encounter all too literally and irks a new set of people, he still manages to harvest the ill-gotten gains of thieves who flee on hearing his voice apparently coming from the "heavens" of the tree branches where he has been resting.[37]

Of the "cuentos" in Richard M. Dorson's *Burying the Wind* following similar patterns, several trickster tales follow either the devious pattern laid down by Pedro Urdemales or the naive bobo pattern. The tales about foolish tricksters bear some resemblance to Jack Tales in which Jack also acts foolishly; they demonstrate, however, a much closer resemblance to the infuriatingly foolish Jewish trickster, Joha, from Spain's Sephardic tradition. Such tales may well originate with the tales about the Sephardic Joha. Thus, for example, when the mother of the literalist Sephardic Joha tells him to "pull the door," that is, close it, when he leaves, he pulls the door off its hinges and carries it with him. Resting in a tree that night and eating nuts he has picked, he speaks out loud, drops shells from his nuts, and frightens away robbers who think there is an evil spirit in the tree. So Joha brings their loot home to his mother but also complains to her that next time she should "just say 'close the door.' "[38] Totally self-absorbed, Joha never realizes that he might have made a mistake.

Fantastic Tricksters

Harold Scheub talks about fantasy tales being "a form of reasoning, a way of looking at events in a context of emotion."[39] The importance of fantasy—and trickster tales are innately fantastic—can hardly be overemphasized. As Jack Zipes points out, in the face of the "relentless progress" of modern consumerism, even modern men and women also use fantasy to make sense of their worlds, sometimes to take time out from dealing with those worlds, and sometime to resist them.[40] Fantasy as resistance comprises a common thread through Latino literature. Not uncommonly, Latino trickster tales belong to the category that Tzvetan Todorov deems "marvelous," calling for "new laws of nature."[41] Although sometimes Latino trickster tales depend on recognizable patterns of human psychology or behavior in order for the trickster to succeed, some belong to a "religious" ambiance assuming an audience capable of accepting the marvelous or supernatural as part of the existing world.[42] When Latino trickster tales do involve the fantastic, they obviously go beyond the natural. In these tales, the physically impossible happens, and the characters in a fantastic Latino story as well as the readers just accept every marvel. Most modern trickster traditions make some use of the fantastic; and when the tricksters with whom modern writers present readers move through fantasy, their actions participate in a carnival-like misrule.[43] This is particularly true of Latino literature where the fantastic is often paired with humor. As one would expect of a culture that has embraced magical realism, the fantastic plays a particularly apparent role in Latino literature.

Among the mix of influences feeding into Latino trickster literature, a bit of the American Indian Coyote peers from around the corner; sometimes a bit of Br'er Rabbit or Jack wafts through the tale. Sometimes the spider Ananse or the Monkey King raise their sly heads in Latino trickster tales, especially in those from the Caribbean.

Prominent if not dominant, the cunning of Pedro Urdemales and his ability to rattle whoever is in charge continue to characterize Latino trickster tales. Yet in spite of the down-to-earth desires and actions of Pedro Urdemales, the primary Latino trickster, the fantastic is also commonplace in a number of Latino trickster stories.

Situated as they are on multiple borders, Latinos and the tricksters they produce take on the coloration of many influences, yet as a group they are still distinctive. So what does the most prominent trickster tradition, the Pedro Urdemales of oral culture, lead readers to expect of Latino literary tricksters as a whole? Pedro Urdemales shares Jack's arrogant self-confidence. So readers can be assured that the behavior of Latino tricksters, like that of Pedro Urdemales, will be at least mischievous, in his case maliciously so. Latinos have a long history of unjust political, economic, and social oppression to resent. Their tricksters crave payback. Thus readers can also expect that Latino tricksters will be irreverent toward anyone in authority. Readers might also recall that for all of Pedro Urdemales's grounding in a realistic world, he is more than a culture hero; he is an unstoppable force of nature. Thus, the flights into fantasy found in the Latino oral tales still seep into modern trickster stories.

It turns out that all three elements from the oral Latino trickster tradition—rough mischief, irreverence, and fantasy—abound in Latino literary trickster tales though the relative emphasis on each varies from one work to another. In the trickster fiction of Rudolfo Anay, Ron Arias, and Nina Marie Martínez, for example, a fantastic mythopoetic world is made more down-to-earth through humor.

TRANSLATING THE TRICKSTER INTO CONTEMPORARY SCENES: MYTHOPOETIC AND REALISTIC APPROACHES

Rudolfo Anaya's Tricksters

Although tricksters are common in Rudolfo Anaya's fiction, their tricksterism can be central or peripheral to the plot. Thus, for example, though the central character in his atmospheric 1995 *Zia Summer* is a formulaic private detective, Rudolfo Anaya's Sonny Baca also demonstrates plenty of trickster traits. Much of what makes him more than a cutout is related to his trickster core: his recognition that he identifies with the errant spouses he has been hired to track down; his status as a *small-time* detective; his vanity; his inability to succeed at pedestrian marriage or at high school teaching; his comfort living on the margins. In addition, Sonny hangs out with three old but apparently unstoppable *duendes*—imps—whom he affectionately calls Snap, Crackle, and Pop. Like other tricksters, Sonny always somehow escapes. His animal spirit—as Lorenza Villa, a curandera, tells him—is the coyote. The one opponent who comes close to defeating him is another trickster called Raven.

Traditional and Modern: Rudolfo Anaya's "B. Traven" (1979)

Many readers identify Rudolfo Anaya with the "folklore, myth, and dream in a lyrical narrative"[44] of his *Bless Me, Ultima*. That novel, however, written in the 1960s and published in the early 1970s presents a different face than the far more consciously literary and sophisticated short story, "B. Traven Is Alive and Well in Cuernavaca," republished in his 2006 collection of short stories, *The Man Who Could Fly*.[45] Starting with its title, "B. Traven" is replete with trickster discourse. The "real" B. Traven was the secretive and apparently consciously duplicitous author of a 1927 novel published in German, later translated into English, and eventually used as the basis for John Huston's 1948 film *The Treasure of Sierra Madre* starring Humphrey Bogart. Almost all sources agree on the year of Traven's death. Various biographies disagree about his birthplace, parentage, native language, aliases, exploits, even his name. Since Traven refused to give interviews and seemed to make a habit of laying false trails about his background, no one can know who he really was. As the narrator of Anaya's story says, "While [Traven] lived he remained unapproachable, anonymous to his public, a writer shrouded in mystery."[46]

What is certain is Traven's style: to quote *Britannica Online*, his "works are harsh, filled with descriptions of danger, cruelty, and physical and emotional suffering, but his lean, direct prose has a hypnotic immediacy, and the narratives are clear and compelling."[47] So the character named in Anaya's title was himself a trickster—and already dead in 1979 when the story was first published. But like all tricksters, he is still going along. Mexican students encounter his work in required readings for their classes; his books are read and enjoyed throughout Mexico. According to the narrator, travelers quite commonly encounter "a yellowed thumb-worn novel by Traven" in some "dusty niche."[48] Finally, his legend lives on, propagated by the cantina denizens and taxi drivers who insist that they knew him and by the men and women who are sure he still lives in Mexico.

Justino, the gardener of the narrator's host in the Cuernavaca home, also has more than a bit of trickster in him. The story itself has a double frame reminiscent of Charles Chesnutt's "Po' Sandy," a story told to the well-meaning but oblivious Northerner narrator by a supposedly simple Uncle Julius in *The Conjure Woman*.[49] As in Chesnutt's story, the story within the story and the character Justino reflect back on the framing action and themes. Anaya's and Chesnutt's stories share subversive trickster qualities and question past and present social orders. Anaya's story, however, is primarily about the role of imagination: Traven's, Justino's, and the narrator's. The story is about other things as well including the submerged violence and potential for revolution that always exists in an oppressed population. These were Traven's themes as well. The narrator meditates on the role of time and puzzles over a series of clues—including a letter addressed to B. Traven and dated March 26, 1969, the day most sources agree Traven died. Toward the end of the story, the narrator meets a Traven avatar, recognizes the importance of Justino—the peon and trick-ster—as his inspiration, and leaves the metaphoric dryness of a liter-ary gathering to go off and write a story. The narrator needs to return imaginatively to the Pozo of Mendozo, a literal well and the site of Justino's story but also a metaphoric wellspring.

As the elderly tertulia guest (*perhaps* B. Traven himself), another writer with what *may* be a Germanic accent, tells the narrator, Justino once served as his guide. In those earlier years while Justino wandered in search of adventure, the now elderly man searched for stories.[50] What is important to both writers is that "People like Justino are the writer's source"[51] because he "knows the campesino very well."[52] The narrator already realizes that Justino is "a rogue with class,"[53] "a wild Pan."[54] Justino is a trickster who would rather be "a movie actor or an adventurer, a real spirit"[55]; however, as reality in the form of his many children "appeared,"[56] he has settled instead for relatively pedestrian life as a gardener—with a wife, two mistresses, close friendships with a the women from bordellos, and the habit of deceiving his employer. Justino embodies the campesino/trickster's response to his society's willful ignorance of economic inequities. Dogs bark in the night; well-to-do men like the narrator's host build high fences. Rather than risk encountering the poor and oppressed of his society in any meaningful way, the host chooses distraction and closes himself off from the hint of danger. Advised by Justino, the narrator's host also leaves a radio on at night playing soft music; and the employer sleeps soundly while the gardener lolls in his employer's car or in his pool with chosen friends. The narrator, on the other hand, who hangs out with Justino, eventually learns to recognize his implicit message and then passes that message on to his readers.

Harking Back to the Oral Tradition: Anaya's "The Native Lawyer" (2004)

A sense that the simple, uneducated "folk" are often in touch with primeval wisdom continues to pervade Anaya's twenty-first-century short story, "The Native Lawyer." The story's brevity and uncomplicated narrative resembles what readers expect from an oral tale and, in fact, the story derives from an oral tale.[57] In "The Native Lawyer," by an odd twist of fate, a good but poor man, Manuel, accepts a friend's gift of 25 pesos to buy a dozen eggs for a meal. The honest man and his wife eat the eggs when his friend, Rufo, does not return to share them; but Manuel then buys more eggs and raises the chicks they hatch. He plans to give to his friend half of whatever he earns. Over time, Manuel parlays the chicks he raised into riches. Years later when Rufo returns, he takes Manuel to court, demanding all of what is now a comfortable competence. After a lifetime of hard work, the peasant is about to be stripped of his gains; a native lawyer, however, his "good neighbor, Salvador,...[uses] common sense [and beats] the educated lawyers."[58] Salvador makes the judge realize that just as baked beans cannot grow into crops, the cooked eggs could not have produced chicks.

As his name implies, Salvador is, of course, a savior; but he is also a trickster. Both he and Manuel belong to the class of "los de abajo," despised by the powerful and those who are used to manipulating the law in their own favor. This time, however, the scorned outwit those who would take advantage of them. Although the characters are given names, they could be anyone. Manuel's and Rufo's names are generic and Salvador's almost as much so.

A REFUSAL TO ADMIT BARRIERS: *THE ROAD TO TAMAZUNCHALE* (1987)

The narrators in "B. Traven" and "The Native Lawyer" utilize imagination and trickster responses to thwart the rich and powerful. Ron Arias's Fausto Tejada uses similar tools as he faces an even greater challenge. At first, the central character in Ron Arias's *The Road to Tamazunchale* seems an ordinary old man; yet trickster-like, Fausto breaks down all limitations. The novel makes an old man's final journey to death not just the completion of a full life but an engaging journey. Not only Fausto but also most of the other characters live in their imaginations as well as the "real" world that Fausto's Sancho Panza-like sidekick insists on. Fausto Tejada takes on and vanquishes almost every possible limitation. Given that he is unbound by time and space and identity and age and nationality, the sense that his death also feels transitory suits his trickster persona. The women in his life, his dead wife Evangelina and his niece Carmela, remind him to take his pills and offer him meals; but Fausto cannot be bothered with such mundane matters or even his immanent death. Instead, he travels through parks, drive-ups, and freeways in present-day Los Angeles to seventeenth-century Peru and Spain and mid-twentieth-century Mexico. His name and questing closely associate Fausto with other literary characters such as Christopher Marlowe's Dr Faustus and Miguel de Cervante's Don Quixote, who also refuse to be confined by limitations. Fausto's imagination simply disallows limits: subjected to a bout of seemingly all too real diarrhea while on a bus trip to seventeenth-century Cuzco, "Fausto ignore[s] the driver's refusal to stop and simply descend[s] from the machine of noise, odors of urine and grimy bodies."[59] In his world, colonial icons and Spanish "foot soldiers, arquebusiers and lancers" inhabit the same time and space as "[t]elephone poles along the train tracks" and "a billboard advertising Cuzqueña beer."[60]

Ron Arias, the story's interlocutor, crafts his tale to echo elements of *Dr. Faustus* and *Don Quixote* and also—in a nod to early practitioners of magical realism[61]—elements of the twentieth-century short stories by Gabriel García Márquez and William Faulkner. For instance, the first of the novel's mojados[62] recalls Estéban, "The Handsomest Drowned Man in the World," when Fausto's neighbors in *Road* adopt their own drowned "David." Later, the spinster Mrs Rentería's infatuation with his corpse reminds readers of Rose Grierson and Homer Barron in "A Rose for Emily." In both short stories, as it does in Arias's novel, imagination surmounts the pedestrian and mundane.

It seems that Fausto does "die," yet in Arias's novel Fausto's death is almost beside the point. The novel supplies a couple of "death" scenes, first when the priest and doctor and curandera all come to visit his deathbed during or perhaps after the staged bus trip to Tamazunchale. In the course of the bus trip, all the other passengers and even the driver get off the bus; but only Fausto and a little girl take the final walk. As they walk along, they talk about why they have to go to Tamazunchale and what it is like. Presumably, Tamazunchale, the Mexican town of

Fausto's origin, is also the final end for both him and the little girl; as he explains to her, it is "like any other place"; [nonetheless] "a few things are different…if you want them to be."⁶³ It need not be fearful. As Fausto explains it, "Tamazunchale *is* our home. Once we're there, we're free, we can be everything and everyone. If you want, you can even be nothing."⁶⁴ In this trickster world, imagination can overcome even death, and in the novel's earlier pages, Fausto has been practicing up. The second "death" scene occurs on the last page where "Fausto set[s] himself down beside his wife, clap[s] some life into his cold hands, then crosse[s] them over his chest and [goes] to sleep."⁶⁵

This second scene offers the sort of clichéd "closure" about which news organizations always prattle; yet the novel contradicts that notion of "the end." Many stories end with a trickster's "death," and then in the next story, he starts all over again. Implicitly, Fausto too will begin all over again.

REALISTIC URBAN TRICKSTERS BLENDING INTO THE CITYSCAPE

Both Anaya and Arias tap into the fantastic tricksters inherited by Latinos from American Indian oral lore. In contrast, the tricksters of Dagoberto Gilb and Junot Díaz update the gritty, recognizably realistic resentment of Pedro Urdemales. One striking aspect about tricksters written by Latinos living in the United States during the last 20 years is the manner in which their tricksters are blending in with others in the American cityscape. In the Southwest of the United States, Latino tricksters take on American Indian touches. Those from the Caribbean blend in African and Asian elements. Those found in the city become city tricksters; and if their neighbors are African American, they borrow bits of the African American trickster. The ambiance of, for example, stories by Dagoberto Gilb ("Churchgoers" and "Love in L.A." from *The Magic of Blood*—1993) and Junot Díaz ("Edison, New Jersey" from *Drown*—1996) is indisputably Latino, with Latino concerns such as racism, class, and gender that are also American concerns; nonetheless, the writers have moved beyond the tricksters of an earlier Latino tradition to forge new trickster characters suited to exploring the tensions of contemporary American culture. The characters look, act, and function as Latinos; yet they also meld into the American cityscape so that readers recognize the characters and their concerns as urban American characters and American concerns.⁶⁶

"Churchgoers" and "Love in LA" (1993)

Although more often than not, Dagoberto Gilb's characters are hard-working blue-collar family men,[67] characters with an edge and the potential to upset everything are not uncommon. Smooth, for example, the lowly laborer who takes on and defeats the power-hungry boss in "Churchgoers" is also a trickster whose ability to teach "a lesson…about the danger of messing with a man's working life"[68] makes his fellow workers a "congregation of men"[69] elated and vindicated at seeing rough justice dealt to a petty tyrant. Smooth does not even show up until almost the last third of "Churchgoers." First, the narrator establishes that the construction job's superintendent is a bully. Although not overly competent, the superintendent—whose name is O.K.—seems to take sadistic pleasure in ragging the workers, flaunting his power to fire any of them at will. In the course of the story, O.K. does fire many of the men who know, as the narrator's black partner reminds him, that quitting is only "for rich white boys. When the boss brings you a layoff check, you say, 'Thank you so very much, sir.' Then you be on your way, not before."[70] Gilb also sketches a short scene where, instead of being pleased to see them, O.K. intimidates his wife and small son who have stopped by to visit him at work. O.K.'s mean-spirited temper extends to everyone within his power.

The workers manage to live under O.K.'s petty tyranny because their jobs are "our pride, who we were…Employed, it was what we were never ashamed of."[71] Ultimately, however, they also believe "like some religious tenet held by construction workers," that "[w]hat goes around, comes around" (lines reordered).[72] That happens when the loose canon, Smooth, convinces O.K. that he has the boss in his gun sights and manages to reduce him to a "pained, fearful, even embarrassed slump,"[73] "pale and scared, friendless."[74] Smooth, the trickster "little guy" defeats Goliath; and he is relatively little, "a small man in his mid-twenties, five-eight or less, a featherweight."[75] But he talks big and according to scuttlebutt has already gotten away with at least one murder. He strikes fear into a big foreman who has been watching him work; the man quits rather than having to give Smooth a layoff check. Smooth ultimately scares all of the "white hats." In time he stops working entirely and instead taunts O.K., but even O.K. does not dare hand Smooth his final paycheck. While the police eventually walk Smooth off the work site, everyone on the site is convinced that he will return in his own time and deliver the "something I got for you" (quotation rearranged)[76] to O.K. Tricksters are outsiders.

Smooth is successful because he does not care if he gets a couple of bullets in his shoulder as long as he can defeat his opponent.

In "Love in L.A." Gilb presents another trickster, Jake the fast-talking womanizer checking out possibilities. Self-deceived, Jake destroys his own chances through his need to pretend. Like all true tricksters, Jake is basically shiftless. He wants a newer, better car—but not enough to hold down a regular job. He wants to connect on a personal level with the young woman whose new car he has smacked into—but not enough to tell the truth. He gives her his first name, but everything else he hands her is a lie. He makes up a fake last name and address. He gives his victim "the name of an insurance company an old girlfriend once belonged to."[77] Even the license plates on his old beater are a lie: He has "taken [them] off a junk because the ones that belonged to his [Buick] had expired so long ago."[78] Jake's true passion is his desire to be unencumbered by any responsibility.[79]

Jake's performance is both admirable and despicable. He is superb at what he does—acting irresponsibly. He has caused the accident because he is inattentive, happily considering his lack of employment and the fact that he does not usually have to deal with the morning commute in gridlocked traffic. The only reason he does not leave the scene of the accident is that the traffic is too heavy for him to get away safely. Instead of taking responsibility, however, through a series of pickup lines, he tries to impress the young woman driving the Toyota he has literally bumped into. He "sound[s] genuine," fully knowing that his chances are "unlikely, but there was always possibility."[80] Tricksters live in possibility. In some cases, their self-centered focus on themselves aids others. Sometimes it does not. The young woman he tries to pick up smiles but then goes on to bat down his series of inventive lures; regardless, he is still going to leave her with the cost of paying for the damage to her car: "the trunk lid, the bumper, a rear panel, a taillight."[81] Readers hear the cash register toting up her bill. On the other hand and from another perspective, as John McKenna notes,[82] Jake is the underdog, caught up in consumerism and frustrated economic aspirations—and thus an apt trickster using wile to deal with an inherently unequal situation.

The ambiance of Gilb's stories is Latino, but above all, it is urban and working class. Men and women from blue-collar families will recognize the accuracy of his depictions though, for the most part, the perspective is unrelentingly male. Working men of all races inhabit Gilb's landscape.[83] Work—or in the case of Jake, avoiding work—is the center of the lives of Gilb's characters.

"Edison, N. J." (1996)

The Dominican American tricksters of Junot Díaz's short-story collection *Drown* are complicated by their increased awareness of the
influence of class and color in American society. As in the United
States, the connection between race and especially gradations of color
in Latin America has ties with the history of slavery in the Americas.[84]
While some Latin countries have smaller numbers of people of African
descent than others, "Racism prevailed through the hemisphere."[85]
Díaz's stories spell out that continuity in the late twentieth century
and "the cultural effects of long-term patterns of exclusion."[86]

Consonant with their being tricksters, however, characters are often
blind to the ugliness of sexism. This is particularly true for the black-
skinned men and women in *Drown*, a book of linked short stories that
take place in the Dominican Republic and in East Coast cities of the
United States. Díaz's stories are grittier and more hard-edged than
those of Gilb. His characters are at best marginally employed, often as
minor drug dealers. Drugs, violence, and poverty pervade the world
the characters inhabit. If Gilb's Jake lives in an innately inequitable
world, that is all the more true for Díaz's characters.

In addition to all their other frustrations, Díaz's characters are
caught between languages: The book opens with a poignant inscription from Gustavo Pérez Firmat in which the speaker tells listeners
that the very fact he is communicating in English "falsifies" what he
wants to say. Nonetheless, having already crossed the divide from his
"mother tongue," he now belongs "nowhere else."

Díaz's characters drop letters and parts of syllables in both English
and Spanish and use words from one language to mask their discomfort in the other. Díaz comments that he incorporates Spanish
into his English text to force English-speaking readers to grapple
with some of the violence and frustration he encountered in having to speak English when he first came to the United States.[87] In
any case, the mixture of English and Spanish reflects the trickster's
position in between cultures and languages. As multiple Latinos in
the United States attest, moving beyond this state means a further
loss—to become literally monolingual and culturally displaced.

Most of the stories in *Drown* deal with social and economic
oppression exacerbated by drugs and violence; without a great deal
of success, characters seek ways to get ahead and to forge meaningful human relationships. One story is titled "Aguantando"—roughly
translated "sticking it out, bearing up, enduring." The title reflects
the lives of most of the characters in the book. In "Edison, New

Jersey," the narrator does have a job, not much of a job, but a job. As he spells out for the reader/listener, it would take him two and a half years to buy the sort of pool table he delivers to people who can afford one. Even that calculation is predicated on not buying underwear and eating only pasta.[88] Anger against such economic inequity underlies much of the rambling narrative.

Although he says he is "philosophical,"[89] the narrator still resents his dead-end job and inequities he can never overcome. He is angry with his former girlfriend who has moved on to someone "better," a *zángano*—drone[90]—with a job at a record store. Even the dark-skinned Dominicana for whom he risks and almost loses his job returns to her wealthy boss, perhaps lover. In retaliation, the narrator takes pleasure in his income from thievery. He steals from the cash register in his business's showroom, managing "a hundred-buck haul"[91] on a good day; he pilfers cookies, razors, and sometimes condoms from the wealthy homes to which he is delivering pool tables. The class divide in this story is high and harsh. The wealthy customers seem able to buy anything they want including expensive toys such as the pool tables he delivers; nonetheless, if they have "been good and tipped good, we call it even and leave."[92] Apparently, the narrator can, if not forgive them, at least leave them alone. If they have not acknowledged that he is "owed," he manages to leave their toilets plugged up or a smelly decaying horseshoe crab in the garage. The revenge he practices is at once petty and disdainful.

The narrator in Junot Díaz's "Edison, New Jersey" shows the trickster's threatening face. His response to his marginalization is sabotage, minor womanizing, glib excuses, occasional drunkenness, and gambling. He has no interest in the job his former girlfriend's father offers him even though the job is a "real one that you can build on."[93] Instead, he buys lottery tickets on Thursdays and makes a game of pretending to his partner that he can predict where their next delivery will be. Although he has no idea where they will be sent on the following day, at the end of the story, he tells his partner that on the next day they will be delivering to Edison, New Jersey. He just drifts along. While he bears them no particular animosity, he does not particularly care about anyone either; so he does whatever suits him.[94] The threatening tricksters in Gilb's and Díaz's stories are—as is true of all tricksters—amoral. They do not think in terms of right and wrong. They live in society, but they are not social creatures. Their loyalty is only to themselves.

Most readers realize that the bored and uninvolved glance of the threatening Latino trickster reflects objective social and economic realities. Reports in weekly newspapers during early February of 2007, for example, carried one story[95] on the "perceived barriers" that Chicano high school students face while another story on racial disparities in the juvenile justice system in the United States spoke of "a sea of black and brown faces, dressed in orange or blue jumpsuits, with only a scattering of whites in between."[96] From an early age, poor Latino youths are bound to recognize that their lives are likely to face multiple barriers.

THE CULTURAL ELEPHANT IN THE LIVING ROOM: MACHISMO THROUGH MULTIPLE LENSES

Machismo is an inescapable reality of Latino culture. In his five-page encyclopedia article, Gabriel Estrada keeps his definition of *machismo* simple and nonevaluative, referring to machismo as "masculinity and male-identified social roles."[97] Whether men and women view machismo as a stimulus to living honorably or as an impetus to bullying, it is so central to Latino culture that is bound to be an important element in trickster discourse about the culture's potentially oppressive elements.[98] Latino writers use trickster discourse to pay tribute to its positive effects, to question its negative effects, and sometimes to ruminate on its complex role in Latino lives. Tricksters in Latino literature not only point out the friction-causing imbalances and barriers that machismo produces, but their antics also often suggest how to deal with them. While the tricksters in the fiction of Gilb, Díaz, and Anaya hone in on economic and social inequities, Arias follows the adventures of an ordinary man who becomes extraordinary as he confronts and finally crosses the final barrier in his life. Works by Arturo Islas, Marcos McPeek Villatoro, Denise Chávez, and Nina Marie Martínez explore the role of machismo. As Islas, Chávez, and Martínez make clear in their fiction and as Alfredo Mirandé and Richard T. Rodríguez make clear in their analyses, unexamined glorification of machismo marginalizes gays, lesbians, and, indeed, all women. How writers deal with machismo reflects how they view the role of machismo in Latino culture. Some writers use it to show how machismo can be a healthy part of being responsible for oneself and one's community while others use the trickster's penchant for mischief, irreverence, and fantasy to explore its dark side.

North Americans from the United States, especially Euro-Americans, tend to think of machismo, exaggerated masculinity, in terms of violence and aggression, particularly toward women, as well as ludicrous self-centeredness; during the 1960s and 1970s, sociological studies by Euro-Americans appeared to validate the stereotype. Since Alfredo Mirandé's 1997 *Hombres y Machos: Masculinity and Latino Culture* was published, however, non-Latinos have been encountering a more nuanced picture. Unlike his predecessors, Mirandé measured the masculinity of men of Latin American origin through culturally specific means. Using bilingual interviewers, Mirandé's study found considerable complexity among Latinos in their attitudes toward machismo. As the study illustrated, Latino men are not "all of a type."[99] As a whole, the disparate men he studied admired the macho's role in standing up for political rights and his responsibility in providing for the family. They did not admire the stereotypical authoritarianism and aggression associated with machismo. In addition, Mirandé found that Latino machos, whether bullies or defenders of the community—and in contrast to Euro-American men—demonstrated an appealing willingness to express emotion and recognize familial relationships as central to a man's life. This latter difference generally means that Latinos will be more openly affectionate with their children.

The diversity and complexity of machismo and Latino attitudes toward machismo is reflected in the work of their writers. Marcos McPeek Villatoro's *The Holy Spirit of my Uncle's Cojones*, for example, depicts a narrator who needs to embrace his machismo in order to live a full and healthy life while Nina María Martínez uses female tricksters to poke fun at and ultimately marginalize blatantly macho characters in *¡Caramba!*. Both Arturo Islas in *La Mollie and the King of Tears* and Denise Chávez in *Loving Pedro Infante* present more balanced, thoughtful depictions of how machismo affects Latino culture. Of particular note is the fact that all the last three novels give prominent roles to gay characters and the cult of machismo's effect on them.

Latino Trickster as Macho—*The Holy Spirit of My Uncle's Cojones* (1999)

Marcos McPeek Villatoro, the author of *The Holy Spirit of my Uncle's Cojones,* grew up in small Tennessee towns with an Appalachian father and an El Salvadoran mother, so he is heir to two major trickster traditions: the "always seeking his fortune" Appalachian Jack and slyly mischievous Pedro Urdemales. Many readers know McPeek Villatoro as the author of a popular series of detective stories featuring Romilia Chacon.

In Marcos McPeek Villatoro's *The Holy Spirit of my Uncle's Cojones*, the novel's narrator, Tony McCaugh (or Antonio McCaugh

Villalobos) is fortunate in his association with his Uncle Jack (Juan Villalobos),[100] a classic trickster. At the opening of the novel, a inscription quotes Pablo Neruda with a translation by Alastair Reid; the inscription evokes the energy of Jack's machismo but also inter-twines that with his trickster core.[101] The speaker in Neruda's poem—and by extensions, Jack—has lived so fully that he is unforgettable and needs to be "forcibly" forgotten, erased from the blackboard of life because his "heart" [is] "inexhaustible." In *The Holy Spirit of my Uncle's Cojones*, Villatoro[102] intertwines trickster attitudes with Latino machismo[103] implying that both are healthy aspects of "loosen[ing] up a bit"[104] and living life to the full. To everyone who knows him, Jack, who embodies both traits, has always seemed larger than life. In fact, when the novel opens, his family and friends are amazed that he has died in his fifties of a mere heart attack. "No gunshot wound. He wasn't beaten, No signs of poisoning. No one ran over him. Nothing."[105] None of these latter causes would have surprised anyone. As it turns out "The funeral home did not need to hide one scar. No slit on his neck, no bullet hole in his forehead, no car grille markings on his face. Nothing."[106] Although pleased, his sisters are astonished.

The narrator recalls how, years earlier, conflicted by his dual Appalachian/El Salvadoran heritages and oppressed by adolescent angst, he had visited San Francisco with his mother so that he could spend "some time with"[107] his uncle Jack. His intended quiet after-noon with his uncle—purportedly to run some minor errands and "see some of the city"[108]—turns into a violent encounter with a drug dealer and his thugs, a flight to Mexico, and a series of initiation experiences for the teenaged Tony. These experiences culminate in the 16-year-old Tony's proving that, as Jack has told him, "Even if another man's dick [or presumably any other weaponry] is bigger than yours, you [can] make him believe differently."[109]

With the present and past reflecting on one another, the novel's action moves between the mid-1990s and recollections of that sum-mer of 1978 in San Francisco. In 1978, Tony was an immature teen-ager, insecure about his sexuality and caught between two heritages, doubting his self-worth, barely surviving a botched suicide attempt. By the 1990s, he thinks he has moved beyond his earlier malaise: He teaches part time at several colleges in the Knoxville area, has pub-lished a book, and has a live-in girlfriend. Nonetheless, his present is actually a variant of his earlier life: Once again, he has lost touch with his Latino family and heritage; the writing he loves is being pushed aside by his overloaded teaching schedule; and his girlfriend is using him as a meal ticket but cuckolding him with her tennis partner. Now with the more mature perspective of a man in his mid-thirties, Tony returns to San Francisco for his uncle's funeral; while there, he revisits the people he met during that earlier summer and recalls his experiences. He also develops further insight into the ongoing relevance of his uncle's trickster-like machismo.

Uncle Jack incarnates the Latino trickster in late-twentieth-century California. Jack has been macho, but more specifically a trickster, from childhood. Even at five years of age, flashing the *"jodido*[110] grin" that irks his older sister, Jack has "that wild-ass tendency about him."[111] Throughout his life, he is strong despite being shorter and thinner than most men. Since he is a character in a piece of realistic fiction, Jack is a mix of the "legendary"[112] and believable and he smokes and drinks to excess, yet by his fifties, he realizes that his earlier excesses have diminished his health. And his strong body matters to him: He does 300 sit-ups and 300 push-ups every morning. Nonetheless, he smokes marijuana regularly and occasionally chews mescaline-laced mushrooms. In fact, as a favor to a friend, he supplements his income as an electrician by selling marijuana. He is also reliably loyal to his family; without question, he would sacrifice himself for them. He loves Ricarda Guerra, his *compañera*, as long as he lives, yet they divorce and he leaves a string of illegitimate children up and down the West Coast.

One indication of Jack's trickster status is that he is "not grown up."[113] This comment of the narrator does not just emerge from a lack of understanding. Jack has many admirable qualities; but though his sisters defend his role as a *mujeriego,*[114] the fact that "he slept with every woman he could"[115] typically characterizes the preadolescent psychology of the trickster. Tricksters do not develop a moral sense much beyond the stage of "I want it; therefore, it must be good." Unlike his manipulative daughter Felícita, Jack does not try to take advantage of his family; but he treats any woman outside his family—including his childhood friend's mother, wife, and daughter—as fair game. Another indication of Jack's trickster nature comes in that his most enduring female attachments are with his aged mother, and after her death, with the wise woman Chucharonna, a local curandera and the grandmother of his boyhood friend Chucho. Chucharonna seems to embody the Chicano wise woman of oral literature, what one writer identifies as the "Toltec-Aztec Spiderwoman goddess,..., the sun-god's agent of creation and grandmother of the human race."[116]

Tricksters are basically indestructible; Jack's family recognizes that "of course" his nephew will get in trouble if he hangs out with Jack. 'But the strangest thing about him, he's [Jack's] got some angel or somebody watching over him. He never gets too badly hurt. Oh, maybe a bullet in his back, but he still gets out of the situation."[117] His mother tells Tony, "Stay next to him. I mean right next to him. Then you'll be protected too."[118] Jack does suffer setbacks; he is wounded and scarred, yet like other tricksters, he keeps going along. Even after having his finger cut off by a drug dealer, Jack—as his nephew realizes—"regained his fearlessness. Perhaps it had even become stronger, knowing how great the risks were, yet still willing to live with them."[119] While the novel begins after Jack's death, he lives on—in the tales people tell about him and the truth that his nephew needs to relearn: that Tony too needs to plug into the wild side of his own nature if he is to deal successfully with people like the homicidal neo-Nazi Southerner he encounters on the way to the Knoxville airport[120] and his user of a girlfriend or even his own fear of flying. Tony needs to live his Jack's growl, "A man's dick is only as big as his life."[121]

Tricksters are characterized by their immoderate appetites, and so is Uncle Jack. More than a caricature, however, Jack lives in a realistic world. His love of his family and Ricarda, his whole-hearted embrace of life, his ability to hold down a job and do it well, and to have deep friendships—these qualities make him more than an irrationally virile trickster. But still, his trickster core makes him a vibrant character.

All tricksters alter the landscape. Their stories often explain how things came to be the way they are. They can also warn about the consequences of doing something wrong. But tricksters are culture heroes because they use their imagination and always stretch—sometimes break down—limits, to show what *could* be. Jack is such a character, and his nephew needs such a role model.

Female Tricksters Undercutting Machismo—*¡Caramba!* (2004)

While Marcos McPeek Villatoro glorifies the macho's admirable qualities, Nina Marie Martínez makes fun of macho characters in *¡Caramba!* who believe that, because of their gender, they are entitled to precedence. As trickster stories often are, Martínez's novel is irreverently funny and assumes that female tricksters, not males, make the world what it is. Her novel turns the machismo tradition on its head as the women characters take advantage of their presumed secondary importance to pull strings and make their worlds function as they want.[122] Even the macho trickster father of one of the two central women characters, the man whose extended stay in purgatory impels one of the women on a quest to her friend's Mexican birthplace, is treated with neither respect nor apprehension but a kind of indulgent amusement. After Natalie's success in getting him out of purgatory, where he has had to study English for 27 years, Don Pancho becomes the patron saint of drunks and prostitutes. In life after all, he had been closely allied with both.

In *¡Caramba!*, women are in charge, but they rule by wile rather than brawn. In a reversal of tradition, as Latino men have depended on machismo, these women use their femininity to dominate.[123] The central pair of women characters Consuelo and Natalie, have been friends since second grade. Martínez's two principal characters are mischievous rather than malicious tricksters. They enjoy life and they enjoy language and seemingly enjoy sharing the fun of both the absurdities in life[124] and language even though others may be taken either too seriously to find the fun in them. The women are quirky; apparently satisfied with their part-time jobs at the town's major industry, The Big Cheese Plant,[125] and indulgent with the hordes of ranch hands and day laborers with whom they flirt and dance at successive venues. In a typically gender-bending play on words, Consuela sleeps in a king-sized bed "fit for a queen."[126] Natalie defies not only Consuelo's dead father who tries to manipulate her dreams but also "all men who try to keep a girl down."[127] Natalie tells her friend that she is "the sorta girl that can't do without the affection of a man." In a reversal of the philandering *male* trickster's role, however, "it don't have to be the same man."[128]

Typical of as yet unsocialized tricksters, at 27, Consuelo and Natalie still exhibit the interests and ambitions of preadolescence. Buying new shoes satisfies their needs when they encounter disappointment; driving a restored Cadillac satisfies their ambitions; wearing ludicrous costumes to give tours to school children is no bother; their primary emotional ties are with one another. In their way, they are powerful; their employer, Cal, implicitly acknowledges this when he wills the bulk of his holdings to Consuelo and makes her and Natalie his executors. Still, they do not need his wealth and are in control well before Consuelo receives her inheritance. At the novel's conclusion, they are doing what all tricksters do—moving along. They have broken the hold of the compulsion that once kept Consuelo within a 30-mile radius of home, and they are driving out of town.

Although Consuelo and Natalie dominate center stage, their circle of friends—especially Lulubelle; her born-again mariachi son, Javier;

his cocaine-dealing girlfriend/possibly half-sister, Lucha; and the transvestite beautician True-Dee—bustle through the novel contributing their own pieces of trickster discourse. Throughout the novel, what stays with readers is the breaking down of categories: sexual, mortal, moral, linguistic, identity, religious, and national. Sometimes, the ruptures of categories seem to be thrown in merely for laughs: Javier and his mariachi band know only a few songs, so these are what they play—including a "Tex-Mex version of 'Jesus Loves Me'" and "'Just a Closer Walk with Thee' sung to a bolero rhythm"[129] when they perform at the Lava County Women's Correctional Facility.

Some of Martínez's romps with categories seem more serious; she plays a great deal with sexual categories. The most overtly feminine character in the novel is True-Dee, a transvestite beautician; she and her transvestite friends are fabulously successful at arousing the heterosexual men at the local tavern, El Aguantador. The irony of True-Dee's name vies with her preoccupation with a stereotypical femininity. Another poke at gender expectations occurs early in the novel when a group called the Mariachi Macho picks a fight with an all-girl mariachi group, "beautiful elegant ladies" whom the Mariachi Macho do not realize are drag queens.[130] The Mariachi Macho lose the fight.

Probably, the most important border crossing in the novel, however, is linguistic. Although written in English, the novel also makes use of various visuals, Spanish, Spanish typographical conventions, and Spanglish. The novel takes its form from Mexican Loteria cards. Martínez herself refers to Loteria as "just a jazzy form of bingo."[131] The novel plays with reminders of the place of popular culture in contemporary American life with its frequent use of the ® symbol after brand names. Throughout the novel, Martínez employs sketches and visuals that illustrate and comment on the action. These pictographic symbols become still another literary "sign."[132] Each short chapter and the novel itself open with a Spanish *dicho* and a translation into English. The novel is, nonetheless, in English. Just as Natalie and Consuelo lack a deep cultural sense of Mexico itself,[133] their first language is English, but English with a border accent. Wearing her trickster cap, Martínez ignores linguistic and formal literary barriers. Throughout *¡Caramba!*, Martínez employs multiple puns often in English and Spanish, sometimes in Spanglish, playing the sound and meaning in one language off of the other.[134] Early in the novel, for example, once readers have learned that at 18, Consuelo had legally changed her name from Consuelo Constancia González Contreras to Consuelo Sin Vergüenza, Javier comments to Natalie, "There's a reason that girl's middle name is Sin."[135] The Big Cheese is the name of the factory where Natalie and Consuelo work and also the role to which their diminutive male boss pretends. Don Pancho is referred to as DP, which are his initials, but the letters also accurately depict his uncomfortable status as a displaced person. In ¡Caramba!, language is just another structure to play with.

The Trickster in the Mirror—*La Mollie and the King of Tears* (1996)

Arturo Islas plays a riff on the absurdities, including machismo, inherent in his culture's norms. *La Mollie and the King of Tears* is the second novel Islas wrote, but published posthumously and after his two other, semiautobiographical, novels. Although superficially romantic, *La Mollie* implicitly asks its Euro-American readers to look into the mirror that its narrator holds up to them and to Mollie, the woman he loves despite her flaws. Islas uses a narrative frame with his central character, Louie Mendoza, speaking into the tape recorder of an academic researcher in the waiting room of a large public hospital. Readers too become his auditors as he tells about his experiences and implicitly urges them to reconsider what makes satisfactory institutional care for traumatized veterans, what are healthy family and sexual relations, what leaves someone educationally or culturally "disadvantaged," what is true religion, and what makes for effective language. Unabashedly macho with a big heart, Louie is still a king of tears because he cares deeply not just about Mollie and his birth family but also for all the broken people of the world. Such love is costly. Yet earthy, resilient, and full of life, Louie is in love with jazz, language, movies, trees, and a pampered Anglo woman—a feminine surrogate for the whole United States—who mistakes political correctness for effective action. Kindly assessments would assert that her heart is in the right place. Because Louie is apparently a marginally educated *pachuco* from El Paso[136] making a marginal living as a saxophonist in 1973 San Francisco, strangers might mistake him as intellectually inferior to his beloved Mollie, her smug friends, and the dominant culture they represent. Yet, her privileged economic and educational background cannot protect her from a range of pre-packaged ideas and opinions and her certitude that the return of the comet Kahouteck spells the end of the world. On the other hand, Louie's hit-and-miss education in addition to the painful experiences of his life have made him someone who can at least effectively deal with his own *cucuy*s, which are "kinda like a Mexican bogey man, only lots worse."[137]

Despite occasional encounters with a *cucuy*, Louie retains a sense of humor. The novel quickly establishes him as a typical trickster pretending ignorance, for example, in the company of Mollie's well-heeled friends from Pacific Heights. As he says,

> You know, man, when anyone—specially another guy—treats me like a dumb Mexican cause of the way I talk, I just go ahead and act like one. That lets em stay all smug, and I can laugh at em for being so stupid. I been conning the gringos like that for years and they never catch on.[138]

Islas, the narrator behind the narrator, is himself a trickster.[139] The genesis of the novel comes from an assignment he had given his students one summer in El Paso and that he attempted himself. His students were to write a story with a narrator as different from themselves as possible. Thus, Louie is barely a high school graduate while Islas distinguished himself in high school and won an Alfred P. Sloan scholarship to Stanford where he went on to earn first a BA and then in 1971, a PhD in English, and finally taught for 20 years. Louis is conspicuously heterosexual while Islas was homosexual. Almost all of Louie's family is dead; throughout his life, Islas remained in sometimes problematic contact with his family. As Frederick Luis Aldama's biography shows, small details in the novel often have their sources in Islas's life;[140] however, they have been significantly altered.

The whole novel presents a chicano trickster commentary on American inequities. Several sections of the novel reflect on homosexuality and its incomprehensibility from the standpoint of the hetero Louis. Nonetheless, Louie says at one point, "I'm telling you, man, these sissies have a hard life. I'm serious."[141] Later on, Louie ruminates on a sadomasochistic homosexual hangout where he has gone in search of his brother Tomás. Louie finds what he encounters in the bar "so sad."[142]

> [It's] Kinda like being hungry, only the kinda hunger you feel when you ate plenty but you're still starving. Like there's lotsa food in front of you on the table and you don't really wanna eat no more, but you just put the nearest goodie in your mouth and chew away till it's gone anyways. And then you find the goodies are still there even after you eat em, so you start again.[143]

The sly trickster-narrator also takes aim at institutions that for the most part fail their clients. This is particularly true of the high school Louie attends, despite the valiant efforts of his English teacher, Leila P. Harper, who harps on Shakespearean insights,[144] and the inadequate way mental hospitals, in this case a Veteran's Administration hospital where Louie has spent time after the Korean War, deal with traumatized veterans. The hospital's main treatment appears to involve the administration of Thorazine and unlimited supplies of cigarettes. Again, however, a lone unappreciated intern, Mr Angel, struggles to engage the men and draw them out of their torpor. Organized religion too comes in for disdain though Louie contrasts the harshness of institutional religion with the innocent goodness of his friend Sonia's parents and the open-handed generosity of Joyce O'Leary, a one-eyed ex-nun who works as a checker at a local grocery store and personally pays for the groceries of street people.

Additionally, Louie's tale illustrates his reflections on language,

> I don't want everybody to speak like me—that would be boring—but I don't want no one telling me I can't talk this way neither. And all this caca about which is the real mother tongue—our language is accents, man... There's only one language that counts anyway... The language of the heart.[145]

Louie despises the "robot words" that Mollie's friends use.[146] For the most part, theirs is a world of sophomoric theories, shaped from third-hand Freud, pseudo-psychology, and pseudo-Marxism. Instead of reasoned reflection, their words reproduce what "everybody" in their group "knows."

Louie's most scathing criticism is for Mollie's friends who, caught up in their own sense of entitlement, are convinced that their standard English and expensive educations grant them superiority to the rest of society while they are blind to the ironies of their sheltered positions in society. A book read by la Mollie, her friend whom Louie nicknames Dracula, and "the other rich bloodsuckers" convinces them that Russians are "more spiritual than the American materialists."[147] Mollie and her friends can afford their high-minded opinions since Dracula makes a fortune each year defending drug dealers, and la Mollie is a trust-fund baby. They are not working stiffs and unlike Joyce O'Leary, they do not allow their theories to interfere with their lifestyle.

Islas makes Louie a surprisingly self-aware trickster recognizing, for instance, how foolish he has been—as when he once borrowed one girlfriend's car to take another on a date. In retrospect, he recognizes what could be said of almost any trickster following his desires rather than his head, "How come it don't even come to me that my life is in danger? Cause I'm in love and eating cotton candy clouds."[148]

A FEMALE TRICKSTER COMING TO GRIPS WITH MACHISMO—*LOVING PEDRO INFANTE* (2002)

Over 50 years ago, Pedro Infante [Cruz] epitomized the best and perhaps the worst of machismo. A handsome, talented actor and singer, the charming Infante headlined Mexican movies throughout their heyday during the 1940s and 1950s until his death at 50 on April 15, 1957, when the plane he was piloting crashed in the Yucatán peninsula. His cinematic persona and the cult of the man himself marked him as a macho trickster: a womanizer, larger than life, dead but still loved, particularly by his female fans. His movies offered celluloid dreams with just enough gritty reality for audiences to dream about how their lives might also be touched by Pedro Infante's screen magic. As the narrator ruminates, "He's the man we want our men to be. And he's also the man we imagine ourselves to be if we are men. The man we want our daughter to have loved. Pedro's the beautiful part of our dreaming."[149]

Denise Chávez's *Loving Pedro Infante* explores what it means to be caught up in those dreams nurtured and contradicted by twenty-first-century life in a small Southern border town. Recognizing that by her thirties, she is already "gastada, apagada, jodida"[150]—roughly translated—spent, wiped out, screwed, Tere admits she has "a degree in living."[151] The novel's central character as well as narrator, Tere, as Teresina Avila Ambriz is known, grasps at dreams. The narrative follows her affair with Lucio Valadez as if it were a contagion from first infection though viral fever and finally a slow, painful recovery until it comes to a "fin."[152] The object of her lust is an insecure womanizer, small in spirit as well as stature, whom Tere, after seeing him interact with his third-grade daughter, mistakes for a true macho.

The novel weaves a number of tropes and themes though the narrative as it explores the roles of national borders but also those among classes, different ages, races, languages, and genders as they affect the lives of the characters. The novel is concerned with the importance of knowing and being true to oneself and one's culture, the vulnerability of someone as rootless as Tere who has cut herself adrift from the certainties of her mother's generation without yet finding anything else to moor herself to. With humor and compassion, the novel deals with the foibles and follies of Tere and her friends. It weaves the themes of dreaming and forgetting as both helpful and foolish in the characters' lives. In the persons of her comadre Irma and Tere's other close friend, a gay man named Ubaldo, the novel proposes a couple of significant character foils to Tere. While she can not talk with her lover Lucio anymore than she could with he long-gone youthful husband, Tere can talk with Ubaldo and Irma. Thus, the novel offers numerous means of analytical approach; however, in conjunction with *The Holy Spirit of my Uncle's Cojones* and *¡Caramba! Loving Pedro Infante*, it also offers a third female trickster path to recognizing true machos. Accepting the macho veneer, Tere comes to recognize, short-changes a woman. As even Tere realizes early in the novel, after she and the rest of the audience sigh through the end of another Pedro Infante film, "All is well. All is safe. All is as it should be. For the men. A'lo Macho Bravo"[153]—but not necessarily for the women in his life.

Although she says she is picky about men, in fact, for much of the novel, Tere lacks the trickster's healthy self-centeredness; she is blind to who and what is admirable about the apparently macho men in her life. Chávez told an interviewer that in *Loving Pedro Infante*, she intended "to write about love, deceiving love, and the angst of loving the wrong person."[154] As the novel opens, Tere is put off by the idea of connecting even temporarily with the losers she used to meet at La Tempestad, a local bar. Since she does not want to leave her hometown, however, and for all practical purposes, Cabritoville offers only La Tempestad or the Dairy Queen as Friday and Saturday night entertainment, Tere and her friend Irma regularly find themselves drawn back to the stagnant world of La Tempestad. When Tere encounters Lucio, he seems a better choice than the men from La Tempestad: true he is married, but he is macho like Pedro Infante, "with strength and pride and ability to carry out responsibility."[155] Tere's early impression is wrong, of course, but she takes and inflicts on herself a good deal of abuse before she realizes that. (He does not listen to her. They have almost nothing in common besides sexual passion. He is drawn to her earthy qualities at the same time he seems to despise her. He has her slinking around to a sleazy motel and avoids ever being seen in public with her. He disparages her at almost every turn. He needs to build himself up by making her feel inferior. Basically, Lucio takes from Tere without giving anything back.)

Tere learns from her experiences with Lucio;[156] but she also learns from her foils. Ubaldo, her self-deceived gay friend, keeps destructively hooking up with Pedro Infante look-alikes. In contrast, Tere's *comadre*, Irma, has been widowed since her marriage to one stable man; and in the course of the novel, she meets and marries another imperfect but good man. Watching Irma, Tere comes to recognize that marrying someone imperfect need not be so much an abdication as the beginning of a series of negotiations. Tere has trickster qualities to move her beyond the stalemate in her life. For example, she ignores social boundaries and national borders. Her sexual passion has earned her a well-earned reputation in Cabritoville though her sexual exploits have not led to parenthood. Her clothes' sense reflects a modern-day "principle of motley." Except for the sexually ambiguous Ubaldo, her best friends, rather than sexual partners, are all women. Throughout the novel, Tere's tendency to interpret her current reality through the prism of Pedro Infante's movies certainly breaks down distinctions between reality and reflection. The novel suggests that after letting Lucio feed on her passion, she comes to question even her dreams about Pedro Infante. Instead, Tere finally muses, "No one is perfect. Not even Pedro."[157] Chago, who has not been the man of her dreams but actually fits her own definition of macho, is looking better and better. As Chávez says in an interview and her character Tere comes to realize, "to be macho is a complimentary term because [he is] responsible, [he is] an upright human being who takes care of family and kin and all of [his] affairs and everything."[158] That describes Chago. The novel ends with Tere playing a game of catch with Irma's little dog, but then she realizes, "The game would never end until I grew tired and finally decided to stop. At some point you just have to stop."[159] While still enamored with the *dream* of Pedro Infante, Tere is no longer going to settle for one of his stand-ins.

MULTIFACETED TRICKSTERS REFLECTING MULTIPLE HERITAGES

Latino tricksters live on multiple borders, and the works they appear in demonstrate the burden and excitement produced by that placement. As border dwellers, Latino writers call on different trickster heritages depending on what perceived imposition they are speaking to. They use these heritages to throw light on social conundrums as specific to Latino culture as machismo and as common to human life as mortality. Thus, the tradition of Pedro Urdemales lurks in most works dealing with social or economic inequity; on the other hand, especially in writing from the American Southwest, the spirit of American Indian tricksters like Coyote raises its head in tales that serenely slip into fantasy and humor. Latino tricksters sometimes literally translate linguistic borders; they play with both Spanish and English. But they also play with the vagaries of popular and academic culture and can as easily poke fun at Spanglish as at the arrogance of high culture. All too aware of their placement between different entities though part of them both, Latino writers and their tricksters refuse pigeonholes. Yet, the threat of rough mischief, irreverent laughter, and the sense that anything *can* happen stalks through stories about Latino tricksters.

CONCLUSION

"We, the People of the United States" named in the Constitution face a perennial challenge to understand one another in order to function as a "we" rather than an "I" and a multitude of "others." We can, however, access each group's trickster tradition, bridges that help us understand one another better. Ethnic tricksters offer "outsiders" insight into a group's understanding of the world and their part in it. Both oral and literary trickster stories are fascinating in themselves; in part because, as chips of unvarnished human nature, they offer glimmers about what makes others, the people who produce and listen to them, tick. While these tricksters speak most clearly and are best understood by the audience for which they were intended—fellow members of a racial/ethnic group, their stories—often antics—also allow the larger community of Americans to "listen in" to the ways a group "remembers" events, makes sense of their surroundings, and hopes to achieve its goals. Given Americans' diversity, this contribution is invaluable.

An ideal as much as a political reality, the United States of America works best when all its people are recognized and recognize themselves as citizens with all the rights and responsibilities implied in the word. As Parker J. Palmer reminds his fellow Americans, "The benefits of diversity can be ours only if we hold our differences with respect, patience, openness, and hope, which means we must attend to the invisible dynamics of the heart that are part of democracy's infrastructure."[1] Each trickster tradition is part of those invisible dynamics. As happens with other healthy organisms, the United States is energized as well as challenged by its inherent tensions. Recognized and valued, instead of despised, differences among its peoples can be a source of the country's strength. Their most clichéd, popular war movies illustrate American unity where a group of unlikely companions, recognizing their common goal, bond together and willingly sacrifice for the whole.

Quotidian reality in America is messy where the twin pulls of egalitarianism and individualism struggle against one another. Making the struggle all the more challenging, the egalitarian model touted by the country's founding documents has been further strained by the nation's choice to accept multitudes of different peoples into its fold. The United States is a country whose people already find it hard enough to accept as peers others who are pretty much like themselves; the country finds further challenge in acknowledging the equal status of peoples with different skin hues, different accents, different histories, and many different values. Yet, Americans have had opportunities to turn to socialism, for instance, and have consistently refused that direction; they have also repudiated the virulent capitalism represented by nineteenth-century robber barons. Rather than an egalitarian culture, perhaps more realistic and in accord with its history and ideals, the aspiration should be a community that communicates, a commonwealth that encourages all of its members to achieve individually.

Tricksters are universal, and—as Barbara Babcock and others point out—they share some characteristics. Each tradition, however, reflects the history, concerns, and discontents of a particular people who therefore emphasize different aspects of the trickster; and by doing so, they tell others a great deal about themselves. Each group's trickster helps a specific ethnic group to deal with the challenges of being part of the disparate whole called the United States of America because African American, American Indian, Euro-American, Asian American, and Latino/a tricksters, for example, act differently from one another and so set themselves apart.

To illustrate, following centuries of African American slavery and racial discrimination, their tricksters are even more distrustful than other tricksters. They take even more pleasure than other tricksters in language, the only resource that never failed them, even during slave times. Br'er Rabbit is not about to trust Br'er Bear. With considerable reason, Toni Morrison's Son and Walter Mosley's Easy maintain Br'er Rabbit's distrust.

Setting them apart, American Indians, with their still fresh sense of the loss of their land, have produced tricksters who continue to value the earth. Yet those who tell American Indians trickster stories are more willing than other traditions to laugh at their tricksters' quirks—and presumably at their own; their jokes, however, can be as cruel and unforgiving as nature itself. Although they are always trying to cut through limitations, they recognize that as in nature, limitations do exist. Coyote and Raven adapt to circumstances; their fictional human descendants—Leslie Marmon Silko's Tayo, as well as Louise Erdrich's Nanapush, for example—also recognize limitations they cannot change and therefore adapt in order to hold on to what they value the most, the land and the community it nourishes.

More than other tricksters, Euro-American tricksters are identifiably human, with human flaws but also human self-confidence. Still, their self-confidence often tends toward naiveté rather than arrogance. Their success is tied to their individualism and also sometimes to magical good fortune. Although European tricksters often took the form of a cat or a fox, the most universal early Euro-American trickster takes the form of the youthful Jack, out to seek his fortune. In the nineteenth century, Mark Twain reintroduced Jack as Huckleberry Finn; but in the twentieth century, elements of Jack reemerge in as disparate a crew as Saul Bellow's Morris Selbst, Ken Kesey's Randle Patrick McMurphy, and Mark Childress's Lucille Vinson. Contemporary Euro-American tricksters are often recognizable for the chaos that trails them.

The most recent arrivals on American soil and forced to change almost everything in their worlds, Asian American tricksters, at least Chinese American tricksters, are the ultimate transformers. In common with American Indian tricksters, they demonstrate the effort needed to balance the self and the group. The Chinese Monkey King could change himself 72 different ways. Chinese American immigrants and their descendants in the United States have demonstrated similar flexibility. Maxine Hong Kingston's Wittman Ah Sing is a particularly good example of a twentieth-century trickster in the tradition of the Monkey King, but so is Gene Luen Yang's twenty-first-century Jin/Danny whose very name changes in his new home.

Both caught between worlds and exploiters of that position, Latino/a tricksters, inheritors of multiple trickster traditions and thus borderers, are especially influenced by a Euro-American peasant trickster from Spain, an underdog always working against those who possess the goods of this world. Regardless of its source, modern trickster tales also often demonstrate a strong element of fantasy. So Latino/a tricksters often follow the tradition of Pedro Urdemales repeatedly challenging economic or social oppression; however, Latino/a tricksters are additionally often characterized by an imaginative power exceeding that of the Pedro Urdemales tales. Rudolfo Anaya's short story "B. Traven Is Alive and Well in Cuernavaca" combines the trickster approaches, but others—such as Ron Arias's *The Road to Tamazunchale*—rely more on fantasy while the work of Dagoberto Gilb and Junot Díaz is firmly in the realistic resistance tradition of Pedro Urdemales.

These characteristics do not define each ethnic trickster in the sense of limiting them, but they do set each trickster apart from the others. The United States is heir to multiple trickster traditions even though the five analyzed in this text are particularly prominent. Each tradition tells Americans as a whole something more about who they are; and when the country as a whole takes seriously the words of the Declaration of Independence and the Preamble to the Constitution, the *whole* population plays a part in everyone's good and is part of a *common*wealth.

APPENDIX I: THE MONKEY KING

W u Ch'êng-ên's *The Journey to the West* depicts multiple Monkey Kings and more than one trickster. In the first ten chapters, the Monkey King is an emotional child, mischievous, totally self-centered character, gluttonous for food but also for honor and glory. Smart and powerful, he easily outwits and overcomes a series of demigods and even the leaders of the heavens until he is overcome and incarcerated by the Buddhist Patriarch Tathagata. The first ten chapters are about the unfettered trickster who lacks self-control and has to be finally subdued by forces.

The early books of *The Journey to the West* establish the Monkey King's initial greedy self-absorption, his indolence, and his need for self-glorification. He epitomizes the unsocialized individual in a society where everyone has a foreordained place and a role, and everything in life is bound by precedent. The world of the immortals reflects the mortal world. In both, "[e]very class has its proper place and direction."[1] The Monkey King, however, refuses to accept a proper place. Nonetheless, while the Monkey King of the early book admits no limitations, over the course of the tale, he becomes a culture hero who marshals his considerable gifts to aid the quest of Hsuän-tsang, the T'ang monk. In fact, along with the T'ang monk, in the last chapters, the Monkey King becomes a Buddha. Before that, however, the Monkey King goes through multiple changes: Born a stone egg, he is transformed into a stone monkey. In no time, he becomes the leader of the monkeys and discovers a magical place for them behind the waterfall; the rest of the monkeys acknowledge him as Handsome Monkey King.

That is just the start. Dissatisfied with the limitation of mortality, the Monkey King travels over oceans and through two continents in order to study with a Patriarch who gives him a new name—Sun Wu k'ung. The Patriarch teaches him magical arts, and also recognizes that he has "entered into the divine substance" (I: 89). However, recognizing in addition the Monkey King's aptitude for action before thought, the wise Patriarch asks only that the Monkey King not "get into trouble and involve me" (I: 92). The next five chapters do not find the Monkey King involving the Patriarch, but he gets into plenty of trouble.

Acknowledging no one's prerogatives but his own, the Monkey King easily defeats a monster who has been afflicting his monkeys during his absence and then steals armor as well as weapons for his monkeys from one of the oceanic dragon kings. He even forces the dragon king at the bottom of the Eastern Ocean to give him the dragon king's magical "Compliant Golden-Hooped Rod" (I: 105). "That piece of iron—a small stroke with it is deadly and a light tap is fatal! The slightest touch will crack the skin and a small rap will injure the muscles!" (I: 107). This wondrous rod comes to be identified with the Monkey King.[2] Still dissatisfied, the Monkey King then forces the brothers of the dragon king to outfit him with martial clothing: "cloud-treading shoes,...a cuirass of chainmail made of yellow gold,...and a cap with erect phoenix plumes made of yellow gold" (I: 107). In time, the Monkey King's depredations bring him to the notice of the Emperor of Heaven. His early adventures have prepared him, however, to take on even heaven.

Since the Monkey King is already immortal, at first the Jade Emperor of heaven tries to placate him. So Monkey King is put in charge of the imperial stables, but he quickly realizes and resents that his heavenly appointment is at the "meanest level" (I: 122). Defeating one heavenly champion after another, the Monkey King then receives "an empty title...rank without compensation"; he is named "Great Sage, Equal to Heaven" (I: 131). In a further attempt to neutralize the Monkey King's rambunctious behavior, the emperor entrusts the Monkey King with temporary care of the Garden of Immortal Peaches. The Monkey King's response is to gorge himself on the Immortal Peaches, eating "to his heart's content" (I: 136). Using trickery and magic, he also steals and eats most of the rest of the "dainties" and "delicacies" (I: 143) prepared for the Queen Mother's Peach Festival feast. Still worse, when he encounters five gourds of Lao Tzu's concentrated divine elixir, "he pour[s] out the contents of all the gourds and [eats] them like fried beans" (I: 141). All of this renders him *almost* invulnerable. After horrendous battles, however, the Monkey King is subdued by Lao Tzu's diamond snare. But even imprisoned in the Brazier of Eight Trigrams, the Monkey King is refined rather than destroyed. So by "[t]his time our Monkey King ha[s] no respect for persons great or small; he lashe[s] out this way and that with his iron rod, and not a single deity c[an] withstand him" (I: 168). He is at a crossroads because

He could be good;
He could be bad;

Present good and evil he could do at will.
Immortal he'll be in goodness or a Buddha,
But working ill, he's covered by hair and horn. (I: 170)

According to Yu's endnote, this last phase means that "he is reduced to an animal" (I: 511).

The Jade Emperor of heaven appeals to the Buddhist Patriarch Tathagata who first demonstrates to the Monkey King his relative insignificance (I: 174) and then has him imprisoned for 500 years, pinned down in a "kind of stone box" (I: 195) on the Mountain of Five Phases until the Monkey King learns the "meaning of penitence" (I: 195) and is "willing to practice religion" (I: 195). His confinement does not convince the Monkey King; he is not particularly penitent. He is smart enough, however, to recognize a superior force; so he tones down his impetuosity. Actually, at the beginning of his journey with the T'ang monk, the Monkey King demonstrates that he has been only partially cowed. The T'ang monk holds him in check primarily by a golden fillet on his head; when the T'ang monk recites a sutra, the fillet afflicts the Monkey King with implacable headaches. He does not want to serve any master, but he is not self-destructive; so he does start to help the T'ang monk.

Nonetheless, in the course of their journey, the Monkey King changes.[3]

The Monkey King changes so much that by the end of the pilgrims' journey, he is worthy to be "the Buddha Victorious in Strife" (IV: 425). In contrast, the T'ang monk's second disciple, who embodies the trickster's more earthy qualities, Pa-chieh, barely achieves enlightenment. Although the T'ang monk is the putative head of the group, both he and his other disciples—Chu Pa-chieh, Sha Monk, and the dragon horse—depend primarily on the Monkey King's phenomenal power, talents, and wits to deliver them from an exhausting series of trials.

When the T'ang monk and the Monkey King, now called Pilgrim, first encounter him, Pa-chieh—though like Monkey actually an incarnation of another marvelous creature—is married, a glutton, and generally swine-like.[4] Although Pa-chieh's name means "eight commandments" and refers to the first eight of Buddhism's ten commandments—against killing, stealing, immorality, lying, the use of cosmetics and other personal comforts such as a fine bed, strong drink, the use of music and dancing, and eating outside of regulation hours, Pa-chieh indulges in all of these prohibited activities. Particularly identified with his outsize appetite for food,[5] Pa-chieh also grumbles and complains throughout the journey, has no sense of what is proper, is always ready to abandon the T'ang monk, and at one point actually does leave him. Pa-chieh retains his interest in women; in general, he lacks self-control. He is fundamentally slothful, callow, and venal. He makes so many stupid comments and choices that the T'ang monk and Pilgrim regularly address Pa-chieh as "Idiot." Athough often the butt of Pilgrim's tricks, Pa-chieh also pulls sly tricks on his "elder brother." In short, he remains lecherous and greedy, a typical earthy trickster. All of the travelers retain their natural bent. Pilgrim develops his wiliness, however, and places his talents at the service of the T'ang monk while Pa-chieh retains the trickster's earthy, animal-like qualities. Pilgrim has twice Pa-chieh's talent at transformation, but both are gifted.

Usually in a doltish fashion, Pa-chieh is also funny. Even in horrendous situations, he can demonstrate a wry humor as when a fiend counsels other fiends to tie up the captured Pa-chieh, drop him in a pond, then "[w]hen his hairs are soaked off," rip him open, cure him with salt, and finally sun-dry him because then he will be "good with wine when it turns cloudy." Hearing this, Pa-chieh complains, "I've run into a fiend who's a pickle merchant" (IV: 9). In keeping with Pa-chieh's clownish role, *The Journey* portrays his situation as ludicrous rather than dangerous. When Pilgrim spies Pa-chieh and before rescuing him, the narration comments that "our Idiot [is] half floating and half submerged in the pond, with his four legs turned upward and his snout downward, snorting and blowing water constantly . . . a laughable sight indeed, like one of those huge black lotus roots of late autumn that has cast its seeds after frost" (IV: 9).

By the end of the pilgrims' journey, even Pa-chieh has changed though not as much as the Monkey King. The two tricksters retain their powers of self-transformation, but now they are in control of themselves—and therefore of their powers as well. They serve the greater good embodied in the T'ang monk's leadership.

NOTES

1 INTRODUCTION

1. Ralph Ellison, *Invisible Man* (New York: Random House, 1952; rpt. 2002), 435–436.
2. Full of trickster discourse, *The Invisible Man* (1952) falls too early for the parameters of this study. It is interesting, however, that both Ellison's novel and the other great trickster novel of the twentieth century, Saul Bellow's *The Adventures of Augie March* (1954), were published a decade before a major flowering of trickster discourse in American letters during the 1960s.
3. Related to this fact is that, as a recent Associated Press story noted, interracial marriages in the United States now average a 1 in 12. Hope Yen, "Interracial Marriages in U. S. Reach Record," *Wisconsin State Journal* (February 16, 2012), A9.
4. In a review and commentary on Simon Schama's *The American Future: A History* (New York: Ecco, 2009), Louis P. Masur, "The American Character: Bucking Scholarly Trends, Simon Schama Argues It Has a Bright Future," *The Chronicle Review*, January 16, 2009, http://chronicle.com/weekly/v55/i19/19b00601.htm (accessed January 12, 2009) outlines the arguments of major players in the history of American exceptionalism.
5. Langston Hughes, "Theme For English B." *The Collected Poems of Langston Hughes*, ed. Arnold Rampersad and David Roessel (New York: Vintage, 1994), 409–410.
6. William T. May, *Testing the National Covenant: Fears and Appetites in American Politics* (Washington, DC: Georgetown University Press, 2011), 137.
7. Niigonwedom James Sinclair, "Trickster Reflections, Part I," 21–58, in *Troubling Tricksters: Revisioning Critical Conversations*, ed. Deanna Reder and Linda M. Morra (Waterloo, Ontario [Canada]: Wilfrid Laurier University Press, 2010), 23.
8. Toni Morrison, "Unspeakable Things Unspoken: The Afro-American Presence in American Literature," *Michigan Quarterly Review* 28, no. 1 (Winter 1989): 9–34; rpt. in *Modern Critical Views*, ed. Harold Bloom (New York: Chelsea House Publishers, 1990), 208.
9. Richard Conniff, "Close Encounters of the Sneaky Kind," *Smithsonian* (July 2003): 66–70. In this article, Conniff follows the

apparent success via stealth of weaker, less well-endowed male birds in impregnating the most valued females, 3, 66.

10. Barbara Babcock-Abrahams, " 'A Tolerated Margin of Mess': The Trickster and His Tales Reconsidered," *Journal of the Folklore Institute*, 11 (1974): 159–160: rpt. in *Critical Essays on Native American Literature*, ed. Andrew Wiget (Boston, MA: G.K. Hall, 1985), 162–63, outlines commonly accepted trickster characteristics when she notes the following:

In almost all cases, and to a greater or lesser degree, tricksters

1. exhibit an independence from and an ignoring of temporal and spatial boundaries;
2. tend to inhabit crossroads, open public places (especially the marketplace), doorways, and thresholds. In one way or another they are usually situated between the social cosmos and the other world or chaos;
3. are frequently involved in scatological and coprophagous episodes which may be creative, destructive, or simply amusing;
4. may, similarly, in their deeds and character, partake of the attributes of Trickster-Transformer-Culture Hero;
5. frequently exhibit some mental and/or physical abnormality, especially exaggerated sexual characteristics;
6. have an enormous libido without procreative outcome;
7. have an ability to disperse and to disguise themselves and a tendency to be multiform and ambiguous, single or multiple;
8. often have a two-fold physical nature and/or a "double" and are associated with mirrors. Most noticeably, the trickster tends to be of uncertain sexual status;
9. follow the "principle of motley" in dress;
10. are often indeterminate (in physical stature) and may be portrayed as both young and old, as perpetually young or perpetually aged;
11. exhibit a human/animal dualism and may appear as human with animal characteristics or vice versa; (even in those tales where the trickster is explicitly identified as an animal, he is anthropomorphically described and referred to in personal pronouns);
12. are generally amoral and asocial—aggressive, vindictive, vain, defiant of authority, etc.;
13. despite their endless propensity to copulate, find their most abiding form of relationship with the feminine in a mother or grandmother bond;
14. in keeping with their creative/destructive dualism, tricksters tend to be ambiguously situated between life and death, and good and evil, as is summed up in the combined black and white symbolism frequently associated with them;

15. are often ascribed roles (i.e., other than tricky behavior) in which an individual normally has privileged freedom from some of the demands of the social code;

16. in all of their behavior, tend to express a concomitant breakdown of the distinction between reality and reflection.

Sometimes, however, is it easier to recognize tricksters by "characteristics common to many tricksters—shape shifting, cross-dressing, disruption, playfulness, and liminality" that Bradley John Monsma mentions in " 'Active Readers...Obverse Tricksters': Trickster Texts and Cross-Cultural Reading," *Modern Language Studies* 26, no. 1 (Fall 1996): 83.

11. Babcock-Abrahams, "A Tolerated Margin of Mess," 156.

12. Ibid., 161.

13. See note 4.

14. Although not necessarily so, tricksters are usually male.

15. Babcock-Abrahams, "A Tolerated Margin of Mess," 168.

16. While Gerald Vizenor uses this phrase repeatedly in his publications, he explicitly titles an essay in the summer 1990 issue of the *American Indian Quarterly*, "Trickster Discourse," 286. Vizenor is intrigued by the trickster's linguistic role in culture. Toward the end of this essay, he encapsulates his meaning when he says, "the trickster animates human adaptation in a comic language game." When I use the phrase, I have in mind both the tales that incorporate tricksters and the underlying attempt by relatively powerless speakers to name uncomfortable truths to those in power.

17. In "The Seriously Funny Man." *Time* (July 14, 2008): 47, Richard Lacayo quotes Twain writing this line in an unpublished rejoinder to Matthew Arnold.

18. William G. Doty, "Native American Tricksters: Literary Figuras of Community Transformers," in *Trickster Lives: Culture and Myth in American Fiction*, ed. Jeanne Campbell Reesman (Athens: University of Georgia Press, 2001), 5, also connects tricksters and freedom, seeing them as symbolic of "the freedom [they] ultimately represent," and that freedom as requisite to participating gracefully in cultural life.

19. One might think of tricksters as situational ethicists; however, the tricksters of oral literature in particular are not that sophisticated. They are amoral; they do not think in terms of either moral principles or the present "good." Emotionally, the tricksters of oral literature live in a stark world and function at the emotional level of immature ten-year-olds: the fact that they want something provides sufficient motivation for their pursuit of that object. For the tricksters of oral literature, morality is beside the point. Modern writers, however, depict tricksters in a more complicated moral universe, so the characters they offer readers come with complex motivations.

Many of these characters are situational ethicists; representatives of oppressed minorities, tricksters in modern literature feel that their situation justifies their defying authorities, transgressing hierarchies, and breaking not just social rules but ethical rules. In common with their forebears, many modern literary tricksters are just amoral.

20. Lewis Hyde, *Trickster Makes This World: Mischief, Myth, and Art* (New York: Farrar, Straus and Giroux, 1998), 13.

21. Ralph Ellison, *Shadow and Act* (New York: Random House, 1964), 57.

22. Most famously in *Shadow and Act*, 57, Ralph Ellison vehemently objects to trickster-hunting in modern, realistic fiction. He insists that "if the symbols appearing in a novel link up with those of universal myth they do so by virtue of their emergence from the specific texture of a specific form of social reality." However, as Carl Jung, "On the Relation of Analytical Psychology to Poetry," Vol. 15, Pars. 97–132, note 7, in *The Spirit in Man, Art, and Literature. Collected Works*, trans. R. F. C. Hull, Vol. 15, Bollingen Series 20 (Princeton, NJ: Princeton University Press, 1980) notes, sometimes even realistic literature "pay[s] tribute to the overwhelming impression" tricksters have made on the human psyche. (Following the customary usage, references to Jung's work published in his collected works are cited by volume number and paragraph rather than page number.)

23. Robert D. Pelton, *The Trickster in West Africa: A Study of Mythic Irony and Sacred Delight* (Berkeley, CA: University of California Press, 1980), 243. The quotation continues "hermeneutics in action,...probing ceaselessly all opacity for hidden designs, and forever rejecting every form of muteness. One is permitted to believe that he [the trickster], like every hermeneut, is doomed to failure, but not before immersing oneself in the specific language of his dance."

2 AFRICAN AMERICANS AND AN ENDURING TRADITION

1. In *Folklore in New World Black Fiction* (Columbus, OH: The Ohio State University Press, 2007), 134, Chiji Akoma argues that while the spoken word is central in African literary expression, in "the interrogation of the oral form through writing," both African and African American writers extend the skilled oral performances admired by folk audiences, making written work "more usable and relevant for contemporary audiences."

2. John W. Roberts, "The African American Animal Trickster as Hero," in *Redefining American Literary History*, ed. A. LaVonne Brown Ruoff and Jerry W. Ward (New York: MLA, 1990), 110.

3. Ibid., 110–111.
4. Ibid., 112.
5. Ibid., 112.
6. Susan Feldman, "The Rabbit and the Antelope," in *African Myths and Tales* (New York: Dell Publishing, 1963), 141–144.
7. Feldman, "Introduction," in *African Myths and Tales*, 13–15.
8. A similar verve and gusto for life in the face of belittlement appears in one of BarbaraNeely's Blanche White mysteries where the dark-skinned third-person narrator thinks about her black-skinned community's "marriage of color and style for the sheer purpose of expressing personality." *Blanche among the Talented Tenth* (New York: Penguin Books, 1994), 58.
9. Annette Gordon-Reed, *The Hemingses of Monticello: An American Family* (New York: W. W. Norton, 2008), 56.
10. Ibid., 17.
11. Jay D. Edwards, *The Afro-American Trickster Tale: A Structural Analysis*, Vol. 4, Monograph Series of the Folklore Publications Group (Bloomington, IN: Folklore Institute of the University of Indiana, 1978), 70.
12. As William Bernard McCarthy, compiler and editor, shows in *Cinderella in America: A Book of Folk and Fairy Tales* (Jackson, MI: University Press of Mississippi, 2007), 242, even what Americans think of as the quintessential African American animal trickster, Br'er Rabbit, has added to his own mischief-making other tricks that are elsewhere attributed to European tricksters such as Reynard the Fox, Jack, and Pedro.
13. Edwards, *The Afro-American Trickster Tale*, 78. The "trickster turns his marginal status against the system by separating himself from that system and then by using its internal constraints to his advantage."
14. Roberts, "The African American Animal Trickster as Hero," 106.
15. Feldman. "Introduction," *African Myths and Tales*, 17.
16. Pelton, *The Trickster in West Africa*, 4.
17. Ibid., 17.
18. Ibid., 26.
19. Ibid., 27.
20. Ibid., 27–28.
21. Robert D. Pelton, "West African Tricksters: Web of Purpose, Dance of Delight," in *Mythical Trickster Figures: Contours, Contexts, and Criticism*, eds. William J. Hynes and William G. Doty (Tuscaloosa, AL: University of Alabama Press, 1993), 138.
22. Although other parts of Africa also had trickster traditions, those of West Africa had the greatest influence on Caribbean and North America traditions because the slaves transported to the Caribbean and North America were primarily from West Africa.

23. Laura Makarius, "The Myth of the Trickster: The Necessary Breaker of Taboos," *Mythical Trickster Figures*, 73.
24. Ibid., 82.
25. Ibid., 83.
26. Roberts, "The African American Trickster as Hero," 104.
27. Ibid., 110.
28. Ibid., 111.
29. Mel Watkins, *On the Real Side: Laughing, Lying, and Signifying— The Underground Tradition of African-American Humor that Transformed American Culture, From Slavery to Richard Pryor* (New York: Touchstone Books, 1994), 53.
30. See, for example—to choose just a few among many texts—those found in Roger D. Abrahams, ed., *Afro-American Folktales: Stories from Black Traditions in the New World* (New York: Pantheon, 1985): 179–217; Richard M. Dorson, collector, *American Negro Folktales* (1958; rpt. New York: Fawcett, 1970): 66–102; Charles C. Jones, *Negro Myths from the Georgia Coast* (Boston, MA: Houghton Mifflin, 1888); Willliam J. Faulkner, *The Days When the Animals Talked: Black American Folktales and How They Came to Be* (Chicago: Follett, 1977), 72–178; J. Mason Brewer, *American Negro Folklore* (Chicago, IL: Quadrangle Books, 1968): 4–19; and Joel Chandler Harris, *Uncle Remus: His Songs and His Sayings* (rev ed. 1895; rpt. New York: Appleton & Company, 1921), 3–174; and McCarthy, compiler and editor, *Cinderella in America*, 241–292.
31. Roberts, "The African American Animal Trickster as Hero," 112, writes of a late-nineteenth-century collector of animal trickster tales being "*repulsed* (emphasis added) by the enthusiasm and delight expressed by her informant for what she viewed as the immoral antics of the wily trickster." As Roberts also explains, for the most part, even those stories a white person might encounter were "permeated…with the cajoling and flattering that made the masters susceptible to manipulation," (112).
32. Bruce D. Dickson, Jr., "'The John and the Old Master' Stories and the World of Slavery: A Study in Folktales and History," *Phylon* 35 (1974): 427.
33. Nigel H. Thomas, *From Folklore to Fiction: A Study of Folk Heroes and Rituals in the Black American Novel* (New York: Greenwood Press, 1988), 82.
34. John W. Roberts, *From Trickster to Badman: The Black Folk Hero in Slavery and Freedom* (Philadelphia, PA: University of Pennsylvania Press, 1989), 52.
35. A 2001 monograph by John Minton and David Evans, *"The Coon in the Box": A Global Folktale in African-American Tradition* (Helsinki: Academia Scientiarum Fennica, 2001), demonstrates in detail that while this tale has roots in a multipart tale told in second-century India, in America, the tale has morphed into a uniquely

African American tale. In illustration of Minton and Evans's point, Miriam Behnam's retelling of "Shankar the Fortune-teller," 170–80, in *Heirloom: Evening Tales from the East* (New York: Oxford University Press, 2001), uses the same punch line with only a slight variation, "I never expected Froggy to be trapped inside the box," 180. Behnam grew up in Southern Iran and now lives in the Bastaki community of Dubai, United Arab Emirates.

36. Zora Neale Hurston, *Mules and Men* (New York: Lippincot, 1935; rpt. New York: Harper, 1990), 81. Although in this case, John is just the recipient of dumb luck, the case also illustrates that *sometimes* the trickster wins regardless of the odds.

37. Brewer, *American Negro Folklore*, 29.

38. Roberts, *From Trickster to Badman*, 55.

39. Alan Dundes, *Mother Wit from the Laughing Barrel: Readings in the Interpretation of Afro-American* Folklore (Englewood Cliffs, NJ: Prentice-Hall, 1973), 551.

40. Dorson, *American Negro Folktales*, 148.

41. Ibid., 149. This tale continues to circulate today appearing as recently as 1998 in *Secrets*, Nuruddin Farah's novel of Somalia's civil war. The narrator relates that his childhood friend once told him "a folktale her father had learnt from a Nigerian fellow seaman." In the tale, a hunter encounters a talking skull who warns the hunter, "Beware of divulging secrets, because that is what got me where I am, dead." Of course, the hunter cannot resist telling his wife and friends about this wonder. The news filters to the king who visits the skull, but the skull will not speak. Furious, the king has the hunter beheaded and his head left there, unburied. After everyone leaves, the talking skull asks the hunter's unburied head how he came to be there. The unburied skull replies, "Divulging secrets got me here, dead." (New York: Arcade Publishing, 1998; rpt. New York: Penguin Books, 1999), 17. The tale is extremely widespread appearing in the most unlikely places. In the Irish novelist Peter Murphy's novel *John the Revelator*, for example, an African immigrant to Ireland tells a variant with a skull warning a young man, "Foolishness killed me, but I will kill thee"; since the young man tells of the encounter, he is indeed killed (Boston, MA: Houghton Mifflin Harcourt, 2009), 207.

42. Hurston, *Mules and Men*, 89.

43. Ibid., 90.

44. Jake Mitchell and Robert Wilton Burton, *De Remnant Truth: The Tales of Jake Mitchell and Robert Wilton Burton*, collected by Kathryn Sport and Bert Hitchcock (Tuscaloosa, AL: The University of Alabama Press, 1991), 45.

45. Ibid., 29.

46. Ibid., 33.

47. Thomas, *From Folklore to Fiction*, 83–109.

48. Both books, Mel Watkins's *Stepin Fetchit* and Champ Clark's *Shuffling to Ignominy*, are reviewed in John Strausbaugh's "How a Black Entertainer's Shuffle Actually Blazed a Trail," *New York Times* (December 7, 2005) www.nytimes.com/2005/12/07/books /07stra.html?emc+eta1&pagewanted=print.

49. One of Red Foxx's lines was, "They say Negroes carry knives. That's a lie. My brother has been carrying an ice pick for years," quoted in Mel Watkins, *On the Real Side*, 516. Pryor developed a character called Oilwell who said, "I don't take no ass whuppin's, and don't know nothin' about being unconscious…you got to *kiilll* me," quoted in Mel Watkins, *On the Real Side: Laughing, Lying, and Signifying*, 552.

50. Barbara Hambly, *Dead Water* (New York: Bantam, 2004), 2.

51. Gillian Johns, "Going Southwest: American Humor and the Rhetoric of Race in Modern African-American Fiction and Authorship" (Diss. Temple University, 2000), xxiii.

52. Ibid., xxviii.

53. William Bernard McCarthy, ed. and compiler, *Cinderella in America*, 241–242.

54. Nellie McKay, "An Interview with Toni Morrison," 153, in *Conversations with Toni Morrison*, ed. Danille Taylor-Guthrie (Jackson, MI: University Press of Mississippi, 1994).

55. I do not want to bore the reader with repetition of material found in the Introduction. So I am not repeating in this or other chapters why these works and the characters in the works illustrate trickster discourse. Readers who are not familiar with tricksters and trickster discourse would do well to review the so-called both-and characteristics of all tricksters as listed in Barbara Babcock-Abrahams's "A Tolerated Margin of Mess." Cf. note 10 of the Introduction to this work.

56. Since this is a modern "realistic" play, Ted Shine provides "motivation" when he has Mrs Love tell her grandson, "The Bible says love and I does. I turns the other cheek and I loves 'til I can't love no more. (*Eugene nods*) Well…I reckon I ain't perfect. I ain't like Jesus was; I can only bear a cross so long. I guess I've 'had it' as you young folks say. Done been spit on, insulted, but I grinned and bore my cross for a while. Then there was peace—satisfaction. Sweet satisfaction." Ted Shine, "Contribution," *The Best Short Plays of 1972*, ed. Stanley Richards (York: Equinox Books, 1972), 38–39.

57. Ibid., 41.

58. Ibid., 35.

59. Ibid., 42.

60. Ishmael Reed, *Flight to Canada: A Novel* (1976; rpt. New York: Atheneum, 1989), 38.

61. Monsa " 'Active Readers…Obverse Tricksters': Trickster Texts and Cross-Cultural Reading," 83–98, also makes connections between these two writers and Maxine Hong Kingston.

62. In fact, Reed insists "the main thing about my writing is that it is not like any other. I have always strived to be original." Rebecca Carroll, *Swing Low: Black Men Writing* (New York: Crown Publishers, 1995), 193. Nonetheless, the trickster is so rooted in Reed's tradition that he does not need to advert to it.
63. The two writers' use of trickster is so similar that in examining Reed's work, it is useful to refer to what Vizenor has to say about trickster. In the prologue to his 1988 comic novel *The Trickster of Liberty*, Vizenor emphasizes the ties among the trickster, imagination, and language. According to Vizenor, trickster writing and trickster reading breaks down set forms and calcified thinking. By nature and choice, tricksters exist on the margins; Vizenor finds a virtue in what others have often found restrictions. He repeatedly praises the role of mixed bloods because they are neither/nor; he also validates other forms of ambiguity. Vizenor gleefully explores one form of absurdity, one sort of "what if?" after another. He glories in the situations his fictions imagine as "the trickster liberates the mind in comic discourse," *The Trickster of Liberty: Tribal Heirs to a Wild Baronage* (Minneapolis, MN: University of Minnesota Press, 1988), xii.
64. Laura L. Mielke, " 'The Saga of the Third Word Belle': Resurrecting the Ethnic Woman in Ishmael Reed's *Flight to Canada*," *MELUS* 32, no. 1 (Spring 2007): 7, also explores Reed's own "role [as] a trickster-author."
65. Patrick McGee, *Ishmael Reed and the Ends of Race* (New York: St. Martin's Press, 1997), 39.
66. Reed, *Flight to Canada*, 7.
67. Babcock-Abrahams, " 'A Tolerated Margin of Mess': The Trickster and his Tales Reconsidered," in *Critical Essays on Native American Literature*, ed. Andrew Wiget (Boston, MA: G.K. Hall, 1985), 158.
68. Louis Henry Gates, *The Signifying Monkey: A Theory of African-American Literary Criticism* (New York: Oxford University Press, 1988), 244.
69. Ibid., xxvii.
70. Reed, *Flight to Canada*, 178.
71. Robert Elliot Fox, *Conscientious Sorcerers: The Black Postmodernist Fiction of LeRoi Jones/Amiri Baraka, Ishmael Reed, and Samuel R. Delaney* (New York: Greenwood Press, 1987), 3.
72. Reed, *Flight to Canada*, 20.
73. Gates, *The Signifying Monkey*, 35.
74. This is particularly true of African Americans since the tale belongs to that group of "forms, conditions, and ideas" that Trudier Harris, following Stephen Henderson's concept of "saturation," says are "so thoroughly enmeshed in the African-American psyche and culture that they are instinctively, intuitively recognizable when they appear

in literary form." *Fiction and Folklore: The Novels of Toni Morrison.*
(Knoxville, TN: The University of Tennessee Press, 1991), 10.

75. In common with other tales from oral literature, "Br'er Rabbit and
the Tar Baby" can have many meanings. Son politicizes the tale and
gives it a racialized meaning: in his retelling, the tar baby has been
crafted by a white farmer to catch the rabbit. In an interview with
Thomas Leclair, " 'The Language Must Not Sweat': A Conversation
with Toni Morrison," in *Toni Morrison: Critical Perspectives Past
and Present*, ed. Henry Louis Gates and K. A. Appiah (New York:
Amistad, 1993), 372, Morrison adds a note of gender and says that
as she grew up, "tar baby came to mean the black woman who can
hold things together."

76. Toni Morrison, *Tar Baby* (1981; rpt. New York: A Plume Book,
1987), 305.

77. Ibid., 120.

78. Ibid., 113.

79. Ibid., 290.

80. Ibid., 291.

81. Ibid., 31.

82. Ibid., 39.

83. Ibid., 59.

84. Ibid., 87.

85. Ibid., 6.

86. Toward the end of a 1977 interview, Morrison talks about how she
envisions the novel she is working on, *Tar Baby*:
I was always terrified by the story...and I never knew why. But it's
an example of black folklore as history. It's incredible, but it's right
there on the surface—both as prophecy and as a reflection of the
past. It's a love story, really: the tar baby is a black woman; the rabbit is a black man, the powerless, clever creature who has to outwit
his master. He is determined to live in that briar patch, even though
he has the option to stay with her and live comfortably, securely,
without magic, without touching the borders of his life.
Do you think she would go into that briar patch with him?...Well,
that's what it's all about. If there is any consistent theme in my
fiction, I guess that's it—how and why we learn to live this life
intensely and well." Mel Watkins, "Talk with Toni Morrison," *The
New York Times* (September 11, 1977): 50.

87. Morrison underscores this element of choice in her interview with
Christina Davis. "Interview with Toni Morrison," in *Toni Morrison:
Critical Perspectives Past and Present*, ed. Henry Louis Gates and
K. A. Appiah (New York: Amistad, 1993), 419, where she talks
about Son's having to choose from among possibilities and readers
also having to choose. Morrison says, "You don't end a story in the
oral tradition—you can have a little message at the end, your little

moral, but the ambiguity is deliberate because it doesn't end, it's an ongoing thing and the reader or listener is in it and you have to THINK."

88. Toni Morrison, "Unspeakable Things Unspoken: The Afro-American Presence in American Literature," *Michigan Quarterly Review* 28, no. 1 (Winter 1989): 9–34; rpt. in *Modern Critical Views*, 227.

89. Keith Byerman makes this point in *Fingering the Jagged Grain: Tradition and Form in Recent Black Fiction* (Athens: University of Georgia Press, 1985), 161.

90. Gates, *The Signifying Monkey*, 29.

91. Alice Walker, *The Color Purple* (1982; rpt., Orlando: A Harvest Book, 2003), 273.

92. Gates, *The Signifying Monkey*, 6.

93. As Gates explains at length in Chapter 2 of *The Signifying Monkey*, black Signification—which he indicates with an upper case S—represents "a concept remarkably distinct from that concept represented by the standard English signifier, 'signification' " (45). As Gates uses the word, Signification refers to the ways African American writers pick up and use a "rhetorical principle in Afro-American vernacular discourse" (44) to react to and revise the work of other writers. Particularly apparent in this process is the use of pastiche and parody.

94. Gates, *The Signifying Monkey*, 15.

95. Ibid., 6, 16.

96. Mentioned by Gates as constituting a "partial list," the trickster's "characteristics" include "Individuality, satire, parody, irony, magic, inderterminacy, open-endedmess, ambiguity, sexuality, chance, uncertainty, disruption and reconciliation, betrayal and loyalty, closure and disclosure, encasement and rupture" (6). In *The Color Purple*, it is the women characters who demonstrate these qualities.

97. Edwards, *The Afro-American Trickster Tale*, 73.

98. Jacqueline Bobo, "Sifting through the Controversy: Reading *The Color Purple*," *Callaloo: An Afro-American and African Journal of Arts and Letters* 2 (1989): 332–342. Bobo outlines the stages of the controversy surrounding *The Color Purple*—first as a novel (in 1982), as a film (in 1985), as a theatrical production (at the beginning of 1987), and as a video (in July of 1987)—and shows how successive releases stirred further backlash so that many of the most vocal male critics of the film were responding to what *they* perceived that the novel and film said rather than the general population perceived. In fact, for the most part black audiences did not consider the film offensive. Nonetheless, the novel and the various works that followed the novel do take aim at sexism and racism. This did

upset men who would rather ignore sexism in African American culture.

99. "Facing It," first published in Yusef Komunyakaa's *Dien Cai Dau* (Hanover, NH: Wesleyan University Press, 1988); rpt. *Pleasure Dome: New and Collected Poems* (Middletown, CT: Wesleyan University Press, 2001), 234, reflects on the speaker's own and his country's involvement in the Vietnam War even as he literally faces his reflection in the Vietnam memorial.

100. In fact, Alvin Aubert calls the persona of "I Apologize," the speaker in the poem from which *I Apologize* gets its title, "a ludicrously bumbling trickster figure" (122). "Yusef Komunyakaa: The Unified Vision—Canonization and Humanity," *African American Review* 27 (1993): 119–123.

101. *Pleasure Dome*, 141.

102. Ibid., 87.

103. Ernest Suarez, *Southbound: Interviews with Southern Poets* (Columbia, MO: University of Missouri Press, 1999), 140.

104. In addition to referencing Roger D. Abrahams, "Joking: The Training of the Man of Words in Talking Broad," Mel Watkins, *On the Real Side*, 453–455, dedicates several pages to distinguishing among several types of "broad talk, " including the dozens.

105. On the other hand, in "Walter Mosley, Detective Fiction and Black Culture." *Journal of Popular Culture*, 32:1 (Summer 1998): 141–50, Mary Young, makes a good argument for Easy being the trickster and Mouse the traditional badman—often a variant of the African American trickster. In any case, Young shows that Mosley's first three novels demonstrate at least as much debt to African American folklore as to traditional hardboiled fiction.

106. See, for example, *Some Things I Thought I'd Never Do* (New York: One World, 2003) and *Baby Brother's Blues: A Novel* (New York: One World, 2006).

107. Roberts, *From Trickster to Badman*, 215.

108. The African American belief in the legal system's being tilted away from their favor persists into the Easy novels. As a narrator living in 1967, Easy comments, "I lived in a world where many people believed that laws dealt with all citizens equally, but that belief wasn't held by my people. The law we faced was most often at odds with itself." Walter Mosley, *Blond Faith* (New York: Little, Brown and Company, 2007), 75.

109. Jerry H. Bryant, *"Born in a Mighty Bad Land": The Violent Man in African American Folklore and Fiction* (Bloomington, IN: Indiana University Press, 2003), 2. Bryant also notes that African American literary writers—and that includes the writers in this chapter—tend to make the badman someone who has graduated from the undisciplined violence of the "bad nigger" celebrated by oral folk literature (e.g., Stagolee, Devil Winston, John Hardy, Dupre, Railroad Bill

and others) to a man who has acquired a modicum of middle-class values (7).

110. Walter Mosley, *Bad Boy Brawl Brawly Brown* (Boston, MA: Little, Brown and Company, 2002), 237.

111. To quote only one among a multitude, Easy tells a woman who offers him a drink, "Whiskey for me is like having an allergy to aspirin along with the worst headache you could imagine." Walter Moseley, *Blonde Faith*, 93.

112. The first Easy Rawlins novel takes place in the years after World War II, and the last takes place in 1967 when Easy is 47 years old.

113. John G. Cawelti, *Adventure, Mystery, and Romance: Formula Stories as Art and Popular Culture* (Chicago, IL: University of Chicago Press, 1977).

114. In a throw-away comment during a 1981 interview first published in *Essence*, Toni Morrison says that she thinks Black male writers "have been addressing white men when they write. And it's a legitimate confrontation—they're men telling white men what this is." Wilson, "A Conversation with Toni Morrison," in *Conversations with Toni Morrison*, 132. In his novels, although Mosley is speaking to an African American reading public too, he is also speaking to a much larger Euro-American—usually male—reading public. Walter Mosley's mysteries are steeped in machismo. In contrast, in her mystery series featuring a dark-skinned domestic named Blanche White, Barbara Neely updates the African American trickster as a woman rather than a man with a starring role for Queen Latifa rather than Denzel Washington.

115. In comparing him with heroes from earlier hardboiled popular fiction, Helen M. Whall even calls Easy "This *modern prophet*... [who] also struggles against the same moral decadence, political corruption, and police stupidity which failed to thwart Spade and Marlowe" (emphasis added). "Walter Mosley and the Books of Ezekiel," *Paradoxa: Studies in World Literary Studies* no. 16 (2001): 196.

116. Walter Mosley, *Devil in a Blue Dress* (New York: W. W. Norton, 1990; rpt. New York: Pocket Books, 1991), 97.

117. Walter Mosley, *The Best of NPR: Writers on Writing* (audiotape reissued in New York: Time Warner Audio Books, 1998). The interview with Mosley starts on Side 2 of the audiotape.

118. Ibid.

119. Many critics, for example, among the essayists featured in Owen E. Brady and Derek C. Maus's *Finding a Way Home: A Critical Assessment of Walter Mosley's Fiction* (Jackson, MI: University Press of Mississippi, 2008), argue who is the bad nigger, who takes on the badman role in Mosley's fiction. Although I lay out what I consider is a reasonable interpretation, I realize that others parse the trickster discourse in the novels differently.

120. George Tuttle, "What Is Noir?" *Mystery Scene* 43 (1994): 35+; "What Is Noir," http:noirfiction.info/what.html (accessed July 22, 2009); "Noir Fiction," www.geocities.com/SoHo/Suite/3855 (accessed July 22, 2009).

121. One of the essayists who explores the "fit" and "lack of fit" between the works of Mosley and writers such as Raymond Chandler, Dashiell Hammet, and John McDonald is Albert U. Turner, Jr., " At Home on 'These Mean Streets': Collaboration and Community in Walter Mosley's Easy Rawlins Mystery Series," 109–120, in Brady and Maus, *Finding a Way Home*.

122. Jerry H. Bryant, "Born in a Mighty Bad Land," 151.

123. Mosley often draws erudite, if self-taught, African American characters; his own ability to signify on the work of other African American writers reflects wide reading. His academic and early employment history includes a disparate background in political science, art, and computer programming before turning to writing. In 1991, Mosley received a MA in creative writing from City University of New York (CUNY). The same school later awarded him an honorary doctorate in Humane Letters.

124. Walter Mosley, *Fear Itself* (Boston, MA: Little, Brown and Company, 2003), 75.

125. Ernest Suarez, *Southbound*.

3   COYOTES AND OTHERS STRIVING FOR BALANCE

1. Even though the earliest written versions of American Indian oral tales were translated by Euro-Americans such as Henry Schoolcraft as well as Christian missionaries and though transcribers actually altered the stories by adding their own scrim of Euro-American values and understanding to the tales they wrote down and published, the emphasis on balance—the necessity to consider the good of the community as well as the self—remains such a universal and perduring value in the tales that I think it can be attributed to precontact culture. American Indian tricksters can be at once ludicrous and admirable. Their stories can also be warnings about what not to do. Thus, for example, listeners to oral tales may admire the inferior suitor who uses trickery to gain a wife but also laugh at his absurd self-absorption as he forgets the limitation of his trick and reveals himself as an imposter. American Indian tricksters are at once powerful and flawed. Louise Erdrich's Nanapush too can be cruel and is certainly self-serving; but he is still admired for using his trickery to save the remnant of the Pillagers in the persons of Fleur and then her daughter Lulu. Nanpush is enjoyed as a figure of fun and admired for his trickery: He is a culture hero. Yet his community recognizes that he is also flawed and dangerous.

NOTES 189

2. Sherman Alexie, *The Absolutely True Diary of a Part-Time Indian* (2007; rpt. New York: Little, Brown and Company, 2009), 173.
3. Franchot Ballinger, *Living Sideways: Tricksters in American Indian Oral Tradition* (Norman, OK: University of Oklahoma Press, 2004). 39.
4. Hartwig Isernhagen, *Momaday, Vizenor, Armstrong: Conversations on American Indian Writing* (Norman, OK: University of Oklahoma Press, 1999), 82.
5. Paula Gunn Allen, *Spider Woman's Granddaughters* (New York: Fawcett Columbine, 1989), 9.
6. Jarold Ramsey, *Coyote Was Going There* (Seattle, WA: University of Washington Press, 1977), xxxi.
7. Alan R. Velie, "Gerald Vizenor's Indian Gothic," *MELUS* 17 (1991): 79, suggests one explanation of the trickster's complicated nature by mentioning an Ojibwe tradition which says that the trickster Nanabozho was the son of a spirit and a mortal woman. But the trickster's complicated nature is, however, probably more attributable to his belonging to the time before humans walked the earth than simple ancestry.
8. Ballinger, *Living Sideways*, 21, argues that the real danger from the Indian Trickster is that he puts his ego, his self, before communal needs. In a culture that values an orderly social fabric and values community over individual needs, he is "an insider gone awry." In fact, "Trickster represents...a comic cautionary social image of potentially dangerous human behavior," 20.
9. Paula Gunn Allen, ed., *Spider Woman's Granddaughters*, 130–134.
10. Willliam Bright, *A Coyote Reader* (Berkeley, CA: University of California Press, 1993), 60–64.
11. Deward Walker, Jr., in collaboration with Daniel N. Matthews, *Nez Perce Coyote Tales: The Myth Cycle* (Norman, OK: University of Oklahoma Press, 1998), 135–138.
12. Roger L. Welsch, *Omaha Tribal Myths and Trickster Tales* (Chicago, IL: Sage Publications, 1981), 23–24.
13. Ibid., 63–65. Almost incidentally, the tale also explains why plums are covered with a gray haze. Ictinike has rubbed his semen on the plums.
14. Paul Radin, *The Trickster: A Study in American Indian Mythology* (1956. rpt. New York: Schocken, 1972), 53.
15. Penny Petrone, ed., *Northern Voices: Inuit Writing in English* (Toronto: University of Toronto Press, 1988), 52–54. A variant retelling of the tale, this time in a children's book, appears in Gerald McDermott's *The Raven: A Trickster Tale from the Pacific Northwest* (San Diego, CA: Harcourt Brace & Company, 1993).
16. Walker, *Nez Perce Coyote Tales: The Myth Cycle* (Norman, OK: University of Oklahoma Press, 1998), 124.

17. Bobby Lake-Thom (Medicine Grizzly Bear), *Spirits of the Earth: A Guide to Native American Nature Symbols, Stories, and Ceremonies* (New York: Plume Books, 1997), 74.
18. Malcolm Margolin, ed. *The Way We Lived: California Indian Stories, Songs and Reminiscences* (Berkeley, CA: Heyday Books, 1981; rev. 1993), 140.
19. Ibid., 147.
20. Ibid., 141.
21. While many writers list characteristics of the Indian trickster, David Walker, Jr., in *Nez Perce Coyote Tales*, 184, objects that one cannot generalize across many Indian cultures. What Walker does instead is draw a "descriptive interpretation of coyote's character" as can be inferred from Nez Perce Coyote tales. In defense of my generalizations, all I can do is acknowledge with others that although I realize that different tribes think of trickster energy in somewhat different ways, I still think some commonalities, such as the trickster's resilience and adaptability, emerge in an examination of multiple American Indian tales.
22. Larry Ellis, "Rabbit and Big Man-eater: Identity Shifts and Role Reversals in a Creek Indian Trickster Tale," *Thalia* 18, No. 1–2 (1998): 3–20.
23. Ibid., 9.
24. Ibid., 14.
25. In 2007, for example, Ellen Datlow and Terri Windling collected *The Coyote Road: Trickster Tales* (New York: Viking), bringing together tales drawing upon multiple traditions but written by contemporary writers.
26. My text is concentrating on literature—primarily literary, but also popular and oral literature. However, the "wry and ironic humour" of American Indians is literally visible in visual arts such as those reproduced in Allan J. Ryan's *The Trickster Shift* (Vancouver: University of British Columbia Press, 1999), xi. The appearance of the trickster Coyote is notably illustrative in Rebecca Belmore's "Coyote Woman, 1991," 65, Harry Fonseca's "Wish You Were Here, c. 1986," 160, Diego Romero's "Coyote and the Disciples of Vine Deloria J, American Highway Series, 1993," 260, and Harry Fonseca's pen and ink drawing of Coyote, 284. Yet all the prints in Ryan's book demonstrate similar approaches to/attitude toward American Indian history and current circumstances.
27. Clarissa Pinkola Estés, *Women Who Run with the Wolves* (New York: Ballantine Books, 1992), 340.
28. Peter Blue Cloud, *Elderberry Flute Song: Contemporary Coyote Tales* (Trumansburg, NY: Crossing Publication, 1982), 14.
29. Ibid., 113–115.
30. David Lee Smith, *Folklore of the Winnebago Tribe* (Norman, OK: University of Oklahoma Press, 1997), 40–41.

31. One of my students, whose ancestry is part Ho-Chunk, told me that when he was a child, at bedtime his father told him trickster tales as well as garden variety "Cinderella" tales.
32. Welsch, *Omaha Tribal Myths and Trickster Tales*, 19.
33. In her memoir, Wilma Mankiller also uses a tale about the Cherokee Rabbit to illustrate and make sense of her sense of displacement when as an adolescent, she moved with her family to San Francisco. Referring to her people's stories, she says, "Remembrances can be powerful teachers. When we return to our history, those strong images assist us in learning how not to make identical mistakes. Perhaps we will not always be doomed to repeat all of our history, especially the bad episodes," 78.
34. Among Barbara Babcock-Abrahams's list of characteristics for the tricksters is his tendency to "find their most abiding form of relationship with the feminine in a mother or grandmother bond." " 'A Tolerated Margin of Mess': The Trickster and his Tales Reconsidered," in *Critical Essays on Native American Literature*, ed. Ed. Andrew Wiget (Boston, MA: G.K. Hall, 1985), 163. For the most part, Thomas Builds the Fire fits this pattern.
35. As James Cox. "Muting White Noise: The Subversion of Popular Culture Narratives of Conquest in Sherman Alexie's Fiction," *Studies in American Indian Literature* 9, No. 4 (Winter 1997): 66, says, "Alexie revises the narratives from the perspective of the invaded, and the cultural conflict becomes a battle of stories, or more precisely, a battle between storytellers."
36. During the nineteenth and early twentieth centuries, the oral tales of American Indians had been written down and subtly, if unconsciously, altered by "people of good will" such as Henry Rowe Schoolcraft and a host of anthropologists. In the process, American Indians, relegated to the status of a "vanishing people," had ceased to represent "America"; but in Thomas Builds the Fire's (and Alexie's) stories, they take center stage and tell their own story.
37. Alexie's characters do need to cobble together their story. The Spokane/Coeur d'Alene Indians from the American Northwest in Sherman Alexie's work are the most contemporary of the American Indians examined in this chapter and seemingly more disassociated from their aboriginal cultures than most of the Indians in other texts. In fact, Alexie makes fun of a common assumption that modern American Indians are steeped in traditional culture. In his story, "Do You Know Where I Am?" *Ten Little Indians: Stories* (New York: Grove, 2003), 150–151, for example, Alexie has his narrator muse, "I suppose, for many Indians, garage sales and trashy novels are highly traditional and sacred." According to John Purdy, "Crossroads: A Conversation with Sherman Alexie," *Studies in American Indian Literatures* 9, No. 4 (Winter 1997), 13, Sherman Alexie insists that he has relatively weak ties to his traditional culture;

nonetheless, bedrock trickster lore remains engrained in his and his characters' psyches. In both fiction and poetry, Alexie consistently and wittily merges kitsch and traditional tricksters as his characters attempt to supply for the loss of an integrated cultural tradition that would help them deal with their losses. Watching Alexie trade jibes with Stephen Colbert on a video clip from a 2008 Colbert Report provides a quick illustration of Alexie's ability to be serious while he is apparently only joking around, www.colbertnation.com/the -colbert-report-videos/189691/october-28–2008/sherman-alexie.

38. Although Erdrich and Vizenor both have Ojibwe roots, they come at the trickster differently.

39. Gerald Vizenor was born in 1934. Leslie Marmon Silko in 1948, Louise Erdrich in 1954.

40. Among other essays, Laurie Ferguson's section in "Trickster Shows the Way: Humor, Resiliency, and Growth in Modern Native American Literature," PhD diss., Wright Institute Graduate School of Psychology, 2002, 109–119, is particularly insightful on "tricking the trickster."

41. Leslie Marmon Silko, *Ceremony* (New York: Viking, 1977; rpt. New York: Penguin, 1986), 254.

42. Ibid., 258.

43. A useful working definition of *witchery* in this context appears in Louis Owens's *Other Destinies* (Norman, OK: University of Oklahoma Press, 1992), 233–234, "the misuse of knowledge for the benefit of the individual alone rather than the community as a whole." Obviously, such an approach tears down the balance essential in community.

44. Gretchen Ronnow's essay, "Tayo, Death, and Desire: A Lacanian Reading of *Ceremony*," 69, appears in Gerald Vizenor's collection, *Narrative Chance: Postmodern Discourse on Native American Indian Literature* (Norman, OK: University of Oklahoma Press, 1993), 69–90.

45. In "Trickster Discourse: Comic and Tragic Themes in Native American Literature," in *Buried Roots and Indestructible Seeds*, ed. Mark A. Linquist and Martin Zanger (Madison, WI: The University of Wisconsin Press, 1994), 34, Vizenor says, "tribal cultures have been largely unimagined by the social scientists." Many other readers would also accept Laurie L. Ferguson's contention that until recent times, anthropologists in particular often missed the "spirituality, ritual, liveliness, social necessity and...unequivocal truth" of American Indian myths, "Trickster Shows the Way," 38.

46. Laura Coltelli, *Winged Words: American Indian Writers Speak* (Lincoln, NE: University of Nebraska Press, 1990), 161.

47. Ibid., 169.

48. Ibid., 170.

49. Vizenor, "Trickster Discourse," 196.
50. Gerald Vizenor, *The Trickster of Liberty: Tribal Heirs to a Wild Baronage* (Minneapolis, MN: University of Minnesota Press, 1988), x.
51. "Introduction," in *Narrative Chance*, 9.
52. Ibid., 13.
53. Vizenor, "Trickster Discourse," 187.
54. Ibid., 194.
55. Vizenor published an earlier version of *Bearheart* in 1978 as *Darkness in Saint Louis Bearheart*; but Elizabeth Blair, "Text as Trickster: Postmodern Language Games in Gerald Vizenor's *Bearheart*," *MELUS* 20 (1995): 5, believes that the later novel is more than a revision as it emphasizes "the continuity of the Native American struggle." Regardless of the changes from one text to the next—and Blair has laid these out meticulously, even exhaustively—as the last published *Bearheart* is the text discussed in this chapter. In any case, as Blair also notes, "Vizenor's oeuvre consists of a house of word mirrors in which passages and characters reappear from work to work, wearing distortions reminiscent of the fun house mirror," 7.
56. Coltelli, *Winged Words*, 180.
57. Gerald Vizenor, *Griever: An American Monkey King in China* (Normal, IL: Illinois State University Press, 1987), 3.
58. Ibid., 228.
59. Coltelli, *Winged Words*, 182.
60. Vizenor, *The Trickster of Liberty*, x and xviii.
61. Gerald Vizenor, *The Heirs of Columbus* (Hanover, NH: Wesleyan University Press, 1991), 126.
62. Relying heavily on Mikhail Bakhtin's concepts of chronotype, 123, polyglossia, 125, and interlocutor, 136, as well as Vizenor's own mythic verism, 131, and holotrope, 131—both terms found in "Trickster Discourse: Comic Holotropes and Language Games" from *Narrative Chance*, 187 and 200—in "The Trickster Novel," 121–140, in *Narrative Chance*, Alan Velie delineates ways in which *Darkness in St. Louis Bearheart* (and the later *Bearheart: The Heirship Chronicles*) uniquely blend traditional and postmodern forms. Paula Gunn Allen, *The Sacred Hoop* (Boston, MA: Beacon Press, 1986), 97, also believes that Vizenor "reconciles the opposing forces of good and evil" in his 13-pilgrim trickster and produces "the funniest and most brutal American Indian novel written."
63. Coltelli, *Winged Words*, 166.
64. Blaeser, "Trickster: A Compendium," *Buried Roots and Indestructible Seeds: The Survival of American Indian Life in Story, History, and Spirit.* Ed. Mark A. Lindquist and Martin Zanger (Madison, WI: The University of Wisconsin Press, 1994), 47–66, 185.
65. *Bearheart: The Heirship Chronicles* (Minneapolis, MN: University Minnesota Press, 1990), 9.

66. Vizenor, *Bearheart*, 15.
67. Isernhagen, *Momaday, Vizenor, Armstrong*, 125.
68. Vizenor, *Bearheart*, 217–218.
69. Isernhagen, *Momaday, Vizenor, Armstrong*, 132. Shortly later in the Isernlhagen interview, Vizenor says, "I think an enormous amount of violence takes place in Western civilization because it is aestheticized and disguised," 133.
70. In the "Afterword" to *Saint Louis Bearheart*, Louis Owens offers his definition of terminal creeds: "beliefs that seek to impose static definitions upon the world," *Bearheart*, 249.
71. Owens, *Other Destinies*, 229.
72. Kimberly M. Blaeser, *Gerald Vizenor: Writing in the Oral Tradition* (Norman, OK: University of Oklahoma Press, 1996), 170, suggests that Vizenor's use of allusion and symbolism—including symbolic names—offers "the reader a playful entrance into the text."
73. Vizenor, *Bearheart*, 118.
74. Paul Pasquaretta's essay, "Sacred Chance: Gambling and the Contemporary Native American Indian Novel," *MELUS* 21, No. 2 (1996): 21–33, effectively lays out ways in which tricksters—Proude, the hero of *Bearheart*, as well as Tayo in *Ceremony* and Lipsha in *Love Medicine*—use traditional Indian gaming to resist "the demands of colonial occupation," 21. Upon occasion, the "chance and uncertainty," 23, these tricksters face could easily annihilate them.
75. Vizenor, *Bearheart*, xiii.
76. Vizenor, *Darkness in Saint Louis Bearheart*, xiv.
77. Indian creation myths from the American Southwest feature a series of increasingly better, more recognizably human worlds as the creatures gain wisdom and understanding.
78. Since writing this cycle, Erdrich has continued to write fiction but focused instead on books for juveniles, such as the series in which *The Porcupine Year* appears, and exploration of emotional dramas such as *The Plague of Doves* (2008), *Shadow Tag* (2010), a tragic story about a mutually enabling couple moving toward the final wreckage of their marriage, and *The Round House* (2012), a novel about injustice and violence and, afterward, a family picking up the pieces of their lives. Even so, *The Porcupine Year* includes a couple of trickster tales, one explicitly about Nanabozho.
79. A matter-of-fact local news story, "Tribal Land to be Open to the Public," from the AP in the *Wisconsin State Journal*, A5, on December 29, 2011, includes the information that Red Cliff and the Apostle Islands are considered the hub of Ojibwe culture. But the 14,000-acre reservation, established in 1863, was distributed in parcels to tribal members by 1896 and became fragmented as original members lost properties. Today, the tribe and its members hold 8,000 acres within the reservation that stretches for 14 miles around the top of the Bayfield peninsula.

80. Erdrich, *The Last Report on the Miracles at Little No Horse* (New York: HarperCollins Publishers, 2001), 223.
81. Margaret Coel, *Killing Raven* (New York: Berkeley Books, 2003), 132.
82. Ibid., 349.
83. Susan Perez Castillo, "Postmodernism, Native American Literature, and the Real: The Silko-Erdrich Controversy," *The Massachusetts Review* 32, No. 2 (Summer 1991), notes the suggestion that the Adares' father might have been an American Indian; since Jack Mauser's mother came from June Kaspaw's reservation, *Tales of Burning Love*, 5, he too has Indian heritage. Presumably, Jack Mauser is a descendant of Fleur and the John James Mauser who bought the Ojibwe land after having its owners "declared incompetent," *The Last Report on the Miracles at Little No Horse*, 106. Jack Mauser is probably the son of the strange, soft, white "boy Fleur brought back to the reservation," *The Last Report on the Miracles at Little No Horse*, 261, presumably her unnamed son, *Four Souls*, 200. Jack's parents would be Awun, "Mist," Mauser, and Mary Kashpaw.
84. Catherine M. Catt, "Ancient Myth in Modern America: The Trickster in the Fiction of Louise Erdrich," *The Platte Valley Review* 19 (1991): 79.
85. Other common names for the trickster of the northern Midwest and Great Lakes region include Manabozho, Naanobohzo or Nanabozho, and Wenebojo or Winabojo. Presumably, the variant spellings reflect variant pronunciations as Euro-Americans wrote down what they thought they heard.
86. Louise Erdrich, *Tracks* (New York: HarperCollins Publishers, 1988), 113.
87. Ibid., 38.
88. Ibid., 48.
89. Louise Erdrich, *Four Souls* (New York: HarperCollins Publishers, 2004), 138.
90. By distributing Indian reservation lands via discrete parcels to individual tribesman, with the Dawes Severalty Act (Feb. 8, 1887), the US Congress attempted to turn nomadic Indians who thought in communal terms into individualist farmers. Originally sponsored by Senator Henry L. Dawes of Massachusetts, the act was finally passed in February of 1887. The act resembled most homesteader legislation; each head of a household was to receive 160 acres and each unmarried adult, 80 acres. No one could sell the land for 25 years. The act also made anyone who accepted an allotment a US citizen and thus subject to local, state, and federal laws. One reason it took several sessions to pass the act was that the bill needed the support of land speculators. They did support the bill after it included the caveat that land left over after allotments were made

could be sold at a public sale. Senator Dawes and his supporters intended to assimilate American Indians and help them to achieve a standard of living similar to that of Euro-American settlers. The bill's supporters did not, however, consider who was to receive an allotment. Nomadic Indians were unprepared to become farmers. Many were simply swindled out of their land. The hodgepodge of land acquisition broke up the continuity and communal nature of the reservation. By 1932, Euro-Americans had acquired two-thirds of the 138,000,000 acres Indians held in 1887. Returning home for a funeral, a character in *Love Medicine* (rev. ed. New York: HarperPerennial, 1993), 11, muses that, "The policy of allotment was a joke. As I was driving toward the land, looking around, I saw as usual how much of the reservation was sold to whites and lost forever."

91. Louise Erdrich, *Four Souls* (New York: HarperCollins Publishers, 2004), 180.

92. Erdrich, *Tracks*, 146.

93. Ibid., 177.

94. Ibid., 196.

95. Of Fleur's years in the Twin Cities pursuing revenge, Nanapush muses "Time is the water in which we live, and we breathe it like fish. It's hard to swim against the current. Onrushing, inevitable, carried like a leaf, Fleur fooled herself in thinking she could choose her direction. But time is an element no human has mastered and Fleur was bound to go where she was sent," *Four Souls*, 28. In *The Bingo Palace*, Fleur's grandson Lipsha, still another colossally gifted gambler, also suffers his most painful blunders when he overreaches.

96. Erdrich returns repeatedly to some characters. Nanapush is one of these. As her 2001 novel, *The Last Report on the Miracles at Little No Horse*, relates the last days of Nanapush, in *The Round House* (New York: Harper, 2012), 179–183, 184–187, 212–215, Erdrich inserts a series of tales told by old Mooshoom about Nanapush's formative early adolescence. An old buffalo woman has told him that he has survived by being contrary, and so Nanapush decides "that in all things he would be unpredictable. As he had completely lost trust in authority, he decided to stay away from others and to think for himself, even to do the ridiculous things that occurred to him," 214.

97. While the racism, cultural insensitivity, and alcoholism that continue to dog American Indians are also part of the novel's landscape, the central injustice perpetrated against the novels' Indian characters is the theft of their land. News stories continue to attest that the Chippewa/Ojibwe, in particular, associate the land as well as their oral and cultural traditions with their communal identity. A

1994 article in *The Progressive* (Tim King, "Native Americans Take Back Land," August 1994: 14), for example, featured Anishinabe (Ojibwe) efforts to recover land alienated from the tribe over a period of 50 years. A low point in their struggle occurred during the 1930s with the creation of the Tamarac Wildlife Refuge out of land that had been assured to the tribe by treaty. In recent years, Wisconsin papers regularly have run stories concerning tribal efforts to assert the fishing and gathering rights ceded to tribes during the nineteenth century. For most contemporary Euro-Americans, moving is an ordinary way of life. The first Anglo-Americans called themselves pilgrims, and most of their spiritual descendants continue to be more commonly sojourners than settled. Familiar statistics note that most Americans average at least five different jobs during their working careers and move residences even more often. The man or woman who stays in the same town all of his or her life is the exception rather than the rule. All of this mitigates against a close attachment to the land. American Indian culture, on the other hand, identifies the people with the land. In Erdrich's novels, losing the land serves as a root evil to which many later evils can be traced. Erdrich herself writes of "people and place" being "inseparable" in traditional culture, "Where I Ought to Be: A Writer's Sense of Place," *New York Times Book Review* (July 28, 1985), sec. 7:1; thus, to lose one's place is to lose one's self. Erdrich also refers to Eudora Welty's speculation that people who lack a sense of place may also lose much of their human response to events, "Where I Ought to Be," 23. Since American Indians have lost so much—land; language; relatives killed by alcoholism, disease, or violence, for example—Erdrich sees the role of contemporary American Indian writers as having to connect the "core of the cultures"—such as the trickster tradition—and the "stories of contemporary survivors." Louise Erdrich, "Where I Ought to Be," 23.

98. Louise Erdrich, *The Bingo Palace* (New York: HarperCollins Publishers, 1994), 139.
99. Ibid., 143.
100. Erdrich, *Four Souls*, 197.
101. Ibid., 46.
102. Ibid., 46.
103. Erdrich, *The Bingo Palace*, 145.
104. Ibid., 221.
105. Ibid., 272.
106. Louise Erdrich, *Love Medicine* (1984; rpt. New York: Bantam Books, 1989), 83. Unless otherwise noted, page numbers refer to the original (1984) edition of *Love Medicine*.
107. From *The Beet Queen*, readers recognize Jude Miller as Mary and Karl Adare's younger brother who was also abandoned by their

mother but then raised by a childless Euro-American couple in St. Paul. Weaving characters through the novels, Erdrich achieves the pattern of interconnectedness that Gerry Nanapush espies in the universe, *The Bingo Palace* (New York: HarperCollins Publishers, 1994), 226.

108. Although biologically Lulu is the child of Fleur and Eli (or one of the rapists or just maybe the powerful water spirit Misshepeshu), Lulu's birth certificate lists Nanapush as her father.

109. Louise Erdrich, *Love Medicine* (1984; rpt. New York: Bantam Books, 1989), 221.

110. Kimberly Blaeser, "Trickster: A Compendium," 52.

111. Erdrich, *Love Medicine* (rev. ed. New York: HarperPerennial, 1993), 80.

112. Ibid., 201.

113. Ibid., 200.

114. Ibid., 201.

115. Ibid., 202.

116. Erdrich, *The Bingo Palace*, 226.

117. Generally a foolish trickster, Lipsha also is a notable gambler—winning at bingo and cards, saving his father, but often wrecking his own good fortune by overreaching.

118. Louise Erdrich, *Love Medicine* (1984; rpt. New York: Bantam Books, 1989), 362.

119. Katrina Schimmoeller Peiffer, *Coyote at Large: Humor in American Nature Writing* (Salt Lake City, UT: University of Utah Press, 2000), 4.

120. A folk group, according to Alan Dundes, quoted in Karen E. Beardslee, *Folklore Foundations: Selfhood and Cultural Tradition in Nineteenth- and Twentieth-Century American Literature.* (Knoxville, TN: The University of Tennessee Press, 2001), xvii–xviii, is "any group of people whatsoever who share at least one common factor," such as a common occupation, language, or religion. Agnes/Damien comes to share multiple "dynamic interactions" with the Ojibwe.

121. Louise Erdrich, *The Last Report on the Miracles at Little No Horse* (New York: HarperCollins Publishers, 2001), 135.

122. As Nancy Peterson notes in "Indi'n Humor and Trickster Justice in *The Bingo Palace,*" *The Chippewa Landscape of Louise Erdrich*, ed. Allan Chavkin (Tuscaloosa, AL: University of Alabama Press, 1999), 163–166, what she calls "Indi'n humor" goes beyond the tragic romanticism of often sentimental nineteenth-century fiction to demand redress for injustices. Seen in this light, Indian gaming offers one means of leveling historic imbalances. John S. Slack, "The Comic Savior: The Dominance of the Trickster in Louise Erdrich's *Love Medicine,*" *North Dakota Quarterly* 61 (1993): 119, even sees Erdrich's trickster characters as "comic savior[s]," who

preserve the "very human, humorous side of life." So many critics note that this aspect of Erdrich's work has become a truism. For example, Katrina Schimmoeller Peiffer in *Coyote at Large: Humor in American Nature Writing* (Salt Lake City, UT: University of Utah Press, 2000), ix, categorizes Erdrich as a "comic moralist"; and Sharon Manybeads Bowers, "Louise Erdrich as Nanapush," in *New Perspectives on Women and Comedy*, ed. Regina Barreca (Philadelphia, PA: Gordon, 1992), 140, mentions the important link between humor and critical commentary because "Humor is the social sanction to look at things differently." In an interview, Hertha D. Wong, "An Interview with Louise Erdrich and Michael Dorris," *The North Dakota Quarterly* 55 (1987): 214, Erdrich herself has linked humor and what some of her critics found "devastating" moments.

123. Erdrich, *Four Souls*, 210.

4   Trickster Seeking His Fortune

1. Peter Edelman, *So Rich, So Poor: Why It's So Hard to End Poverty in America* (New York: The New Press, 2012) focuses on the increasing income disparities American citizens have witnessed since the 1970s and how the current economy has held down wage growth for the lower half of America's workers, including Euro-Americans. Edelman's attitude is encapsulated in an introductory statement: "The American economy did not stagnate over the past forty years: it grew, but the fruits of that growth went to those at the top," xvii. He argues that government policies have battered lower economic classes in the United States; even though this harm has fallen disproportionately on people with darker skins, even Euro-Americans have lost 16 percent of their median wealth during, for example, the downturn between 2005 and 2009, Edelman, 25. Charles Murray, *Coming Apart: The State of White America, 1960–2010* (New York: Crown Forum, 2012), looks at the growing separation during the last half century of Euro-American upper and lower classes and how, he believes, core behaviors and values among the two groups have contributed to increasing economic inequality. Murray believes that since the early 1960s, Euro-Americans have lost the sense that— across class, gender, and social lines—theirs is common enterprise. But both scholars start from the real economic and social looses suffered by numbers of Euro-Americans since 1960.

2. Folklorists categorize many European trickster tales as *märchen* or magical wonder tales. Although sometimes called fairy tales, neither folk nor literary *märchen* necessarily feature fairies; they do, however, feature marvels and enchantment. Some of the characters or objects in *märchen* are endowed with magic or supernatural

powers. These are the stories some of us listened to during "story hour" when we were small children. "Cinderella" is a märchen; so is *The Wizard of Oz*.

3. Murray, *Coming Apart*, 12.

4. Daniel S. Traber, *Whiteness, Otherness, and the Individualism Paradox from Huck to Punk* (New York: Palgrave Macmillan, 2007), 2, further confines the dominant group to "straight white males (the group poised to benefit the most from the status quo)." Bolstering his contention that white people are "the group consistently named as the dominant culture's self-anointed arbiters of Culture and Truth," 12, Traber goes on to quote Richard Dyer's *White* (New York: Routledge, 1997), 10, that " 'the right not to conform, to be different and get away with it is the right of the most privileged groups in society' who 'depend upon an implicit norm of whiteness' to rebel against," 13.

5. Sarah Delany and A. Elizabeth Delany with Amy Hill Hearth, *Having Our Say: The Delany Sisters' First 100 Years* (New York: Kodansha International, 1993), 11.

6. Ralph Ellison, *Shadow and Act*, 54.

7. Ibid., 56.

8. Quoted in Winifred Morgan, *An American Icon: Brother Jonathan and American Identity* (Newark, DE: University of Delaware Press, 1988), 139. The cartoonist may also be poking a subtle jab at Jonathan's ignorance of the earth's circumference. Even in Connecticut, a traveler going either east or west would have to circumnavigate closer to 18,000 than a 1,000 miles around the globe. So the American know-it-all making fun of the English traveler is himself not quite as knowledgeable as he thinks. (At the equator, the earth's circumference is 24,859 miles. At Massachusetts and Connecticut—presumably the traveler is moving to either to the east or west—the earth is 18, 820.5 miles around.)

9. In *How to Tell a Story and Other Essays* (New York: Harper & Brothers, 1897), 8, Twain says,

> To string incongruities and absurdities together in a wandering and sometimes purposeless way, and seem innocently unaware that they are absurdities, is the basis of the American art…Another feature is the slurring of the point. A third is the dropping of a studied remark apparently without knowing it, as if one were thinking aloud. The fourth and last is the pause.

The speaker or writer who follows Twain's directions is a trickster and, though not invariably, his tales are often trickster tales.

10. Nell Irvin Painter, *The History of the White Race* (New York: W. W. Norton, 2010). Painter shows that while the term *race* is a misnomer, over the last 500 years or so, supported by historical hegemony

and pseudo-science, white skin has come to be associated with beauty and intelligence.

11. Hyde, *Trickster Makes This World*, 227.

12. Elizabeth Ammons, "Introduction," *Tricksterism in Turn-of-the Century American Literature: A Multicultural Perspective* (Hanover, NH: University Press of America, 1994), ix.

13. Ammons speaks of tricksters and trickster energy serving to "articulate a whole order, [an] independent cultural reality and a positive way of negotiating multiple cultural systems" so that members of a minority population can "pull together conflicting world views and sets of values into coherent, new identit[ies]," xi.

14. Hyde, *Trickster Makes This World*, 7.

15. Richard M. Dorson, *American Folklore* (Chicago, IL: University of Chicago Press, 1959), 61.

16. Ibid., 132.

17. Consider, for example, the ongoing popularity of the *Ocean's Eleven* franchise and the 2012 Academy Award winner *Argo*.

18. Paul V. A.Williams *The Fool and the Trickster: Studies in Honour of Enid Welsford*, ed. Paul V. A. Williams (Totowa, NJ: Rowman & Littlefield, 1979), 1, says, "One thing is clear: the fool, whoever and whatever he is, is not merely foolish, and the trickster does more than trick."

19. Despite the challenge in tracing popular culture tricksters to oral roots, an unpublished 1965 Master's thesis demonstrates ties that several of the popularizers of the Brother Jonathan persona—the most frequently used name for the Yankee peddler—had with John Wesley Jarvis, a witty ante-bellum American painter and raconteur known for his stories about Yankee peddlers and tricksters. Joseph John Arpad, "David Crockett: An Original," MA Thesis (Iowa City, IA: University of Iowa, 1965), 36–39. In addition, H. E Dickson, "A Note on Charles Mathews' Use of American Humor," *American Literature* 12 (1940): 78–83, also shows that at least one stage Yankee, a comedian named Charles Mathews, was indebted to Jarvis for at least part of his repertoire of American sketches.

20. Traditional oral tales about a character called Jack surface in Virginia, West Virginia, Tennessee, Kentucky, Pennsylvania, New York, Missouri, and Arkansas, but these disparate tales lack the coherence of the Beech Mountain tales first published in Richard Chase's 1943 collection, *The Jack Tales* (Boston, MA: Houghton Mifflin, 1943). Whether or not Chase's collection reflects a larger collection of coherent tales remains arguable. See also William Bernard McCarthy, ed., *Jack in Two Worlds: Contemporary North American Tales and Their Tellers* (Chapel Hill, NC: University of North Carolina Press, 1994), xxi.

21. Dan Piraro, "While Jack Makes a Fortune Stealing from the Giant, His Neighbors Live in Terror of Falling Beans," *Bizarro. Wisconsin State Journal* (Madison) (August 31, 2003). Comics.
22. Wiley Miller, *Non Sequitur. Wisconsin State Journal* (Madison) (March 28, 2004). Comics, 2. Less clearly tied to Jack, in a popular series of comic strips, the not fully socialized—or perhaps not happily socialized—trickster child in every human being also flowers into Bill Watterson's comic strip trickster Calvin in *Calvin and Hobbes.*
23. William Bernard McCarthy, ed., *Jack in Two Worlds*, xiv, xxxii, 8, 60.
24. Donald Davis, *Jack Always Seeks His Fortune: Authentic Appalachian Jack Tales* (Little Rock: August House, 1992), 163–177.
25. Ibid., 65–72.
26. As a number of sources, including Henry Glassie, "Three Southern Mountain Jack Tales," *Tennessee Folklore Society Bulletin* 30 (1964): 82, 83, note, several ethnic groups settled in the Appalachian Mountains; the Jack Tales represent a merging of multiple traditions especially Scotch-Irish and German traditions, but also French and, of course, British traditions. As early as 1939, Richard Chase notes parallels to Jack Tales in Germanic sources, "The Origin of 'The Jack Tales,' " *Southern Folklore Quarterly* 3 (1939): 190–192. W. F. H. Nicolaisen titles his essay "English Jack and American Jack," *Midwestern Journal of Language and Folklore* 4 (1978): 27, as he compares two traditions from English-speaking parts of Europe. Implying a single national source, an early journal presents the text of three versions of "How Jack Went to Seek His Fortune" and is titled "English Folk-Tales in America," *Journal of American Folklore* 2, No. 6 (1889): 213. H. Pomeroy Brewster authored the following essay, "The House that Jack Built," 209–212, so presumably, he is the collector of the three versions. Carl Lindahl notes in William Bernard McCarthy' collection, *Jack in Two Worlds*, xvii, that multiple English, Scottish, and Irish "streams" fed into American Jack Tales.
27. Nonetheless, as C. Paige Gutierrez points out, in the Beech Mountain tales she examined, Jack's success in half of the Jack Tales depends on magic rather than "trickery and quick-thinking," "The Definition of a Folk Tales Sub-Genre," *North Carolina Folklore Journal* 26 (1978): 98.
28. Glassie, 82.
29. "Jack and His Lump of Silver," 25–26, in Charles L. Perdue, Jr.'s *Outwitting the Devil: Jack Tales from Wise County, Virginia* (Santa Fe, NM: Ancient City Press, 1987).
30. Richard M. Dorson, *Burying the Wind: Regional Folklore in the United States* (Chicago, IL: University of Chicago Press, 1964), 173.

31. In fact, weighing heavily on Jungian archetypal symbolism, Charles Thomas Davis, III, in "Jack as Archetypal Hero," *North Carolina Folklore* (Raleigh) 26, No. 2 (1978): 134, finds "cosmic and psychological dimensions" in the Jack Tales.
32. Davis, *Jack Always Seeks His Fortune*, 133–148.
33. McCarthy, *Jack in Two Worlds*, xxvii.
34. Joan N. Radner, "AFS Now and Tomorrow: The View from the Stepladder: AFS Presidential Address, October 28, 2000, *Journal of American Folklore* 114 (453): 275.
35. Chase, *The Jack Tales*, 67–75.
36. Ibid., 75.
37. Perdue, Jr., *Outwitting the Devil*, 119–131.
38. The Jack of this and other tales is still another trickster whose closest connection is to an older woman.
39. Despite Daniel Traber's contention, 3, that "self-interest grows into a reigning principle," only during the Gilded Age, it is already at least implicit in the Jack Tales.
40. Although only a couple of examples are reprinted here, my *An American Icon* provides ample further illustration of this point.
41. Royall Tyler, *The Contrast* (Philadelphia, PA: Pritchard & Hall, 1790) (rpt. New York: The Dunlap Society, 1887), 44.
42. Quotd. in Morgan, *American Icon*, 134.
43. William E. Lenz, *Fast Talk and Flush Times: The Confidence Man as a Literary Convention* (Columbia, M: University of Missouri Press, 1985), 1.
44. While shelves of information on the humor engendered by the tricksters of the Old Southwest exist, an abbreviated but accurate summary from a Washington State University site posted by Donna Campbell can be found at http://public.wsu.edu/~campbelld/amlit/swhumor.htm (accessed January 4, 2013). A further, more extensive site, created by John Molinaro and posted on the University of Virginia's Crossroad's site can be found at http://xroads.virginia.edu/~HYPER/DETOC /sw/front.html (accessed January 4, 2013).
45. Lenz, *Fast Talk and Flush Times*, 1.
46. Lenz, 59, speaks of the period from about 1830 through 1861 being a "literary high tide" of the confidence man in the Old Southwest with a "particular imaginative matrix," 64, emerging in the 1840s.
47. Kenneth S. Lynn. *Mark Twain and Southwestern Humor* (Boston, MA: Little, Brown and Company), 1959, 27.
48. Lenz, *Fast Talk and Flush Times*, 116.
49. Lynn, *Mark Twain and Southwestern Humor*, 85.
50. Joseph G. Baldwin, *The Flush Times of Alabama and Mississippi: A Series of Sketches* (New York: D. Appleton & Company, 1854), 139.
51. Lenz, *Fast Talk and Flush Times*, 93. In page 92, Lenz notes that critics of the period viewed Suggs as "a new stable form...a literary convention."

52. George Washington Harris, "Mrs. Yardley' Quilting," 72, in *Sut Lovingood: Yarns Spun* [*by a "Nat'ural Born Durn'd Fool"*], 1846 (rpt. Whitefish, MT: Kessinger Publishing, n.d.).
53. Harris, "Sicily Burn's Wedding," 43, in *Sut Lovingood*.
54. Lynn, *Mark Twain and Southwestern Humor*, 131.
55. For example, in "The Corn Cob Pipe: A Tale of the Comet of '43," Dr O. B. Mayer's 1848 tale, 117–131, in *Fireside Tales: Stories of the Old Dutch Fork*, edited by James Everett Kibler Jr. (Columbia, SC: Dutch Fork Press, 1984), Nancy Happerduckes is being courted by an Ichabod Crane-like suitor whom her father at first prefers. Nancy, rather than her preferred suitor Habakkuk Trummel, engineers her father's approval of the match she wants.
56. Augustus Baldwin Longstreet, *Georgia Scenes: Characters, Incidents, etc. in the First Half Century of the Republic* (1835; rpt. New York: Sagamore Press, 1954), 21.
57. Lynn, *Mark Twain and Southwestern Humor*, 148.
58. Harris, "Parson John Bullen's Lizards," 22–29, in *Sut Lovingood*. Sut, "a poor innersent youf," 22, gets in trouble with Parson Bullens for finding a quiet shady place to "converse" with a girl; so he gets back at the parson by letting lizards up Bullen's legs during a meeting and embarrassing the grossly fat preacher who disrobes in front of his congregation in order to get rid of the lizards. The description of the camp meeting is memorable. Parson Bullen is perhaps the same "Ole Bullen" who tints his white lightning with run-off from his barn.
59. Johnson Jones Hooper, *Some Adventures of Capt. Simon Suggs* (1848; rpt. Upper Saddle River, NJ: Literature House, 1970), 12.
60. Carolyn See, "Book World: Characters of Every Stripe," rev. of *Crazy in Alabama* by Mark Childress. *Washington Post* (August 27, 1994): C2.
61. Dorie Larue, rev. of "*Crazy in Alabama*," *Southern Quarterly* 32, No. 2 (Winter 1994): 161.
62. Mark Childress says that he thinks of himself as a storyteller rather than an "Artist," Bill Caton, *Fighting Words: Words on Writing from 21 of the Heart of Dixie's Best Contemporary Authors* (Montgomery, AL: Black Belt Publishers, 1995), 39. As a storyteller, Childress falls heir to the Southern oral tradition that has always included a strong admixture of trickster exaggeration.
63. Clyde Edgerton, *Walking across Egypt*. (Chapel Hill, NC: Algonquin Books; rpt. New York: Ballantine Books, 1987), 167.
64. W. Todd Martin makes the case that Edgerton's protagonists have a lover's quarrel with Southern Baptists as the tricksters force "other characters…to confront the limitations of their views," "Where Trouble Sleeps: Clyde Edgerton's Criticism of Moralistic Christianity" *Renascence* 53 (2001): 260, because these characters' views focus on respectability rather than—to paraphrase Isaiah

6:10—turning their hearts to be healed. Any biblical reference in this text is from *The New English Bible*.
65. Clyde Edgerton, *Killer Diller* (Chapel Hill, NC: Algonquin Books; rpt. New York: Ballantine Books, 1992), 188.
66. Ibid., 241.
67. William Nelson, "The Comic Grotesque in Recent Fiction," *Thalia* (Ottawa, Ontario) 5, No. 2 (Fall, Winter 1982).
68. "Redeeming Blackness: Urban Allegories of O'Connor, Percy and Toole." *Studies in the Literary Imagination* 27, No. 2 (Fall 1994): 29–40.
69. According to *Publishers Weekly,* each of those copies now sell for $2,000 in the rare book market, Bob Summer, "Honoring Dunces," *Publishers Weekly* (March 20, 2000): 23. A more recent blog from *The Chronicle of Higher Education* carries a story that quotes Mary Katherine Callaway, the director of LSU Press, who spells out just how well the novel has done for the press. "The novel is, quite simply, a phenomenon. It has sold steadily since its first year, spurred on by winning the Pulitzer Prize for Fiction in 1981, and by word of mouth from countless readers…Today, the press continues to sell the book in hardcover and large-print hardcover editions, and we have licensed translations in over 26 languages, as well as English paperback, audio, and e-book editions." " 'A Confederacy of Dunces,' Still Strong at 30," http://chronicle.com/blogPost /A-Confederacy-of-Dunces/24140/?sid+at&utm_source=at&utm _medium=en (accessed May 21, 2010).
70. *A Confederacy of Dunces* (Baton Rouge: Louisiana State Press, 1980), vi.
71. Toole wrote his MA Thesis on John Lyly's sixteenth-century *Euphues*, a text known for its ornate convoluted prose, and presumably enjoyed parodying the style in Reilly's pretentious "pensées."
72. Ken Kesey, *One Flew over the Cuckoo's Nest* (New York: Viking Press, 1962; rpt. New York: Penguin Books, 2003), 13.
73. Barbara Babcock might see McMurphy's growth into a tragic figure as a normal progression as in the Winnebago [Ho-Chunk] cycle where the trickster also grows and integrates into society, " 'A Tolerated Margin of Mess': The Trickster and His Tales Reconsidered," Andrew Wiget, ed., *Critical Essays on Native American Literature.* (Boston, MA: G. K. Hall, 1985), 178–179. In the Winnebago cycle she analyzes, Babcock finds a "process of increasing biological, psychic, and social awareness" leading to a character who is "almost thoroughly socialized." This process also reflects, according to Babcock, the human need to learn through experimentation.
74. Kesey, *One Flew over the Cuckoo's Nest*, 13.
75. Although critics sometimes employ words such as savior and Christ-figure with reference to McMurphy, the scaffolding for the argument

feels shakey. Nonetheless, he does become a pathmaker, showing Chief Bromden and the other men how to alter their lives.
76. Kesey, *One Flew over the Cuckoo's Nest*, 279.
77. Henry David Thoreau, 1849, "On the Duty of Civil Disobedience," in *Walden; and Civil Disobedience*. (New York: Penguin Books, 1983). "If...the machine of government...is of such a nature that it requires you to be the agent of injustice to another, then, I say, break the law."
78. Wolfe reflects this aim when he says, "I have tried not only to tell what the Pranksters did but to re-create the mental atmosphere or subjective reality of it." *The Electric Kool-Aid Acid Test* (New York: Farrar, Straus and Giroux, 1968; rpt. New York: Bantam Books, 1969), 371.
79. Ibid., 114.
80. Kevin T. McEneaney, *Tom Wolfe's America: Heroes, Pranksters, and Fools* (Westport, CT: Praeger, 2009), 52, finds among other, lesser effects, three principal cultural effects brought about by the Pranksters: "The revitalization of Western pop music through the creation of acid rock, the creation of unusual dramatic happenings known as the Acid Tests which influence popular theater of the period, and the spiritual attention upon Eastern wisdom as a prophetic indication of what the future holds."
81. McEneaney, *Tom Wolfe's America*, 33, also notes the ways in which "freak" and "freaky" have come to be used as the Pranksters used the words.
82. Bolstered by Larry McMurty's recollection, Kevin T. McEneaney, 31, recounts a more nuanced explanation of the incident.
83. Ellison, *Shadow and Act*, 57.
84. The reviewers such as Philip Marchand, "John Irving: Author with an Attitude: No Apology for Writing Another Long and Involved Novel," *The Toronto Star*, Final Edition, August 28, 1994, Spotlight, B1, who admire Irving's Dickensian plot, characters, and "socially significant details" have no problem with the adjective; and Irving himself, mentions in his "notes," *A Son of the Circus* (New York: Random House, 1994), vii, that he spent more than four years working on the novel. In his review, Philip Marchand credits Irving with giving five years and five months to the novel.
85. Sean Piccoli, "John Irving's "Circus' Goes to Strange and Funny Places," *The Washington Times* (September 18, 1994). Final Edition, Part B, Books, 88.
86. One might argue, of course, that while John Irving is a Euro-American, his character is not. Nonetheless, *A Son of the Circus* is a Euro-American novel; his characters are crafted by the author's frame of reference.
87. Complicating what might otherwise be a fairly straightforward trickster tale, Bellow draws upon his Jewish heritage and makes the story

at once humorous and thoughtful. Bellow himself characterized Jewish literature as "so curiously mingl[ing] laughter and trembling that it is not easy to determine the relations of the two." Ruth R. Wisse, "Jewish American Renaissance," *The Cambridge Companion to Jewish American Literature*, ed. Michael P. Kramer and Hana Wirth-Nesher (Cambridge, UK: Cambridge University Press, 2003), 204, rpt. from "Introduction," *Great Jewish Short Stories*, 12. This quotation has been rearranged. First published in *The New Yorker* (September 25, 1978), "The Silver Dish" is reprinted in Bellow's short-story collection, *Him with His Foot in His Mouth* (1984).

88. Nathan Ausubel, *A Treasury of Jewish Humor* (Garden City, NY: Doubleday & Company, Inc.), xvi.
89. Ibid., xvii.
90. Ibid., 381. Thanks to Professor Henry Sapoznik, I found these definitions of *schmiggege* in Leo Rosten's *The Joys of Yiddish* (New York: Pocket Books/Washington Square Press, 1968), 358: "1. An unadmirable, petty person, 2. A maladroit, untalented type, 3. A sycophant, a shlepper, a whiner, a drip."
91. Ausubel, *A Treasury of Jewish Humor*, 381–382.
92. Saul Bellow, "A Silver Dish," *Him with His Foot in His Mouth and Other Short Stories* (New York: Harper, 1984), 205.
93. Ibid., 222.
94. Ibid., 193.
95. Ibid., 193.
96. Ibid., 196.
97. Ibid., 216.
98. Could Woody's full first name be Woodrow—an ironic glance at an American President known for his sometimes self-defeating rectitude?
99. Bellow, *Him with His Foot in His Mouth and Other Short Stories*, 217.
100. Richard Chase, "Jack and the Varmits," *The Jack Tales* (Boston, MA: Houghton Mifflin, 1943), 58–66. The Jack tale, in turn, recalls a number of English folk tales such as the one about the little tailor who killed seven (flies) at once and became a successful hero. http://fairytales4u.com/story/sevenat.htm (accessed January 30, 2012).
101. Elmore Leonard, *Pagan Babies* (New York: Delacorte Press, 2000), 263.

5 HEIRS OF THE MONKEY KING

1. Since the bulk of Asian immigration to the United States has occurred since the McCarran-Walter Act of 1952 eliminated race as a barrier to immigration, and national quotas were ended in 1965, facilitating Asian immigration, at this time much of Asian-American literature is still, de facto, immigrant literature.

2. When, for instance, a local Madison, Wisconsin, daily newspaper decided to feature a series retelling an Asian trickster story for children, it retold the first part of the Monkey King's adventures. *Wisconsin State Journal*, Madison, January 25, 2010–May 17, 2010.

3. Sau-ling Cynthia Wong, *Reading Asian American Literature: From Necessity to Extravagance* (Princeton, NJ: Princeton University Press, 1993), 5.

4. Ibid., 7. Wong further insists that their "subsumption of identity as Chinese, Filipino, Korean, Japanese, etc. in a larger pan-Asian identity has to be *voluntarily adopted* and highly *context-sensitive* in order to work," 6.

5. Sau-ling Cynthia Wong and Stephen H. Sumida, eds., *A Resource Guide to Asian American Literature* (New York: Modern Language Association of American, 2001), 6.

6. Elaine H. Kim, "Foreword," in *Reading the Literatures of Asian America*, Shirley Geok-lin Lim and Amy Ling, eds. (Philadelphia, PA: Temple University Press, 1992), xii. Kim goes on to further note that "class, gender, sexual orientation, national origin, nativity, place of residence, generation, and so forth" have been also ignored by a dominant American culture that lumps *all* Asians and Asian Americans together.

7. As Jennifer Gonzalez notes in a *Chronicle of Higher Education* article, "Asian-American and Pacific Islander Students Are Not Monolithically Successful, Report Says," June 27, 2011 (accessed June 29, 2011) http://chronicle.com/article/Asian-AmericanPacif ic/128061/?sid+pm&utm_source+p&utm_medium+em. In fact, while four-fifths of East and South Asians who enter college go on to earn at least a bachelor's degree, 55–66 percent of all adults have not attended any form of postsecondary education; and Southeast Asians and Pacific Islanders are particularly less likely to attend college or to persist to graduation. Given the tie between education and financial rewards, these numbers are significant.

8. Chinese laborers were often allotted jobs dealing with explosives, for example, since no one worried too much when they were maimed or died during the frequent blasting accidents.

9. This is not a universal, of course, as Robert G. Lee's *Orientals: Asian Americans in Popular Culture* (Philadelphia, PA: Temple University Press, 1998), illustrates in detail. See, in particular, Chapter Three, 83–104, "The Third Sex."

10. So Sax Rohmer's Fu Manchu stood in for all mysterious and dangerous Oriental villains. In a parallel development, the Charlie Chan movies and Hollywood comedies featuring ludicrous Asian servants popularized the notion that Asian American men were smart enough to handle limited and carefully defined tasks but for the most part docile and lacking sexual threat. In fact, before World War II, the tendency was to portray Asian males "as witless, sexless,

NOTES 209

and therefore harmless." James S. Moy in Shirley Geok-lin Lim and
Amy Ling, *Reading the Literatures of Asian America* (Philadelphia,
PA: Temple University Press, 1992), 352. This stereotype persisted
in popular culture through at least the first half of the twentieth
century. Colleen Lye, *America's Asia: Facial Form and American
Literature, 1893–1945* (Princeton, NJ: Princeton University Press
2004), 11, even argues that the Asian stereotypes found in early
twentieth-century American literature depicting individuals in
terms of some *part* of who they were—for example, the type of
work they did—fed into "today's stereotypical Asian American."
This perception has changed only in recent years. In 2006, *USA
Today* writer Ann Oldenburg still considered it newsworthy when
an Asian American actor on the television show *Lost* emerged as
a sex symbol. Ann Oldenburg, "Kim Surfaces as Sex Symbol on
Lost," *USA Today* (March 22, 2006), Life, 1d. In contrast, from
the start Asian females were seen as sexually seductive. Few Asian
women were allowed into the United States until after World War
II, and many early Asian American women immigrants were forced
into prostitution. Amy Ling, *Between Worlds: Women Writers of
Chinese Ancestry* (New York: Pergamon Press, 1990), 13. Aware
of the potency in these popular culture perceptions, in *Tripmaster
Monkey: His Fake Book* (1989; rpt., New York: Vintage, 1990), 299,
Maxine Hong Kingston builds upon this past when she mockingly
quotes a Kiplingesque foray into Chinatown.

11. As Robert G. Lee, notes, 146 and 150+, designating Asian
Americans as the model minority offered a certain convenience to
the dominant culture bothered by obstreperous demands by African
Americans, for example, and men and women who were advocating
for more open ways of dealing with gender roles.

12. Zeng Li, "Diasporic Self, Cultural Other: Negotiating Ethnicity
through Transformation in the Fiction of Tan and Kingston,"
Language and Literature 28 (2003): 7.

13. As Anthony C. Yu makes clear in the introduction to his four-volume translation of *The Journey to the West* (Chicago, IL: University
of Chicago Press, 1977), I, 21, Wu Ch'êng-ên's authorship is at
most probable; however, "despite scholarly objection to date," that
attribution "remain[s] the most likely."

14. Anthony C. Yu, "Introduction," I: 279.

15. Although *The Journey to the West* is pure fantasy, Hsüan-tsang was
a historical figure who lived from 596 to 664 and did journey—as
did several other Buddhist monks—from China to India. After an
even longer period of time than the 14-year pilgrimage related in
the *Journey* of Wu Ch'êng-ên's T'ang monk, the historical Hsüan-
tsang returned to China with many Buddhist scriptures.

16. Anthony C. Yu, I: 262. This attitude certainly accords with Francis
L. K. Hsu's contention, *American and Chinese: Two Ways of Life*

(New York: H. Schuman, 1953), 239, that—at least before the Communist revolution—Chinese attitudes toward religion were fundamentally polytheistic. Nonetheless, not all religions are valued equally: Muslims, for example, are lumped together among "barbarians, Muslims, tigers, wolves, and leopards," bothersome adversaries the pilgrims have to contend with on their pilgrimage. Anthony C. Yu, I: 329.

17. Shu-yan Li, "Otherness and Transformation in *Eat a Bowl of Tea* and *Crossings*," *MELUS* 18, No. 4 (1993): 99, uses the phrase "a transitional generation of immigrants" to characterize post–World War II Asian Americans in the years before immigration laws were reformed and before Asian Americans developed a new sense of themselves as both Asian and American during the 1960s and 1970s.

18. Louis Chu, "Introduction," *Eat a Bowl of Tea* (New York, NY: Lyle Stuart, 1961; rpt. Seattle, WA: University of Washington Press, 1979), 8. Of course, many others regard Onoto Watanna's *Miss Numé of Japan* the first Asian American novel. Onoto Watanna was the pen name of Winifred Eaton who shared the same Chinese American heritage with her older sister, Edith Eaton. As Onoto Watanna, Winifred Eaton published about a dozen "Japanese" romance novels. While under the pen name of Sui Sin Far, Edith Eaton had been publishing work dealing with Chinese immigrants since 1896, she published only one book and that was not a novel. Huining Ouyang, "The Trickster Narrative in *Miss Numè of Japan*: A Japanese-American Romance," in *Doubled Plots: Romance and History*, ed. Susan Strehle and Mary Paniccia Carden (Jackson, MI: University Press of Mississippi, 2003), 105, believes both sisters used but disabused the tenets of the popular oriental romance during the late nineteenth and early twentieth centuries. Ouyang says that *Miss Numè of Japan*, for example, "exemplifies turn-of-the century minority women's literary tricksterism."

19. Although in another dialect, the "Ah" tacked to the beginning of "Ah Song" might indicate that the community considers him inconsequential. Although Tsai Chin, *Daughter of Shanghai* (New York: St. Martin's Press, 1989), 26, mentions a Chinese practice of tacking "Ah" onto "the names of inconsequential people," the characters in *Eat a Bowl of Tea*, belong to a predominantly Cantonese community. In Cantonese, "Ah" is a term of endearment added to a person's first name for closeness in communication among family and friends. Although not exactly the same, the practice is somewhat similar to the use of diminutives in many European cultures as a "Joan," for example, becomes a "Joanie" or a "John" becomes a "Johnny." In English and other languages, the diminutive can be used disparagingly.

20. Chu, *Eat a Bowl of Tea*, 95.

21. Ibid., 96.
22. Ibid., 216, 222.
23. Ibid., 137.
24. Ibid., 242.
25. In contrast to most American interpretations, Shu-yan Li's reading, "Otherness and Transformation," 106, draws on Chinese classics such as *The Water Margin* and *Tien Pong Mei* as well as popular sentimental tales to cast Mei Oi in a less positive light. Yet Li accepts that Chu's novel remains an "alternate reading of the Pan story" in the *Water Margin*. Despite her failings, the Mei Oi of Chu's novel is not the sly and manipulative woman of *The Water Margin*. Ruth Y. Hsiao, "Facing the Incurable: Patriarchy in *Eat a Bowl of Tea*," 160, in *Reading the Literatures of Asian America*, ed. Shirley Geok-lin Lim and Amy Ling (Philadelphia, PA: Temple University Press, 1992) also finds Mei Oi lacking, a product of "both the Western and the Chinese patriarchal caricatures of Asian women." As such, of course, she is incapable to taking on the trickster's deeply subversive role.
26. Cheng Lok Chua, "Gold Mountain: Chinese Versions of the American Dream in Lin Yutang, Louis Chu, and Maxine Hong Kingston." *Ethnic Groups* 4 (1982): 41.
27. Chua, "Gold Mountain," 56, concludes with the sweeping generalization that "through the works of our selected authors [Lin Yutang, Louis Chu, and Maxine Hong Kingston], we see that Chinese Americans, in their pursuit of the better life, of family continuity, of personal happiness, and of individual as well as communal identity are centering themselves in the dreams of America and the realities of being Americans without reservations."
28. Ibid., 232.
29. Jinqi Ling, "Reading for Historical Specificities: Gender Negotiations in Louis Chu's *Eat a Bowl of Tea*," *MELUS* 20, No. 1 (1995): 46.
30. Francis L. K. Hsu, xi. Later on the same page and in the same paragraph, Hsu says, "The human being in whom two such contrasting cultures [Chinese and American] meet, moves, as it were, along the margin of each. He paces the border where they confront each other within himself, and he can reach out to touch both."
31. Chin, *Daughter of Shanghai*, 197.
32. Chuang Hua, *Crossings* (New York, NY: Dial Press, 1968; rpt. Boston, MA: Northeastern University Press, 1986), 81.
33. Ibid., 196.
34. Ibid., 197.
35. As Paul Radin notes, *The Trickster: A Study in American Indian Mythology* (1956; rpt. New York: Schocken Books, 1972), xxiv, as a rule, "[l]aughter, humor, and irony permeate everything Trickster does." Of course, Radin is describing *American Indian* tricksters;

nonetheless, all tricksters belong to the comic rather than tragic realm.

36. Shu-yan Li, "Otherness and Transformation in *Eat a Bowl of Tea* and *Crossings*," 102.

37. Ruth Y. Hsiao, in Shirley Geok-lin Lim and Amy Ling, 151, sees Chinese American writers as *either* "agreeing with the value of [patriarchy]" *or* "designing its collapse with a subversive plot." Yet Chuang Hau's narrator does not entirely come to grips with one or the other.

38. Huining Ouyang, "Rewriting the Butterfly Story: Tricksterism in Onoto Watanna's *A Japanese Nightingale* and Sui Sin Far's 'The Smuggling of Tie Co,' " *Alternative Rhetoric*, ed. Laura Gray-Rosendale and Sibylle Gruber (Albany, NY: State University of New York Press, 2001), 204.

39. Joan Chiung-huei Chang, *Transforming Chinese American Literature: A Study of History, Sexuality, and Ethnicity* (New York: Peter Lang, 2000), 138.

40. Edward Said, *Orientalism* (New York: Vintage Books, 1979), 5.

41. David Henry Hwang, "Worlds Apart." *American Theatre* (January 2000): 50.

42. In a parallel development, David Roediger's work, *The Wages of Whiteness: Race and the Making of the American Working Class* (London: Verso Books, 1991) traces how—encouraged by politicians and members of economic elites—during the nineteenth-century working-class men constructed their self-image as mainstream, *not* marginal (and thus "better") in terms of their *not* being black nor red nor yellow; and Roediger's insight is certainly relevant here. In fact, during the early decades of the nineteenth century, "[m]uch popular energy was in fact expended to make the literal legal title of *freeman* absolutely congruent with *white* adult maleness" (58). The onus of "race" as a construct continues to haunt Americans from all backgrounds.

43. *M. Butterfly* opened on Broadway in March of 1988 and won that year's Tony for best play. A cinematic version appeared in 1993. Hwang also wrote the screenplay although—as he repeatedly tells interviewers—he had little control over the final cinematic product.

44. David Hwang, *M. Butterfly, M. Butterfly* (New York: Plume, 1989), 95, himself refers to the work as "a deconstructivist *Madame Butterfly*."

45. Ibid., 7.

46. Ibid., 59.

47. Douglass Kerr, "David Henry Hwang," in *Asian Voices in English*, ed. Mimi Chan and Roy Harris, (Hong Kong: Hong Kong University Press, 1991), 44, 45, refers to Gallimard's added "essential ignorance of the Asian reality" and to his "willful gullibility."

48. David Belasco's play, the opera that Puccini built on that play, and Kwang's play are built on power balances between countries and genders. Douglas Kerr in Chan and Harris, 151, refers to the reversal of Butterfly's situation in *M. Butterfly* as "revenge"; but the reversal can also denote that Gallimard—and much of his world—cannot envision the world in any terms but those of dominance and subordination.

49. David L. Eng, "In the Shadows of a Diva: Committing Homosexuality in David Henry Hwang's *M. Butterfly*," *Amerasia Journal* 20, No. 1 (1994): 111.

50. See, for example, A. Esther Álvarez Lopez, "Gender and Genre Illusion: Man/Woman, Theatre, and *M. Butterfly*," *Proceedings of the 20th International AEDEAN Conference*, ed. P. Guardia and J. Stone (Barcelona, Spain: Universidat de Barcelona, 1997); Hsiao-hung Chang, "Cultural/Sexual/Theatrical Ambivalence in *M. Butterfly*," *Tamkang Review: A Quarterly of Comparative Studies between Chinese and Foreign Literatures* 23 (Fall–Summer 1992–93): 15–34; and Tina Chen, "Betrayed into Motion: The Seduction of Narrative Desire in *M. Butterfly*," *Hitting Critical Mass: A Journal of Asian American Cultural Criticism* 1, No. 2 (1994): 129–154.

51. Hwang, "Worlds Apart," 56.

52. Quoted in Bonnie Lyons, " 'Making His Muscles Work for Himself': An Interview with David Henry Hwang," *The Literary Review* 42 (Winter 1999): 235.

53. Hwang, *M. Butterfly*, 92.

54. Quoted in Bonnie Lyons, "Making His Muscles Work for Himself," 231.

55. The subtitle of Maria Degabriele's "From Madame Butterfly to Miss Saigon: One Hundred Years of Popular Orientalism," *Critical Arts Journal* 10, No. 2 (1996): 105–119. EBSCOhost (accessed May 5, 2004), refers to a long line of "Butterfly" stories that have appeared in fiction and on stage from 1887 through the Broadway success of *Miss Saigon* in 1989. Robert K. Martin calls the Puccini libretto a "paradigm for Western romanticizing." "Gender, Race, and the Colonial Body: Carson McCuller's Filipino Boy, and David Henry Hwang's Chinese Woman," *Canadian Review of American Studies* 23, No. 1 (Fall 1992): 4 (accessed December 7, 2010).

56. Jeanne Rosier Smith, *Writing Tricksters: Mythic Gambols in American Ethnic Literature* (Berkeley, CA: University of California Press, 1997), 31.

57. Maxine Hong Kingston, quoted in an interview with Marilyn Chin," *MELUS* 16, No. 4 (Winter 1989–90): 61.

58. Ling, "Reading for Historical Specificities," 152.

59. Maxine Hong Kingston, *Tripmaster Monkey: His Fake Book* (New York: Knopf, 1989; rpt. New York: Vintage Books, 1990), 320.

60. Ibid., 326–327.
61. Ibid., 314.
62. Maxine Hong Kingston, quoted in Marilyn Chin, "A MELUS Interview," 64.
63. Zeng Li, "Diasporic Self, Cultural Other," 9, points out that Wittman's last name, Ah Sing, also echoes the name of a couple of nineteenth-century Chinese caricatures by Brete Harte and Mark Twain, thus setting up "a critical comment on the split between the socially constructed image of Chinese American and what really exists."
64. Kingston, *Tripmaster Monkey*, 9, has Wittman mentioning, for instance, not just Ambrose Bierce but also Bierce's less well-remembered journalist friend Gertrude Atherton.
65. Ibid., 213.
66. Ibid., 337.
67. Ibid., 339.
68. Li, "Diasporic Self, Cultural Other," 12.
69. Chin, "A MELUS Interview," 59.
70. Kingston, *Tripmaster Monkey*, 340.
71. Chin, "A MELUS Interview," 73.
72. Kingston, *Tripmaster Monkey*, 340.
73. Ibid., 340.
74. A parallel is found in the Winnebago trickster, Wakdjunkaga. According to one of Paul Radin's informants, though Wakdjunkaga was responsible for just about everything in the Indian's world, "Yet one thing he never did: he never went on the warpath, he never waged war," *The Trickster*, 147. The trickster sometimes acts foolishly but never that foolishly.
75. Reaction to Kingston's novel included comments referring to Wittman's acerbic self as "a character who doesn't always evoke one's compassion or affection," Gail Caldwell, "Playing Fast and Loose with a Playwright," rev. of *Tripmaster Monkey: His Fake Book*, by Maxine Hong Kingston, *Boston Globe* (April 16, 1989). Michiko Kakutan, "Books of the Times: Being of 2 Cultures, and Liking and Loathing It," rev. of *Tripmaster Monkey: His Fake Book*, by Maxine Hong Kingston, *New York Times* (April 14, 1989), Late City Final Ed.: C: 30, considers the narrative a series of self-indulgent "shaggy dog stories." According to Bharati Mukerjee, "Wittman at the Golden Gate," rev. of *Tripmaster Monkey: His Fake Book*, by Maxine Hong Kingson, *the Washington Post (April 16 1989)*, Kingston's novel is "bloated." Le Anne Schrieber, "The Big, Big Show of Wittman Ah Sing," *New York Times Book Review* Final Ed: Book World: 11 (April 2, 1989): 9, says of Wittman, "Sometimes he is spellbinding; too often he is just a windbag." The reviewers' complaints about Wittman might be said of his predecessor, the Monkey King; Kingston's novel shares the sprawling nature of the sixteenth-

century *Journey to the West*. Despite my emphasis on the Monkey King and *the Journey to the West* in *Tripmaster Monkey*, Kingston actually weaves bits of several other Chinese classics including *The Romance of the Three Kingdoms, the Water Margin,* and *The Dream of the Red Chamber* into *Tripmaster Monkey*. For a more positive review by Gerald Vizenor who had, after all, spent time in China and whose own fictions are also imaginatively inventive, see his April 23, 1989, *Los Angeles Times Book Review*.

76. Predicating her argument on the postmodern structure of *Tripmaster Monkey*, Patricia Lin, "Clashing Constructs of Reality: Reading Maxine Hong Kingston's *Tripmaster Monkey: His Fakebook* as Indigenous Ethnography," in *Reading the Literatures of Asian America*, ed. Shirley Geok-lin Lim and Amy Ling (Philadelphia, PA: Temple University Press, 1992), 345, 335, 345, finds "transformational 'monkey power' " in what she considers Kingtson's "ethnographic enterprise." For Lin, "the act of self-retrieval from amidst a morass of pre-fabricated representations [in *Tripmaster Monkey*] is accompanied by rejection of the idea that there is finality or permanence of any text, truth, or representation." Derek Parker Royal, "Literary Genre as Ethnic Resistance in Maxine Hong Kingston's *Tripmaster Monkey: His Fake Book*," *MELUS* 29, No. 2 (Summer 2004): 142, also focuses on the pastiche of other stories and genres undercutting the novel's structure and believes that the dramatic presentation in the last three chapters takes "a well-established genre in Western, drama, and transforms it into a narrative vehicle that violates or transcends its assumed boundaries." While Royal is interested primarily in Kingston's use of structures within the novel to achieve ethnic resistance, he is describing what all tricksters do-breaking down boundaries.

77. A number of critics demonstrate Kingston's debt to Chinese and popular sources in *Tripmaster*, for instance, as Elliott H. Shapiro, "Authentic Watermelon: Maxine Hong Kingston's American Novel," *MELUS* 26 (Spring 2001): 11, sees it, Kingston's use of allusions and sources is part of Kingston's "claim to any [popular or literary genre; European, American, or Chinese] cultural artifacts she might find useful." He believes that the richness her American and European literary sources contribute to the novel's "communal choir."

78. Specifically, Hsiao-hung Chang, "Gender Crossing," *MELUS* 22 (1997): 20, believes that "the female author-narrator in *Tripmaster Monkey* skillfully positions herself in the (post)gender and (post)ethnic mapping of minority literature." Jeanne Rosier Smith, *Writing Tricksters* (Berkeley, CA: University of California Press, 1997), 66–67, also sees the shifting narrative perspectives as a trickster means of undercutting the reader's sense of either male or female self-assurance.

79. David Leiwei Li, *Imagining the Nation: Asian American Literature and Cultural Consent* (Stanford, CA: Stanford University Press, 1998), 68, refers to Kingston's "narrative recognition of Chin [in the novel]…[as] an inclusive act of an excluded figure, at once a jazzy improvisation and a kung fu challenge of his fake book/original score."

80. Chang, "Gender Crossing," 19.

81. Bette Bao Lord, *The Middle Heart* (New York: Fawcett Columbine, 1996), 400.

82. Ibid., 170.

83. Ibid., 280.

84. Ibid., 288.

85. Lord's Mountain Pine echoes Alexander Solzhenitsyn's Dr Zhivago. His focus is on a livable life rather than a heroic stance.

86. *The Middle Heart* presents an eerie parallel between the excesses of New England Puritanism and the irrationalities perpetuated under Mao. Both societies were built on ideals: a perfectly moral society on earth and a perfectly egalitarian culture. Once the external enemies of the Chinese Communists—the Japanese and the Kuomintang—had been beaten, communism should theoretically have delivered utopia. Instead, Mao's Great Leap Forward in the late 1950s led to the starvation of 20 million people, and the Cultural Revolution of the 1960s and 1970s caused major economic disruptions. In response to clear failures, both the Puritans and the Chinese Communists insisted that internal enemies must be sabotaging their perfect societies. Since neither set of leaders could accept the idea that a flaw might exist in their theories, they had to clamp down on even whispers of dissent. For a while, youths were used as surrogates to accuse dissenters during the New England witch trials of the 1690s and the Red Guards accused suspected Revisionists among Mao's deputies and others during the 1970s. With Mao's death, of course, Chinese leadership purged its most radical elements represented by the Gang of Four; however, even this more "balanced" leadership cannot, as the world witnessed with the death of hundreds of reform-minded students in Tiananmen Square during early 1987, admit dissent.

87. Jan Alexander, "Casualties of History," rev. of *The Middle Heart*, by Bette Bao Lord, *Far Eastern Economic Review* (May 30, 1996), 37. Actually, Alexander's review is scathing, not even granting the novel the status of "a good historical potboiler" (38). For the most part, reviewers did not pay much attention to the novel.

88. Yang's *American Born Chinese* was a 2006 National Book Award finalist in the young people's literature category, and it won the American Library Association's 2007 Michael L. Printz Award for Excellence in Young Adult Literature. Yang teaches computer science at a Catholic prep school in Oakland.

89. Gene Luen Yang, *American Born Chinese* (New York: First Second, 2006), 31.
90. Ibid., 179.
91. Ibid., 149.
92. Binfin Fu kindly translated the characters for me.
93. "Reimagining the Monkey King in Comics: Gene Luen Yang's *American Born Chinese*," in *Oxford Handbook of Children's Literature*, ed. Julia Mickenberg and Lynn Vallone (Oxford: Oxford University Press, 2011).
94. As Binbin Fu explains in his translation of the Chinese character identifying Tze-Yo-Tzuh on page 84 of *American Born Chinese*, the character literally means "the one who is self-made" or "self possessed." It is a term Yang uses to replace Sakyamun, the ultimate figure of Buddhism. Sakyamuni is better known as Prince Siddhartha or Gautama Buddha. As Fu further notes "I am who am" comes from Exodus 3:14.
95. Yang, *American Born Chinese*, 215.
96. Jeff Chu and Nadia Mustafa. "Between Two Worlds." *Time* (January 16, 2006: 64–68).

6 ROUGH MISCHIEF, IRREVERENCE, AND THE FANTASTIC

1. Not everyone agrees on names: *Hispanic*—a name derived for the Latin *hispanicus*—meaning Spanish refers to people who either speak Spanish or many of whose ancestors spoke Spanish. An Associated Press wire service story appearing in newspapers around the United States during the summer of 2006 offers a popular definition: "Hispanic is a term for people with ethnic backgrounds in Spanish-speaking countries. Hispanics can be of any race, including white," Scott Bauer, "State Is Now 4.5% Hispanic," *Wisconsin State Journal* (Madison, August 15, 2006): B 1–2. Nonetheless, although the United States Census Bureau and popular print media use that term, critics of that nomenclature argue that the term *Hispanic* valorizes only one part of Latino/a heritage. The term *Latino* is also problematic. The choice of *Latino* is as much a political as a descriptive term. There is no perfect solution. However, in a clear and articulate essay, "By Any Other Name," Demetria Martínez, *Confessions of a Berlitz-Tape Chicana* (Norman, OK: University of Oklahoma Press, 2005), 50, explains her preference for the term *Latino* over *Hispanic*. She believes that the poor and powerless recognize that only through political power do they stand a chance against an economically stacked deck. In solidarity with the powerless, she and many others prefer *Latino* because the term hints at political action and pushing back against unjust structures. Furthermore, since

they feel ignored by the use of the inclusive *Latino*, many North American women prefer *Latino/a* to *Latino*. I have been tempted to use *Latino/a;* however, that is not yet the more common usage; so for the most part, I am using *Latino*.

2. Richard M. Dorson, *Burying the Wind: Regional Folklore in the United States* (Chicago, IL: University of Chicago Press, 1964), 421.
3. Rolando J. Romero, "Border of Fear, Border of Desire," *Borderlines: Studies in American Culture* 1, No. 1 (1993): 62.
4. Henry A. Giroux, "Paulo Freire and the Politics of Postcolonialism," *Journal of Advanced Composition* 12, No. 1 (Winter 1992): 17.
5. Ibid., 17.
6. Ibid., 20.
7. The holographic metaphor comes from D. Emily Hicks, "Deterritorialization and Border Writing," *Ethics/Aesthetics: Post-Modern Positions*, ed. Robert Merrill (Washington, DC: Maissoneuve, 1988), 47–58.
8. Scott Michaelsen and David E. Johnson, *Border Theory: The Limits of Cultural Politics* (Minneapolis, MN: University of Minnesota Press, 1997), 3.
9. Benjamin Alire Sáenz, "In the Borderlands of Chicano Identity, There Are Only Fragments," in *Border Theory*, ed. Scott Michaelsen and David E. Johnson (Minneapolis, MN: University of Minnesota Press, 1997), 71, recognizes, for example, that *chicanismo* has been "formed by racist discourse." Yet, Sáenz also realizes that asserting difference reflects a rooted awareness of a complex reality. In common with most of his students, Sáenz refuses "to be completely contained by that homogeneous, devouring word *American*," 79. Many writers and the people they write about choose to stay in the borderlands where circumstances have placed them.
10. Eduardo Barrera Herrera, "Apropiación y tutelaje de las frontera norte," *Puentelibre* 4 (Spring 1995): 13.
11. Ibid., 14.
12. In support of his contention that "the U.S-Mexico [border]...has become a symbolic stage upon which the nation's insecurities and fear, hopes and dreams, are projected for public consumption," the Princeton socialist Douglass Massey, "Borderline Madness," *The Chronicle of Higher Education*, June 30, 2006, B11, summarizes in a fairly short space a clear and accurate picture of Mexican immigration to the United States over the last century.
13. Robert MacNeil and William Cran, "Hispanic Immigration: Reconquest or Assimilation?" *Do You Speak American?: A Companion to the PBS Television Series* (New York: Doubleday, 2005). Héctor Tobar, *Translation Nation: Defining a New American Identity in the Spanish-Speaking United States* (New York: Riverhead Books, 2005), 28, even says that "The *paisanos* of Mexico, Guatemala, El

Salvador, California, Texas and other places where Spanish is spoken
freely have pushed so far into the interior of North America that
you could say a new Latin Republic of the United States is being
born."
14. Quoted in Delia Poey and Virgil Suarez, eds. "Introduction."
    Iguana Dreams: New Latino Fiction (New York: HarperPerennial,
    1992), xvii.
15. Demetria Martínez, *Confessions of a Berlitz-Tape Chicana* writes
    about all speakers of Spanish—whatever their family's country of
    origin—having a "familial" bond in the language; yet as Michael
    Scherer noted in the March 5, 2012, issue of *Time*, 26, as "a com-
    mon ancestral language," Spanish "binds nationalities, family his-
    tory and geographic allegiances. But that's about it."
16. Undocumented immigrants are intent on remaining invisible, so
    reliable numbers on their presence in the United States are noto-
    riously difficult to ascertain. A couple of lines from a June 2006
    Madison, Wisconsin, weekly newspaper suggests why. "In Dane
    County, there are at least 20,000 Latinos [in a total population of
    under 250,000], although a recent survey by the United Way says
    the number is likely twice that. Many of them are illegal." Vikki
    Kratz, "The Promised Land," *Isthmus* (June 30, 2006): 10–13.
17. According to the third edition of the *Hispanic American Almanac*,
    Sonia Benson, ed. (Detroit: Thomson Gale, 2003): 214–225,
    Mexican Americans made up 58.5 percent of the Hispanic popula-
    tion in the United States, Puerto Ricans 9.6 percent, and Cubans
    3.6 percent.
18. Rudolfo Anaya and R. S. Sharma, "Interview with Rudolfo Anaya,"
    Prairie Schooner 68, No. 4 (Winter 1994): 177–187, *Contemporary
    Literary Criticism*. Gale Group. Madison, WI: Edgewood College
    Libr. http://infotrac.galegroup.com (accessed February 7, 2007).
19. Chen Pan, *Monkey Hunting* (New York: Knopf, 2003), 241.
20. Chávez, Denise, *Face of an Angel* (New York: Farrar, Straus, and
    Giroux, 1994; rpt. Warner, 1995), 36.
21. Diogenes Céspedes, "Fiction Is the Poor Man's Cinema: An
    Interview with Junot Díaz," *Callaloo* 23 (Summer 2000): 904.
22. The first chapter of Héctor Tobar's *Translation Nation: Defining
    a New American Identity in the Spanish-Speaking United States*
    (New York: Riverhead Books, 2005), illustrates this quite well as
    Tobar describes his 1970s' childhood grounding in both his father's
    admiration for the radicalism of Che Guevara and his unquestion-
    ing acceptance of North American values.
23. Rafaela G. Castro's book *Chicano Folklore* (New York: Oxford
    University Press, 2001), 183, offers another translation of
    Urdemales's name. An alternate name (Pedro Ordimales) would
    mean "Peter of the holy water font"—probably with a bit of irony.
    Castro's book also includes a concise overview of the character. A

further, quite complete source for both the tales and their background can be found in María Cristina Brusca and Tona Wilson's book for children, *Pedro Fools the Gringo and Other Tales of a Latin American Trickster* (New York: Henry Holt and Company, 1995).

24. "Introducción," *Veinte cuentos de Pedro Urdemales* www.libros maravillosos.com/veintecuentos/index.html (accessed February 11, 2012).

25. Carlos René García Escobar, "Pedro Urdemales y los bandidos mágicos en Guatemala," rev. of *Cuentos populares de bandidos mágicos en Guatemala: Las hazañas de Pedro Urdemales* by Celso A. Lara Figueroa. *Folklore Americano* (January 1999): 297. Thompson /Gale. South Central Lib. System (WI) www.galenet.com (accessed July 11, 2006). Among other qualities, the Pedro Urdemales of the oral tales retold by Celso A. Lara Figueroa is capable of more than human efforts and perhaps is in league with the devil. He is certainly ineradicable. Changed into a stone, he becomes a force of nature.

26. Ramon A. Laval, "La piedra del fin del mundo." *Veinte cuentos de Pedro Urdemales.* www.librosmaravillosos.com/veintecuentos /index.html (accessed February 11, 2012).

27. Ramon A. Laval, "La flauta que rescuscitaba muertos." *Veinte cuentos de Pedro Urdemales.* www.librosmaravillosos.com/veintecuentos /index.html (accessed February 11, 2012).

28. Brusca and Wilson, *Pedro Fools the Gringo and Other Tales of a Latin American Trickster*, 25–27.

29. Richard M. Dorson, *Burying the Wind: Regional Folklore in the United States* (Chicago, IL: University of Chicago Press, 1964), 429–434.

30. Genevieve Barlow, "Las Aventuras de Juan Bobo," *Leyendas Latino-Americanas* (Lincolnwood, IL: National Textbook, 1995), 38–42.

31. Barlow, "¡Pobre Inocente!" *Leyendas Latino-Americanas*, 20–22.

32. In "Don Peanut and Doña Peanut," for example, 442–444, in Dorson, *Burying the Wind*, Don Peanut fakes out a bully by just suggesting that the bully will be the one-hundredth man he has defeated. Another time, in the same series of tales, he gets his opponents in a card game to fold rather than raise him when he tells Doña Peanut to bring his small money bag since she would not be strong enough to carry the large one even though Don Peanut has only one peso left.

33. Barlow, "El Cabo Montañez," *Leyendas Latino-Americanas*, 20–22.

34. The year 1492 marks both Christopher Columbus's first voyage to American and Ferdinand and Isabella's royal edict expelling Jews from Spain. Surely many Jews and their tales, whether "converted" or not, fled to the New World.

35. This definition comes from a headnote to "Las Aventuras de Juan Bobo," 38, in Genevieve Barlow's *Leyendas Latino-Americanas*.

36. I cannot recall even one female.
37. Barlow, "Las Aventuras de Juan Bobo," *Leyendas Latino-Americanas*, 38–42.
38. Cf. "Joha, Pull the Door," 208–210, in Matilda Koén-Sarano, *Folktales of Joha, Jewish Trickster* (Philadelphia, PA: The Jewish Publication Society, 2003).
39. Harold Scheub, *Story* (Madison, WI: University of Madison Press, 1998), 29.
40. Jack Zipes, *Relentless Progress: The Reconfiguration of Children's Literature, Fairy Tales, and Storytelling* (New York: Routledge, 2009), 46, 48.
41. Tzvetan Todorov, *The Fantastic: A Structural Approach to a Literary Genre*, trans. Richard Howard (Ithaca, NY: Cornell University Press, 1975), 41.
42. Rosemary Jackson, *Fantasy: The Literature of Subversion* (London: Methuen, 1981), 24, notes this distinction between traditional cultures that accept the marvelous and supernatural as opposed to secular ones that can accept the fantastic only as uncanny. Later in the same text, 44, Jackson says that themes in fantastic literature work to make "visible the un-seen" and "articul[ate] the un-said." That, of course, is the role of trickster discourse.
43. Jackson, 16, finds modern fantasies less communal than those from oral culture; yet since the trickster, seemingly the ultimate loner, actually exists only in an ethnic setting, even his modern tales are communal.
44. The phrase from his introduction, xi, to the 1994 reprinting of the novel is Anaya's own.
45. The collection includes stories written over a 30-year period. "B. Traven" has a long publication history beginning with an appearance in *Escolios* 4, No. 1–2 (May–November 1979): 1–12, but then going on to be reprinted seven more times in various collections and anthologies.
46. Rudolfo Anaya, *The Man Who Could Fly and Other Stories* (Norman, OK: University of Oklahoma Press, 2006), 87.
47. *Encyclopaedia Britannica*, 2007, s.v. "Traven, B." Encyclopaedia Britannica Online, http://0-www.search.eb.com.oscar.edgewood.edu:80/eb/article/-9073253 (accessed 24 Feb. 2007)
48. Anaya, "B. Traven," 87.
49. In frame stories, the author retells a story presumably heard from someone else who may have heard the story from still another person. The ultimate trickster is the author. The "lesson" is intended for the one who is listening. In stories with a frame within a frame, the person who was first told the story and then retells it may or may not understand the point; but the reader who hears the story is supposed to recognize the point. In Chesnutt's story, *Atlantic Monthly* 61 (1888): 605–611, a former slave, Uncle Julius, tells a tale about

the injustice endured by the overworked Sandy and his conjure second wife who attempts to protect him by turning him into a pine tree. The story has its elements of humor as when the hounds set to hunting down Sandy keep baying at the pine tree; but even as a tree, Sandy is set upon repeatedly; and finally, the slave owner has the tree chopped down and sawed into lumber for a cookhouse. The new owner, retelling the story Uncle Julius has told him, realizes he is being manipulated since Uncle Julius now wants to use the shack for an little church. The new owner does not, however, recognize or empathize about how the story is metaphorically also a story about the inescapable horrors of slavery.

50. Anaya, "B. Traven," 100.
51. Ibid.
52. Ibid.
53. Ibid., 92.
54. Ibid., 96.
55. Ibid., 89.
56. Ibid.
57. Anaya has a clear oral source for this short story in "The Smart Indian Lawyer," 447–448, reprinted in Richard M. Dorson's *Burying the Wind*, where an Indian lawyer makes the same defense for a poor man brought before the law. A headnote mentions that examples of the motif are also extant in Dutch and Jewish sources.
58. Rudolfo Anaya, "The Native Lawyer," *Sudden Fiction Latino: Short-Short Stories from the United States and Latin America*, ed. Robert Shapard, James Thomas, and Ray Gonzalez (New York: W. W. Norton & Company, 2009), 162.
59. Ron Arias, *The Road to Tamazunchale* (Reno, NV: West Coast Poetry, 1975; rpt. Tempe, AR: Bilingual, 1987), 32–33.
60. Ibid., 33.
61. D. Emily Hicks, "Deterritorialization and Border Writing," in *Ethics/Aesthetics: Post-Modern Positions*, ed. Robert Merrill (Washington, DC: Maissoneuve,1988), 49, argues that *magical realism* is a misnomer, wrongly valorizing the realistic in literature. She believes that what others see as magical realism reflects ways in which *border writing*—and tricksters invariably inhabit the borders—disconcert readers who expect linear narratives reflecting traditional patterns of dominance. Hicks's major objection is that the term *magical realism* tends to "depoliticize the text."
62. Wetbacks.
63. Arias, *The Road to Tamazunchale*, 107.
64. Ibid., 108.
65. Ibid., 125.
66. Although Gilb and Díaz come from quite different Latino traditions and parts of the country, the fiction of each writer is urban-based. Both men came intellectually alive as undergraduates. Both

concentrate on the concrete; Gilb talks, for example, about having "the image of the end" before he actually writes a short story, *Conversations with Texas Writers*, ed. Frances Leonard and Ramona Cearley (Austin, TX: University of Texas Press, 2005), 114, while Díaz refined his fiction by trying—unsuccessfully—to write screen plays. Yet, he says that the experience taught him "how to deal with concrete images and externalities," Diogenes Céspedes, "Fiction Is the Poor Man's Cinema," 903.

67. Gilb's personal background is unashamedly working class, and in 1995, he told an interviewer with the *Austin Chronicle* about his surprised euphoria over the prizes *The Magic of Blood* won and then Grove press's acceptance of his first novel. At that time, he was also thinking about a third novel "centering on the constructions world," Alvaro Rodriguez, "The Magic of Gilb." *The Austin Chronicle* (January 6, 1995): 24.

68. Dagoberto Gilb, *The Magic of Blood* (Albuquerque, NM: University of Mexico Press, 1993; rpt. New York: Grove, 1994), 117.

69. Ibid., 118.

70. Ibid., 108. For Gilb and his characters, racism is an inherent part of the American scene, an irritant but unavoidable. For most of his life, Gilb has worked as a stock boy, a laundry worker, and finally for 16 years as a journeyman carpenter. Many of his coworkers were black or Latino, as are the characters in his fiction. His fiction, however, does not seem to be as frustrated and angry with the racism he encountered in those jobs as what he has met as a writer. He talks in an interview, for example, of the "racist" attitudes he has met in editors and the "patronizing" responses of some—particularly Texan—reviewers, Frederick Luis Aldama, *Spilling the Beans in Chicanolandia: Conversations with Writers and Artists* (Austin, TX: University of Texas Press, 2006), 110.

71. Ibid., 117. Demetria Martínez, 127, reflects on the similar thinking of an "illegal" she meets in Albuquerque: "No work was beneath him. Quite the opposite. Work, any work, was a gift from God. It gave him dignity, defined him as a man. Work allowed him to survive." No matter how hard or dirty their jobs are, these men find validation and self-worth in them. It proves their manhood.

72. Gilb, "*Churchgoers*," 109.

73. Ibid., 116.

74. Ibid., 117.

75. Ibid., 110.

76. Ibid., 113.

77. Gilb, "Love in L.A.," 202.

78. Ibid., 202.

79. In one of Terry Gross's "Fresh Air" interviews on NPR, "Writer Dagoberto Gilb." *Fresh Air from WHYY. National Public Radio.* March 8, 2001. www.npr.org/templates/stry/story.

php?storyId=1119629&sc+emaf (accessed February 10, 2007), Gilb offers glimpses of his own hard scrabble upbringing in Los Angeles and leaves readers no doubt that, even if he has chosen another route than Jake, he has known plenty of characters like Jake.
80. Gilb, "Love in L.A.," 201.
81. Ibid., 201
82. John J. McKenna, "Teaching Trickster Figures in Short Fictions," *Eureka Studies in Teaching Short Fiction* 2, No. 1 (Fall 2001): 9.
83. In an interview where he rails against Mexican American stereotypes, Gilb also makes a point that "real good stories come from stories that happen." Elisabeth M. Mermann-Jozwiak, "My Grandmother Makes the Best Tortillas," 103, in *Conversations with Mexican American Writers*, ed. Elisabeth M. Mermann-Jozwiak and Nancy Sullivan (Jackson, MI: University of Mississippi, 2009). His years as a construction worker lend authenticity to Gilb's fiction.
84. Robert J. Cottrol's essay-length review of *Afro-Latin America*, "From Emancipation to Equality: The Afro-Latin's Unfinished Struggle," rev. of *Afro-Latin America, 1800–2000*, by George Reid Andrews, *American Quarterly* 57 (June 2005): 573–581, makes this connection quite clear.
85. Ibid., 576.
86. Ibid., 579.
87. Céspedes, "Fiction Is the Poor Man's Cinema," 904.
88. Junot Díaz, *Drown* (New York: Riverhead Books, 1996), 128.
89. Ibid., 121.
90. The word could also mean a lazy oaf; however, the disparaging bee-like "drone" seems to better fit the narrator's attitude.
91. Díaz, 125.
92. Ibid., 123.
93. Ibid., 127.
94. In his analysis of works by two Chicano writers, Vincent Perez, " 'Running' and Resistance: Nihilism and Cultural Memory in Chicano Urban Narratives," *MELUS* 25, No. 2 (Summer 2000): 134, analyzes their "postmodern experience" in terms of nihilism and sees the story's young men using nihilism "as a form of resistance to the threat of social erasure and exclusion" and "a resonant counterdiscourse for disenfranchised Chicanos in their struggle to overcome the dauntingly oppressive forces" they face daily. He might as easily have considered their choices as trickster responses. "Running," one of his key words and concepts, is characteristic of the trickster.
95. Lauren Smith, "Mexican-American High-School Students Perceive Many More Barriers to College Than Do Their White Peers," *The Chronicle of Higher Education* (February 13, 2007). http://chronicle.com/daily/2007/02/200702134n.htm (accessed February 13, 2007).

96. Nell Bernstein, "Report: Racial Disparity in Juvenile Justice," *National Catholic Reporter*, February 2, 2007.

97. Gabriel Estrada, "Machismo," *The Oxford Encyclopedia of Latinos and Latinas in the United States*, ed. Suzanee Oboler and Deena J. Gonzáles (New York: Oxford University Press, 2005), Vol. 3, 32–36.

98. Machismo is related to *la familia*, which Richard T. Rodríguez, *Next of Kin: The Family in Chicano/a Cultural Politics* (Durham: Duke University Press, 2009), 176, refers to as "the gendered hierarchies particular to the domestic sphere" and "an organizing principle for Chicano/a cultural politics."

99. Alfredo Mirandé, *Hombres y Machos: Masculinity and Latino Culture* (Boulder, CO: Westview Press, 1997), 17.

100. Calling Juan Villalobos *Jack* in the United States might be a nod to the Euro-American Jack Tales. However, the dominant trickster tradition accessed in the novel seems to be that of the Latino Pedro Urdemales.

101. In Villatorro's *Holy Spirit*, machismo and tricksterism entwine in a way similar to the manner in which male "cool" and tricksterism entwine in the African American mystery novels of Walter Mosley. From this point of view, both machismo and cool reflect being comfortable in one's skin and indifferent to other's rules.

102. In a 2001 interview with Jim Minick, Marcos McPeek Villatoro mentions that when he was growing up in Tennessee, he was known as Mark McPeek. Then, following a stay in Nicaragua, he made *Marcos McPeek Villatoro* the legal name on his California driver's license, "an obvious adherence to the Latino roots without forgetting the Appalachian." Villatoro says, "It's a mouthful of a name, but it fits me" (211).

103. In an interview with Nancy Sullivan, in "¡Ay, El Inglés Tan Bonito!" *Conversations with Mexican American Writers*, ed. Elizabeth Mermann-Jozwiak and Nancy Sullivan (Jackson, MS: University Press of Mississippi Press, 2009), 151, Denise Chávez notes that despite the derogatory connotations of *macho* in the United States, "In México and Latin America, to be macho is a complimentary term because you're responsible, you're an upright human being who takes care of family and kin and all of your affairs and everything."

104. Marcos McPeek Villatoro, *The Holy Spirit of My Uncle's Cojones* (Houston, TX: Arte Público, 1999), 137.

105. Ibid., 2.

106. Ibid., 112.

107. Ibid., 63.

108. Ibid., 94.

109. Ibid., 139.

110. Smirky or knowing; or to use the street vernacular, fucking.

111. Villatoro, *The Holy Spirit of My Uncle's Cojones*, 64.

112. Ibid.
113. Ibid., 115.
114. Womanizer, ladies man.
115. Villatoro, *The Holy Spirit of My Uncle's Cojones*, 115.
116. Paul Beekman Taylor, "Chicano Secrecy in the Fiction of Rudolfo A. Anaya." *Journal of the Southwest* 39, No. 2 (Summer 1997). Gale. Madison, WI: Edgewood College Library, http://infotrac.galegroup.com. (accessed February 1, 2007).
117. Villatoro, *The Holy Spirit of My Uncle's Cojones*, 144–145.
118. Ibid., 145–146.
119. Ibid., 275.
120. In the same interview with Jim Minick, "Latino Hillbilly: An Interview with Marcos McPeek Villatoro," *Appalachian Journal: A Regional Studies Review* 28, No. 2 (Winter 2001): 218, McPeek Villatoro mentions that this event alone comes from his own experience of "this guy with road rage…follow[ing] me for a good ten miles as if he were going to kill me."
121. Villatoro, *The Holy Spirit of My Uncle's Cojones*, 280.
122. With a light touch, Martínez's novel offers readers a type of "feminist fabulation" such as Marleen B. Barr, *Feminist Fabulations* (Iowa City, IA: University of Iowa Press, 1992), 10, writes about. *¡Caramba!* proposes for readers "a world clearly and radically discontinuous from the patriarchal one."
123. While Natalie and Consuelo's transvestite cosmetician friend True-Dee worries about a "conspiracy of the highest order designed to deprive women of their most volatile asset: their femininity," Nina Marie Martínez, *¡Caramba!* (New York: Knopf; rpt. Anchor, 2004), 98, the women in this novel prove more than able to defend themselves.
124. Since she was four-years-old, Consuela has taken to heart her aunt Concha's counsel, "You only get one life chica. Live it up." Nina Marie Martínez, 4.
125. In a typically sly bit of irony, the Big Cheese Plant is owned and run by the local "Big Cheese," a sickly, undersized man from the East, Cal McDaniel.
126. Martínez, *¡Caramba!*, 74.
127. Ibid., 85.
128. Ibid., 251.
129. Ibid., 27.
130. Ibid., 33.
131. Lynn Andriani, "¿A Novel with Pictures? Si, Senor!; PW Talks with Nina Marie Martinez," *Publishers Weekly* (February 16, 2004): PW Forecasts; Fiction; 152. Edgewood College Libr. Madison, WI. http://web.lexis-nexis.com (accessed March 17, 2007).
132. Martínez's "signs might also remind readers who have seen them of visual works such as Ojibwa artist Rebecca Belmore's 1991 pencil

sketch, 65. depicting a sexy, sly, and dangerous 'Coyote Woman.' Belmore's comment that "the work I'm doing has a serious message somewhere in it but there's a lot of humor," Allan J. Ryan, *The Trickster Shift: Humor and Irony in Contemporary Native Art* (Vancouver: University of British Columbia Press, 1999), 146, applies to Martinez's novel as well.

133. At one point after her return from Mexico, Natalie tells Consuelo, "Sway, this is how they do it in Mexico." Martínez, *¡Caramba!*, 301. Looping arms with someone of the same sex would not come naturally to them as it would to women in most Latin countries.

134. In the spring 2007 issue of *MELUS*, Lourdes Torres, "In the Contact Zone: Code-Switching Strategies by Latino/a Writers," further explores various means of code-switching commonly utilized by Latino writers and suggests some possible motivations.

135. Martínez, *¡Caramba!*, 15.

136. Louie speaks the same *caló* street dialect that Islas's father spoke on the job as a policeman back in El Paso.

137. Arturo Islas, *La Mollie and the King of Tears: A Novel* (Albuquerque: University of New Mexico Press, 1996), 37.

138. Ibid., 22. The lines bring to mind Luis Valdez's "Los Vendidos."

139. Islas intended to write a "picaresque novel" and thus engage in trickster discourse; however, his trickster models were literary, Lazarillo de Tormes and Thomas Nashe, rather than the oral tradition of Pedro Urdemales or Jack. Frederick Luis Aldama, *Dancing with Ghosts: A Critical Biography of Arturo Islas* (Berkeley, CA: University of California Press, 2005), 51.

140. The name of Louie's tough gay high school friend, Virgil Spears, for example, conflates a literary reference with the name of a man from Islas's father's past as well as Islas's former lover. Aldama, *Dancing*, 53.

141. Islas, *La Mollie and the King of Tears*, 71.

142. Ibid., 145.

143. Ibid., 145.

144. This is another example of Islas altering his background as grist for the novel. He based Leila P. Harper on one of his high school teachers, but El Paso High—where he attended high school—had a strong program that prepared him well for Stanford.

145. Islas, *La Mollie and the King of Tears*, 137. Tough as he is in other respects, Louie can be romantic. His language, of course, is processed so that it gives the appearance rather than the reality of someone who is street-educated.

146. Ibid., 65.

147. Ibid., 25.

148. Ibid., 53.

149. Denise Chávez, *Loving Pedro Infante: A Novel* (New York: Washington Square Press, 2002), 9.

150. Ibid., 11.
151. Ibid., 51.
152. Ibid., 300.
153. Ibid., 16.
154. Nancy Sullivan, "¡Ay, el inglés tan bonito!" 150.
155. Chávez, *Loving Pedro*, 52.
156. Lucifer is also associated with light.
157. Denise Chávez, *Loving Pedro*, 316–317.
158. Nancy Sullivan, in "¡Ay, El Inglés Tan Bonito!" *Conversations with Mexican American Writers*, ed. Elizabeth Merman-Jozwiak and Nancy Sullivan (Jackson, MS: University Press of Mississippi, 2009), 151.
159. Chávez, *Loving Pedro*, 320.

CONCLUSION

1. Parker J. Palmer, *Healing the Heart of Democracy: The Courage to Create a Politics Worthy of the Human Spirit* (San Francisco, CA: Jossey-Bass, 2011), 13.

APPENDIX I: THE MONKEY KING

1. This and all quotations from *The Journey to the West* are from Anthony C. Yu's four-volume translation of Ch'êng-ên Wu's text (Chicago, IL: University of Chicago Press, 1977), II: 100.
2. A Freudian would immediately associate the Monkey King's rod with a penis. In *The Journey to the West*, however, even as the story begins and the Monkey King breaks every taboo he encounters, he is a remarkably asexual creature.
3. Mao T'se-tung reputedly enjoyed *The Journey to the West* and especially the Monkey King. Presumably, Mao admired the early rebellious and ever-inventive early Monkey King rather that the compliant Pilgrim that he becomes.
4. Pa-chieh is often called Hog.
5. At one point, for example, "Pa-chieh ate with abandon like a hungry tiger, so terrifying those holding dishes and trays that their hearts quivered and their gallbladders shook" (IV: 195).

BIBLIOGRAPHY

Abrahams, Roger D., ed. *Afro-American Folktales: Stories from Black Traditions in the New World*. New York: Pantheon, 1985.

Adelman, Peter. *So Rich, So Poor: Why It's So Hard to End Poverty in America*. New York: The New Press, 2012.

Akoma, Chiji. *Folklore in New World Black Fiction: Writing and the Oral Traditional Aesthetics*. Columbus, OH: The Ohio State University Press, 2007.

Aldama, Arturo J. "Borders, Violence, and the Struggle for Chicana and Chicano Subjectivity." *Race, Gender, and the State*. Ed. Arturo J. Aldama. Bloomington, IN: Indiana University Press, 2003, pp. 19–38.

Aldama, Frederick Luis. *Brown on Brown: Chicano/a Representations of Gender Sexuality and Ethnicity*. Austin, TX: University of Texas Press, 2005.

———. *Dancing with Ghosts: A Critical Biography of Arturo Islas*. Berkeley, CA: University of California Press, 2005.

———. "Ethnoqueer Rearchitexturing of Metropolitan Space." *Nepantla: Views from the South*, 1:3 (2000): 581–604.

———. *Spilling the Beans in Chicanolandia: Conversations with Writers and Artists*. Austin, TX: University of Texas Press, 2006.

Alexander, Jan. "Casualties of History." Rev. of *The Middle Heart* by Bette Bao Lord. *Far Eastern Economic Review* (May 30, 1996): 37.

Alexie, Sherman. *The Absolutely True Diary of a Part-Time Indian*. Art by Ellen Forney. 2007; rpt. New York: Little, Brown and Company, 2009.

———. *The Lone Ranger and Tonto Fistfight in Heaven*. New York: Atlantic, 1993.

———. *Reservation Blues*. New York: Warner, 1996.

———. *The Summer of Black Widows*. Brooklyn, NY: Hanging Loose, 1996.

———. *Ten Little Indians: Stories*. New York: Grove, 2003.

Allen, Paula Gunn. *The Sacred Hoop: Recovering the Feminine in American Indian Traditions*. Boston, MA: Beacon Press, 1986.

——— ed. *Spider Woman's Granddaughters: Traditional Tales and Contemporary Writing by Native American Women*. New York: Fawcett Columbine, 1989.

Álvarez López, M. Esther. "Gender and Genre Illusion: Man/Woman, Theatre, and *M. Butterfly*." *Proceedings of the 20th International AEDEAN Conference*, edited by P. Guardia and J Stone. Barcelona, Spain: Universidat de Barcelona, 1997.

Amato, Jean. "Bette Bao Lord." *Asian American Novelists: A Bio-Bibliographical Critical Sourcebook*. Ed. Emmanuel S. Nelson. Westport, CT: Greenwood Press, 2000.

Ammons, Elizabeth and Annette White-Parks. *Tricksterism in Turn-of-the-Century American Literature: A Multicultural Perspective*. Hanover, NH: University Press of New England, 1994.

Anaya, Rudolfo. *Bless Me, Ultima*. New York: Warner, 1972; rpt. 1994.

———. "B. Traven Is Alive and Well in Cuernavaca." *The Man Who Could Fly and Other Stories*. Norman, OK: University of Oklahoma Press, 2006, pp. 87–102.

———. "The Native Lawyer." *Serafina's Stories*. University of New Mexico Press, 2004. Rpt. *Sudden Fiction Latino: Short-Short Stories from the United States and Latin America*. Ed. Robert Shapard, James Thomas, and Ray Gonzalez. New York: W. W. Norton & Company, 2009, pp. 158–162.

———. *Zia Summer*. New York: Warner, 1995.

Anaya, Rudolfo and R. S. Sharma. "Interview with Rudolfo Anaya." *Prairie Schooner* 68:4 (Winter 1994): 177–187. *Contemporary Literary Criticism*. Gale Group. Edgewood College Libr. Madison, WI. February 7, 2007, http://infotrac.galegroup.com.

Andriani, Lynn. "?A Novel with Pictures? Si, Senor!; PW Talks with Nina Marie Martinez." *Publishers Weekly* (February 16, 2004): PW Forecasts; Fiction; 152. Edgewood College Libr. Madison, WI. March 17, 2007, http://web.lexis-nexis.com

Arias, Ron. *The Road to Tamazunchale*. Reno, NV: West Coast Poetry, 1975; rpt. Tempe, AR: Bilingual, 1987.

Arpad, Joseph John. "David Crockett: An Original." MA Thesis. University of Iowa, Iowa City, 1965.

Aubert, Alvin. "Yusef Komunyakaa: The Unified Vision—Canonization and Humanity." *African American Review* 27 (1993): 119–123.

Ausubel, Nathan, ed. *A Treasury of Jewish Humor*. Garden City, NY: Doubleday & Company, Inc., 1951.

Babcock-Abrahams, Barbara. " 'A Tolerated Margin of Mess': The Trickster and His Tales Reconsidered." *Journal of the Folklore Institute* 11 (1974): 147–86; rpt. in *Critical Essays on Native American Literature*. Ed. Andrew Wiget. Boston, MA: G.K. Hall, 1985, pp. 153–185.

Badami, Anita Rau. *The Hero's Walk: A Novel*. New York: Ballantine Books, 2002.

Baldwin, Joseph G. The Flush Times of Alabama and Mississippi: A Series of Sketches. New York: D. Appleton & Company, 1854.

Ballinger, Franchot. *Living Sideways: Tricksters in American Indian Oral Traditions*. Norman, OK: University of Oklahoma Press, 2004.

Barlow, Genevieve. *Leyendas Latino-Americanas*. Lincolnwood, IL: National Textbook, 1995.

Barr, Marleen S. *Feminist Fabulation: Space/Postmodern Fiction*. Iowa City, IA: University of Iowa Press, 1992.

Barrera Herrera, Eduardo. "Apropiación y tutelaje de las frontera norte." *Puentelibre* 4 (Spring 1995): 13–17.

Barthes, Roland. "Myth Today." *A Barthes Reader.* Ed. Susan Sontag. New York: Hill and Wang, 1982, pp. 93–149.

Beardslee, Karen E. *Folklore Foundations: Selfhood and Cultural Tradition in Nineteenth- and Twentieth-Century American Literature.* Knoxville, TN: The University of Tennessee Press, 2001.

Behnam, Mariam. "Shankar the Fortune-teller." *Heirloom: Evening Tales from the East.* New York: Oxford University Press, 2001, pp. 170–180.

Bellow, Saul. "A Silver Dish." *Him with His Foot in His Mouth and Other Short Stories.* New York: Harper, 1984, pp. 191–222.

Benson, Sonia, ed. *The Hispanic American Almanac,* 3rd ed. Detroit, MI: Thomson Gale, 2003.

Bergmann, Johannes Dietrich. "The Original Confidence Man." *American Quarterly* 21 (Fall 1961): 560–577.

Bernstein, Nell. "Report: Racial Disparity in Juvenile Justice." *National Catholic Reporter* (February 2, 2007): 13.

Bierhorst, John. *The Mythology of North America.* Oxford: Oxford University Press, 2001.

Blackwell, Angela Glover, Stewart Kwoh, and Manuel Pastor. *Uncommon Common Ground: Race and American's Future.* New York: W. W. Norton & Company, 2010.

Blaeser, Kimberly. "Trickster: A Compendium." *Buried Roots and Indestructible Seeds: The Survival of American Indian Life in Story, History, and Spirit.* Ed. Mark A. Lindquist and Martin Zanger. Madison, WI: The University of Wisconsin Press, 1994, pp. 47–66.

Blaeser, Kimberly M. *Gerald Vizenor: Writing in the Oral Tradition.* Norman, OK: University of Oklahoma Press, 1996.

Blair, Elizabeth. "Text as Trickster: Postmodern Language Games in Gerald Vizenor's *Bearheart.*" MELUS 20 (1995): 75–91.

Blue Cloud, Peter. *Elderberry Flute Song: Contemporary Coyote Tales.* Trumansburg, NY: Crossing Publication, 1982.

Bobo, Jacqueline. "Sifting through the Controversy: Reading *The Color Purple.*" *Callaloo: An Afro-American and African Journal of Arts and Letters* 2 (1989): 332–342.

Bowers, Sharon Manybeads. "Louise Erdrich as Nanapush." *New Perspectives on Women and Comedy.* Ed. Regina Barreca. Philadelphia, PA: Gordon, 1992.

Brady, Owen E. and Derek C. Maus, eds. *Finding a Way Home: A Critical Assessment of Walter Mosley's Fiction.* Jackson, MS: University Press of Mississippi, 2008.

Brewer, J. Mason. *American Negro Folklore.* Chicago, IL: Quadrangle Books, 1968.

Brewster, H. Pomeroy. "English Folk-Tales in America." *Journal of American Folklore* 2:6 (1889): 213.

Brewster, H. Pomeroy, Collector. "The House that Jack Built." *Journal of American Folklore* 2:6 (1889): 209–212.

Bright, Willliam. *A Coyote Reader.* Berkeley, CA: University of California Press, 1993.

Brown, Claude. *Manchild in the Promised Land.* New York: Macmillan, 1965.

Brusca, María Christina and Tona Wilson. *Pedro Fools the Gringo and Other Tales of a Latin American Trickster.* A Redfeather Book. New York: Henry Holt and Company, 1995.

Bryant, Jerry H. *"Born in a Mighty Bad Land": The Violent Man in African American Folklore and Fiction.* Bloomington, IN: Indiana University Press, 2003.

Byerman, Keith E. *Fingering the Jagged Grain: Tradition and Form in Recent Black Fiction.* Athens, GA: University of Georgia Press, 1985.

Carroll, Rebecca. *Swing Low: Black Men Writing.* New York: Crown Publishers, 1995.

Castillo, Susan Perez. "Postmodernism, Native American Literature, and the Real: The Silko-Erdrich Controversy." *The Massachusetts Review* 32:2 (Summer 1991): 285–294.

Castro, Mariellos. "Pedro Urdemales: De la oralidad a la escritura." *Istmica: Revista de la Faculdad de Filosofía y Letras,* Universidad Nacional, UNA. 5:5 (2000): 142–157.

Castro, Rafaela G. *Chicano Folklore: A Guide to the Folktales, Traditions, Rituals and Religious Practices of Mexican Americans.* New York: Oxford University Press, 2001.

Caton, Bill. *Fighting Words: Words on Writing from 21 of the Heart of Dixie's Best Contemporary Authors.* Montgomery, AL: Black Belt Publishers, 1995.

Catt, Catherine M. "Ancient Myth in Modern America: The Trickster in the Fiction of Louise Erdrich." *The Platte Valley Review* 19 (1991): 71–81.

Cawelti, John G. *Adventure, Mystery, and Romance: Formula Stories as Art and Popular Culture.* Chicago, IL: University of Chicago Press, 1977.

Céspedes, Diogenes. "Fiction Is the Poor Man's Cinema: An Interview with Junot Díaz." *Callaloo* 23 (Summer 2000): 892–907.

Chang, Hsiao-hung. "Gender Crossing in Maxine Hong Kingston's *Tripmaster Monkey.*" MELUS 22 (1997): 15–34.

———. "Cultural/Sexual/Theatrical Ambivalence in M. Butterfly." *Tamkang Review: A Quarterly of Comparative Studies between Chinese and Foreign Literatures* 23 (Fall–Summer 1992–1993): 735–755.

Chang, Joan Chiung-huei. *Transforming Chinese American Literature: A Study of History, Sexuality, and Ethnicity.* New York: Peter Lang, 2000.

Chase, Richard. *The Jack Tales: Folktales Told by R.M. Ward and His Kindred in the Beech Mountain Section of Western North Carolina and by Other Descendants of COUNCIL HARMON (1803–1896) Elsewhere in the Southern Mountains; with Three Tales from Wise County Virginia.* Boston, MA: Houghton Mifflin, 1943.

———. "The Origin of 'The Jack Tales.' " *Southern Folklore Quarterly* 3 (1939): 190–192.

Chávez, Denise. *Face of an Angel.* New York: Farrar, Straus, and Giroux, 1994; rpt. Warner, 1995.
————. *Loving Pedro Infante: A Novel.* New York: Washington Square Press, 2002.
Chen, Tina. "Betrayed into Motion: The Seduction of Narrative Desire in *M. Butterfly.*" *Hitting Critical Mass: A Journal of Asian American Cultural Criticism* 1.2 (1994): 129–154.
Chesnutt, Charles W. "Po' Sandy," *The Conjure Woman.* 1899; rpt. Ann Arbor, MI: The University of Michigan Press, 1969, pp. 36–63.
Childers, J. Wesley. *Tales from Spanish Picaresque Novels: A Motif-Index.* Albany, NY: State University of New York Press, 1977.
Childress, Mark. *Crazy in Alabama.* New York: Ballantine Books, 1993.
Chin, Marilyn. "A MELUS Interview: Maxine Hong Kingston." *MELUS* 16:4 (Winter 1989–1990), pp. 57–74.
Chin, Tsai. *Daughter of Shanghai.* New York: St. Martin's Press, 1989.
Chu, Louis. *Eat a Bowl of Tea.* New York: Lyle Stuart, 1961; rpt. Seattle, WA: University of Washington Press, 1979.
Chua, Cheng Lok. "Gold Mountain: Chinese Versions of the American Dream in Lin Yutang, Louis Chu, and Maxine Hong Kingston." *Ethnic Groups* 4 (1982): 33–59.
Cleage, Pearl. *Baby Brother's Blues: A Novel.* New York: One World, 2006.
————. *Some Things I Thought I'd Never Do.* New York: One World, 2003.
Coel, Margaret. *Killing Raven.* New York: Berkeley Books, 2003.
Cooksey, Thomas L. " 'Hero of the Margin' The Trickster as Deterritorialized Animal." *Thalia: Studies in Literary Humor* 18:1–2 (1998): 50–61.
Coltelli, Laura. *Winged Words: American Indian Writers Speak.* Lincoln, NE: University of Nebraska Press, 1990.
Conley, Robert J. *The Dark Way.* Norman, OK: University of Oklahoma Press, 2000.
Contreras, Sheila Marie. *Blood Lines: Myth, Indigenism, and Chicana/o Literature.* Austin, TX: University of Texas Press, 2008.
Cottrol, Robert J. "From Emancipation to Equality: The Afro-Latin's Unfinished Struggle." Rev. of *Afro-Latin America, 1800–2000,* by George Reid Andrews. *American Quarterly* 57 (June 2005): 573–581.
Cox, James. "Muting White Noise: The Subversion of Popular Culture Narratives of Conquest in Sherman Alexie's Fiction." *Studies in American Indian Literature* 9.4 (Winter 1997): 52–70.
Datlow, Ellen and Terri Windling, eds. *The Coyote Road: Trickster Tales.* New York: Viking Books, 2007.
Davis, III, Charles Thomas. "Jack as Archetypal Hero." *North Carolina Folklore* (Raleigh) 26:2 (1978): 134–145.
Davis, Donald. *Jack Always Seeks His Fortune: Authentic Appalachian Jack Tales.* Little Rock: August House, 1992.
Degabriele, Maria. "From Madame Butterfly to Miss Saigon: One Hundred Years of Popular Orientalism." *Critical Arts Journal* 10:2 (1996): 105–119. EBSCOhost. Accessed May 5, 2004.

Delany, Sarah and A. Elizabeth Delany with Amy Hill Hearth. *Having Our Say: The Delany Sisters' First 100 Years.* New York: Kodansha International, 1993.

Díaz, Junot. "Edison, N. J." *Drown.* New York: Riverhead Books, 1996, pp. 121–140.

Dickey, Jerry R. " 'Myths of the East, Myths of the West': Shattering Racial and Gender Stereotypes in the Plays of David Henry Hwang." *Old West—New West: Centennial Essays.* Ed. Barbara Howard Meldrum. Moscow, ID: University of Idaho Press, 1993. 272–80.

Dickson, Jr., Bruce D. "The 'John and Old Master' Stories and the World of Slavery: A Study in Folktales and History." *Phylon* 35 (1974): 418–429.

Dickson, H. E. "A Note on Charles Mathews' Use of American Humor." *American Literature* 12 (1940): 78–83.

DiGaetani, John Louis. "*M. Butterfly:* An Interview with David Henry Hwang." *TDR: The Drama Review: A Journal of Performance Studies* 33:3 (Fall 1989): 141–153.

Dong, Lan. "Reimagining the Monkey King in Comics: Gene Luen Yang's "*American Born Chinese.*" *Oxford Handbook of Children's Literature.* Ed. Julia Mickenberg and Lynn Vallone. Oxford: Oxford University Press, 2011, pp. 231–251.

Dorson, Richard M. *American Folklore.* Chicago, IL: University of Chicago Press, 1959.

———, collector. *American Negro Folktales,* 1958; rpt. New York: Fawcett, 1970.

———. *Burying the Wind: Regional Folklore in the United States.* Chicago, IL: University of Chicago Press, 1964.

Dundes, Alan. *Mother Wit from the Laughing Barrel: Readings in the Interpretation of Afro-American Folklore.* Englewood Cliffs, NJ: Prentice-Hall, 1973.

Dyer, Richard. *White.* New York: Routledge, 1997.

Edelman, Peter. *So Rich, So Poor.* New York: The New Press, 2012.

Edgerton, Clyde. *Killer Diller.* Chapel Hill, NC: Algonquin Books; rpt. New York: Ballantine Books, 1992.

———. *Walking across Egypt.* Chapel Hill, NC: Algonquin Books; rpt. New York: Ballantine Books, 1987.

Edwards, Jay D. *The Afro-American Trickster Tale: A Structural Analysis.* Vol. 4. Monograph Series of the Folklore Publications Group. Bloomington, IN: Folklore Institute of the University of Indiana, 1978.

Ellis, Larry. "Rabbit and Big Man-Eater: Identity Shifts and Role Reversals in a Creek Indian Trickster Tale." *Thalia* 18:1–2 (1998): 3–20.

Ellison, Ralph. *Invisible Man.* New York: Modern Library, 1952; rpt. New York: Random House, 2002.

———. *Shadow and Act.* New York: Random House, 1964.

Eng, David L. "In the Shadows of a Diva: Committing Homosexuality in David Henry Hwang's *M. Butterfly.*" *Amerasia Journal* 20: 1 (1994): 93–116.

Erdoes, Richard and Alfonso Ortiz. *American Indian Trickster Tales*. New York: Viking Press, 1998.

Erdrich, Louise. *The Absolutely True Diary of a Part-Time Indian*. Art by Ellen Forney, 2007; rpt. New York: Little, Brown and Company, 2009.

———. *The Beet Queen*. 1986; rpt. New York: Bantam Books, 1989.

———. *The Bingo Palace*. New York: HarperCollins Publishers, 1994.

———. *Four Souls*. New York: HarperCollins Publishers, 2004.

———. *The Last Report on the Miracles at Little No Horse*. New York: HarperCollins Publishers, 2001.

———. *Love Medicine*. 1984; rpt. New York: Bantam Books, 1989.

———. *Love Medicine*, rev. ed. New York: HarperPerennial, 1993.

———. *The Plague of Doves*. New York: HarperCollins Publishers, 2008.

———. *The Porcupine Year*. New York: HarperCollins Publishers, 2008.

———. *The Round House*. New York: Harper, 2012.

———. *Shadow Tag*. New York: HarperCollins Publishers, 2010.

———. *Tales of Burning Love*. 1996; rpt. New York; HarperPerennial, 1997.

———. *Tracks*. New York: HarperCollins Publishers, 1988.

———. "Where I Ought to Be: A Writer's Sense of Place." *New York Times Book Review* (July 28, 1985), sec. 7: 1+.

Estés, Clarissa Pinkola. *Women Who Run with the Wolves*. New York: Ballantine Books, 1992.

Estrada, Gabriel. "Machismo." *The Oxford Encyclopedia of Latinos and Latinas in the United States*. Ed. Suzanee Oboler and Deena J. Gonzáles. Vol. 3. New York: Oxford University Press, 2005, pp. 32–36.

Farah, Nuruddin. *Secrets*. New York: Arcade Publishing, 1998; rpt. New York: Penguin Books, 1999.

Faulkner, William J. *The Days When the Animals Talked: Black American Folktales and How They Came to Be*. Chicago, IL: Follett, 1977.

Feldman, Susan, ed. *African Myths and Tales*. New York: Dell Publishing, 1963.

Ferguson, Laurie L. "Trickster Shows the Way: Humor, Resiliency, and Growth in Modern Native American Literature." PhD diss., Wright Institute Graduate School of Psychology, 2002.

Fox, Robert Elliot. *Conscientious Sorcerers: The Black Postmodernist Fiction of LeRoi Jones/Amiri Baraka, Ishmael Reed, and Samuel R. Delaney*. New York: Greenwood Press, 1987.

Franco, Dean J. *Ethnic American Literature: Comparing Chicano, Jewish, and African American Writing*. Charlottesville, VA: University of Virginia Press, 2006.

Fu, Binbin. "Revisualizing the (In)visible: Male Subjectivity in Three Asian American Graphic Novels." *Coloring America: Multi-Ethnic Engagements with Graphic Narrative*. Ed. Derek Parker Royal. Jackson, MS: University of Mississippi Press. 2013.

———. Rev. of *American Born Chinese*, by Gene Luen Yang. *MELUS* 32:3 (Fall 2007): 274–276.

García, Cristina. *The Agüero Sisters.* New York: Knopf, 1997.
———. *Monkey Hunting.* New York: Knopf, 2003.
García Escobar, Carlos René. "Pedro Urdemales y los bandidos mágicos en Guatemala." Rev. of *Cuentos populares de bandidos mágicos en Guatemala: Las hazañas de Pedro Urdemales* by Celso A. Lara Figueroa. *Folklore Americano* (January 1999): 297. Thompson/Gale. South Central Lib. System (WI) www.galenet.com, July 11, 2006.
Gates, Henry Louis Jr. *The Signifying Monkey: A Theory of African-American Literary Criticism.* New York: Oxford University Press, 1988.
Gates, Henry Louis Jr., and K. A. Appiah, eds. *Toni Morrison: Critical Perspectives Past and Present.* New York: Amistad, 1993.
Gilb, Dagoberto. "Churchgoers," pp. 101–117, and "Love in LA," pp. 199–202. *The Magic of Blood.* Albuquerque: University of New Mexico Press, 1993; rpt. New York: Grove, 1994.
Giroux, Henry A. "Paulo Freire and the Politics of Postcolonialism." *Journal of Advanced Composition* 12.1 (Winter 1992): 15–26.
Glassie, Henrie. "Three Southern Mountain Jack Tales." *Tennessee Folklore Society Bulletin* 30 (1964): 82–102.
Gordon-Reed, Annette. *The Hemingses of Monticello: An American Family.* New York: W. W. Norton & Company, 2008.
Grove, James. "Anne Tyler: Wrestling with the 'Lowlier Angel.' " *Southern Writers at Century's End.* Ed. Jeffrey J. Folkes and James A. Perkins. Lexington, KY: University of Kentucky Press, 1997, pp. 134–150.
Gutierrez, C. Paige. "The Jack Tale: A Definition of a Folk Tale Sub-Genre." *North Carolina Folklore Journal* 26 (1978): 85–110.
Halttunen, Karen. *Confidence Men and Painted Women: A Study of Middle-Class Culture in America, 1830–1870.* New Haven, CT: Yale University Press, 1982.
Hambly, Barbara. *Dead Water.* New York: Bantam Books, 2004.
Hamilton, Patrick L. *Of Space and Mind: Cognitive Mappings of Contemporary Chicano/a Fiction.* Austin, TX: University of Texas Press, 2011.
Hanrahan, Heidi M. "Funny Girls: Humor and American Women Writers." *Studies in American Humor.* New Series 3, No. 24 (2011): 9–13.
———. " 'Kiss My Foot! Here's Whar I Wuz Bred an' Born': Wags in Sherwood Bonner's Short Fiction." *Studies in American Humor* 3:19 (2009): 45–61.
Harris, George Washington. *Sut Lovingood: Yarns Spun [by a "Nat'ural Born Durn'd Fool"].* 1846; rpt. Whitefish, MT: Kessinger Publishing, n.d.
Harris, Joel Chandler. *Uncle Remus: His Songs and His Sayings,* rev ed. 1895; rpt. New York: Appleton & Company, 1921.
Harris, Trudier. *Fiction and Folklore: The Novels of Toni Morrison.* Knoxville, TN: The University of Tennessee Press, 1991.
Heredia, Juanita. "From Golden Age Mexican Cinema to Transnational Border Feminism: The Community of Spectators in *Loving Pedro Infante.*" *Aztlán* 33:2 (2008): 37–58.

Hernández, Ellie D. *Postnationallism in Chicana/o Literature and Culture.* Austin, TX: University of Texas Press, 2009.

Hicks, D. Emily. "Deterritorialization and Border Writing." *Ethics/ Aesthetics: Post-Modern Positions.* Ed. Robert Merrill. Washington, DC: Maissoneuve, 1988, pp. 47–58.

Hobbs, Michael. "Living In-Between: Tayo as Radical Reader in Leslie Marmon Silko's *Ceremony.*" *Western American Literature* 28:4 (1994): 301–312.

Holditch, W. Kenneth. "Another Kind of Confederacy: John Kennedy Toole." *Literary New Orleans in the Modern World.* Ed. Richard S. Kennedy. Baton Rouge, LA: Louisiana State University Press, 1998, pp. 102–122.

Holley, Joe. "Dagoberto Gilb." *Conversations with Texas Writers.* Ed. Frances Leonard Ramona Cearley. Austin, TX: University of Texas Press, 2005, pp. 109–117.

Hooper, Johnson Jones. *Some Adventures of Capt. Simon Suggs* (1843–1851). Upper Saddle River, NJ: Literature House, 1970.

Hsu, Francis L. K. *American and Chinese: Two Ways of Life.* New York: H. Schuman, 1953.

Hua, Chuang. *Crossings.* New York, NY: Dial Press, 1968; rpt. Boston: Northeastern University Press, 1986.

Hughes, Langston. "Theme For English B." *The Collected Poems of Langston Hughes.* Ed. Arnold Rampersad and David Roessel. New York: Vintage, 1994, pp. 409–410.

Hurston, Zora Neale. *Mules and Men.* New York: Lippincot, 1935; rpt. New York: Harper, 1990.

Hwang, David Henry. *M. Butterfly.* New York: Plume, 1989.

———. "Worlds Apart." *American Theatre* (January 2000): 50–56.

Hyde, Lewis. *Trickster Makes This World: Mischief, Myth, and Art.* New York: Farrar, Strauss and Giroux, 1998.

Inge, M. Thomas and Ed Piacentino, eds. *Southern Frontier Humor: An Anthology.* Columbia, MO: University of Missouri Press, 2010.

Isernhagen, Hartwig. *Momaday, Vizenor, Armstrong: Conversations on American Indian Writing.* Norman, OK: University of Oklahoma Press, 1999.

Islas, Arturo. *La Mollie and the King of Tears: A Novel.* Ed. and Afterword, Paul Skenazy. Albuquerque: University of New Mexico Press, 1996.

Jackson, Rosemary. *Fantasy: The Literature of Subversion.* London: Methuen, 1981.

Johns, Gillian. "Going Southwest: American Humor and the Rhetoric of Race in Modern African-American Fiction and Authorship." Diss. Temple University, 2000.

Johnson, David E. and Scott Michaelsen, eds. *Border Theory: The Limits of Cultural Politics.* Minneapolis, MN: University of Minnesota Press, 1997.

Jones, Charles C. *Negro Myths from the Georgia Coast.* Boston, MA: Houghton Mifflin, 1888.

Jung, Carl G. "On the Psychology of the Trickster Figure." *The Trickster: A Study in American Indian Mythology.* Ed. Paul Radin, New York: Schocken Books, 1972, pp. 195–211. Rpt. from *The Archetypes and the Collective Unconscious,* 2nd ed. Translated by R. F. C. Hull. Bollingen Series 20. Vol. 9, Pt.1. Princeton, NJ: Princeton University Press, 1959. Pars. 456–488.

———. "On the Relation of Analytical Psychology to Poetry, Vol 15." *The Spirit in Man, Art, and Literature: Collected Works.* Translated by R. F. C. Hull. Bollingen Series 20. Princeton, NJ: Princeton University Press, 1980, pars. 97–132.

Jurich, Marilyn. *Scheherazade's Sisters: Trickster Heroines and Their Stories in World Literature.* Westport, CT: Greenwood, 1998.

Kerr, Douglass. "David Henry Hwang." *Asian Voices in English.* Ed. Mimi Chan and Roy Harris. Hong Kong: Hong Kong University Press, 1991.

Kesey, Ken. *One Flew over the Cuckoo's Nest.* New York: Viking Press, 1962; rpt. New York: Penguin Books, 2003.

Kevane, Bridget and Juanita Heredia. *Latina Self-Portraits: Interviews with Contemporary Women Writers.* Albuquerque: University of Northern Mexico Press, 2000.

Kibler, Jr., James Everett, ed. *Fireside Tales: Stories of the Old Dutch Fork.* Columbia, SC: Dutch Fork Press, 1984.

Kim, Elaine H. *Asian American Literature: An Introduction to the Writings and Their Social Context.* Philadelphia, PA: Temple University Press, 1982.

———. "Asian Americans and American Popular Culture." *Dictionary of Asian-American History.* Ed. Hyung-Chan Kim. Westport, CN: Greenwood Publishing, 1986, pp. 99–114.

Kingston, Maxine Hong. *China Men.* New York: Vintage Books, 1989.

———. *Tripmaster Monkey: His Fake Book.* New York: Knopf, 1989; rpt. New York: Vintage Books, 1990.

———. *Woman Warrior: Memoirs of a Girlhood Among Ghosts.* New York: Knopf, 1976.

Koén-Sarano, Matilda, collector and ed. *Folktales of Joha, Jewish Trickster.* Trans. David Herman. Philadelphia, PA: The Jewish Publication Society, 2003.

Komunyakaa, Yusef. *Pleasure Dome: New and Collected Poems.* Middletown, CT: Wesleyan University Press, 2001.

Lake-Thom, Bobby (Medicine Grizzly Bear). *Spirits of the Earth: A Guide to Native American Nature Symbols, Stories, and Ceremonies.* New York: Plume Books, 1997.

Lakhnavi, Ghalib and Abdullah Bilgrami. *The Adventures of Amir Hamza: Lord of the Auspicious Planetary Conjunction.* Trans. Musharraf Ali Farooqi. New York: Modern Library, 2007.

Larue, Dorie. Rev. of "*Crazy in Alabama.*" *Southern Quarterly* 32:2 (Winter 1994): 161.

Laval, Ramon A. *Veinte cuentos de Pedro Urdemales*. www.librosmaravillo sos.com/veintecuentos/index.html (accessed February 11, 2012).

Lee, Robert G. *Orientals: Asian Americans in Popular Culture*. Philadelphia, PA: Temple University Press, 1998.

Lenz, William E. *Fast Talk and Flush Times: The Confidence Man as a Literary Convention*. Columbia, MO: University of Missouri Press, 1985.

Leonard, Elmore. *Pagan Babies*. New York: Delacorte Press, 2000.

———. *When the Women Come out to Dance: Stories*. New York: William Morrow, 2002.

Li, David Leiwei. *Imagining the Nation: Asian American Literature and Cultural Consent*. Stanford, CA: Stanford University Press, 1998.

Li, Shu-yan. "Otherness and Transformation in *Eat a Bowl of Tea* and *Crossings*." *MELUS* 18:4 (1993): 99–110.

Li, Wensin. "Gender Negotiations and the Asian American Literary Imagination." *Asian American Literary Studies*. Ed. Guiyon Huang. Edinburgh: Edinburgh University Press, 2005, pp. 109–131.

Li, Zeng. "Diasporic Self, Cultural Other: Negotiating Ethnicity through Transformation in the Fiction of Tan and Kingston. *Language and Literature* 28 (2003): 1–15.

Lim, Shirley Geok-lin and Amy Ling, eds. *Reading the Literatures of Asian America*. Philadelphia, PA: Temple University Press, 1992.

Ling, Amy. *Between Worlds: Women Writers of Chinese Ancestry*. New York: Pergamon Press, 1990.

Ling, Jinqi. "Reading for Historical Specificities: Gender Negotiations in Louis Chu's *Eat a Bowl of Tea*." *MELUS* 20:1 (1995): 35–51.

Linquist, Mark A. and Martin Zanger, eds. *Buried Roots and Indestructible Seeds: The Survival of American Indian Life in Story, History, and Spirit*. Madison, WI: The University of Wisconsin Press, 1994.

Longstreet, A. B. *Georgia Scenes: Characters, Incidents, etc. in the First Half Century of the Republic. 1835; rpt.* New York: Sagamore Press, 1954.

Lord, Bette Bao. *The Middle Heart*. New York: Alfred A. Knopf; rpt. Fawcett Columbine, 1996.

Lowe, John. "Monkey Kings and Mojo: Postmodern Ethnic Humor in Kingston, Reed, and Vizenor." *MELUS* 21:4 (Winter 1996): 103–26.

Lye, Colleen. *America's Asia: Facial Form and American Literature, 1893–1945*. Princeton, NJ: Princeton University Press, 2004.

Lynn, Kenneth S. *Mark Twain and Old Southwest Humor*. Boston, MA: Little, Brown, and Company, 1959.

Lyons, Bonnie. " 'Making His Muscles Work For Himself': An Interview with David Henry Hwang." *The Literary Review* 42 (Winter 1999): 230–244.

MacKethan, Lucinda. "Redeeming Blackness: Urban Allegories of O'Connor, Percy and Toole." *Studies in the Literary Imagination* 27:2 (Fall 1994): 29–40.

MacNeil, Robert and William Cran. "Hispanic Immigration: Reconquest or Assimilation?" *Do You Speak American?: A Companion to the PBS Television Series.* New York: Doubleday, 2005.

Mankiller, Wilma. *Mankiller, A Chief and Her People.* New York: St. Martin's Press, 1993.

Margolin, Malcolm, ed. *The Way We Lived: California Indian Stories, Songs and Reminiscences.* Berkeley, CA: Heyday Books, 1981; rev. 1993.

Martin, Robert K. "Gender, Race, and the Colonial Body: Carson McCuller's Filipino Boy, and David Henry Hwang's Chinese Woman." *Canadian Review of American Studies* 23:1 (Fall 1992): 95–106. EBSCO (accessed December 7, 2010).

Martin, W. Todd. "Where Trouble Sleeps: Clyde Edgerton's Criticism of Moralistic Christianity." *Renascence* 53 (2001): 257–266.

Martínez, Demetria. *Confessions of a Berlitz-Tape Chicana.* Norman, OK: University of Oklahoma Press, 2005.

Martinez, Nina Marie. *¡Caramba!* New York: Anchor Books, 2004.

May, William T. *Testing the National Covenant: Fears and Appetites in American Politics.* Washington, DC: Georgetown University Press, 2011.

McCarthy, William Bernard, ed. *Cinderella in America: A Book of Folk and Fairy Tales.* Jackson, MI: University Press of Mississippi, 2007.

———. *Jack in Two Worlds: Contemporary North American Tales and Their Tellers.* Chapel Hill, NC: University of North Carolina Press, 1994.

McDermott, Gerald. *Raven: A Trickster Tale from the Pacific Northwest.* San Diego, CA: Harcourt Brace & Company, 1993.

McEneaney, Kevin T. *Tom Wolfe's America: Heroes, Pranksters, and Fools.* Westport, CT: Praeger, 2009.

McGee, Patrick. *Ishmael Reed and the Ends of Race.* New York: St. Martin's Press, 1997.

McGowan, Miranda Oshige and James Lindgren. "Testing the Model Minority Myth." *Northwestern University Law Review* 100:1 (2006): 331–378.

McKenna, John J. "Teaching Trickster Figures in Short Fictions." *Eureka Studies in Teaching Short Fiction* 2:1 (Fall 2001): 2–12.

Mehaffy, Marilyn and AnaLouise Keating. " 'Carrying the Message': Denise Chávez on the Politics of Chicana Becoming." *Aztlán* 26:1 (Spring 2001): 127–156.

Mermann-Jozwiak, Elizabeth and Nancy Sullivan, eds. *Conversations with Mexican American Writers: Languages and Literatures in the Borderlands.* Jackson, MI: University Press of Mississippi, 2009.

Michaelsen, Scott and David E. Johnson, eds. *Border Theory: The Limits of Cultural Politics.* Minneapolis, MN: University of Minnesota Press, 1997.

Mielke, Laura L. " 'The Saga of the Third Word Belle': Resurrecting the Ethnic Woman in Ishmael Reed's *Flight to Canada*," *MELUS* 32 (Spring 2007): 3–27.

Minick, Jim. "Latino Hillbilly: An Interview with Marcos McPeek Villatoro."
    Appalachian Journal: A Regional Studies Review. 28:2 (Winter 2001):
    201–220.
Minton, John and David Evans. *"The Coon in the Box": A Global Folktale in
    African-American Tradition.* Helsinki: Academia Scientiarum Fennica,
    2001.
Mirandé, Alfredo. *Hombres y Machos: Masculinity and Latino Culture.*
    Boulder, CO: Westview Press, 1997.
Mitchell, Jake and Robert Wilton Burton. *De Remnant Truth: The Tales
    of Jake Mitchell and Robert Wilton Burton.* Collected by Kathryn Sport
    and Bert Hitchcock. Tuscaloosa, AL: The University of Alabama Press,
    1991.
Monsma, Bradley John. " 'Active Readers...Obverse Tricksters': Trickster
    Texts and Cross-Cultural Reading." *Modern Language Studies* 26:4 (Fall
    1996): 83–98.
Morgan, Winifred. *An American Icon: Brother Jonathan and American
    Identity.* Newark, DE: University of Delaware Press, 1988.
Morrison, Toni. *Tar Baby.* 1981; rpt. New York: A Plum Book, 1987.
———. "Unspeakable Things Unspoken: The Afro-American Presence in
    American Literature." *Michigan Quarterly Review* 28:1 (Winter 1989):
    9–34; rpt. in *Modern Critical Views: Toni Morrison*, edited by Harold
    Bloom. New York: Chelsea House Publishers, 1990, pp. 201–230.
Mosley, Walter. *Bad Boy Brawly Brown.* Boston, MA: Little, Brown and
    Company, 2002.
———. *The Best of NPR: Writers on Writing.* 1997; New York: Time Warner
    Audio Books, 1998.
———. *Blonde Faith.* New York: Little, Brown and Company, 2007.
———. *Fear Itself.* Boston, MA: Little, Brown and Company, 2003.
———. *Devil in a Blue Dress.* New York: W. W. Norton, 1990; rpt. New
    York: Pocket Books, 1991.
Murphy, Peter. *John the Revelator.* Boston, MA: Houghton Mifflin Harcourt,
    2009.
Murray, Charles. Coming Apart: The State of White America, 1960–2010.
    New York: Crown Forum, 2012.
Newton, John. "Sherman Alexie's Autoethnography." *Contemporary
    Literature* 62:2 (2001): 413–428.
Neely, Barbara. *Blanche Among the Talented Tenth.* New York: Penguin
    Books, 1994.
———. *Blanche Cleans Up.* New York: Viking, 1998.
———. *Blanche on the Lam.* New York: St. Martin's Press, 1992.
Neely, Barbara. *Blanche Passes Go.* New York: Viking, 2000.
Nelson, William. "The Comic Grotesque in Recent Fiction." *Thalia* (Ottawa,
    Ontario) 5:2 (Fall, Winter 1982): 36–40.
Nguyen, Viet Thanh. *Race and Resistance: Literature and Politics in Asian
    America.* New York: Oxford University Press, 2002.

Nicolaisen, W. F. H. "English Jack and American Jack." *Midwestern Journal of Language and Folklore* 4 (1978): 27–36.

Northhouse, Cameron. *Ishmael Reed: An Interview.* Dallas, TX: Contemporary Research, 1993.

Obourn, Megan. "Hybridity, Identity, and Representation in *La Mollie and the King of Tears. American Literature* 80:1 (March 2008): 141–166.

Oehlschlaeger, Fritz, ed. *Old Southwest Humor from the "St. Louis Reveille," 1844–50.* Columbia, MO: University of Missouri Press, 1990.

Ouyang, Huining. "Rewriting the Butterfly Story: Tricksterism in Onoto Watanna's *A Japanese Nightingale* and Sui Sin Far's 'The Smuggling of Tie Co.' " *Alternative Rhetorics.* Ed. Laura Gray-Rosendale and Sibylle Gruber. Albany, NY: State University of New York Press, 2001, pp. 203–217.

———. "The Trickster Narrative in *Miss Numè of Japan*: A Japanese-American Romance." *Doubled Plots: Romance and History.* Ed. Susan Strehle and Mary Paniccia Carden. Jackson, MI: University Press of Mississippi, 2003, pp. 86–106.

Owens, Louis. *Other Destinies: Understanding the American Indian Novel.* Norman, OK: University of Oklahoma Press, 1992.

Painter, Nell Irvin. *The History of the White Race.* New York: W. W. Norton & Company, 2010.

Palmer, Parker J. *Healing the Heart of Democracy: The Courage to Create a Politics Worthy of the Human Spirit.* San Francisco, CA: Jossey-Bass, 2011.

Pasquaretta, Paul. "Sacred Chance: Gambling and the Contemporary Native American Indian Novel." *MELUS* 21:2 (1996): 21–33.

Pegler-Gordon, Anna. "Chinese Exclusion, Photography, and the Development of U.S. Immigration Policy." *American Quarterly* 58:1 (March 2006): 51–77, 267.

Peiffer, Katrina Schimmoeller. *Coyote at Large: Humor in American Nature Writing.* Salt Lake City, UT: University of Utah Press, 2000.

Pelton, Robert D. *The Trickster in West Africa: A Study of Mythic Irony and Sacred Delight.* Berkeley, CA: University of California Press, 1980.

Perdue, Jr., Charles L., ed. *Outwitting the Devil: Jack Tales from Wise County, Virginia.* Santa Fe, NM: Ancient City Press, 1987.

Perez, Vincent. " 'Running' and Resistance: Nihilism and Cultural Memory in Chicano Urban Narratives." *MELUS* 25:2 (Summer 2000): 133–146.

Pérez-Torres, Rafael. *Mestizje: Critical Uses of Race in Chicano Culture.* Minneapolis, MN: University of Minnesota Press, 2006.

Peterson, Nancy. "Indi'n Humor and Trickster Justice in *The Bingo Palace.*" *The Chippewa Landscape of Louise Erdrich.* Ed. Allan Chavkin. Tuscaloosa, AL: University of Alabama Press, 1999.

Petrone, Penny, ed. *Northern Voices: Inuit Writing in English.* Toronto: University of Toronto Press, 1988.

Piccoli, Sean. "John Irving's 'Circus' Goes to Strange and Funny Places." *The Washington Times* (September 18, 1994). Final edition, Part B. Books, 88.

Ping, Wang. *American Visa: Short Stories.* Minneapolis, MN: Coffee House, 1994.

Poey, Delia and Virgil Suarez, eds. "Introduction." *Iguana Dreams: New Latino Fiction.* New York: HarperPerennial, 1992.

Power, Susan. *Grass Dancer.* G. P. Putnam, 1994; rpt. New York: Berkley Books, 1997.

Purdy, John. "Crossroads: A Conversation with Sherman Alexie." *Studies in American Indian Literatures* 9:4 (Winter 1997): 1–18.

Radin, Paul. *The Trickster: A Study in American Indian Mythology.* 1956. rpt. New York: Schocken Books, 1972.

Radner, Joan N. "AFS Now and Tomorrow: The View from the Stepladder" (AFS Presidential Address, October 28, 2000). *Journal of American Folklore* 114 (453): 263–276.

Ramsey, Jarold, ed. *Coyote Was Going There.* Seattle, WA: University of Washington Press, 1977.

———. *Reading the Fire: Essays in the Traditional Literatures of the Far West.* Lincoln, NE: University of Nebraska Press, 1983.

Reder, Deanna and Linda M. Morra, eds. *Troubling Tricksters: Revisioning Critical Conversations.* Waterloo, Ontario: Wilfrid Laurier University Press, 2010.

Reed, Ishmael. *Flight to Canada.* 1976; rpt. New York: Atheneum Publishers, 1989.

Reesman, Jeanne Campbell, ed. *Trickster Lives: Culture and Myth in American Fiction.* Athens: University of Georgia Press, 2001.

Revilla, Linda A. et al., eds. *Bearing Dreams, Shaping Visions: Asian Pacific American Perspectives.* Pullman, WA: Washington State University Press, 1993.

Roberts, John W. "The African American Animal Trickster as Hero." *Redefining American Literary History.* Ed. A LaVonne Brown Ruoff and Jerry W. Ward. New York: MLA, 1990, pp. 97–114.

———. *From Trickster to Badman: The Black Folk Hero in Slavery and Freedom.* Philadelphia, PA: University of Pennsylvania Press, 1989.

———. *The Trickster in West Africa: A Study of Mythic Irony and Sacred Delight.* Berkeley, CA: University of California Press, 1980.

———. "West African Tricksters: Web of Purpose, Dance of Delight." *Mythical Trickster Figures: Contours, Contexts, and Criticism.* Ed. William J. Hynes and William G. Doty. Tuscaloosa, AL: University of Alabama Press, 1993, pp. 122–140.

Rodríguez, Richard T. *Next of Kin: The Family in Chicano/a Cultural Politics.* Durham: Duke University Press, 2009.

Roediger, David R. *The Wages of Whiteness: Race and the Making of the American Working Class.* London: Verso Books, 1991.

Romero, Rolando J. "Border of Fear, Border of Desire." *Borderlines: Studies in American Culture* 1.1 (1993): 36–70.

Rosten, Leo. *The Joys of Yiddish.* New York: Pocket Books, 1968.

Royal, Derek Parker. "Literary Genre as Ethnic Resistance in Maxine Hong Kingston's *Tripmaster Monkey: His Fake Book.*" *MELUS* 29:2 (Summer 2004): 141–156.

Ruoff, A. LaVonne Brown and Jerry W. Ward, eds. *Redefining American Literary History*. New York: MLA, 1990.

Ryan, Allan J. *The Trickster Shift: Humor and Irony in Contemporary Native Art*. Vancouver: University of British Columbia Press, 1999.

Said, Edward. *Orientalism*. New York: Vintage Books, 1979.

Scheub, Harold. *Story*. Madison, WI: University of Madison Press, 1998,

Shapiro, Elliott H. "Authentic Watermelon: Maxine Hong Kingston's American Novel." *MELUS* 26 (Spring 2001): 5–28.

Shine, Ted. "Contribution." *The Best Short Plays of 1972*. Ed. Stanley Richards. New York: Equinox Books, 1972.

Silko, Leslie Marmon. *Ceremony*. New York: Viking, 1977; rpt. New York: Penguin, 1986.

Slack, John S. "The Comic Savior: The Dominance of the Trickster in Louise Erdrich's *Love Medicine*." *North Dakota Quarterly* 61 (1993): 118–29.

Slaughter, Stephany. "The Ambiguous Representation of Macho in Mexico's Golden Age Cinema: Pedro Infante as Pepe el Toro." *Tinta* 7:7 (2003): 23–42.

Smith, David Lee. *Folklore of the Winnebago Tribe*. Norman, OK: University of Oklahoma Press, 1997.

Smith, Jeanne Rosier. *Writing Tricksters: Mythic Gambols in American Ethnic Literature*. Berkeley, CA: University of California Press, 1997.

Spurgeon, Tom. "CR Sunday Interview with Gene Luen Yang" from *the Comics Reporter*, June, 20, 2010. *Graphic Novels and Comic Books*. Ed. Kan, Kat [Katherine]. The Reference Shelf 82:5. New York: H.W. Wilson Company, 2010, pp. 168–175.

Stewart, Michael and Jerry Herman. *Hello, Dolly!* pp. 157–178 in *The Best Plays of 1963–1964*. Ed. Henry Hews. New York: Dodd, Mead & Company, 1964.

Suarez, Ernest. *Southbound: Interviews with Southern Poets*. Columbia, MO: University of Missouri Press, 1999.

Tannen, Ricki Stephanie. *The Female Trickster: The Mask that Reveals: Post-Jungian and Postmodern Psychological Perspectives on Women in Contemporary Culture*. London: Routledge Taylor & Francis Group, 2007.

Taylor, Paul Beekman. "Chicano Secrecy in the Fiction of Rudolfo A. Anaya." *Journal of the Southwest* 39:2 (Summer 1997): 239–265. Gale. Madison, WI: Edgewood College Library, February 1, 2007.

Taylor, Tom. "Our American Cousin." In *British Plays of the Nineteenth Century; An Anthology to Illustrate the Evolution of the Drama*. 1858; rpt. in Ed. J. O. Bailey. New York: Odyssey Press, 1966.

Taylor-Guthrie, Danille, ed. *Conversations with Toni Morrison*. Jackson, MI: University Press of Mississippi, 1994.

Tennyson, Alfred Lord Tennyson. *Idylls of the King: In Twelve Books*. 1885; rpt. New York: St. Martin's Press, 1968.

Thomas, H. Nigel. *From Folklore to Fiction: A Study of Folk Heroes and Rituals in the Black American Novel*. New York: Greenwood Press, 1988.

Thoreau, Henry David. "On the Duty of Civil Disobedience." 1849; rpt. *Walden; and Civil Disobedience*. New York, New York : Penguin Books, 1983.

Tobar, Héctor. *Translation Nation: Defining a New American Identity in the Spanish-Speaking United States*. New York: Riverhead Books, 2005.

Todorov, Tzvetan. *The Fantastic: A Structural Approach to a Literary Genre*. Trans. Richard Howard. Ithaca, NY: Cornell University Press, 1975.

Torres, Lourdes. "In the Contact Zone: Code-Switching Strategies by Latino/a Writers." *MELUS* 32:1 (Spring 2007): 75–96.

Toole, John Kennedy. *A Confederacy of Dunces*. Baton Rouge, LA: Louisiana State Press, 1980.

Traber, Daniel S. *Whiteness, Otherness, and the Individualism Paradox from Huck to Punk*. New York: Palgrave Macmillan, 2007.

Tuttle, George. "...Noir Fiction." www.geocities.com/SoHo/Suite/3855 (accessed July 22, 2009).

———. "What Is Noir?" *Mystery Scene* 43 (1994): 35, 36, 91, 92.

———. "What Is Noir." http:noirfiction.info/what.html (accessed July 22, 2009).

Twain, Mark. *The Adventures of Huckleberry Finn*. New York: Harper & Row.

———. *How to Tell a Story and Other Essays*. New York: Harper & Brothers, 1897.

———. "The Man Who Corrupted Hadleyville." *Collected Tales, Sketches & Essays*, Vol. 2. New York: The Library of America, 1992, pp. 390–438.

Tyler, Anne. *The Accidental Tourist*. New York: Knopf, 1985.

[Tyler, Royall.] *The Contrast*. Philadelphia, PA: Pritchard & Hall, 1790. Rpt. New York: The Dunlap Society, 1887.

Velie, Alan R. "Gerald Vizenor's Indian Gothic." *MELUS* 17 (1991): 75–86. *MLA Bibliography*. http://0-web.ebscohost.com.oscar.edgewood.edu /ehost/resultsadvanced?vid=2&hid=102&sid=ad7dd75f-e929-4d77 -8517-69d9939385f3%40sessionmgr113&bquery=(TI+(Gerald+Vizeno r's+Indian+Gothic))&bdata=JmRiPW16aCZ0eXBlPTEmc2l0ZT1laG9z dC1saXZl (accessed February 6, 2004).

Villatoro, Marcos McPeek. *The Holy Spirit of My Uncle's Cojones*. Houston, TX: Arte Público, 1999.

Vizenor, Gerald. *Bearheart: The Heirship Chronicles*. Minneapolis, MN: University of Minnesota Press, 1990.

———. *Darkness in Saint Louis Bearheart*. Saint Paul: Truck Press, 1978.

———. *Griever: An American Monkey King in China*. Normal, IL: Illinois State University Press, 1987.

Vizenor, Gerald. *The Heirs of Columbus*. Hanover, NH: Wesleyan University Press, 1991.

———, ed. *Narrative Chance: Postmodern Discourse on Native American Indian Literature*. Norman, OK: University of Oklahoma Press, 1993.

———. "Trickster Discourse." *American Indian Quarterly* 14 (Summer 1990): 277–287.

———. "Trickster Discourse: Comic and Tragic Themes in Native American Literature." *Buried Roots and Indestructible Seeds: The Survival of American Indian Life in Story, History, and Spirit*. Ed. Mark A. Lindquist and Martin Zanger. Madison, WI: The University of Wisconsin Press, 1994, pp. 67–83.

———. *The Trickster of Liberty: Tribal Heirs to a Wild Baronage*. Minneapolis, MN: University of Minnesota Press, 1988.

Walker, Alice. *The Color Purple*. New York, NY: Harcourt Brace Jovanovich, 1982; rpt. Orlando, FL: A Harvest Book, 2003.

Walker, Jr., Deward, in collaboration with Daniel N. Matthews. *Nez Perce Coyote Tales: The Myth Cycle*. Norman, OK: University of Oklahoma Press, 1998.

Wallace, Karen L. "Liminality and Myth in Native American Fiction: *Ceremony* and *The Ancient Child*." *American Indian Culture and Research Journal* 20:4 (1996): 91–119.

Watkins, Mel. "Talk with Toni Morrison." *The New York Times* (September 11, 1977): 48+.

———. *On the Real Side: Laughing, Lying, and Signifying—The Underground Tradition of African-American Humor that Transformed American Culture, From Slavery to Richard Pryor*. New York: A Touchstone Book, 1994.

Welch, James. *Fools Crow*. New York: Viking Books, 1986; rpt. New York: Penguin, 1987.

Welsch, Roger L. *Omaha Tribal Myths and Trickster Tales*. Chicago, IL: Sage Publications, 1981.

Whall, Helen M. "Walter Mosley and the Books of Ezekiel." *Paradoxa* No. 16 (2001): 190–202.

Wiget, Andrew. *Native American Literature*. Boston, MA: Twayne Publishers, 1985, pp. 15–21.

Williams, Paul V. A., ed. *The Fool and the Trickster: Studies in Honour of Enid Welsford*. Totowa, NJ: Rowman & Littlefield, 1979.

Wilson, Jr., Charles E. *Walter Mosley: A Critical Companion*. Westport, CT: Greenwood Press, 2003.

Wisse, Ruth R., "Jewish American Renaissance." *The Cambridge Companion to Jewish American Literature*. Ed. Michael P. Kramer and Hana Wirth-Nesher. Cambridge, UK: Cambridge University Press, 2003, pp. 190–211.

Wolfe, Tom. *The Electric Kool-Aid Acid Test*. New York: Farrar, Straus and Giroux, 1968; rpt. New York: Bantam Books, 1969.

Wong, Hertha D. "An Interview with Louise Erdrich and Michael Dorris," *The North Dakota Quarterly* 55 (1987): 107–112.

Wong, Sau-ling Cynthia. *Reading Asian American Literature: From Necessity to Extravagance*. Princeton, NJ: Princeton University Press, 1993.

Wong, Sau-ling Cynthia and Stephen H. Sumida, eds. *A Resource Guide to Asian American Literature*. New York: Modern Language Association of American, 2001.

[Wu, Ch'êng-ên.] *The Journey to the West*. Trans. Anthony C. Yu. Chicago, IL: University of Chicago Press, 1977, 4 vols.

Yang, Gene Luen. *American Born Chinese*. New York: First Second, 2006.

Young, Kevin. *The Grey Album: On the Blackness of Blackness*. Minneapolis, MN: Graywolf Press, 2012.

Young, Mary. "Walter Mosley, Detective Fiction and Black Culture." *Journal of Popular Culture* 32:1 (Summer 1998): 141–150.

Zipes, Jack. *Relentless Progress: The Reconfiguration of Children's Literature, Fairy Tales, and Storytelling*. New York: Routledge, 2009.

Zwagerman, Sean. *Wit's End: Women's Humor as Rhetorical & Performative Strategy*. Pittsburgh, PA: University of Pittsburgh Press, 2010.

INDEX

Note: Locators followed by 'n' denotes notes.

Adelman, Peter, 73
African American tricksters
    and African tricksters, 17–19
    and animal tricksters, 19
    and badman folk hero, 41–2
    characteristics of, 15–17
    and humor, 18–26
    and John and the Massa tales,
        19–23
    and slave tricksters, 18–19
    tradition of, 23–5
    see also Yusef Komunyakaa; Toni
        Morrison; Walter Mosley;
        Ishmael Reed; Ted Shine; Alice
        Walker
Akoma, Chiji, 178n1
Akunin, Boris, 44
Aldama, Frederick Luis, 160
Alexander, Jan, 215n87
Alexie, Sherman, 8, 65, 191n35–6
    The Absolutely True Diary of a
        Part-Time Indian, 48–9
    "Do You Know Where I Am?"
        191n37
    The Lone Ranger and Tonto Fist
        Fight in Heaven, 55
    Reservation Blues, 55
    Smoke Signals, 55
Allen, Paula Gunn, 50, 193n62
American exceptionalism, 2
American Indian tricksters
    characteristics of, 47–51
    and humor, 8, 51, 54, 59, 61,
        65–6, 69, 72
    and oral literature, 51–4

see also Sherman Alexie; Robert J.
    Conley; Louise Erdrich; Leslie
    Marmon Silko; GeraldVizenor;
    JamesWelch
Ammons, Elizabeth, 12, 201n13
Anaya, Rudolfo, 9, 147, 152
    "B. Traven Is Alive and Well in
        Cuernavaca," 143–5, 169
    Bless Me, Ultima, 143
    and linguistic influences, 136
    The Man Who Could Fly, 143
    "The Native Lawyer," 145,
        222n57
    Zia Summer, 142–3
Arias, Ron: The Road to
    Tamazunchale, 9, 142, 145–7,
    152, 169
Arnold, Matthew, 6
Aubert, Alvin, 186n100

Babcock-Abrahams, Barbara, 5, 53,
    168, 182n55, 191n34, 205n73
Bakhtin, Mikhail, 193n62
Ballinger, Franchot, 49, 53, 109,
    189n8
Barlow, Genevieve, 139
Barr, Marleen B., 226n122
Barrera Herrera, Eduardo, 133
Behnam, Miriam, 180–1n35
Belasco, David, 213n48
Bellow, Saul, 169
    The Adventures of Augie March,
        100, 175n2
    "A Silver Dish," 95–8, 206–7n87
Bertolino, James, 28

Blackwell, Angela Glover, 3
Blaeser, Kimberly M., 69, 194n72
Blair, Elizabeth, 193n55
Blue Cloud, Peter, 53–4
Blue Man Group, 10
border writing, 131–4, 222n61
Bowers, Sharon Manybeads, 198–9n122
Brewster, H. Pomeroy, 202n26
Brown, Claude: *Manchild in the Promised Land*, 27
Brown v. Board of Education, 1, 30
Bryant, Jerry H., 42, 44, 186–7n109
Burton, Robert Wilton, 23

Caldwell, Gail, 214n75
Callaway, Mary Katherine, 205n69
Castillo, Susan Perez, 195n83
Castro, Rafaela G., 219–20n23
Cawelti, John G., 43
Cervantes, Miguel de, 146
Chan, Jeffrey, 108
Chandler, Raymond, 44
Chang, Hsiao-hung, 215n78
Chang, Joan, 113
Chase, Richard, 201n20, 202n26
Chaucer, Geoffrey: *Canterbury Tales*, 63, 77–8
Chávez, Denise, 9, 152
  Face of an Angel, 136
  Loving Pedro Infante, 153, 162–4
  on use of the term *macho*, 225n103
Cheadle, Don, 42
Chesnutt, Charles
  The Conjure Woman, 23–4, 44, 144, 221–2n49
  "Po' Sandy," 23–4, 144
Childress, Mark, 8
  on being a storyteller, 204n62
  Crazy in Alabama, 84–5, 100, 169
Chin, Marilyn, 119–20
Chin, Tsai, 110, 210n19
Chinese American tricksters

characteristics of, 103–4
and the "ethnic dilemma," 104–6
and the Monkey King, 103–29
and transformation, 128–9
see also Louis Chu; Chuang Hua; David Henry Hwang; Maxine Hong Kingston; Bette Bao Lord; Wu Ch'êng-ên; Gene Luen Yang
Chu, Louis: *Eat a Bowl of Tea*, 108–10, 113, 211n25
Chua, Cheng Lok, 211n27
Civil Rights Era, 1, 10, 26, 30, 42, 128
Clinton, Bill, 43
Coel, Margaret: *Killing Raven*, 65
Colbert, Steven, 6, 191–2n37
Coltelli, Laura, 59
"confidence man," use of the phrase, 84
Conley, Robert J.: *The Dark Way*, 49, 55
Conniff, Richard, 4–5
Constitution, United States, 2, 6, 167, 170
Cox, James, 191n35
Cullen, Countee, 23

Davis, III, Charles Thomas, 203n31
Davis, Donald, 77–8
Dawes, Henry L., 71–2, 195–6n90
Dawes Severalty Act, 66, 71–2
Declaration of Independence, 2, 6–7, 30, 170
Degabriele, Maria, 213n55
Delany, Bessie, 74
Díaz, Junot, 9, 169, 222–3n66
  "Aguantando," 150–1
  Drown, 150–2
  "Edison, New Jersey," 150–2
  on multiple traditions, 137
Dong, Lan, 127
Dorson, Richard M., 76, 131, 140
Doty, William G., 12

Douglass, Frederick: *Narrative of the Life of Frederick Douglass, an American Slave*, 22
Dunbar, Paul Lawrence, 23
Dyer, Ricahrd, 200n4

Eaton, Winifred (OnotoWatanna), 210n18
Edelman, Peter, 199n1
Edgerton, Clyde, 8, 85, 88–9, 100, 204–5n64
    Killer Diller, 86–7
    Walking across Egypt, 85–6
egalitarianism, 2, 11, 100, 167–8, 216n86
Ellison, Ralph, 25
    on American humor, 75
    Invisible Man, 1, 23, 39, 44, 175n2
    Shadow and Act, 9, 75, 94, 178n22
    on tricksters in modern fiction, 9, 94
Erdoes, Richard, 54
Erdrich, Louise, 8, 13, 56, 63
    The Beet Queen, 64, 71, 197–8n107
    The Bingo Palace, 49, 64, 68–70, 196n95, 197–8n107
    Four Souls, 64, 68, 196n95
    juvenile fiction of, 194n78
    The Last Report on the Miracles at Little No Horse, 64–5, 67, 69, 196n96
    Love Medicine, 64, 69, 196n90
    The Round House, 196n96
    Tales of Burning Love, 64, 70–1
    Tracks, 64, 66–8
Estés, Clarissa Pinkola, 53
Estrada, Gabriel, 152
Euro-American tricksters
    and Brother Jonathan Tales, 80
    characteristics of, 73–6
    and con men tales, 80–5
    and Jack Tales, 77–80, 84, 89–91, 94–5, 98–9

see also Saul Bellow; Mark Childress; Clyde Edgerton; John Irving; Ken Kesey; Elmore Leonard; John Kennedy Toole; Anne Tyler; Tom Wolfe
Evans, David, 180–1n35

Farah, Nuruddin: *Secrets*, 181n41
Faulkner, William, 146
Ferguson, Laurie, 192n40, 192n45
Figueroa, Celso A. Lara, 220n25
Fox, Robert Elliot, 30
Foxx, Red, 6, 24, 182n49
frame stories, 144, 221–2n49
Fu, Binbin, 217n94

gambling, 4, 63–9, 71, 139, 196n95, 198n117
García, Cristina: *Monkey Hunting*, 136
Gates Jr., Henry Louis, 29–30, 36–8, 185n93, 185n96
Gilb, Dagoberto, 9, 150–2, 169
    background of, 222–3n66, 223n67, 223n70, 223–4n79
    "Churchgoers," 147–9
    "Love in L.A.," 147, 149
    The Magic of Blood, 147
    on stereotypes, 224n83
Giroux, Henry A., 132
Glassie, Henry, 202n26
Gonzalez, Jennifer, 208n7
Gordon-Reed, Annette, 16
Gottlieb, Robert, 88
Gutierrez, C. Paige, 202n27

Hambly, Barbara, 24
Harrington, Oliver, 24
Harris, George Washington: "Parson John Bullen's Lizards," 82, 84, 204n58
Harris, Trudier, 183–4n74
Hemings, Elizabeth, 16
Hemings, Sally, 16
Henderson, Stephen, 183–4n74

Hispanic, use of the term, 135,
    217–18n1
Hooper, Johnson Jones, 81–2
Hsiao, Ruth Y., 211n25, 212n37
Hsu, Francis L. K., 110, 209–
    10n16, 211n30
Hua, Chuang: *Crossings*, 110–13,
    117, 128
Hughes, Langston, 24, 44
"Theme For English B," 2
humor, 6, 11–12
    and African American tricksters,
        18–26
    and American Indian tricksters,
        8, 51, 54, 59, 61, 65–6, 69, 72
    and Chinese American tricksters,
        120, 124, 127, 134, 138–42
    and Euro-American tricksters,
        75, 77, 80–4, 94–6
    and Latino tricksters, 160, 162,
        164, 174
Hurston, Zora Neale, 24–5
    Mules and Men, 21–3, 181n36
    Their Eyes Were Watching God, 37
Huston, John, 143
Hwang, David Henry: *M. Butterfly*,
    9, 113–17, 128–9, 212n43
Hyde, Lewis, 6, 11, 13, 75–6, 93
Hynes, William J., 12

immigrants and immigration
    and Asian-Americans, 8–9, 105,
        108–10, 121, 128–9, 169,
        207n1, 208–9n10, 210n17
    and documentation, 135–6,
        219n16
    and Latinos/as, 134–6
    and legislation, 10, 128–9,
        207n1, 210n17
    and transformation, 103, 128
individualism, 2, 8, 37, 48, 62,
    74, 82–4, 86, 101, 167, 169,
    195–6n90
Infante, Pedro, 162
    see also Chávez, Denise: *Loving
    Pedro Infante*

Irving, John: *A Son of the Circus*,
    94–5, 100, 206n84, 206n86
Islas, Arturo: *La Mollie and the
    King of Tears*, 153, 159–62,
    227n136, 227n139–40,
    227n144–5

Jackson, Rosemary, 221n42–3
Johansen, Ruthann Knechel, 12
Johns, Gillian, 25
Johnson, David E., 132–3
Johnson, Lyndon B., 128
Jung, Carl, 4, 203n31

Kakutan, Michiko, 214n75
Keillor, Garrison, 105
Kerr, Douglas, 213n48
Kesey, Ken, 8, 74
    One Flew over the Cuckoo's Nest,
        90–2, 101, 169, 205n73,
        205–6n75
    Sometimes a Great Nation, 92
    see also Wolfe, Tom: *The Electric
    Kool-Aid Acid Test*
Kim, Elaine H., 208n6
Kingston, Maxine Hong, 13, 208–
    9n10, 211n27
    China Men, 117, 121
    Tripmaster Monkey, 9, 117–21,
        128–9, 169, 214–15n75,
        215n76–7, 216n79
    Woman Warrior, 117, 121
Komunyakaa, Yusef
    Copacetic, 40
    "False Leads," 40–1
    *I Apologize for the Eyes in My
    Head*, 39
    influences on, 45
    "Touch-up Man," 39–40
Kwoh, Stewart, 3

Latino, use of the term, 135,
    217–18n1
Latino tricksters
    and bobo tales, 140–1
    characteristics of, 131–4

and *el disimulo*(process of
  concealment), 134–5
and fantastic tricksters, 141–2
and Latino diversity, 135–7
and machismo, 134–5, 152–9,
  162–4
and Pedro Urdemales tales,
  137–42, 147, 153, 164, 169
see also Rudolfo Anaya; Ron
  Arias; Denise Chávez; Junot
  Díaz; Dagoberto Gilb; Arturo
  Islas; Nina Marie Martínez;
  Marcos McPeek Villatoro
Leclair, Thomas, 184n75
Lee, Robert G., 208–9n11
Lenz, William E., 81, 203n46,
  203n51
Leon, Donna, 44
Leonard, Elmore, 8, 95, 98–100
  Pagan Babies, 98
  *When the Women Come out to
    Dance*, 98–9
Li, David Leiwei, 215n79
Li, Shu-yan, 112, 210n17, 211n25
Li, Zeng, 106, 119, 214n63
Lin, Patricia, 215n76
Lindahl, Carl, 77, 202n26
Ling, Amy, 117–18
Ling, Jinqi, 110
Locke, John, 2
Longstreet, Augustus Baldwin:
  "The Horse Swap," 83
Lord, Bette Bao: *The Middle Heart*,
  121–5, 216n87
Lye, Colleen, 208–9n10

machismo, 134–5, 152–9, 162–4,
  187n114, 225n98, 225n101
"macho," use of the term, 225n103
MacKethan, Lucinda, 88
magical realism, 9, 141, 146,
  222n61
Makarius, Laura, 18
Mankiller, Wilma, 191n33
Mao T'se-tung, 121, 216n86,
  228n3

Marchand, Philip, 206n84
märchen(magical wonder tales), 78,
  80, 94, 199–200n2
Margolin, Malcolm, 53
Marlowe, Christopher, 146
Márquez, Gabriel García, 146
Martin, Robert K., 213n55
Martin, W. Todd, 204–5n64
Martínez, Demetria, 217–18n1,
  219n15, 223n71
Martínez, Nina Marie
  *¡Caramba!*5, 153, 156–9,
    163, 226n123, 226–7n132,
    227n133
  and gender bias, 9, 152–3, 156–8
  and humor, 142
  and machismo, 152–3, 156–8
MASH, 76
Massey, Douglass, 218n12`
May, William T.: *Testing the
  National Covenant*, 2–3
McCarthy, William Bernard, 25, 77,
  179n12
McEneaney, Kevin T., 206n80–1
McGee, Patrick, 28
McKay, Nellie, 25
Michaelsen, Scott, 132–3
Minick, Jim, 225n102, 226n120
Minton, John, 180–1n35
Mirandé, Alfredo, 152–3
Mitchell, Jake, 23
Morra, Linda M., 13
Morrison, Toni, 4, 7, 13
  on Black male writers, 187n114
  on choice, 184–5n87
  on retelling of stories, 25
  Tar Baby, 30–6, 168, 184n75,
    184n86
  on *Tar Baby*, 36
Mosley, Walter, 7, 41, 168
  and African American folklore,
    186n105
  Bad Boy Brawly Brown, 42, 44
  Blonde Faith, 43–4
  Devil in a Blue Dress, 42, 45
  and machismo, 187n114

Mukerjee, Bharati, 214n75
Murphy, Peter: *John the Revelator*, 181
Murray, Charles, 73–4, 199n1

Neely, Barbara, 179n8
Nicolaisen, W. F. H., 202n26

O'Connor, Flannery, 88
Old Southwest, 8, 23, 25, 77, 80–4, 203n44, 203n46
Oldenburg, Ann, 208–9n10
Ortiz, Alfonzo, 54
Ouyang, Huining, 113, 210n18
Owens, Louis, 63, 192n43, 194n70
Oxford, Cheryl, 77

Painter, Nell Irvin, 200n10–11
Palmer, Parker J., 167
Paretsky, Sara, 44
Pasquaretta, Paul, 194n74
Pastor, Manuel, 3
Paz, Octavio, 134
Peiffer, Katrina Schimmoeller, 198–9n122
Pelton, Robert D., 13, 17–18
Percy, Walker, 88
Perez, Vincent, 224n94
Perry, Anne, 44
Perry, Lincoln, 24
Peterson, Nancy, 198–9n122–3
Pryor, Richard, 24, 182n49

Radin, Paul, 109, 211–12n35, 214n74
Ramsey, Jarold, 50
Reder, Deanna, 13
Reed, Ishmael, 183n62–3
    Flight to Canada, 27–30, 36, 41
Reesman, Jeanne Campbell, 12–13
Roberts, John W., 15, 20, 41–3, 180n31
Rodríguez, Richard T., 152, 225n98
Roediger, David, 212n42
Rogers, Will, 6, 225n98

Rohmer, Sax, 208–9n10
Romero, Rolando J., 131
Ronnow, Gretchen, 57
Royal, Derek Parker, 215n76
Ryan, Allan J., 190n26

Sáenz, Benjamin Alire, 133, 218n9
Scherer, Michael, 219n15
Scheub, Harold, 141
schmiggege, 96, 98, 207n90
Schoolcraft, Henry Rowe, 71, 188n1, 191n36
Schrieber, Le Anne, 214–15n75
Schuyler, George A., 25
Shapiro, Elliott H., 215n77
Shine, Ted: "Contribution," 25–7, 182n56
"Signification," use of the term, 185n93
Silko, Leslie Marmon: *Ceremony*, 49, 56–8, 65, 72, 168, 192n39
Sinclair, Niigonwedom James, 3
Slack, John S., 198–9n122–3
slaves and slavery, 7, 11, 15–16, 19–30, 36, 150, 168, 221–2n49
Smith, David, 54
Smith, Jeanne Rosier, 13, 35, 117
Sobol, Joseph Daniel, 77
Solzhenitsyn, Alexander, 216n85
Sullivan, Nancy, 225n103
Sumida, Stephen, 104

Thoreau, Henry David, 91, 206n77
    "Resistance to Civil Government," 99
Tobar, Héctor, 218–19n13, 219n22
Tocqueville, Alexis de, 74
Todorov, Tzvetan, 141
Toole, John Kennedy, 8, 205n71
    A Confederacy of Dunces, 88–9, 100
Torres, Lourdes, 227n134
Traber, Daniel S., 200n4, 203n39
Treasure of Sierra Madre, The (film), 143

tricksters and trickster stories
    Ananse (spider), 15, 17–18, 141
    anomalousness of, 5
    and antistructure, 5
    and badman tradition, 41–5
    bobos, 140–1
    as both/and creatures, 5, 117,
        133, 137
    Br'er Rabbit, 4–5, 7, 15–16, 25,
        31, 35, 38, 41–2, 45, 47, 104,
        138, 141, 168, 179n12, 184n75
    Brother Jonathan, 75, 80, 200n8,
        201n19
    "The Coon in the Box," 20–1,
        180–1n35
    Coyote, 5, 7–8, 47–53, 55, 57,
        65, 67, 69, 72, 104, 137–43,
        164, 168, 190n21, 190n26
    definitions and characteristics,
        4–5, 15–17, 47–51, 69, 73–6,
        103–4, 131–4, 176–7n10,
        185n96
    earlier critical attention to, 12–14
    female, 8, 36, 38, 67, 82, 153,
        156–9, 162–4
    Jack Tales, 5, 7–8, 77–80, 84,
        89–91, 94–5, 98–9, 104, 138,
        140–2, 153–6, 169, 201n20,
        202n22, 202n26–7, 203n39,
        207n100
    John and the Massa, 19–23
    and Jungian archetypes, 4–5
    Monkey King, 5, 7–9, 60, 72,
        103–29, 136, 141, 169, 171–4,
        208n2, 214–15n75, 228n2–3
    and morality, 41–5, 83, 86–8,
        98–100, 151, 155, 177–8n19
    Pedro Urdemales, 5, 9, 137–42,
        147, 153, 164, 169, 219n23,
        220n25, 225n100, 227n139
    since 1960, 10–11
    Tar Baby, 4, 16, 30–6, 38,
        184n75, 184n86
    written versus oral, 9–10,
        177–8n19, 184–5n87,
        188–9n1, 191n36

    see also African American
        tricksters; American Indian
        tricksters; Chinese American
        tricksters; Euro-American
        tricksters; humor; Latino
        tricksters
Turner, Jr., Albert U., 188n121
Tuttle, George, 43
Twain, Mark
    Adventures of Huckleberry Finn,
        23, 73, 84, 87, 138, 169
    on American irreverence, 6, 11
    on American joke-telling, 200n9
    "The Celebrated Jumping Frog of
        Calaveras County," 23, 83
    "How to Tell a Story," 23
    humor of, 25, 75
    "The Man That Corrupted
        Hadleyburg," 83
Tyler, Anne: The Accidental Tourist,
        93–4, 100
Tyler, Royall: The Contrast, 80

Velie, Alan R., 189n7, 193n62
Vietnam War, 10–11, 56, 93, 116,
        119–20, 186n99
Villatoro, Marcos McPeek, 152,
        225n102, 226n120
    The Holy Spirit of my Uncle's
        Cojones, 153–6, 225n101
Vizenor, Gerald, 5, 8, 28, 56,
        58–61, 72, 177n16, 192n39
    Bearheart: The Heirship
        Chronicles, 59–64, 193n55,
        193n62
    Darkness in Saint Louis
        Bearheart, 62, 64, 193n55,
        193n62
    and Erdrich, 192n38
    Griever: An American Monkey
        King in China, 59–60
    The Heirs of Columbus, 59, 61
    and symbolism, 194n72
    on tribal cultures and social
        science, 192n45
    on trickster as "kitsch," 49

Vizenor, Gerald—*Continued*
  The Trickster of Liberty, 59–61,
    183n63
  on violence, 194n69

Walker, Alice, 7, 30, 36–8
  The Color Purple (film), 185–6n98
  The Color Purple(novel), 30, 36,
    47, 185–6n98
  Tar Baby, 30
Walker, Jr., David, 190n21
Washington, Denzel, 42, 187n114
Watanna, Onoto, 210n18
Welch, James: *Fools Crow*, 49, 55
Welsch, Roger, 54
Welty, Eudora, 197n97
Whall, Helen M., 187n115
White-Parks, Annette, 12
Williams, Paul, 77
witchery, 57, 192n43

Wolfe, Tom: *The Electric Kool-Aid
  Acid Test*, 91–3, 206n78,
  206n80–1
Wong, Sau-ling Cynthia, 104,
  208n4
World War II, 43, 56–7, 106,
  208–9n10, 210n17
Wright, Richard, 24
Wu Ch'êng-ên: *The Journey to the
  West*, 8, 107–10, 120–1, 127,
  171, 209n15, 214–15n75,
  228n2–3

Yang, Gene Luen: *American
  Born Chinese*, 9, 125–8, 169,
  216n88, 217n94
Young, Mary, 186n105
Yu, Anthony C., 173, 209n13

Zipes, Jack, 141

CPSIA information can be obtained at www.ICGtesting.com
Printed in the USA
LVOW10*0843180114

369937LV00003B/57/P